BLACKSHIRT
CONSPIRACY

BLACKSHIRT CONSPIRACY

AN
AGENTS OF ROOM Z
NOVEL

JASON MONAGHAN

First published by Level Best Books/Historia 2023

This novel is entirely a work of fiction. The names, characters and incidents portrayed in it are the work of the author's imagination. Any resemblance to actual persons, living or dead, events or localities is entirely coincidental.

Jason Monaghan asserts the moral right to be identified as the author of this work.

Author Photo Credit: Alice Turian

First edition

ISBN: 978-1-68512-450-2

Cover art by Level Best Designs

This book was professionally typeset on Reedsy.
Find out more at reedsy.com

For Abigail

Praise for Blackshirt Conspiracy

'In Blackshirt Conspiracy, Jason Monaghan sets a tale of treachery against the extraordinary backdrop of the British Abdication Crisis of 1936. In the real world, a resolute Prime Minister forced a reckless monarch off the throne. In this slice of alternative history, fascist schemers cause events to take a darker turn...'—Martin Edwards

'A powerful and gripping narrative with a shocking outcome.'—Leigh Russell

Dramatis Personae

Characters and organisations listed in italics are based on real historical figures, modified in the interests of fiction. Historical figures mentioned in the story are not listed if they play only a peripheral role.

Department Z

- Hugh Clifton, Commander Z3 Confidential Investigation Section
- Sissy Poe-Maundy, Woman Unit Leader
- Julian Thring, Section Leader
- Danny Hills, Unit Leader
- Lucy Parmentier
- Nigel and Ruth Fritton
- Eleanor Fitzherbert, an ex-debutante
- Julia Sandwell-Hope, an ex-debutante
- Jimmy Walsh, Hugh's driver
- *Major P G Taylor, Director of Intelligence, Department Z*
- Dr Valentine, Commander Z1 Internal Security Section
- Captain Parker, Commander Z2 Special Action Section

British Union of Fascists and National Socialists (British Union)

- *Sir Oswald Mosley, 'the Leader'*
- *'F-H' Neil Francis-Hawkins, Director-General of Operations*
- *William Joyce, Director of Propaganda*
- Melissa Stapleton, Woman Section Leader and fiancée of Julian Thring
- Alf and Enid Hardcastle, Bromley Branch

- Section Leader Clague, Ashford Branch
- Dowager Baroness Rockwell, Sissy's mother

Security services & police

- Marcus Calhoun, *the Security Service (MI5)*, working with 'K' and 'M'
- Detective Inspector Renton, *Special Branch, Metropolitan Police*
- *Inspector Evans, Metropolitan Police*

Other characters

- 'Verity', former MI5 agent
- Bruno Vogel, *German Embassy*
- Nathaniel Isby, emissary of the *Archbishop of Canterbury*
- Arnold Alexander Thorne, 'AA', *Foreign Office*
- Neil Gotobed, brother of Alf Hardcastle
- Leonora D'Auville Clifton, 'Leo', Clifton's wife
- Viscount Lyle, equerry to the king

Historical characters

- *King Edward VIII, 'David'*
- *Mrs Wallis Simpson and Mr Edward Simpson*
- *Stanley Baldwin, Prime Minister*
- *Neville Chamberlain, Chancellor of the Exchequer*
- *Winston Churchill, a Conservative Party backbencher*
- *Herman and Kitty Rodgers, Lord Brownlow, Aunt Bessie: friends of Wallis Simpson*
- *Guy Trundle, Ford Motor Company executive*

A note on British Union ranks and titles

The BU was constantly shuffling its organisation, the titles of its officials and paramilitary ranks. By 1935 a man in charge of a unit roughly ten strong would rank as Unit Leader, while a woman would be Woman Unit Leader. Units were combined into Sections, Sections into Companies, but in this novel to reflect its importance Department Z has three Commanders placed above Section Leaders.

Chapter One

October 1936

I t was a beautiful day for a riot. London is at its best in October, when the summer heat is gone, but the sun remains high enough to penetrate the canyons of streets. Trees in the parks and leafy squares still carry their foliage but are starting to adopt autumn shades.

To mark the fourth anniversary of the founding of the British Union of Fascists, Oswald Mosley's Blackshirts would march through the East End of London. It was no coincidence that this was where Britain's Jews were most concentrated, and Jewish-owned businesses were most prominent. Mosley's rallying call was published in that Saturday's edition of *The Blackshirt*, attempting to justify his fight.

'We did not begin the struggle…the Jews began it.'

Mosley claimed not to be a racialist, and his closest supporters sprung to his defence each time he faced the accusation. 'His fight is an economic one,' they protested when discussion became most heated over the dinner table; 'the Leader wants to free Britain from the stranglehold of international bankers but holds nothing against Jews as a race.' I kept my head down during these debates, taking silent note of which fascists were on which side of the argument. Perhaps one day a wedge could be driven between them.

On the first Saturday in October, I walked quietly through the streets of Stepney, accepting left-wing pamphlets and observing the posters that were

1

springing up on walls.

All Out Against Fascism

London Workers! Anti-Fascists! Peace Lovers!

The Party had been renamed the British Union of Fascists and National Socialists, British Union for short, to distance it from Mussolini's Italian *Fascisti.* Nobody was fooled. The British Union would march, but the left was mobilising to stop them. A woman handed me a proclamation printed by a Jewish organisation complaining a petition to the government to halt the march signed by one hundred thousand people had been turned down.

One leaflet entitled 'The 35 Group: Christians against Fascism' listed biblical injunctions against hatred and discord.

> '...The one who hates his brother is in the darkness and walks in the darkness and does not know where he is going because the darkness has blinded his eyes.'

Walking the sunny side of the street along the route of the march, I saw discreet preparations being made by shopkeepers boarding up their windows. Darkness was not yet come, and they were not blinded to what was likely to happen.

The proposed route was a five-mile horseshoe starting at Mint Street and heading east for a rally at Salmon Lane, Limehouse. The parade would turn north towards the next venues at Stafford Road in Bow, then Victoria Park at Bethnal Green, allowing half an hour between each. In my estimation, this did not leave a great deal of time, as speeches would be made at each halt. Its final leg was a march west to terminate with a meeting at Aske Street, Shoreditch, at 6.30 pm. The route was well advertised, and crowds were expected at each halt, where Mosley and others would speak. I walked it in an hour and a half, which made the official timing optimistic. If the socialist rhetoric was true, the Blackshirts would have to fight for every yard.

I handed over the information I'd gathered at the end-of-day briefing in the Club Room at Black House. Later, I would also apprise my handler within the Security Service, known by some as MI5. Beyond these simple tasks, I had no brief to either stop the march or ensure it succeeded.

Since Christmas, I'd built up a small team of reliable agents, all paid-up fascists but filtered carefully to exclude the most fanatical and dogmatic, the antisemites and would-be Nazis. Lighter shades existed within the Blackshirts. My team arrived at Mint Street in the early afternoon, weaving our way through an impressive number of policemen. The trained units of Blackshirts had been christened stormtroopers in May, with a rank and file retaining the Italian look of tight-fitting collarless shirts even if their peak-capped commanders now dressed more like Germans. Grey-shirted cadets and even more numerous civilian followers formed up behind them.

Such scenes should soon be consigned to photographic archives. The government was preparing a Public Order Act which would ban political groups organising as private armies and parading in uniform. Just maybe the appeal of British Union would wane once they looked like any other fringe political party.

'Hugh!' Julian shouted, then waved to attract my attention.

'Good morning, Section Leader Thring. Eyes watching, so better keep it formal.'

'Commander Clifton.' He brought his heels together, but didn't salute as we were both in working-class civilian clothes.

It was difficult, perhaps even unwise, to class anyone in the movement as a friend, but Julian Thring came close. Dark-haired, with a slight build and boyish looks, he trained as an accountant, so was an excellent choice to recruit into my section. I also wanted him out of the stormtroopers and away from harm's way, as we'd already dodged too many bricks, bottles, and coshes together.

Julian went to reassure his fiancée, who was holding the standard of the Women's Section, its pole resting on the ground. The women were out in force, together with their marching band. Melissa was a healthy-cheeked young woman decked out in a black blouse and grey skirt. Beneath a black beret, her blonde hair was cut back in a severe style, but she was rather shorter than the Nordic Amazons featured in Nazi propaganda films.

Melissa would love to be in a Nazi propaganda film.

Department Z were not in uniform. I spotted Major Taylor but couldn't see his Internal Security agents; they were creatures of the night who liked to lurk unseen. Captain Parker's section were also without uniforms, armbands, or insignia. Almost all his Special Action men were young, many still in their teens. With only his black eyepatch to mark him out from other gang members, Parker pointed to a map in his hand and indicated one Jewish business after another he deemed in need of special action. I ordered the dozen men and women of my own section to scout ahead of the parade, checking the side roads. Enemies had ambushed me from dark alleys too often.

Squad by squad the main body of stormtroopers marched up. Last to take up their position were Mosley's personal bodyguard, now known as the Black Guard. Their newly redesigned uniforms had a military cut and were topped off by peaked caps. Senior officers I knew by sight or repute were dressing their troops, giving orders, exchanging confident smiles. A variety of red brassards worn on the left sleeve proclaimed their now standardised roles, and military-style ranks had been handed out as freely as tombola tickets. This organisation was growing and evolving all the time. When I infiltrated the movement the year before, its pretensions seemed farcical, but not anymore.

Parker came across. 'Nine thousand here and another twelve spread across the four rallies. And they said we were finished after Olympia!' His one eye gleamed at the prospect of action. 'You'd better get moving, Clifton. Kick-off is two thirty.'

Kick-off was an apt euphemism for what I knew would follow.

Julian came over, beaming. 'Splendid, isn't it?'

That wouldn't be my choice of words.

I summoned the rest of my section to join us. Sissy had wanted to march in uniform, but I was now her commander as well as her lover. Sullen, quiet, wearing no make-up, she had dressed down into the dowdiest cardigan, blouse, and skirt she could buy from a street corner stall and pulled on a drab knitted hat to hide most of her dark hair. Camouflaged in dull greys, tans and browns, if all went to hell we could fade away unremarked into the London streets.

'Sissy will be the rallying point,' I said. 'Here, by that pub. Then, after the parade moves off, she'll stay close to the Women's Section. She's got the medical bag.'

Unsmiling and without making a comment, she held up the canvas satchel. She knew jolly well why she'd been given the least dangerous role of the entire operation.

'Right, chaps, ladies, off you go! Julian, with me.'

Police officers were directing traffic away from the route. Julian and I had not even reached Cable Street before a solid phalanx of policemen blocked our way. Officers on foot filled the roadway from one side to the other, dozens of ranks deep, and we had to push past them one by one. How on earth the parade would make any better progress was beyond me.

'I'd turn back, sir,' one helpful copper advised.

'I wouldn't go through there,' warned another.

We stepped aside as a dozen mounted police nudged their way through the throng. Just ahead, a bus appeared to be wedged in a solid mass of people that filled the road beyond the next junction. A police superintendent was out in the open, glancing about nervously as a crowd a few yards down the road raised clenched-fist salutes in defiance. A group of civilians were pushing a contraption of nailed-together boards and corrugated sheeting into place. A white-painted slogan read *They Shall Not Pass*.

'This looks hopeless,' Julian said, downcast. 'Do you think we could go that way?'

He pointed up past Leman Street station. Coaches carrying more police were driving towards us from that direction, followed by what must be every police horse left in London.

'What about along the river?' He pointed in the other direction.

'I can't imagine the reds haven't thought of that,' I said.

'They can't watch every road—how many of them can there be?'

'A hundred thousand, allegedly.'

'Poppycock.'

We made our way swiftly fifty yards or so south down Dock Street towards the Thames. I spotted one of the male and female pairs from my section returning from their reconnaissance, and they confirmed that route would hem the march in against the docks. Julian and I headed back north of the junction, which looked more hopeful. Glass shattered somewhere back towards the mob, and the jeering and singing rose in volume.

'Here.' Julian indicated a right turn beyond the railway station.

I could see we were being watched from windows and doorways, but there were so many more distracting events going on behind us I didn't imagine that two ordinary-looking men would attract much notice. We ventured into the side road, which bent north immediately. It would carry the parade off its intended route but, just possibly, would also take it around the mob.

A woman came into the periphery of my vision. She was hugging the walls and doorways, in and out of view. She pulled out of sight when she saw I'd spotted her.

'We need to turn back,' I said.

'Wait, let's check.' Julian made the mistake of taking out his map and thinking aloud. 'If the police hold the commies in Cable Street, we could come this way.'

In an instant, two men rushed at him from a shop doorway, one swinging a club. I reached for the shoulder holster inside my jacket just as my friend went down to a single blow.

Chapter Two

Pulling out my Walther pistol I levelled it in a two-handed grip, first at one man, then the next.

'Hold right there!'

The men froze. One muttered an oath. I glanced down at Julian, prone and motionless on the cobbles. Just in time I saw motion behind me and dodged to my right. Burning pain cut into my left arm. Staggering back, I switched around and levelled the gun at the new target with my good hand. A cut-throat razor halted mid-action.

'I'll shoot you all. Now, clear off. Go on, run!'

'Comrades!' a woman's voice shouted.

The attackers looked her way, then mine, then coalesced into a single group before backing into the shop once more. I started to cough, an old injury reminding me of another day I'd narrowly escaped with my life.

Now, I switched the gun to face the new threat. She wore a red armband.

'Hugh Clifton?'

I knew that voice; educated and accent-free.

'Verity?'

The last time I'd seen Verity, she'd been a silhouette shooting at me from the dark. She was quick with both knife and gun, so I couldn't give her the slightest opening. I knew little about her other than I was certain she was not called Verity.

'Put that bloody gun away—do you want to start a war?'

I glanced at my torn jacket sleeve, already adorned with a red armband of my own. It felt as though my arm had been sliced off above the elbow, and the rest was on fire. The war had already started.

'I'm not armed,' she said, half raising her hands.

I lowered the muzzle just so far that I could twitch it back in a moment. The blonde woman in the maroon beret moved with a distinctive limping gait, claiming allegiance to the communists with that armband, although I had no idea who she really served.

She came closer. 'I thought it was you. I've been watching you blundering around for the past ten minutes. Anyone else, and I'd have let them finish you.'

'It was your comrades' lives you saved.' I pressed my wrist against my wound, still gripping the gun. I let out a curse followed by another annoying cough.

'My God, is that Julian?' Verity kneeled by the man she'd once cruelly misled and felt the pulse on his neck. 'He's alive, but he's going to wake up with a headache. What does he know about me?'

'He thinks you're dead. But he was hopelessly in love with you—he'll never forgive or forget.'

'Wonderful, a romantic fascist.'

'Everyone still thinks you're dead.'

She glanced up from her attempt at first aid.

'You mean you never told the dogs from Special Branch about me?'

'No.'

'Not even Calhoun, or whoever else in MI5 you claim to be working for?'

'No.' I glanced down anxiously at Julian, but he heard none of this.

'Why?'

'For the same reason I didn't shoot you in the back when you ran off.'

She nodded. 'So you think we have a truce? Stay with him, I'm going to call a flatfoot over.'

As quickly as she was able, Verity limped to the end of the road while I slipped my Walther back into its holster. If that woman didn't choose to kill me, she could betray me, which would amount to the same thing. I lifted Julian's head and tried to coax him back to consciousness.

'Over here!' Verity's shout echoed back. 'A man is hurt. Yes, down here.'

She flapped her arms in annoyance. 'Well, you can rot in hell!'

She returned, flushed. 'The bastards won't help—they assume he's one of us. You'll need to carry him back on your own.'

Verity helped hoist Julian onto my good arm, and I gripped him as if we were two amiable drunks returning from a night on the town.

'I thought I'd have seen you before now,' I said. 'I need to talk to you. I put adverts in the *Daily Worker*.'

My last mock Lonely Heart advert had read:

> VERITY. *Please give me a chance to explain. Write to me please comrade. HC.*

'I saw them—it was a sweet touch, but it smelt like a trap. I'm going back to being dead, understand? And if you're thinking of bringing the jackboots this way, forget it. Go and tell Mosley he's going to have to fight the entire East End if he wants to get through. When they write the history books, this will go down as the day British fascism was defeated.'

Julian may not be the burliest of Blackshirts, but it was still a struggle to move him. With blood dripping out of my left cuff, I struggled back to Leman Street and spotted a St John's ambulance waiting for this very opportunity to do the saint's work.

Two ambulance men took Julian from me.

'He's concussed,' I said.

'And you're hurt,' said a nurse who came to pay me attention.

I stripped off my jacket, and she looked startled as she discovered the shoulder holster.

'We're detectives,' I said.

'You're brave men going over there today.'

She pulled out a pair of scissors and cut away my soggy shirtsleeve. The razor had made a clean cut but stopped short of the bone.

'Ooh. This will need stitches.'

'Can you do it?'

'Not here; you need a hospital.'

'But you can bind me up?'

'I will, but get to a hospital as soon as you can. You can ride along with your friend.'

'No, thank you. I've got more friends in danger, and I have to warn them.'

Friends? What was I saying? With my arm in a sling and my ruined jacket posted over my right arm, then draped over my left shoulder, I worked back through the mass of police. Their cavalry pressed forward into the street beyond, and what must have been several thousand officers on foot poured after them. Batons were flying, and I hoped that one of them caught the razor man around the ear. I could see women on the upper floors above the shops hurling things down. Was that the contents of a chamber pot? A brick sailed through the air and struck down a policeman.

One constable spotted me and broke into a charge, raising his truncheon to add to my pain.

'I'm with Mosley!' I appealed. 'Can't you see I'm hurt?'

He stopped just short of impact, stepped back, and gave a half-hearted fascist salute.

'Back to bashing the Yids, then,' he said before moving back to join the fray.

Here was proof that the East End police were full of fascist sympathisers, despite officers from other divisions having been sent in to redress the balance. I leaned against the pillars of a closed shop and watched the mayhem, head dizzy from the shock of the wound. The police were doing Mosley's job for him. Worse, Verity and her crew were doing the director of Propaganda's job. He would make a meal of this—the communists, the anarchists, and the rest had turned themselves into the villains of the piece.

With difficulty, I reached the spearpoint of the fascist parade, a waving sea of Union flags, black fascist flags, and the new BU standard. With its white circle on blue ground representing industry, a central lightning flash representing action, and a red background, it was mocked by Mosley's enemies as 'the flash in the pan'. A motorcycle swept up, followed by an open-topped Bentley. Out stepped the Leader, and a gang of his chief sycophants sprung to his side at once, the senior men orchestrating his dream of replacing the elected government with a dictatorship. It wasn't my wish to save Mosley's bacon, but there were easily a thousand women assembled plus a greater number of youths following the lead of their fathers or mothers, and all at risk of grievous injury if the parade went ahead.

'Hail Mosley!' someone cried.

Every Blackshirt turned to salute, right arm at forty-five degrees to the sky. Mosley halted to respond.

Without bothering to even feign a fascist salute, I pressed forward to where the Leader stood.

'Sir.'

'Grief, Clifton!' Major Taylor said. 'Look at the state of you!'

Prompted by Taylor, Mosley at last recognised me.

'Commander Clifton, isn't it? Department Z?'

I seldom met men taller than me, so raising my eyes to meet the bright blue piercing gaze of the Leader was unnerving.

'Cable Street is completely blocked,' I panted. 'Half the East End is battling the police down there. It's hopeless.'

'Nonsense,' said Mosley.

'Nonsense,' echoed Major Taylor. 'What are you talking about?'

'And there are razor gangs waiting in the side streets. There's no way round.'

Julian's father was close by Mosley's side. It was the first time I'd seen the colourless Machiavellian accountant wearing a uniform.

'Julian's injured,' I called out.

Thring senior frowned.

'He was knocked out by a cosh, but I think he's going to be fine. An ambulance took him to hospital.'

Julian's father nodded but displayed no more emotion.

'Sorry to hear that, Thring,' Mosley said. 'Your son will march again.' He turned to his assembled staff. 'You know I deplore violence,' he said. 'We'll let the police clear the streets of communists first. We will wait an hour.'

The men of action shuffled. Most didn't deplore violence at all.

'Good work, Clifton. Get that arm seen to.'

What I wanted to do was find Sissy, so headed for the pub that was to be our rallying point. I came across Unit Leader Hills first and asked him to recall as many of my team as he could find. I didn't want to lose anyone else to Verity's razors.

Sissy spotted me and ran over. 'Hugh!' She stopped short when she saw the empty sleeve. 'Goodness! Is your arm broken?'

'No, just cut a bit.'

'Does it hurt?'

'I'd like to pretend it didn't.' I winced as she pulled the jacket gingerly off my shoulder.

'We have to get you to a doctor.'

'No.' I slumped back against the window ledge of the pub. 'I need to stay and see how this plays out.'

She probed the bandage beneath my sling.

'If you start oozing blood, I'm taking you straight to hospital.' The honourable Cecilia Poe-Maundy might be top-shelf English aristocracy, but any squeamishness had been squeezed out through her flirtation with fascism.

'Where's Julian?'

'Hospital.'

She grimaced; they were good friends. I gave her the story of the ambush, omitting the mention of Verity.

'If Mosley decides to march, it's going to be a tough day.'

We watched the Blackshirts fidget for an hour. Hills was a burly ex-copper and keen to stay, but when the others filtered back, I told them all to go home, listen to the radio, pick up the talk in their local bar, buy the evening papers—anything that sounded like useful intelligence work but took them away from the riot. I had no use for agents who were in prison, in hospital, or in the mortuary.

From the rear of the wedge of policemen, a senior officer emerged, mopping his brow. I felt I'd earned the privilege of hearing what he said, so struggled over.

'We have the right to march,' Mosley asserted.

'There's no way through. You'll have to climb over a pile of bodies to reach Limehouse.'

'So be it,' said William Joyce. The director of Propaganda was my age, just thirty, but looked younger, and his zeal was unmatched. His left cheek had been scarred by a communist's razor slash when he was still a teenager, and it both formed and framed his politics.

'No.' The Leader held up his hand. 'British Union upholds the law. We're not revolutionaries. If you order us to march a different way, Commissioner, we will do it.'

'Assistant Commissioner,' the officer corrected the Leader with some hesitation.

Mosley had little time for such pedantry. 'Well, *Assistant Commissioner*, are you ordering us to stop the march?'

'I can't order you, legally. I can just ask. Advise you, implore you. To avoid more violence.'

'If we turn away, the reds will claim a victory,' Joyce said. 'Fourth of October 1936, the day the workers turned back the Blackshirts. They'll sing songs about it.'

Just as Verity had predicted.

'And if they can stop us today, they'll do it every time.'

Mosley turned back angrily, an imposing figure glaring down at Joyce.

'I know about the wedding, but most don't,' Joyce said in a low tone that only a few of us could hear. 'I understand that you wouldn't want to be injured just before your wedding day or miss it entirely because you were arrested—'

'That's nothing to do with it!'

'But how will it look?' Joyce raised his voice and flung his arm dramatically towards the grey-clad cadets. 'How will it look to them?'

Mosley licked his upper lip, and his moustache quivered.

'To us.' Joyce touched his breast with both hands. If Mosley was aiming a knife at the heart of British democracy, Joyce was the poison dripping from the tip.

'Clear the way, copper!' The shout came from a feared East End bruiser whose forehead was caked with blood from an earlier skirmish.

'Let us through! Let us march!' More cries followed, as if Mosley were the school bully being egged on by his mates.

The next to throw weight behind action was Neil Francis-Hawkins, known as F-H. He made no secret of his conviction that the fascists would win power only if they seized it by force. 'The Stormtroopers are ready,' he asserted. 'This is the moment we've trained for.'

'Yes.' The Leader was hardly leading. He hesitated for another moment, winced at another shout from behind, and then made his decision. 'Assistant Commissioner Malherbert, do your duty. Clear the way. We intend to march, as is our right.'

The Assistant Commissioner looked away. His officers were no longer separating opposing forces but were sandwiched between them.

'You know, Malherbert, I was assured that the officer assigned this detail today would not stand in our way,' Mosley said, his tone low. 'Friends of the Party will rise with us.'

'I've got six thousand officers down there already,' Malherbert protested. 'There are no more to send. You must understand—I don't have enough men.'

'We do,' said F-H. 'Call on British Union to assist you in restoring order.'

'I—'

'Call upon the Blackshirts in England's hour of need,' Joyce added.

The policeman nodded, looking at the ground.

A smile slowly came to Mosley's face. He was a man permanently in search of a crisis, and one had been delivered to him by his enemies.

Orders were shouted. The Black Guard came to attention. A black van rumbled forward, its windows shielded by wire mesh, one of the 'armoured cars' ordered for the Russian secret police but bought by the Party once the British government had blocked the export. Stormtroopers opened the back doors to reveal nothing more than an innocent load of wooden laths. The laths only became offensive weapons as the stormtroopers took them in hand.

'Keep violence to the minimum,' the policeman asked meekly.

Chapter Three

Dress like a fascist, talk like a fascist, act like a fascist, and think like a fascist. To continue my mission, and indeed to stay alive, I had to maintain my reputation as a Blackshirt hero I'd won almost accidentally. A former colleague had cruelly advised I should sleep with a fascist to complete my image.

I'd invited Sissy up to Moat Hall in West Yorkshire for Christmas at the end of 1935. The dust was still settling after the dramatic general election where Mosley had enjoyed unexpected success, and she'd accepted warily. Before that, we'd hardly spoken since we'd stood over a bloodied corpse, and she'd learned my true affiliation. With icy rain beating on the window but a fire roaring in the drawing room, we took the chance to bridge the divide between us.

Seated in one of my father's luxurious leather armchairs by the fireside she sipped a sherry. Her dark eyes sparkled with fire. I sat opposite, almost rigid, gripping both arms of my chair until they squeaked.

'What happens now?' she asked. 'Once you ran up here, I presumed you'd forget all about me.'

'I could never forget about you.'

This young woman in a Parisian-crêpe afternoon dress of deepest blue could make or break my mission. If she put a word in the wrong ear, I'd be a dead Blackshirt hero.

'But now I know what you are, how can we possibly keep seeing each other?' she asked.

'Have I ever asked you to stop being a fascist, to stop supporting Mosley?'

'You can ask me now—and I'll say no.'

'Good. I can't ask you to stop believing what you believe.'

'But *you* don't believe it.'

'No.'

She hardened her look. 'So, what do you believe in?'

'I believe in keeping you safe.'

If I had the dedication of one of Stalin's agents or one of Hitler's henchmen, there would be a straightforward way of ensuring my lover never told a soul what she'd learned about me.

'Not many people know exactly what happened in November,' I said, 'and our lives wouldn't be worth much if the detail became common knowledge.'

Her next sip of sherry was more of a glug. She caught my meaning immediately, even if she was not aware of quite how many unpleasant organisations I'd crossed in the previous nine months. If they were in possession of the full facts, the Russians and the Nazis, as well as home-grown communists and fascists would be lining up to kill us. There was an invisible player in the game too, a powerful individual or group I was nowhere near identifying. For some reason, they wanted us to stay alive—for now.

She uncrossed her legs, then shifted pose as she re-crossed them the opposite way.

'Can't your people help?'

'If it suited them,' I said, 'but there are dead bodies to account for and lots of lies to cover up. The Establishment can pin a murder charge on whomsoever they please at the time of their choosing.'

That blow struck below the belt.

'You're saying I need to just forget what I know.' Her voice quivered. 'I'm supposed to just forget you're a traitor to the Party, a spy, a secret agent—'

'Exactly.'

She gazed into the fire. 'This isn't what I wanted. I thought we were building something.'

'Then let's build something. I'm stuck with the Blackshirt hero tag, like it or not, until the world calms down. So, in the meantime, I'll try to do some

16

good with it.'

'Like, bring Mosley down?' she challenged.

'No, no.' I raised a hand as a defence reflex, hoping to calm her. Mosley's scalp would be the supreme prize, but I was in no position to even fantasise about it. 'We build a better Party.'

'We? Is that your new mission? Your orders from whoever it is you work for and can never tell me about?'

'Well, you said it yourself. I can't tell you about it. And I don't work for anyone in the strict sense, I hardly need the money.' Now, I stretched the truth a little. 'My people, as you call them, are more like allies.'

'Don't tell me you're spying on the Party just for fun? Because you got bored up here in the grim north and had nothing better to do?'

In truth, that was a pretty fair summary of how this affair began.

'And if you're not spying on the Party, why are you even still talking to me?'

'You know why I'm talking to you.' I leaned forward but it would take far too great a stretch to touch her hand. 'Mosley's an Honourable Member of Parliament now. Decent, respectable, and out in the open where everyone can see him.'

'You're being ironic. I can hear that ironic tone in your voice.'

'The people at the top of government think fascism isn't a problem and that communism is the biggest threat to the country. Can we agree on that, at least?'

'Agreed.'

'All the big guns are trained on the communists, including Section Z3.'

'What's Section Z3?' asked Sissy.

'Me, Julian, a few others I have in mind. We're expanding Department Z, and Z3 is the Party's new Confidential Investigation Section—it was my idea, but quickly became Major Taylor's idea which suits me fine. Internal Security is now the remit of Z1, under Taylor himself, and Captain Parker has Z2, Special Action, which means he can beat people up to his heart's delight. They're even letting me have Room Z.'

'But what's the point? What's in it for you, or for Julian for that matter?'

'It saves us from being kicked to death in some street brawl.' It might save Julian's soul, too, if it kept him away from Parker's vicious pogroms. 'Look, to be blunt, I joined Z last year to keep their eyes off me and give me a legitimate reason to be inquisitive.'

'You mean spy on us?'

'But that's done with now, that mission is over.' I had to stretch the truth a little more to keep Sissy on my side. 'I want you to join us and bring some of your Women's Section along.'

'Why? Why would I do that? What's in it for *me*?'

'A sense of purpose. Z3 will gather information on the true nature of the communist threat. That suits the Party, it suits my allies, and it would suit you. There are plenty in the Party who think that the Women's Section should be restricted to nursing and cooking.'

'And having babies,' she added, miming a bloated belly. 'Don't forget the babies.'

'Being a confidential investigator would be so much more fun.'

She smiled and finished her sherry. 'Blackshirt detectives?'

As part of my cover as a struggling writer, I'd begun bashing out a pulp novel called *Blackshirt Detective.* Now I was one, and Sissy would be one too.

Chapter Four

A duck flotilla fought a seagull squadron for bread in St James's Park while fascists and anti-fascists continued to slug it out in the East End. I sat on a bench, utterly downcast. People had died at the Battle of Cable Street, hundreds were in hospital, and I couldn't escape replaying events in my mind. Perhaps if I'd acted differently, I would have been able to stop it. On sober reflection, I knew that I overrated my own importance in a world going slowly mad, and there was nothing I could have done. Even if I'd pulled my pistol and shot Mosley, he'd only be replaced by Joyce or someone even more rabid.

My arm throbbed, the razor slash burned, the iodine stung, and the stitches itched. It was difficult to see what I'd achieved after a year of being followed, betrayed, shot at, stabbed, clubbed, stoned, locked up, tied up, and threatened with torture. Worst of all, the outcome of my first mission had been twisted to put Mosley closer to power.

An office worker on his lunch break was tossing crusts into the water. As the ducks saw it arc towards them, they scrabbled across the surface in a race against the gulls diving down from above. I made the score four-three to the ducks so far, but they had numbers on their side. A pair of swans were gliding towards the action to show everyone who were the real bosses of the pond.

A balding man in a greatcoat that failed to contain his spreading waistline was approaching. Commander Calhoun sat down beside me.

'Why's your arm in a sling?'

'Razor slash.' I ran through the story of my Sunday, up to the part when

Sissy bundled me into a taxi and took me to Barts Hospital. I was unable to tell him anything of the pitched battles that followed.

'Chin up,' he said.

'Why?'

'You're alive, it's a fine day, the East End is calming down...'

'The police went over to Mosley,' I said soberly.

'Sir Phillip Gale should have been there,' Calhoun commented. 'But he was called away, so you got that new man Malherbert.'

'Who looks like he's in Mosley's pocket. Did he stop the petition against the march, too?'

'No, that was the Home Secretary. The government is clueless and rudderless. Baldwin's not a well man. He's spent the summer convalescing, so there's nobody running the show at Whitehall.'

'The risks we're running are pointless if Mosley is allowed to do what he likes. I've been risking my life and my friends' lives—'

'Friends?'

'You know who I mean. I'm done, Calhoun, done, mission over. Just let me walk away, and I'll take Sissy off to some sunny island.'

'Sorry, but that's not going to happen,' he snapped. 'So forget it. Your Department Z can do things we can't, go places we cannot, find out what we need to know.'

My Department Z. A little recognition was welcome, even if Calhoun had me trapped.

'You're still not letting me go?'

'No, sorry. You're signed up for the duration, I'm afraid.'

I huffed, looking away, wishing I had the tiniest lever I could use to prise myself out of the cage I'd cheerfully strolled into. 'You must have someone else on the inside by now. You haven't asked about BU finances for months, so I know you've got another agent keeping an eye on the money.'

'I couldn't comment. But I need you and your *friends* up in Room Z more than ever. I can't see Baldwin hanging on as PM beyond the coronation next May, and Neville Chamberlain is manoeuvring for the job. Meanwhile, the rump of the Cabinet is in a flap, staring at a communist revolution on the streets.'

'That's nonsense. The Cable Street riot was a provocation by the fascists, not a revolution; don't believe the *Daily Mail*. Nobody was in charge of that socialist mob. I've been feeding you the intelligence for a year or more—there's no big plan, no Red Front, no communist threat. Tell the Cabinet that.'

He jabbed a finger, stopping just short of my injured arm.

'This looks to me like a pretty painful non-existent communist threat.'

'It wasn't ordered by Moscow.' As I said this, I wondered who Verity was serving now. 'Every anti-fascist demonstration is thrown together at short notice by local workers' groups, unions or whatever. It was the same at the weekend. I picked up leaflets from the Jewish Council and a transport workers' union, not to mention the 35 Group.'

'Who?'

'Never come across them before. The 35 Group, Christians Against Fascism. It's good to know that Christians are against the Jews being persecuted.'

'*Some* Christians. Hopefully, more than thirty-five of them.'

'It may refer to the year they formed.'

Even side on, pretending to be paying more attention to the ducks, he looked unimpressed.

'So, no Red Front? It will take more than a passionate hunch to convince the politicians. I still need whatever you can find on the socialists.'

'Here, have this if you must.' I switched a copy of the *Evening Standard* from where it sat on the bench to let it rest on Calhoun's own newspaper. A typed list sat folded in its pages. 'Northern miners' strike leaders, with home addresses. But the more socialists you arrest, the more support they gain.'

'We don't follow that theory. Cut off enough heads, and the hydra will die.'

'But in some versions of the legend, each time the hydra lost a head, it regrew two more.'

'Is that a fact?' Calhoun rarely looked me in the eye, but now gave me the most disparaging of glances before turning his attention back to the swans, who were bullying the ducks away from the crusts. After watching the avian battle for a few moments, he pulled his *Daily Telegraph* out from beneath my *Standard* and turned to a photograph on page two. 'Your Leader is starting to look remarkably like Herr Hitler.'

'It's no accident.'

'I used to be a submariner,' Calhoun said. He tapped the photograph. 'We can see what Mosley's up to above the surface—he's hardly hiding it—but what's he up to down in the dark? Germany has my paymasters worried. Hitler marches into the Rhineland, and our government just sits back and watches. He won't stop there, as anyone who has read *Mein Kampf* will understand. K keeps asking me for evidence that your Blackshirts are cosying up to the Nazis.'

I'd never met K, who appeared to be Calhoun's boss at MI5.

'Mosley isn't making any official contact with Hitler because it would damage his image.' This must have sounded close to sarcasm. 'But his mistress, Diana, and her sister Unity just so happened to be in Cologne when Hitler arrived in triumph.'

'She's not going to be only his mistress much longer, I hear. Something about a secret wedding in Germany?'

'I heard a rumour—I think it's this week. I didn't know it was in Germany, though. Diana went to the Munich Olympics, and A K Chesterton went to the Nazi Parteitag, but secret wedding or not, Mosley himself is still publicly keeping his distance from the Nazis.'

'K has asked the Treasury for more budget so we can properly assess the fascist risk, but they wouldn't hand out another penny if he screamed till he turned purple. So I'm afraid it's down to you to find the intelligence we need.'

Being a spy gave my life meaning, I supposed. Then, if I could somehow torpedo Mosley, Calhoun would have little need to keep me as a pressed man, and I could find another purpose, preferably a less dangerous one.

'If I'm carrying on this fool's errand, I need to stop wasting time chasing communists and go full tilt at Mosley.'

'Do both,' Calhoun said. 'Department Z is a very, very useful tool with the added benefit that it doesn't need to be funded by the Treasury.'

One of the swans climbed out of the pond to claim a crust that landed on the path. It hissed at an Airedale terrier that dared come too close.

'When I was a child, I saw a swan kill a small dog,' I said. 'They're remarkably strong. I was in a park with my parents and barely believed what I saw, but it stuck with me. There was this great commotion, with a woman in tears and men trying to help her, but this swan just quietly paddled off to join its mate. They look graceful and beautiful, but they're killers. Using the fascists to fight the communists is a mistake. It's like trying to escape a crocodile by mounting a tiger.'

Chapter Five

I was in my first-floor apartment in Havelock Mansions, staring at a nearly empty piece of paper sticking out of my typewriter. Mornings were a good time to write, but today I was rather stumped as to how my hero, Harry Bretton, and his lively girlfriend would get out of the fix I'd thrown them into. Typing one-handed and trying to ignore the pain in my useless arm made the process worse.

My telephone rang to terminate my writing for the day.

'Clifton? Taylor here. I have a case for you.'

It was almost the line that I'd typed in my novel the week before, then crossed out for being unimaginative.

A woman named Mrs Hardcastle had telephoned in a panic saying her house had been burgled by communists. The reds had been after her husband, she said, but he was away fighting some farm dispute deep in Kent. Hardcastle was an activist in the Fascist Union of British Workers.

'This sounds like the very thing we set your section up to handle,' said Taylor. 'Our own ace detective on the scent, what?'

I agreed, of course. When I'd first infiltrated Department Z, I'd put Taylor down as yet another self-important but ineffective officer of the class the BU specialised in appointing. As the year went on, that impression faded. I was by this time certain he'd never actually been a major and suspected that P. G. Taylor was not his real name. He avoided every single group photograph of the senior staff and had even removed his own picture from the Department Z file. Three separate outside telephone lines were installed in his office, and what appeared to be long lazy lunches could be nothing of the sort. Far from being a Colonel Blimp character plucked straight from the pages of the *Evening Standard,* the man who called himself Taylor was something much shrewder and much more dangerous. He wouldn't waste the Department's time on a trivial matter.

Up on the second floor of Black House on the King's Road, a room with slanting ceilings still retained a letter Z on its door from its former days as a teacher training college. Room Z was now mine. As people moved up in the organisation, they moved down a floor, so Taylor had vacated Z in favour of a larger office on the first floor. I'd supported his decision to employ a more matronly and more 'reliable' secretary than the one he left behind.

One of Julian's smart young men was usually on duty in the outer office, but the real work was led by Lucy Parmentier. She was the only person I'd met at Black House with a notion of how to organise an office and do it with a smile. In her own words, Lucy had 'run away from home', escaping some small town in Essex where she'd been badly treated by her father to rediscover herself in London. Her youth, blonde hair, and excitable nature may have made her appear a perfect recruit for the fascists, but in truth, she simply needed to belong.

Sissy habitually rose late and arrived at Black House even later, so I prevailed on Lucy to bring us an early lunch up from the canteen, and it served as Sissy's breakfast. Coffee and corned beef sandwiches was hardly dining at the Ritz, but the BU claimed to be a classless party with no room for snobbery.

'With so much going on, I'm surprised we're bothering with this,' Sissy said. 'Three Blackshirts were killed by communist rioters in London, dozens injured, but downstairs is worried by a burglary in Bromley?'

'Communists are allegedly behind it.'

'Hugh Clifton investigates!' she declared. 'Admit it, this is what you've always wanted to do: be a detective. Like that bloody hero of yours.'

'*Blackshirt Detective* is going to press in time for Christmas,' I reminded her lightly.

'It's a jolly good job your mistress knows a London publisher who supports the Party,' she reminded me, narrowing her eyes to emphasise how much I owed her.

'Does my mistress want her own case? Lead investigator, not just the sidekick or love interest?' It would be an excuse to get Sissy away from the dangerous atmosphere of the capital, and my arm was not yet up to changing gear on a drive down to Kent. 'Woman Unit Leader Poe investigates.'

'That's a horribly clumsy title,' she said.

The BU's new rank titles hardly slipped off the tongue with ease, and the insistence on women wearing different rank badges from the men didn't sit happily with the supposedly forward-looking vision of the Party.

'The Hardcastle house is in Bromley—you could call on your mother afterwards, perhaps.'

'Give me the details, Commander.'

* * *

Julian Thring ran Z3 on a day-to-day basis and was so much more comfortable in an office than me. He'd trained as an accountant and, as his father was a senior and quite dangerous member of the Party, Julian was a useful man to bring onside. With Sissy off on her mission, Julian and I met for dinner at a small French bistro in Knightsbridge which had no particular reputation. It was quite dark, as if the owner were aiming for an intimate candlelit romantic ambience or was simply mean with electricity.

In poor taste, Julian joked that given his head was swathed in a turban of bandages, we ought to go to Veeraswamy, the top-notch Indian restaurant that was one of my favourite haunts. He was not systematically racialist like his fiancée, but simply careless with notions of race and colour as most English people tended to be. When I grimaced at the bad joke, he suggested that another night we should dine at his new club.

'That's not a good idea,' I said.

'I'm sorry you were blackballed,' Julian said. 'I thought you were in with a chance.'

I nodded. Young's was pretty new, and Julian had been keen I joined.

'I've been blackballed by better clubs.'

'I don't know why, honestly. I feel a fool for proposing you now. I'd probably not been there long enough myself, and not in with enough chaps.'

'Never mind.' I honestly didn't mind. If I had spare time, I'd rather be dining out with Sissy, dancing in a club, or catching the latest show or American movie. Drinking and guffawing with a bunch of cigar-touting toffs calling themselves Young Britons was not my idea of a good evening. However, it would have served my intelligence purposes to mix in right-wing circles beyond the BU and get a view back at the organisation. For all its military trappings and imperialist posturing, half the Party's policies differed little from progressive socialism.

'Shame, it's quite jolly.' Julian was clearly disappointed, either for me or what my exclusion meant for his own position. 'There are military types, up-and-coming civil servants, professionals, second sons of the nobility, good men to know.'

'Are there many BU men in there?'

'No, our senior chaps mostly favour White's. Young's is strictly men of our age, capped at forty on entry.'

'But your father recommended you?'

He shrugged. 'Father knows everyone these days. There's Phillip de Vere Challenger on the managing committee; he's the son of that steel magnate.' He gave a laugh. 'Sorry, I always think of steel magnets. We'll probably rope him in on our Industrial Commission when we take power; he's very sharp, exactly the kind of man we need.'

Julian did not often expound his views. During dinner parties, his fiancée would take over the conversation and too often rehearse bigoted and authoritarian views to which he could only echo agreement. In her absence, he loosened up and spoke more honestly.

'And Viscount Lyle,' he continued. 'He's, um, equerry to the king or something.'

He did enjoy dropping names, so I allowed him to continue dropping them.

'Dougie—that's Freddie Douglas, Cabinet Office. And this chap AA from the FO.'

I tried not to frown to betray my feelings. 'Arnold Alexander Thorne, Foreign Office?'

'AA, yes. Know him?'

'Only by repute. Interesting man.' I'd come across AA earlier in the year, mixed up in some unsavoury business in Spain. Either he genuinely didn't like me or knew my true allegiance and covered up his knowledge with feigned hostility.

The waiter arrived with our meals, and I kicked myself for not paying attention when ordering, forgetting that *langue du boeuf* was ox tongue and invariably chewy.

'You see, we boot the old men out and put young men into all the top jobs.' Julian began to slice up what looked like perfectly devilled kidneys. 'Men who really know what they're doing, not just sitting out the last years of their lives. Chaps itching to solve the big issues of the day while the men above them do nothing. And make doing nothing look important.'

He popped a kidney into his mouth and growled contentment. Pulled into the movement by his father, Julian had latched on to the ambition of the fascists to create a corporate state. Tiers of committees and commissions would bring together experts, unions, and consumers to build a better Britain. Democracy, in his eyes, just got in the way of sound business. He showed little interest in the Empire beyond building trading arrangements I found too dull to follow and only supported his fiancée's intolerant rants because she was his fiancée.

'Young men in a hurry,' I said. 'That's what they criticise us for.'

'We must cut the waste, and the corruption and the cronyism, and the "my father went to school with your father" nonsense.' Julian raised one hand to his temple and scowled.

'How's your head?'

'Like I've downed two bottles of claret already. How's your arm?'

'Like there's a woodcutter trying to take it off with a rusty saw—' I halted mid-metaphor as I remembered that somewhere out in London's shadows lurked a communist torture team who did take men's arms off with rusty saws. 'It hurts like blazes. I'm sorry for dragging you into that mess.'

'Don't mention it,' Julian said. 'I'm still working off my debt—you know, after last year.'

'Debt paid, no need to keep apologising.'

'But I let you down. I let you walk into a trap.' He took a sip of wine, often a sign of nerves with Julian.

'It wasn't a trap, just too many men with clever plans falling over each other. This game we're in isn't black against red, us against the communists. There are lots of players, and last year we were both played.'

'By my father?'

'Partly by your father, but things went on behind the scenes I can't lay at his door, and I can't explain them.'

He nodded sagely. 'You never told me what happened that night.'

'Believe me, you don't want to know.'

'I say, old man, we're friends. Thick and thin.'

'Suffice to say the stories in the newspapers about the police busting the big communist plot were just stories.'

'As I thought,' he said. 'The word's got around, somehow. The rank and file think it was you wiping out those communists, busting their plot, not the police. Dead men in cellars, in warehouses, washing up in the river...executed at point-blank range. Was that all you?'

It would do Julian no good to know the truth. I poured him more wine, then refilled my own glass. I always drank faster than he did.

'Let's just regard all that as useful rumour,' I said. 'If people think we kill without hesitation and smash communist plots in the dead of night, it adds to the mystique of Z3. Keep them all guessing. But be careful what you say at your new club. Don't try to impress the *chaps* by letting slip more than you need to.'

'Of course not.'

'Keeping mum keeps us all alive. Going forward, we don't trust anyone.'

Chapter Six

The Honourable Cecilia Maude Elizabeth Poe-Maundy detached herself from her faithless husband's name when she joined Department Z. As Sissy Poe, she felt more the independent woman, although with a cut-glass accent, the most up-to-the-minute couture and a shiny new MG T-Type in daffodil yellow, she could never pass for one of the masses. She had posted a note to Mrs Hardcastle on Friday, then driven out to visit her mother. The Dowager Baroness Rockwell's country house nestled in the Medway valley, offering an easy drive back across to Bromley on Saturday morning.

If the aristocracy provided one source of Mosley's support, far more came from the disaffected working class. Sissy parked in front of a row of pre-war terraced houses representing part of British life she had never experienced. A stocky woman also in her mid-twenties answered the door, wearing the black blouse of the Women's Section in readiness for the visit.

Sissy was not in uniform. 'Mrs Hardcastle?'

The young woman seemed taken aback.

'Sorry,' she said, recovering. 'I can't get used to that name. You must be...'

'Unit Leader Poe, Department Z.'

'Come in. I must say I hadn't heard of this Department Z, but one of my friends said you investigated reds. Alf said I shouldn't have called you, but you're here now. Would you like some tea?'

'Please.'

Mrs Hardcastle led through a narrow hallway to a kitchen. 'I've made some scones too.'

'That's very kind.'

Sissy took a seat at the plain wooden table as her host slipped a floral apron over her uniform before busying with the kettle and a cake tin.

'I've tidied up.'

'You shouldn't have just for me.'

'No, no, I mean since the break-in. Alf came back, checked what was missing, then told me to tidy up.'

Told her, indeed. 'Is he still here?'

'He went straight back to that farm. Lord knows we can't afford train fares; I hope the union pays.'

Sissy's knowledge of how to conduct detective work came principally from reading novels borrowed from Hugh. His coaching sessions for the team suggested his own knowledge was obtained the same way.

'Tell me about the break-in.'

'It was on Thursday. The day after Alf went down to sort out that farm dispute.'

'Where did he go?'

'A village near Ashford. Hang on, I wrote it down.' She ferreted for a note. 'Much Hadley, a tiny place by the sound of it. Anyways, I was out at work and came home to find the back door broken. Things moved here and there. Not a real mess, but everything had been shifted, and every drawer poked into.'

'Did you fetch the police?'

'No, Alf wouldn't want that. It might have been the police who did it for all we know.'

Sissy narrowed her eyes. 'We don't trust them, do we?' She did wonder whether Alf Hardcastle had a specific reason to avoid the interest of the law or whether it was just the natural reticence of the working man.

'I went straight to my sister's round the corner to be safe until Alf came back. Reg from two along—Alf's friend—mended the door for me. After that, I wanted everything straight.'

'What was taken?'

'Not much.' Mrs Hardcastle pulled aside a dusty red velvet curtain to reveal an understairs cupboard stacked with papers and a typewriter. 'Some of his papers, maybe. The worst mess was down on the floor here where they'd just thrown things they didn't want.'

'Have you any idea why communists would break in?'

'Because Alf's important. The communists run the unions, don't they? And Alf's fighting that, making sure we have control, not Moscow.'

'What was his job, outside the Party?'

'He's a typesetter for the local paper. He wanted to be a reporter one day but didn't have enough learning. They let him write for *Blackshirt,* though. His boss lets him have days off to do union work.' She smiled. 'Then the paper don't get no trouble from the union.'

Sissy had never dealt with unions, but from what she'd been told, they operated like criminal gangs.

'Can I look in here?'

'Be my guest. I don't know what you'll find.'

A quick shuffle through the piles of papers was sufficient to reveal they were mostly old copies of fascist newspapers, pamphlets, and handbills. Cuttings from assorted newspapers, British and foreign, were clipped haphazardly together in bundles. Sissy sorted through them on her knees. Nothing original written by Alf Hardcastle remained in the cupboard, in contrast with Hugh's workspace, that was strewn with discarded drafts and ideas for the next chapter.

'Does he usually show you what he was writing?'

'Every time. I look through to see if I can catch him out on his spellings. He gets me to read his finished jobs out aloud to him, in a booming voice like I was Mosley himself, and he sits and listens and nods at his own work. He's a good writer—they should have him writing for the paper.'

'Was he writing about the farm dispute?'

'I imagine. He's gone down there to join the picket, but he'd have run off a story when he got back. He'll offer it to his paper, and they'd say no, as usual, then he'll send it off to *Blackshirt* and maybe make a few bob.'

His typewriter was there, but no carbons that might have betrayed what he'd been working on.

'Where are his letters?'

'In there, in a couple of shoe boxes.'

She could see no shoe boxes. 'Do people write to him?'

'Now and again. The letters should be in there.'

But they were not.

Sissy returned to sit at the table. 'Did he receive any letters recently that worried him? I don't know…possibly threats or demands for money?'

Mrs Hardcastle shook her head. 'He kept them to himself, unless he was proud of one he got from Black House or a big name in the Party.'

'Any trouble with the police?'

'Only the usual.'

Sissy imagined if the police were interested in what Hardcastle was up to, they would have arrived at the front door with warrants and a Black Maria, not kicked in the back door when they knew nobody was in. Spies of the sort Hugh associated with would have been more subtle and left no trace.

'Does he have any enemies?'

'Not for long. He's a tough man.' Mrs Hardcastle smiled. 'Don't get me wrong—he don't start fights for no reason, but he'll finish them if he has to.'

Chapter Seven

Sissy, as Unit Leader Poe, telephoned me from a phone box, glowing with the report of her solo mission. She was concerned over the break-in, and I could see why as we talked it over. It was not a random crime, and we batted ideas back and forth as to whether it was due to Hardcastle's activity as a trade unionist, fascist bruiser or aspiring journalist. The communists would have written him onto their hate list on any or all counts, but it was hard to see what secrets he could hold to justify burgling his house. Sissy discounted spies, but I wondered briefly about the man known as M, Calhoun's secretive colleague and possibly even his boss, who allegedly broke any rule that suited him. This didn't feel right either, as the Security Service had me and, by default, Z3, so had no need to show their hand, so obviously.

The last thing I wanted to do right now was drive down to darkest Kent and interview Hardcastle himself, and I wasn't comfortable sending Sissy out to an obscure little village on her own. A man with enemies who didn't like questions and solved problems with his fists was not someone to be tackled lightly.

Sissy was excited when she arrived at my apartment on Sunday morning. I'd been at home trying to type up more of my mystery sequel. *Bretton's Second Case* was barely Bretton's Second Chapter. She laid down a heavy burden, set aside her hat, stripped off her coat, and kissed me lightly on the cheek.

'Time for a real detective story.' She repeated much of what she'd told me on the telephone. 'Then I thought about you, messy so-and-so.' Sissy pointed to my wastepaper basket. 'Mrs Hardcastle had been staying at her sister's and hadn't emptied her bins—but thank God I didn't have to rummage through old fish heads. They use scrap paper as firelighters. They had one little heap in a box out the back and some bundled up already in the grate.'

Sissy unfolded one sooty sheet. 'He wrote a letter to Cosmo Lang, Archbishop of Canterbury, would you believe? Last week. But see, he's got spelling mistakes here...and here.'

Hardcastle had got no further than the address in which Canterbury was spelled wrong, the date of 5 October, a salutation, and an angry first line.

> I know whats going on with Wallis S. I have received information
> that on what the Chuchr is up to

It was easy to see Hardcastle angrily pulling the paper out of his typewriter at the second typing error, screwing it up, and tossing it towards the grate. He'd missed an apostrophe too. And made a grammatical error.

'It must be an exposé for *Blackshirt*,' she said, 'or perhaps a request for an interview.'

'Any idea who this Wallis is?'

'Mrs Hardcastle didn't know. I asked what else her husband was writing about lately, and she rattled off a list: Jews in the government, spying on the king, and he had a grudge against the Church too. It all rather tumbled out of her as if she'd been only half listening to him.'

'Do you think wives ever do that?'

She gave me a playful slap on my good arm. 'Wallis sounds like a vicar—Hardcastle's probably picked up one of those scandal stories about a cleric having a sordid affair with a parishioner. If he doesn't like the Church, it's a way of rubbing their face in it.'

'Was his wife familiar with this letter?'

'She hadn't seen it. Perhaps he didn't finish it or thought against retyping it.'

'Or its contents were secret. I see you managed to grab his typewriter.'

'She wasn't happy about my taking it. I did play my Department Z card very hard.'

I had a theory and wanted to put it to the test. I put a steel paperclip on the section of two-colour ribbon due to be struck next, then removed both spools.

'The last things he typed would have been over here.'

I took the ribbon to the window. Sissy took one spool, I took the other, and we held it to the light, then across the light so the impressions of the strikes could just be made out on the black strip. My fingers became immediately inky.

'Look,' she said, pointing a fingernail towards the red strip of ribbon.

Office typists used the red ribbon for the heading of final demands or when typing out negative figures on balance sheets. Home typists only used it for novelty or when especially angry. The red ribbon carried black marks left by strikes from the type bar.

'There's an n, g, capital K,' she read. 'And he's underlining something. Little h, another one, capital C.'

'Church,' I guessed. 'But he didn't use red in that letter you found in the grate. Either he was angrier when he revised it, or he's written to someone else.'

'King,' she added, 'n-g-K typed wrong.'

'Might just be the way the letters hit the ribbon,' I surmised. 'Writing to the archbishop is eccentric, but writing to the king and thinking he'd get an answer would be crazy.'

I sat back and sighed. My phone rang, and I took up the receiver half-heartedly. Not many people knew my home number, and most of them were tiresome.

'Hugh Clifton.'

'Clifton, Taylor here.'

Yes, it was the most tiresome man on the list.

'I've been ringing all over the place trying to find you. That union man, you know, Hardcastle, the one burgled by communists. He's been murdered.'

36

Chapter Eight

Map in hand, I served as navigator, letting Sissy know in good time when she should turn off the main road and into the heart of Kent. My powder-blue Alvis tourer swept into the village of Much Hadley, and she steered straight for the half-timbered pub that looked out on a duck pond from one aspect and the village green from the other. Nestling in a dip in the rolling North Downs, it was the perfect advert for the Garden of England. If the Green Man served decent ale, the dream would be complete. A pint of warm brown painkiller was long overdue.

Neither of us was in uniform, but our black leather coats were becoming almost the dress etiquette for Department Z3. Sissy had bought one for me the previous year after admiring the one worn by a rather suave German named Bruno, who I was convinced worked for the Gestapo or some other tentacle of Hitler's security apparatus. In the early autumn, she'd bought one of her own, with a neater fit at the waist and a cut that broadened her shoulders. I still only had one useful arm, so Sissy carried my light case, and I took her rather less light one. I nudged the pub door open with my backside.

The landlord was reading a newspaper on the bar and glanced up reluctantly as if we were interrupting his day. Such a welcome was less warm than I'd expected. Perhaps having the last paying guest meeting a bloody death had soured the atmosphere.

'Clifton. I telephoned about a room.'

'Mr and Mrs Clifton,' the landlord said at last.

Sissy carried a wedding ring she would slip on for such an occasion.

'We've had a room come vacant, as it happens.'

'So I understand.' I counted out the money due onto the bar.

'Best breakfast in Kent,' the landlord said, warming up a little now. 'And dinner, too, if you let me or my wife know.' He pushed the key across the counter, looking from one of us to the other warily. 'Top of the stair, at the front. You get a nice view.'

'The bags?' I prompted.

'Oh, sorry. Shall I help carry your bags, sir?'

'If you would.'

I let him carry the heavy one as he led the way, and I bore the lighter burden. I had to stoop a little to enter the door to the bedroom. The ceiling sloped to one side, and I had to duck again to swing my case onto the bed. The landlord set Sissy's down on the floor with a thump that rattled the windowpanes.

'Did Mr Hardcastle have this room?' I asked.

The landlord looked from me to Sissy, who was standing in the doorway, giving him no polite way of evading the question. He nodded.

'Are you, what, friends of his? Police?'

I took out my badge. 'Commander Clifton, Department Z.'

He studied the brass badge, which was linked to a short chain.

'That's a new one on me, sir.'

'We're going to clean up after the journey, then perhaps I can buy you a drink and talk about what happened to Mr Hardcastle.'

'I don't know about that, sir.'

I hardened my tone. 'Or we could just have a talk.'

* * *

One thing Sissy had managed to uncover about Alf Hardcastle was that he was not born a Hardcastle. His original name had been less hard and less castle-like. I imagine being called Gotobed must have made his schooldays rough, and he'd have grown up fighting.

Late on Saturday evening, he had been knifed to death on the village green, and his body was found just short of the maypole soon after dawn. Sissy and I had a view of the scene of the crime from our otherwise pleasant room, if one distorted by the diamond-paned windows.

We unpacked and changed our clothes. Once my shirt was off, Sissy unwound the bandage and checked my wound. It resembled a zipper rendered by an amateur tattoo artist in purple, black, and pink.

'Another scar to add to the collection.' I tried to smile.

She touched the spider's web mess over my lower right ribcage, my souvenir of a much deadlier scrape.

'Well, you mustn't get any more. Poor Julian's going to have a corker on his forehead—I thought you were going to keep him out of trouble?'

'Trouble found us.'

I had been awarded the new Action Press uniform, available to officers and those who had made notable contributions to the movement. Of course, I had to buy it myself as British Union was still strapped for cash. My new jacket was of military cut, with breast and hip pockets, and worn with a silver-buckled belt. A gold lightning flash on the shoulder straps proclaimed my rank. The uniform came with grey, puffed-out jodhpurs of cavalryman style, and I was now entitled to wear a peaked cap Calhoun said made me look like a bus conductor. Sissy gingerly pulled a red, white, and blue brassard into place up my left arm. She gave it a soft pat, proudly, and stood beside me as I checked the result in the long mirror. I would not look out of place standing beside Hitler, Mussolini, or Europe's latest would-be dictator, *Generalissimo* Franco.

I'd met Franco and was surprised he was still alive, given the violence of the civil war that had erupted in Spain and the quick demise of other senior Nationalists. British socialists were flocking to join the fight against him, but Mosley ordered British fascists to keep out of the fight. Their strength was needed at home.

Sissy buttoned up the very fetching black silk blouse of the Women's Section, then struggled a little with her black tie. As the regulations on skirts were hazy, she favoured a woollen one in grey with a black houndstooth design. For good measure, she also slipped on a red armband with its blue-in-white circle representing industry and white lightning strike symbolising action. A black beret with the same symbol in silver topped off her outfit. The locals who saw us stride from the pub could be forgiven for thinking we were about to impose martial law.

The landlord had given me the directions to Upper Haye Farm, and we found it after only a short drive through high-hedged lanes. Coming up a rise, we anticipated a surprise awaiting us, and Sissy jerked the Alvis to a halt. Our way was blocked by a felled tree, and beyond it a tractor had been turned across the road for good measure. Behind the tree were three men, one holding a pitchfork that was less a weapon, more a symbol of this peasants' revolt.

A Blackshirt stood with the two men who looked like local farmers. He wore the normal fencing-style collarless jacket but clearly couldn't afford matching trousers and had turned out in tan flannels and brown shoes. As I stepped from the Alvis he snapped to attention and saluted. I returned the fascist salute in the lazy way I was perfecting, keeping my elbow crooked and not raising my hand above my head. If anyone ever picked me up for it, I'd say that I'd seen Hitler do it on the newsreels.

I slid over the tree with only a little awkwardness, and it was only polite for us to both offer to help Sissy to cross. She was a perfect recruiting advert for the movement, and the men's gaze followed her every move.

'Who's in charge?' I asked.

'Section Leader Clague, sir. Did you hear what happened to Mr Hardcastle?'

'Yes, I did—that's why we're here.'

Typical of those who had flocked to follow Mosley, the Blackshirt was a young man, barely in his twenties. He led up the lane fifty yards or so, then down a track to a cluster of ragstone buildings. We stepped directly into the kitchen of the farmhouse. Another Blackshirt sat at the table, older than me but not quite as old as the man who sat next to him, worry clouding his features, both hands gripping a tin mug.

'Commander Clifton, Department Z. And this is Unit Leader Poe.'

Salutes were exchanged, and I was pleased that Sissy used the same lazy half-hearted response as I did. She could be too enthusiastic at times. The Blackshirt at the table was the local union branch organiser named Clague, and the farmer was introduced as Mr William Sutton. His wife clearly had a production-line approach to serving tea, as Sissy and I were both enjoying a cup within minutes. Mrs Sutton brought out her best willow pattern china, too.

'I'm tired of this trouble,' Farmer Sutton said, 'I didn't mean it to go so far.'

'How much rent do you owe?' I asked.

'Forty-seven pounds. And for that, they'll take my tractor, my cows, whatever hens they can catch and sell 'em for a pittance.'

'We won't let that happen,' said Clague. 'We'll get every farmer in the district to the auction and bid a penny a lot, no more. Then Mr Sutton can buy it all back for under a pound.'

'It won't settle the debt,' grumbled Mrs Sutton. 'They'll keep coming, and we'll be bested.'

'So why the blockade?' I asked.

'It's the principle,' said Clague. 'The bailiffs will take everything worth taking on this farm, then move on to the next.'

'And the landlord is?'

'The Church.'

I already suspected this, but needed it spoken out loud.

'That's not very Christian,' Sissy said.

'Den of thieves,' Mrs Sutton hissed from over by the sink. 'Keeping the preacher fat while we starve.'

To be fair, neither Mr nor Mrs Sutton looked as if they missed many meals.

'Wheat prices have been at rock bottom for years, and what's your Mosley doing to help us?'

'We're here,' Sissy said.

'Mosley slowed the Tithe Bill in the Commons,' Clague added. 'The NFU are dominated by rich Tories who don't have to worry about tithes. We all went on the march in July, Sutton here and a brace of my men. Giving up a day's wages, paying our own way to London. And Baldwin wouldn't even meet us. Wouldn't even read the petition. The Tories don't care.'

Clague pushed a notice across the table. 'The farm is under distraint. The bailiffs can turn up anytime from tomorrow.'

'How many men have you got?'

'We had twelve of mine, and nine local lads alongside them.'

'And six women,' added Mrs Sutton. 'My daughter is coming tomorrow and bringing her little ones too. Let the police arrest *them*.'

'But...' Sutton gestured towards my armband. 'This isn't helping, it's turning into London down here. It's not the Jews taking our farms. And now Hardcastle's happened...'

'Have you any idea who killed Hardcastle?' I asked sharply.

'No, that was a great shock.'

'Terrible,' Mrs Sutton added.

'He was staying at the Green Man,' Sutton said. 'He left here with a couple of others at the end of their watch on Saturday.'

I asked Clague to come outside, and we walked over to where only a few cows could hear us.

'What was Hardcastle's role in the protest?'

'Well, he was in the Union,' Clague said, more to the cows than to me. 'But he writes for *Blackshirt* too and told us he was starting a story about our fight down here. London gets too much of the front pages.'

'Did you welcome his help?'

'Ah, I see where this is leading—' he eyed me as if already found guilty— 'but I'm going to be straight with you. No, he just turned up out of the blue. We didn't need his help, I had enough lads to make the point. And now I'm half a dozen down—they slunk off yesterday when they heard about Hardcastle. Some of them are not as committed as they should be.'

'Have you got their names? Men who slink off after a murder are always going to be under suspicion.'

'They were Ashford lads in the main, I know 'em.' Clague paused. 'Except one.'

'Except one,' I echoed.

'He was another one just turned up. I don't think Hardcastle knew him.

Bit posh, not from Kent. A doctor, I think he said.'

'A doctor? I need his name.'

Clague nodded. 'I'll try and remember. It was Saturday when he came. He was snooty when I said we don't need help, and Hardcastle joined in. It was a right tug-of-war. I didn't need either of them to do my job for me.'

'And now, here I am, too.'

He huffed out air as if beyond caring about party politics. 'Well, frankly, now we could do with the support. Sutton barely wants us here anymore. If you hadn't come, we might have called the whole thing off.'

I could have suggested he do that, but I was here to investigate a murder, not risk the attention of Black House by assuming more authority than I had.

'Where's this doctor now?'

'Not seen him since. He was staying at the pub, though—they should know his name.'

Clague talked a little more about the unequal fight between small farmers and the might of the Church before I thanked him and wished him good luck.

'We'll see you at dawn tomorrow.'

As soon as we got back to the Alvis, I took off my cap, then removed my armband. Sissy sat beside me, uniform intact.

'We should just pay the forty-seven pounds for them,' she said.

'No, we shouldn't,' I said. 'Clague says there's about a thousand outstanding tithe debts in Kent alone and thousands more all across the south and out in East Anglia. We can't pay them all off.'

'It's disgusting. How can the Church get away with it?'

'Apparently, it's been that way since the time of Queen Anne.'

'Then it's jolly well time we sorted out this rotten country.'

She started the car and set off for the village while I pondered what we were driving into. Each victory for the Church in the rumbling tithe war could mean a farming family going under. Each victory for a protest backed by the Blackshirts would increase support for Mosley. The angels were not on either side.

Chapter Nine

The landlord of the Green Man informed me the man who'd stayed in the small side room at the pub gave the name Dr Valentine. He'd only stayed for one night and returned to London on the Sunday after the police had spoken to him. We gleaned as much as we could about the night of the murder, which was not a great deal. A bunch of Blackshirts had been drinking in the bar, out of uniform, then at some point their number had dwindled. Hardcastle's body had been spotted by the milkman doing his rounds the next morning, who at first thought he was waking a drunk farmer. Sunday had seen a day of frantic police activity in the village, but all seemed calm again.

I had of course read Agatha Christie's *The Murder at the Vicarage* and it could have been set in a place just like Much Hadley. We changed back into civilian clothes before visiting another of those pieces in the English country village jigsaw. I'd sent the landlord's boy over to the vicarage earlier to present my card, so we were sure to be expected.

We took a direct route across the village green. I wondered why the maypole was still in position, but on closer inspection, it was a solid piece of timber well embedded in the ground. The grass hadn't been cut since the end of summer and was lank and damp. Around the maypole, it was heavily trampled from the activity surrounding the murder and its aftermath. I was sure that not all the dark stains were mud. At the end of the green was a loop of unmetalled road, then a hawthorn hedge that masked the whole vicarage below its roof. Immediately beyond rose the church tower in biscuit-coloured ragstone.

A man in fear of his life might have checked behind him, so I did the same. The duck pond began perhaps twenty yards away, with the bank opposite the Green Man backing onto a clump of small trees and bushes. If I were a murderer, I'd hide there, then steal up to the man by the maypole as he looked expectantly towards the vicarage.

I'm not overtly religious in the way I'm not overtly political. Studying ancient civilisations at university, followed by a couple of years mixing with Hindus, Sikhs, and Moslems taught me to be wary of the single truth, the great book, or the great leader. However, that's not to say I'm an atheist, and on high days and holy days, I will belt out a rousing hymn as loudly as the most ardent believer.

We were greeted by the vicar's wife, whose terrified glanced from me to Sissy and back again suggested she believed we were about to eviscerate her and burn the place to the ground. Politely, fearfully, she invited us inside. It was a plainly decorated place in need of a lick of paint on its woodwork, and the sitting room furniture looked tired. I was directed to an armchair and Sissy to a hard fiddle-back affair that looked as though it had been hurriedly brought in from the dining room.

Introductions were barely necessary as the vicar knew who we were, as did the archbishop's representative, who nodded at our arrival. While Reverend Perchard was a fleshy man of advancing middle age who blubbered his words, the man from Canterbury was clean-cut with greenish eyes and a very precise manner in the way he picked up his teacup and replaced it. Mr Isby was equally precise with his choice of words.

'I understand that you are fascists.'

'British Union of Fascists and National Socialists,' I corrected.

'You've changed your party name.'

'It was associated too closely with Mussolini,' Sissy said.

'So instead, you associate with Hitler.' Isby was clearly no fan of Mosley. 'We have no place for fascists in Kent. Nor national socialists.'

'The Leader is upholding Christian decency against communist atheism.' Sissy defended the party line with far more conviction than I could.

'We have no place for communists either.'

'But you do support the old feudal system,' I said. 'Tenant farmers paying their tithes to the Church and doffing their caps to their betters?'

'It works,' stated Isby.

Sissy had flicked open a small notebook bound in black leather and took out a pencil.

'Now, now, this is rather frosty,' said the Reverend. 'What precisely are you good people here for? If I can help in any little way…'

'A family about to lose their livelihood,' I said.

He nodded. 'It's regrettable.'

'Then stop the distraint.'

'That's impossible,' Isby stated.

'It's the only means we have to support—' the vicar raised his hands to indicate his comfortable home—'the church.'

'Your living comes from the tithes?'

'Precisely.'

The vicar's wife reappeared with a teapot and tray. I accepted an empty cup on its saucer, allowed her to pour, then dropped in a cube of sugar using silver tongs.

'Was Mr Hardcastle invited to tea too?' I asked the vicar.

'No, he—'

'Blockaded the gate with a mob of men and hurled abuse,' Isby interrupted. 'His exact words were that the time for talking was over and it was time for action. He thumped his fist into the air at the word *action,* and his mob cheered.'

Sissy scribbled a note. 'When was this?'

'Thursday. We were quite frightened for our lives,' said the vicar. 'I've heard what your people are doing to the Jews.'

'Not my people,' I stated.

'And those riots in London! Throwing that young girl through a shop window, disgraceful!'

I was not going to have the agenda turned around.

'Two nights ago, Mr Hardcastle returned from Upper Haye Farm, took supper in the Green Man, but then the story tails away around ten pm.

Nobody knows why he left the pub.'

'It was a fine evening,' the vicar suggested helpfully, 'for the time of year.'

'Hardcastle doesn't strike me as the kind of man to go for a stroll under the stars. Clearly, he met someone. Any idea who?'

'No, no, I was well ensconced here with my cocoa and a last look over my sermon. Which because of this nonsense, I never had the chance to deliver. Policemen interviewing my parishioners as if they were common criminals. Then turning them away from the church gate.'

'And where were you?' I asked Isby.

'You're behaving like policemen, and you have no authority to behave like policemen,' protested Isby. 'But for the benefit of your little book, madam, I was also here, seated one chair clockwise from the Reverend, catching up on the London newspapers. Then we all retired to bed.'

'And you didn't hear any commotion, no screams or shouts?'

'No,' said Isby.

'It's seventy-seven yards from the maypole to your gate—I paced it. As it was a fine evening, did you have a window open?'

'With all those scoundrels about?' protested the vicar. 'We locked and bolted the doors.'

'Everyone in this house gave a statement to the police,' Isby said. 'The real police. Our dinner went cold as we were speaking to them last night. Now, I'm no amateur sleuth, but I can deduce what happened. Your Mr Hardcastle was out drinking with his Blackshirt friends, one of whom was secretly under orders to kill him. There was no scream because he thought he was with a friend.'

'That's ridiculous,' Sissy objected.

'But that's the way you people work, madam. Your beloved Leader is likely taking a leaf out of Herr Hitler's book. You've heard of the Night of the Long Knives? Hitler had his Brownshirt leaders rounded up and killed. Maybe Mosley has started on his Blackshirts. Now that he's back in Parliament, you embarrass him with your battles in the streets and persecuting Jews.'

It was a remarkably neat piece of speculation, and Isby clearly kept up with European news. What was also clear was that he'd been sent to lend backbone to the distraint order. Without him, the vicar might have succumbed to Christian sentiment or caved in to Hardcastle and his rustic militia. It was certain we'd get no God's truth out of either cleric.

'Are you returning to London tomorrow?' asked Isby.

'No.'

'You should. The law will follow its proper course.'

Chapter Ten

I was not accustomed to being warned off by clerics, no matter how senior, while Sissy left the vicarage fired up by the evils of the Church and the rightness of our crusade. It was an easy decision to rise before dawn the next morning, quickly pulling on our uniforms and missing out on the best breakfast in Kent. Sissy found a field gateway some distance short of the barricade to park the Alvis, and we approached the picket with black leather coats flapping.

Mrs Sutton offered tea and toast, but we were not given time to enjoy it before the cry went up.

'They're here!'

A dozen men set off running for the farm gate. Half were in working clothes, and half wore black shirts over a variety of non-uniform trousers. Mrs Sutton ran after us, but her daughter and babies had not yet arrived to bolster our numbers. I caught up with Clague and a knot of men behind the tractor that blocked the lane. Beyond it, half a dozen policemen were already clambering over the fallen tree. One farmhand stood behind the trunk, shouting defiance. He was immediately grabbed, bundled over the tree, and frog marched away. The police outnumbered us, and behind them were civilian workmen. I could see a red-painted lorry and a police van halted behind the barrier, and more could be waiting beyond the turn of the lane.

A weasel-faced man in a good tweed suit and brown bowler advanced, clutching a piece of paper, and at his side was the archbishop's man Isby. The bailiff bawled out his name, his authority, and an order to disperse.

Around me, the men looked to my rank for a lead.

'No trouble,' I ordered, then worked my way around the tractor. I was not up for another fight.

'It's bloody Adolf Hitler himself,' one of the coppers remarked.

'Commander Hugh Clifton, Dep—'

'Arrest that man,' a police inspector snapped.

Constables surged towards me, and all I could do was raise one hand and half raise the other. The fact that a man had been murdered justified my carrying my Walther PPK that morning, tucked into its shoulder holster, but it now became a liability.

'Bloody hell,' one constable said as another withdrew the weapon and handed it to a sergeant.

'Planning on starting a war, were we, Adolf? Get him in the van.'

I yelled in pain as they grabbed the injured arm.

'Stop squealing, you sissy!'

That first defiant farmer was already sitting in the back of the police van. Clague soon joined us, sporting a puffy red eye and split lip to show he hadn't come along quietly. Three more of our uniformed men were bundled in, and last came Sissy in handcuffs, dressing down each policeman who dared touch her.

'My mother is the Baroness Rockwell!' she protested in a voice that cut through the morning.

'I don't care if she's the Queen of Sheba, get in the van, bitch, or I'll throw you in!'

No local police station was large enough to accept so many prisoners. Our group was taken to the nearest and spread across two cells. Clague told me it was the sixth time he'd been arrested, and I confessed it was only my second, barring a misunderstanding while at university too juvenile to retell. Sissy was trembling with rage, muttering all forms of revenge. People she knew in high places would swoop mercilessly on the men responsible and peck out their eyes. As soon as we were allowed near a phone, I'd need to call Black House in London and arrange for one of their solicitors to come down and represent us. With all the chaos in London, they'd be having a busy time.

After an hour or two had dragged by, the cell door opened.

'You—and the posh girl,' said a sergeant.

We followed him into a little office where a constable was stirring a tin mug of tea. The station, wherever it was, was too small to boast the luxury of an interview room. I was surprised that the inspector wasn't present, but perhaps he was still rounding up rebels.

The sergeant was looking at the identity cards that had been confiscated.

'Company Commander Clifton and Woman Unit Leader Poe. Nice titles.' He prodded his own sleeve chevrons. 'Rank has to be earned, not given away like sweeties.'

'We're investigating the murder of Alf Hardcastle,' I said, with maximum pomposity.

'No, you're not, the police do that. And those guns are going to get you into trouble.'

Sissy had carried her Walther in her satchel.

'I hope you have firearms certificates and a good reason to be carrying weapons in the street.'

'A man was murdered,' Sissy said. 'That's reason enough.'

'We are legally permitted to carry pistols for self-defence,' I added. 'We didn't use them to resist arrest. We didn't even draw them.'

'And I bet you've got a very clever brief,' said the sergeant. 'Who's going to pick his way through every letter of the law to try to get you two off the hook.'

'Several,' said Sissy.

'Right. I want written statements, then it's going to be the Magistrates Court on Thursday.'

'Do you have a pencil and paper?' I asked.

The sergeant pushed both towards me. I wrote down a London telephone number.

'Ring that number.'

He glanced at it, creased his chin in dismissal, then passed the number over to the constable.

'Bloody hell, sarge, that's Scotland Yard.'

'Give that back.' The sergeant frowned, and his lips moved as he silently read the number.

'Ring it,' I said. 'Ask for Detective Inspector Renton.'

'Never heard of him.'

'Special Branch—the man who cracked the communist plot to disrupt the election.'

The sergeant eased back in his chair. 'Ah, I see your game. You're going to claim this 'ere Detective Inspector Renton is your best friend, and he's going to lean on me to let you go.'

'Everyone and their aunt is going to lean on you.'

'Including my aunt,' said Sissy. 'I've got a dozen numbers to call the moment I'm out of here. My mother is Baroness Rockwell.'

'You've said. Baroness who?' His expression mocked her. 'You know what? I'm going to call your bluff, Miss High-and-Mighty and Mister Commander Clifton.' He turned to his constable. 'Call the number.'

Chapter Eleven

I arrived late for the meeting at Black House and was the only one of the five men in the room wearing civilian clothes.

'Sorry, sir.' As the only free chair was furthest from the door, I had to pass both Major Taylor and Captain Parker to find a seat. My new rank of company commander served me well, as former second lieutenant did not carry much gravitas.

'You're not in uniform.' William Joyce MP spoke from the top of the table. His scar twitched up from the corner of his mouth, turning what might be a rebuke into a macabre smile.

I whipped off my trilby. 'We're the Confidential Investigation Section, so I try to stay confidential. It's best not to advertise.'

My conviction that Major Taylor had never, in fact, been a major came after a contact had quietly checked military records and only found a corporal in the Pay Corps. Odd things had happened in the 1920s, though, and men had acquired rank for services not spoken about.

Partly balding but sporting a military moustache befitting his assumed rank, Taylor glared at me.

'Were you arrested again?' he demanded.

'Occupational hazard.'

'And how did you get off?'

'Baroness Rockwell is a very good friend of the Chief Constable of Kent.'

It wasn't wise to mention Inspector Renton.

Taylor chuckled, but Joyce fidgeted impatiently.

'Captain Parker has just summarised his strategy for building on our success to contain the Jewish threat.'

Parker also bore a scar on his cheek, mostly hidden today by the large black patch over his ruined left eye. His men had enjoyed a few busy evenings since the Battle of Cable Street and no doubt taken a lead role in the Mile End Pogrom.

'We mustered twelve thousand men at Bethnal Green yesterday,' said Joyce. 'And we're going on the offensive against the communists at last. Which means we need more names and addresses from you.'

Prior to the Battle of Cable Street, the Party had avoided outright attacks on political opponents, attempting to pose as the victim each time violence erupted. Calhoun had told me explicitly I should never break the law, but in contradiction, also hinted that if Blackshirt hooligans were to smash up a left-wing political office, I should make sure that one of my team was on hand to grab any paperwork that might be of use.

I wondered who the fifth man was, older and taller than Joyce with a wide, shiny forehead. He watched me intently through little round glasses. I told the group enough of what they wanted to hear about our investigations into certain trade unionists and the new leaders of communist groups that had arisen to replace those arrested since the election. What I didn't tell them was how extensive my network of agents was becoming. The Party was a paranoid organisation full of petty rivalries, and I'd be safer blending in than standing out.

'And this murder. Was that the communists?' Taylor asked.

'I don't know. It makes little sense in the context of a dispute over a fifty-quid debt, rather, it feels like it should be more part of a pattern.'

'The Leader was shot at in Hull,' Parker said.

'His car was hit by a bullet,' I corrected, 'which isn't the same thing. A single shot doesn't feel like a serious assassination attempt, and didn't I hear that his car was bulletproof? Which takes us back to last year. Incompetent terrorists whose attacks only helped our cause. Did *we* orchestrate the attack on Alf Hardcastle?'

'Don't be ridiculous!' Taylor said.

'I'm asking the question because we're all friends here. And we all have our sources.'

William Joyce was always well-informed and clearly had some network beyond Department Z that fed information to him and only him.

'If the killing was planned from within the Party, one of our teams will find out about it, sooner or later. We're not amateurs.' I was egging the pudding a little now, but nothing works better than confirming a bunch of men's views of their own importance. 'I don't want my men to accidentally sabotage one of our own plots.'

One looked to another.

'Well, I've heard nothing,' Parker said immediately.

'He wasn't sacrificed to the cause in the hope we'd win sympathy in the shires?'

'We wouldn't do that,' Joyce said.

Oh yes, they would and had done so before. Indeed, Joyce wouldn't have won his Parliamentary seat by 89 votes the previous November without that fortuitous last-minute collapse in both the Labour and Conservative vote.

'It's not as though he was a traitor. Although someone is.' Joyce spoke icily, then let his words hang.

Was this the purpose of the meeting? I'd missed the start and had no idea of the agenda.

'Special Branch has an informer within Department Z.' Again, Joyce let his words fall with the weight of lead. He looked directly at me. 'You have a Special Branch contact.'

'I have a phone number. I was interrogated by an inspector named Renton last year, so I give him a bell when communists need arresting. Quid pro quo. It gets them off the streets.'

'Does this Inspector Renton pay you for information?'

'I hesitate to mention it, but I'm heir to a mining fortune, so he'd have to pay me an awful lot.'

Joyce had been a part-time English tutor and Parker a debt collector before they joined the staff at Black House. They were paid about a fiver a week, and for once, I didn't mind being the nouveau-riche dilettante in the room.

'Renton doesn't trust me, and I don't trust him. I get the idea that he'd smash the Party as soon as he's finished smashing the reds and take me down with the rest of you.' All this was true, so I could say it with a straight face and as much nonchalance as I could muster. 'How do we know the police have put a spy in our midst?'

'Because we have friends in the police, and more each day.' Joyce said. 'I want this traitor found. And, Clifton, I also want that Kent killer found. If he's a Jew or a communist, so much the better.' He paused. 'Or a gypsy,' he added with a shrug.

If I'd been a lazy detective and a true fascist, I'm sure I could have found someone who'd fit the frame.

'But with regard to finding this traitor, I should introduce our new Deputy Director of Intelligence.'

Taylor shuffled as if this weren't his idea, but the silent man in the round-rimmed glasses smiled.

'Ah, Hugh Clifton, Commander of Z3,' Taylor said. 'May I introduce Dr Valentine.'

My mouth went dry.

Chapter Twelve

Valentine was another worry to add to my list—and to the Party's accommodation problem. The BU had outgrown its Chelsea headquarters and in addition to an office in Curzon Street for the regional officers, there was now another in Westminster, favoured by the fascist MPs and their assistants. After a tug-of-war with Joyce, Black House was left firmly in the grip of Neil Francis-Hawkins and the militarist wing of the Party. It also remained the hub for the printing and distribution of *Blackshirt*, *Action*, and various pamphlets and posters.

Before leaving Kent, I'd telephoned Cecil Lewis, editor of *Blackshirt*, and asked that his staff arrange for my office to have a copy of every edition for our reference. Almost casually, I rounded off by asking whether Alf Hardcastle wrote many articles. I detected no edginess in Lewis's reply at all. He had a legal mind, so was never vague when he didn't intend it. I told Lewis that Hardcastle had been murdered, as it was hardly a state secret.

As arranged, Sissy and I met a fresh-faced young man called Nigel Fritton at the door of the *Blackshirt* office at the back of the building. Fritton's uniform shirt rather dangled from his slight frame.

'Department Z?' he asked nervously, almost in an excited voice. 'I've started collecting the old editions of *Blackshirt*, but there are rather a lot. I'm not sure we have them all yet.'

'Thanks. Bundle up what you have, and one of my men will collect them.'

'I've found some pieces by Alf Hardcastle already.'

As the editor had freely shared the name, it suggested he was not culpable in trying to cover anything up.

'Are you investigating his murder?' Fritton asked in awe. 'Do you think it was the communists?'

'It could be.'

'I remember Hardcastle writing about trade unions in the print industry. And the Kent farmers, of course.'

'What do you do here?' I asked.

'Bit of everything,' he said. 'Subeditor, we call it in the trade. I read things that are sent in, and I write a few pieces myself. For the arts pages in *Action*. It's more middle class, you know, more my thing if you don't mind me saying so.'

'Show me what you've found by Hardcastle.'

Fritton led us to an inky side table and brought over three copies of *Blackshirt* from earlier in the year. One Hardcastle piece concerned the Kent farmers. His strident tone fitted the *Blackshirt* perfectly as his blunt, unsophisticated English would chime with the target audience. Another article was a puff piece on the fascist trade union movement containing little substance. The third was a glowing account of the new king's visit to a Bromley boys' school then an old soldiers' hospital, which betrayed merely that Hardcastle was a proud monarchist. None of the pieces justified the author meeting a grisly death.

'Do you publish everything people send in?' asked Sissy.

'Oh no, some of it is frightful rubbish. Badly written with no concept of grammar. Sometimes, it doesn't fit with Party priorities, and sometimes it's repetitious. We get an awful lot of pieces bashing on about the Jews.' He screwed up his nose. 'Sorry, but it's not an issue of interest outside London. We have to weed them out.'

'Who sees the pieces first? The editor?'

'No, no, we filter the worst rubbish first. Then, the editors of *Action* and *Blackshirt* choose what we'll use and what edition it will go in. There's not a lot of space after our regular writers have sent in their copy.'

'Have you rejected anything by Hardcastle recently?'

'Ah, I can't recall.'

'Do you maintain a file of the articles you reject?'

'We keep the ones that might be useful for future editions.' He looked apologetic. 'But we throw the rest away.' A sweep of his hand indicated the limited space amid the chaos of newsprint, heaps of the latest run, and bundles of returned stock destined to light fire grates.

'Has anyone else from Department Z shown any interest?' I asked. 'I don't want to tread on any toes. Not Dr Valentine, for example?'

'I've never met Dr Valentine.'

It felt like a wild goose chase as we walked back to Sissy's sporty yellow car and removed our armbands. The most crucial decision left that afternoon was where to dine later.

Fritton emerged from the building, craning his head this way and that in an obvious hunt for us. He hurried after us.

'I say, I hope you don't mind, but I heard you're recruiting men for Department Z.'

I turned. 'Reliable men.'

'And women,' added Sissy.

'I've asked upstairs before. I asked Major Taylor, but he said I wasn't cut out for it.'

'It can be a dangerous job,' I said.

'But Department Z3 is different, everyone says. You don't do so much fighting.'

'No fighting at all, if we can help it. But we only take people with special skills. What are yours? Why would you want to join us?'

'I want to be an investigating reporter one day and work for a Fleet Street newspaper. *Blackshirt* is just... Well, there's not a lot of investigating.'

'Who poses the bigger threat to the country—communists or Jews?' I asked.

He knew there was an even chance his answer would see him fail.

'Communists,' he said, then put his head up proudly and defiantly at his answer. 'I'm sorry, but our readers in the regions find the Jewish thing... embarrassing. So that shows...' He paused. 'They're not much of a threat.'

I liked the honesty and the courage that came with it.

'We can't pay you,' I warned.

'They don't pay me at *Blackshirt*. I've a little legacy set aside so I can learn my trade.' Fritton spoke with the typical accent of a middle-class Londoner, but with a strong hint of the East End. 'My father, rest his soul, wanted me to study law, but I'm not…bright enough. There, I said it. Always best to be honest.'

'Unless you're a confidential investigator, then too much honesty can get you killed.'

He nodded rapidly. 'I understand.'

'And what made you join the Party?' Sissy asked.

'I want to restore public decency. Order, the proper way of things. Keep England as it is—or as it was.'

'Not to clear your area of Jews?' I asked. 'I can hear the East End in your voice.'

'As I said.' He gave a shrug.

A young man such as Fritton could easily be led down the wrong path by men who stoked his ideals and dangled promises before him, but he was fresh to the game and ripe to be led down a different path entirely.

'You're right in that we need more men,' I said. 'Men who think and can blend into a crowd and keep quiet when they need to. There's a pub on the Fulham Road opposite the town hall called the King's Head. Be there at six tonight, and I'll introduce you to Unit Leader Hills. We'll see what he makes of you.'

'Oh super, oh wonderful.' Fritton turned to Sissy. 'If you need women… Can my sister Ruth come too?'

'I'd certainly like to meet her. Bring her along.'

Sissy waited until Fritton was gone from earshot.

'He's far too nice to be in Department Z. He looks like he's just out of school.'

'Which makes him perfect,' I said. 'Was your first impression *fascist secret agent*?'

'No, I suppose not. I wonder if his sister is the same?'

'We could use his choirboy looks to start the hunt for Hardcastle's dodgy vicar.'

She clicked her finger. 'Ah, I was going to say. Wallis isn't a vicar. I've been a complete dunce. I should have twigged earlier. We girls had a drink or two last night, Julia and Eleanor, the usual goss, and a name came up.' She bit her lip to tease me.

'Are you going to keep me in suspense?'

'Remember that huge soirée of Lady Cunard's that you hated? A woman was pointed out to us as being the Prince of Wales's mistress. She looked about forty and not that pretty, and I think I said something catty about her dress.' She paused for dramatic effect. 'Wallis Simpson.'

Chapter Thirteen

'And with one bound, he was free,' he said.

Commander Marcus Calhoun had come to my apartment at Havelock Mansions, Bloomsbury, which was unusual. It was raining too heavily to meet in a park and presumably, he didn't want to risk being overheard in one of the little back-street cafes that were his staple foul-weather rendezvous. I'd put him off until late morning as I had an appointment down at Barts to have my stitches taken out. I lounged in my favourite armchair as he ran his eyes over my two bookshelves packed with detective stories, mysteries, and adventures.

'Do you owe your freedom to Baroness Rockwell pulling strings, by any chance?'

'And Detective Inspector Renton. He owed me a favour from last year.'

'You're my man, not his.'

'Would you have broken me out?'

He made a lemon-sucking face, confirming my assertion.

'Carrying that gun around is going to land you in hot water one day.'

'I'll stop carrying it when people stop trying to kill me.'

'But be on notice that carrying guns for self-defence will be made illegal next year, if the bill gets through, so not even your bosom friends at Special Branch will be able to help you then. And in the meantime, do be careful with Renton. Remember your little parable about riding on a tiger to escape the crocodile?'

'I will, I will.'

Calhoun stopped looking at my books and took the other chair. He waved away my suggestion that I make him a drink.

'My list of people to be wary of grows longer,' I said. 'Joyce is on a witch hunt and says there's a Special Branch spy in the camp.'

'I'd be surprised if there weren't. Everyone's got agents inside your party. Even the chief rabbi.'

'The rabbi? Are you certain?'

'He's set up his own intelligence unit, and it won't be for checking that kosher butchers are following the rules.' Calhoun started rummaging in the briefcase he'd brought with him.

'I hear that a lot of Jews are joining the communists,' I said. 'Although it doesn't stop the fascists claiming they're all millionaire capitalists plotting to buy the world.'

'Antisemitic logic doesn't make much sense, and there are Jews and others on the inside now, so just take care you don't expose the wrong man' Calhoun took out a bundle of newspapers. 'Or woman.'

'Joyce has set up a man named Dr Valentine as Witchfinder General,' I said. 'Ring any bells?'

I waited for some nod of recognition, but Calhoun puckered his chin and shook his head.

'This Valentine has the bit between his teeth, and there's another man worrying me: Isby. He does something in the archbishop's office. Both Valentine and Isby were near the scene of the murder last Saturday.'

Calhoun looked thoughtful before his next question. He indicated the C section of my bookshelf with one of his newspapers.

'What is it about the Hardcastle murder that's triggered your Agatha Christie instincts?'

'This isn't our usual day or our usual venue, so I might ask the same. It wasn't the name Wallis Simpson that brought you here, by any chance?'

He nodded reluctantly. 'Do you read the continental newspapers?'

'From time to time.'

'Mrs Wallis Simpson shared the king's carriage at Ascot back in June.'

'Yes.'

Sissy had reminded me of the event.

'And she shares much more of him too, the whispers say.'

King Edward had succeeded his father in February. He hadn't yet been crowned, so his public image was still very much the dashing playboy prince.

Calhoun picked out one of the newspapers and passed over a copy of a Chicago paper I was unfamiliar with.

'Just about every small-town rag in America is carrying the story.'

I quickly scanned the piece speculating whether this American woman would become the next queen of England.

'Are they making this up? I mean, it says here the king and Mrs Simpson spent the summer yachting round the Med together. How did *The Daily Express* miss that?'

'There's a gentleman's agreement between the press barons to keep it out of the British newspapers.'

'Really?' I was almost frightened that a small bunch of wealthy men had the power to keep the wool pulled firmly over the eyes of the nation. And that this story was considered of such importance that they would stoop to such tricks. 'To be fair, the king is single,' I said, frowning at a second paper Calhoun passed over. 'He needs a queen and an heir.'

'Well, she won't be queen and won't be producing an heir.'

'Because she's American?'

'Primarily because *Mrs* Simpson is still married to *Mr* Simpson. Who, it seems, is turning a blind eye to his wife becoming *de facto* the new royal mistress.'

'Ah,' I said. 'So, if the king can't marry her, where's the problem? When he was merely a prince, he had mistresses, girlfriends, call them what you like. Royal mistresses have a long and noble tradition. I thought MI5's role was military intelligence, not policing public morals.'

Calhoun nodded. 'When Edward was Prince of Wales his female companions were usually wealthy titled ladies, but Simpson is a nobody.'

'So this is what, snobbery?'

'She has no family or money of her own and is neither young nor especially beautiful. Now suddenly, she pops up as the king's favourite.'

The intelligence world did not like things happening suddenly.

'It was her husband that excited the most interest at first. Special Branch put their top detective on his tail.'

'Renton?' I guessed.

'No, Superintendent Canning. I've read his report. Simpson has shipping interests. He's often in Hamburg. Sound familiar?'

'Go on.'

'His business is struggling, so that makes him vulnerable, and he must have contact with the Nazis. The report also makes a great deal of his Jewish ancestry.'

'As though that gives him a black mark.'

'In the wisdom of Special Branch, it does.'

'Nazis, Americans, and Jews,' I said with a sigh. 'We only have to add communists and Freemasons to the mix to satisfy all popular prejudice.'

'Simpson is a Freemason,' Calhoun added, totally deadpan.

I could not avoid laughing, then supressed a cough. This was becoming more ridiculous by the moment.

'The king likes being popular with the masses,' Calhoun said. 'We know he's fond of Germany and may even have fascist sympathies, so one could deduce that the crew he gathers around him feel the same. People in the know say he's easily flattered and, I guess, easily seduced. The last thing we need is our new king going to bed with a Nazi spy, so we're going to keep a close eye on Mrs Simpson and her husband to see what they're up to. And when I say we...'

'You mean me.'

Chapter Fourteen

RHC Limited, a newly formed subsidiary of R T Clifton Limited, had bought the Fulham Bakery, not so far from the King's Head pub and a mile and a half west of Black House. My father had been delighted by my sudden interest in commerce and was only too keen to diversify his own empire to include a subsidiary company acquiring London properties. The enterprise might even turn a profit, but what drew my eye was the excessive amount of office space on its first floor and the yard at the rear, large enough to accommodate half a dozen vehicles. Bakers' vans proved ideal for moving small numbers of agents around the capital unremarked.

When recruiting for Section Z3 I avoided diehards in thrall to the words of Mosley, Joyce, or Hitler. Instead, I looked for the outcasts, those for whom fascism offered the last hope or a route out of their disappointments. Men and women who, with a different political indoctrination, might easily have signed up for the communists or taken the Red Train for Spain to rediscover a purpose in life.

Sissy used the freedom, money, and authority that came with being of the landed gentry to run our women's section. Women were easily overlooked by the kind of man who expected police and government agents to be men. Female fascists needed a different kind of care when I was selecting them, so I chose starry-eyed idealists like Lucy, who simply wanted a better world, or those bored with a woman's lot, such as a pair of Chelsea housewives whose husbands worked in the City.

The bakery was merely a front for Section Z3. I inhabited Room Z to maintain appearances and to give me an excuse to be in Black House whenever I wanted, but I needed to keep my agents away from there as much as possible. Lucy and Sergeant Hills were on the payroll of the bakery, while the rest worked for nothing more than the dream of a fascist Britain and the occasional free bun. Section Z3 never wore uniforms at the bakery, partly to remain inconspicuous and partly so I could wean my recruits away from jackbooted fantasies. There would be no saluting and minimum reference to ranks.

By noon, the bakers' working day was over, and only a couple of shop staff remained downstairs. This was convenient given that most of my men were only free in the late afternoons and evenings as they either held down jobs or were looking for jobs. Lunchtime was the time to forsake Room Z, remove my uniform, and drive down the King's Road to where the real work was done. Lucy often spent the whole day there, entering by the back gate, as did bakery staff and fascist agents alike.

The bakery office was spartan, with some walls being cream-painted brick, others plastered but peeling here and there. Furnishings were cheap and utilitarian. An L-shaped plywood partition with a half-glazed end wall served as my barely private office.

Lucy bobbed her head round the insubstantial and rather wobbly door. 'Visitor, sir.' She hardly ever called me sir.

The man she led into my office was rake-thin, his hair wispy above his broad forehead once he had removed his hat and smoothed it back. He moved with short steps, his glasses catching the light as he looked left and right, holding his hat in one hand and tapping it with the other.

I stood to greet him. 'Dr Valentine.'

Lucy closed the office door behind him but continued to watch us through the glass partition.

'Good afternoon, Clifton. Interesting retreat. I see none of your staff are in uniform.'

'No.'

'Why; ashamed?'

'We don't advertise. The reds could easily burn the place to the ground.

One Molotov cocktail would be enough. And you yourself aren't in uniform either, so you also don't want to advertise.'

'Some people don't like the idea that you've set up your own separate headquarters.'

'Which people? Name a few.'

He ignored my question. 'What have you against Black House?'

'It was getting crowded, and it's an obvious place for our enemies to watch, make notes of faces, take photographs, follow people. Their spies can't be everywhere, so down here we have more chance of escaping surveillance. You should understand that—how long have you been with Z1?'

'Oh, I'm here to ask the questions.'

I leaned forward. 'I've also got questions. We don't just bake bread here.'

'My turn first. Any idea who the traitor is?'

I shook my head very slowly.

'With all your leads, all your informants? We know what you're doing. Planting agents in every town. Why is that?'

'Keeping an eye on communist activity.' It was pointless denying what I'd been up to.

'That all?'

'Any activity that threatens the Party. Including members being murdered.'

'Hardcastle, yes. Unfortunate.'

'And bloody mysterious. Why were you down there?'

Valentine paused, possibly to compose an official line. 'We were not sure about him.'

'And are you sure now? Dead martyr or dead traitor?'

He shrugged.

'Look,' I said. 'We're supposed to be on the same side. If it was you, your men, or Parker's who did away with Hardcastle because he was some sort of traitor, just tell me. I'll close the case and move on.'

Valentine shook his head. 'The police also thought it was us.' He pinched his eyes and whispered, 'No imagination.'

'Were you the last to see him alive?'

'Not the last one, clearly. He was still in the bar when I turned in, and he wasn't alone. Nasty little hovel, that hotel; they gave me a poky little room at the side. Hardcastle made sure he had the best one.'

He took out a crocodile-skin cigar case, but I frowned, tapping my chest. 'War wound, lungs.'

'Very well.' He put his case away.

'Have you got any suspects of your own?'

'That man Clague wasn't happy to see us,' Valentine said, 'and nor was Farmer Sutton who we were there to help. Not the local NFU man either, nor the TPA man—they're the anti-tithe campaigners. It's a classic nest of vipers down there, and none of them wanted Hardcastle's help.'

'Did you meet a Mr Isby? He's some lackey of the Archbishop of Canterbury.'

'No.' Valentine sounded certain. 'Frankly, as the village was crawling with police by Sunday lunchtime, I came away as soon as I could. And as you said, it's your case now. Investigate away.'

'And meanwhile, your job is to hunt traitors in our midst?'

'Communist agents, Special Branch informers, trade union plants. The movement has grown so quickly anyone could have sneaked in before we started looking. So, let's start with your troops out there? Do you trust them?'

'With my life in a couple of cases.'

'Yes, you've been in some scrapes, I hear. Well, Joyce wanted me to bring some posters to inspire your team. You could even put some up in the neighbourhood after dark.'

Valentine produced a small bundle of handbills from his coat pocket, half-foolscap size. Even upside-down, I could see it featured a caricature of a Jewish banker lighting a cigar with a pound note and the exhortation *Jews Out!*

'Or is it not your style?' He drew the pile back.

'Thank you,' I said, accepting the pile and setting it to one side.

'Traitor,' he said.

'What?'

'All your ears and eyes, looking for the traitor.'

It would punch a hole in the Party if someone senior could be framed as a Special Branch agent and usefully stoke their paranoia, but it would weaken the police's surveillance if I managed to finger the right man.

'Strictly speaking, hunting traitors is Z1's task,' I said. 'I don't want to steal your trade—what would the secret police union say?'

He stiffened.

'I've my hands full with communist plots,' I said. 'And a murder.'

'Don't worry. I'll find him.' His eyes bore into me as if wanting to read my mind, or at least the poker hand I hid from his sight.

'I have no idea who you are, Dr Valentine, or why the fates conspired to put you right on the spot when Hardcastle was killed. But if you're adding me to your suspect list, be aware that I've added you to mine.'

Chapter Fifteen

I t had seemed a good wheeze to join Major Taylor's fledgling
intelligence unit, but now Department Z was investigating Department
Z. Who watches the watchmen, indeed.

The bakery office had been nearly empty when Valentine made his
unwelcome visit, but Sissy's women arrived soon after he left, and the
men drifted in one by one. One of the Chelsea Wives arranged the meeting
room chairs, and the other put both kettles on. Nigel and Ruth Fritton sat
themselves at the front, full of anticipation and not a little funk.

I half sat, half stood as I began the briefing, resting against the desk in
the meeting room with one foot upon the floor. One of my form teachers
used to perch in that manner when explaining some trivial new school
rule, to give the impression that he was really on the side of the boys. I
cultivated informality to encourage the team to think and act like private
detectives, not the Metropolis automata the stormtroopers were becoming.
Not everyone was present, so we numbered exactly a baker's dozen. One of
my coughs came unbidden, and I took a sip of water.

'Welcome all, and a special welcome to Nigel Fritton and his sister Ruth.
Fritton will be in Thring's section, Ruth will be with Sissy.'

Everyone looked at the newcomers. Nigel Fritton appeared the more
nervous, ducking his head as his name was mentioned. Slightly older, a plain
mousey blonde in a knitted cardigan, Ruth showed the more confidence of
the two, turning to smile at her new unit leader.

'We have a few items on the menu this afternoon.' I held up a finger. 'One,
Black House is on the hunt for a traitor. He or she may actually exist, in

71

which case we may discover that person in the course of our work. Whoever it is won't see Christmas, so my ears first, understood? If that traitor doesn't exist, one may be found anyway *pour encourager les autres*.'

'You know I don't speak Frenchie, guv,' Hills objected. He was a big square-set disgraced copper needing to claw back some self-confidence. He was also the oldest member of the team.

'Joyce wants to make an example of someone, so be on your guard. Make sure it's not you. And if you come across a Dr Valentine, he's with Z1 and is leading the hunt, so mind your p's and q's.'

I added a second finger to the first.

'Two, someone is killing Blackshirts. Again, make sure it's not you next. The murder of Alf Hardcastle was unusual, and the Kent police are not on our side. Hardcastle was killed quietly, possibly professionally, so Hills—gangsters. Was he mixed up in anything beyond politics?'

Hills nodded. His eyes often carried a blank, faraway look, but now I saw the spark of engagement.

'And three,' I said. 'And this is very, very confidential.'

Both the Frittons nodded enthusiastically, but the tall red-haired ex-debutante Eleanor Fitzherbert shrugged, as if I were teaching her to suck eggs. She removed her gold-rimmed Oxford glasses and started to wipe the lenses.

Slowly, I drew the Chicago newspaper off the desk I was half sitting on. I'd folded the newspaper in such a way as to make a photograph prominent.

'This is Mrs Wallis Simpson, the king's new mistress. And it's absolutely top secret.'

'But she's in the newspaper,' Lucy objected.

'An American newspaper. Someone is sitting on the British press...' I paused. 'Which makes me suspicious.'

'We've known about this affair for months,' Eleanor declared, nudging Julia. 'She was with him when he was just a prince.'

'Not everyone is invited to the kind of parties you two attend.'

The pair had been at school together. The stockier brunette, Julia, was by far the more dependable one and most of the reason I kept Eleanor on board.

'There's been a lot of gossip,' Julia added, 'but it's gossip, yah?'

Sissy was the only member of my team privy to the fact that Hardcastle had also taken an interest in the growing scandal, and for the moment, I was keeping it that way.

'Clearly, Mrs Simpson is a friend of the king's,' I said, 'and it's not a state secret if every ex-deb in town knows it.'

The two ex-debutantes grinned.

'So what does the Establishment want to hide?' I growled, deliberately channelling William Joyce. 'What are they afraid of? The king is a good friend of the Party, so it would be very useful if we found out.'

'Did this assignment come from Joyce?' asked Julian, spotting my tone.

'No.' I tapped my own head, which the team could interpret how they pleased. 'It might be nothing, but time spent gathering intelligence is seldom wasted. We're going to need to find someone with access to the king's court. He's not moved into Buckingham Palace yet and is living at Fort Belvedere out in Windsor Great Park. We need a flunky, maid, hanger-on, but someone we can trust to keep quiet.'

'I'll start asking among my friends. Discreetly,' said Sissy. 'Eleanor, Julia, you must know someone.'

The two young women nodded, clearly pleased they had something to offer.

I waved the paper again. 'And there's also a Mr Edward Simpson, so let's ferret out what we can about him. Hills, another one for your boys. Find out where he lives and see if you can spot any reporters sniffing round.'

Hills nodded.

'And we want to know where his money comes from, who his friends are, what club he goes to. That sounds like one for you, Julian. He's in shipping, commerce....'

'It will make a change from dreary communists,' Julian said.

'Let's keep this in-house as far as we can. Employ the people you must, but tell them nothing more than they need to know.'

'Shall I open a file?' Lucy asked.

'And subscribe to a few foreign newspapers. Let's see what they're saying about our king.'

Chapter Sixteen

Baroness Rockwell had pulled enough strings for Sissy and I to escape prosecution for our part in the farm fracas, and the local hands were let off with a warning, but a magistrate handed out fines to Clague and all his Blackshirts for unlawful assembly, obstruction, and other petty offences. Without a body on the mortuary slab, that should have been the end of things.

Sutton's confiscated chattels were to be auctioned in Ashford, an attractive little town with a historic centre of half-timbered buildings. I was amused to drive past a Great War tank installed as a memorial. This emphasised that the town was at the very heart of England and everything it stood for. I took the new boy, Fritton. We turned up in our civilian clothes and split up soon after I parked at the edge of the marketplace.

Clague had mustered two dozen men for the occasion. He saluted me, but I didn't return the compliment.

'I'm not in uniform,' I said. 'No need to salute.' It was as good an excuse as any. I'd even left my black leather coat at home so as to blend in more.

'I–I wasn't in the army, so don't get the rules.'

Clague's men were still a rag-tag bunch, if more numerous than at the farm siege. They lacked the aggressive look of the drilled stormtrooper units but, even so, cast a shadow over the marketplace. Farmers and locals stood apart from them, even Farmer Sutton.

A cluster of demonstrators on the opposite side protested not against the fascists but against the bailiffs. A placard declared them to be the Tithe Payers Association. A placard read *Stop cheap imports! British food for British people!*

I suggested that Fritton drift across. 'That's the TPA. The only man I recognise is the older chap next to the one with the placard. That's Sutton, the one whose farm is under distraint. Mingle, see what you can pick up.'

He nodded and put his head down as if to become more inconspicuous.

I drew Clague aside. 'A quiet word, if you please?' I offered my usual script on the importance of Department Z in keeping a lid on communism. 'And we keep an eye out for anything unusual.'

'Such as what?'

'Hardcastle's death is an outstanding example.'

'I see.'

'Once we're in power, we'll need eyes and ears in every town in the country.'

He nodded.

'Will you be the eyes and ears of Department Z for Ashford? You'd keep it secret, of course—you wouldn't want to end up like Hardcastle.'

'He wasn't—'

'No, he wasn't part of Department Z.'

I explained how Clague could send information to me via a post office address. I gave him my card. He smiled, looking delighted to be asked. The fact I'd recommended him for the

prestigious Action Press uniform and even paid for it probably helped his decision.

'Yes, yes. Department Z. Gosh.'

'But don't bandy it around. We are the *Confidential* Investigation Section. Any more contact from that Dr Valentine?'

'No, none.'

For all my wish to extend the reach of Z3, this was what I really wanted to know. I moved over towards the largest group of civilians clustered around a National Farmers' Union banner. One man looked at me sharply.

'Are you with them?' He nodded towards the black-shirted locals. 'Or that lot?' His disdain switched to the TPA. 'Or are you with the General Stealers?'

'I'm here to support you,' I said.

He snatched a handbill from a colleague and thrust it at me. I gave it a quick glance, noting it promoted the NFU and attacked the distraints orders.

'Are you losing members to the British Fascist Workers' Union?'

He glared at me.

'It's an honest question.'

He tapped his own chest. 'The National Farmers' Union is the real farmers' union. We've been fighting the tithes since before half of those Blackshirts were born.'

I nodded, I smiled. I was not here to make either converts or enemies. A stocky woman was working the crowd, handing out a different leaflet. I went across and allowed myself to be given one, expecting it to be from one of the other campaign groups.

'Christians Against Fascism,' I read aloud.

'Yes,' she said.

'Not Christians Evicting Farmers?

'This is no time for levity, young man.' Her face quivered, and she raised an arm to point at Clague and his followers. 'They are damned. Read the words.' Now she jabbed a finger at the paper she'd given me.

'I will, thank you, ma'am.'

She turned away, flushed with the impression she'd won a convert. In truth, I was warmed by the idea that Mosley was not just being opposed from the left. I glanced at the latest edict again. Unlike the leaflets I'd been given before the Battle of Cable Street, there was no mention of the 35 Group, whoever they'd been.

I moved to rejoin Fritton. 'Have you come across these Christians Against Fascism?'

He studied the latest biblical injunction for a moment. 'I've seen leaflets like this.'

'The ones in London were printed by people calling themselves the 35 Group. It would be interesting to know who they are.'

'I'd guess they were formed in 1935.'

It tallied with my own guess.

'But perhaps they're only in London,' he added helpfully. 'Not here.'

It was a tiny detail, but I was on the alert for tiny details.

Fritton pulled my attention to more immediate issues. 'There's a bunch of socialists over there. They've spotted our interest in the countryside and want to beat us to it.'

'Over the bodies of the Tory landowners, I expect,' I said. 'Ay up, we're on.'

The auctioneer mounted the dais and began to read out the lots, his every word drowned out by catcalls and jeering.

'Lot 1, a two-year-old Holstein heifer. Shall I start the bidding at ten shillings?'

Silence descended. The auctioneer looked around, hopefully.

I put my hand up. 'Sixpence.'

There was a roar of laughter. I had no idea of the value of a cow, but it had to be a few pounds.

'Who will offer ten shillings?' Pause. 'Nine shillings?'

'Sixpence,' I repeated.

'Sixpence ha'penny,' one of the farmers outbid me to more roars of laughter.

The auctioneer began to sweat. This had happened to him before, and he knew it would happen again. Confident I wouldn't be driving home with a cow in tow, I moved around the arena as the charade continued. So many different parties were locking horns in this quiet corner of England, I was not surprised when I spotted another—and he spotted me.

'Mr Isby.'

He was well turned out in tweeds, almost as well tailored as my own.

'I suppose you and your fascist friends think you're being very clever. The debt will still stand.'

'Judas sold the Lord for only thirty silver pieces,' I muttered. 'So a cow can't be worth more than sixpence.'

'Do not take the Lord's name in vain. You and your ungodly multitude over there, bringing your city anarchy out here. What do you want?'

'A quiet word. Without any vicars or bailiffs in earshot.'

We walked to the edge of the crowd and beyond.

'Is this you?' I showed him the Christians Against Fascism leaflet.

'I'm aware of the movement,' he said. 'It's an inevitable response to Mosley's barbarism.'

'Can you tell me more about who publishes these pamphlets?'

'So you can do what? Smash up their printing press and attack their staff?'

'No, so I can understand their argument. For example, the ones I saw in London were published by the 35 Group. Ever come across them? I imagine they were founded last year.'

'Ah, the ignorance of fascists. Deuteronomy, the Song of Moses, Verse 35. "In due time, their foot will slip; their day of disaster is near, and their doom rushes upon them."'

'Good old Deuteronomy. If only our Leader would take it to heart and give up trying to save the country.'

'In layman's terms, judgment awaits. Your so-called Leader will make a mistake, and he will fall. And in due course, he will be judged.'

That was fine by me, but I wouldn't share this sentiment with Isby.

'Can I contact this 35 Group?'

'I'm not sure they're still around,' Isby said. 'There is a time for everything, a season for every activity—'

'Ecclesiastes,' I said. 'I've been to enough funerals to know that one.'

'Movements come, and movements go, as yours surely will.'

'And judgment awaits,' I said. 'Speaking of which, I'm still interested in the murder of Alf Hardcastle. A time to kill—that's another chunk of Ecclesiastes.'

'Oh, police detectives are dealing with that,' Isby said. 'I've spoken to them. They have actual legal authority.' He grinned, aware of my limited locus.

'So if you had nothing to do with the murder, I'm still intrigued as to why a senior member of the Church of England is expending so much time and effort here, punishing a family over such a paltry sum of money.'

'Did you serve in the War?'

'No.'

'Of course you didn't. You upstarts will steal the peace won by the sacrifice of my generation. We had to fight for every inch of ground. Men died to gain inches, or to save inches being lost. In the war between light and darkness we don't give the Devil an inch.'

'But Sutton is a farmer. He's not even a member of our party. And it's his ground you're taking!'

'It is, in truth, the Church's ground.'

'And you take, what, three million pounds a year across the country?' I'd done my research. 'Render unto Caesar what is Caesar's? Perhaps I got the quote right.'

'Without the tithe there is no Church of England, and without its Church, England will slide into a new Dark Age. Led by your Mosley. You are truly consorting with the Devil.'

'Did you know before he died Hardcastle wrote a letter to your archbishop?'

'The joy of your absurdly named Department Z having no authority is that nobody has to answer your questions.'

'If we're the minions of evil you paint us to be, do you imagine we stop at polite enquiries?'

'I imagine you don't. And if an uncultured illiterate like your Mr Hardcastle wrote to Canterbury, I doubt the archbishop would have even been passed the letter to read. I can only imagine the rubbish a man such as that would write.'

'You imagine a lot. It must be better than lying, given lying is a sin.'

'So is wrath.'

I'd pushed Isby further than most men would go. The Great War veteran didn't look to be a feeble man, not as effete as his biblical utterings would suggest, and his pupils had shrunk to a pinprick. This was no place for a brawl.

I tipped my hat. 'Give my regards to the archbishop.'

Chapter Seventeen

On my drive back, I took a detour to Bromley. I told Fritton to remain in the car. He was untested, and there were many things he did not need to know. A paper notice in the window of the Hardcastle house read: *To Let—No Irish*.

The widow answered her door almost as soon as I'd stepped out of the Alvis.

'I see from the sign you're moving, Mrs Hardcastle.'

She hesitated for a moment. 'Yes, the landlord is letting the place.'

'Doesn't he like the Irish?'

She shrugged. 'He can let to who he likes. I'm moving to my sister's.'

'Is she close?'

'Round the corner. Why do you need to know that?'

'Because we're investigating Alf's murder and should stay in touch.'

'Glad someone cares. The police won't let me have a funeral. The bastards are still fiddling with his body.' She retreated a few steps into her hall, and I followed her. 'And I'd thought his brother Neil would have come by now. They were close. And Neil cared for family, too.'

'Did he have far to travel?'

'No, only Surrey. He could have done it on the train in an hour or two.'

'Perhaps he couldn't get time off work. Times are hard.'

'He's only a groundsman. They can let the grass grow for a day.'

'Has he written to you?'

'No, not even that. And he can't pretend he doesn't know because it's been in all the papers and my sister wrote to him too.'

'Yet you said they were close.' Most murders I'd read about were committed by family members, colleagues, or friends.

'That's what hurts. It's not like 'im.'

'Where is he a groundsman?'

'I'm sorry, I need to get on with packing my things.'

'Where does he work?' I insisted.

She looked hurt by my tone. 'A golf club at Virginia Water. He lives on the London Road.'

'Address?'

She told me, and I wrote it down.

'Neil Hardcastle?'

'No, he's still called Gotobed.' She pronounced it Goterbid. 'But Alf had our name changed when he joined the Party. Said he hated that name. It don't bother Neil. He's a gentle soul.'

I wondered quite how gentle.

* * *

The following afternoon Sissy and I drove out to the village of Virginia Water in Surrey, where Wentworth's Club had been established in the twenties. After a drive through trees, I pulled up by the clubhouse, a giant mock-medieval folly of turrets and crenelations.

A steward came immediately to the door of the Alvis.

'Good afternoon, sir.'

'We're not members,' I said, sparing the man the embarrassment of asking. 'Oh, but sir...'

'I'm looking for the greenkeeper, Neil Gotobed.' I tried to pronounce the name in the way it sounded less ridiculous.

'Mr Gotobed isn't the greenkeeper. He's just one of the groundsmen.'

'Could I see him, please? It's most urgent.'

'This is very irregular, sir—he'll be busy.'

'And so are we.'

It took some time to locate the greenkeeper, who explained that he hadn't seen Gotobed since the Friday of the week before and was minded to give him notice when he finally showed up. He rented a cottage by the very edge of the parkland near London Road.

'Last Friday,' Sissy said as I drove off. 'The day before Hardcastle was murdered.'

The day was advancing when we drew up outside the cottage, a single-storey building standing alone and only slightly set back from the main road. From its stone-built, symmetrical construction, I guessed it might once have played a role on the country estate taken to form the golf club. It faced across to Windsor Great Park, and Virginia Water would lie beyond the trees. I swung the car around and parked it by the side of the road a hundred yards back towards London. We returned on foot.

The afternoon was gloomy and turning to dusk before its time. Traffic ground past, making for the capital before nightfall or escaping it.

'Someone's in,' Sissy said.

Gotobed didn't answer my knock on his front door, but most working-class people habitually used only a side or back door.

'I did see someone.' Sissy peered into one of the front windows, then moved to look through the other.

I prowled carefully around the back, thinking for a moment I heard movement.

'The front door is locked,' she said, rejoining me.

I shushed her. 'Someone round the back,' I whispered. Edging around the corner, I glanced through a window into what looked like a bedroom, then pushed the green-painted back door open.

'Hello!' I called. Groundsmen might just possibly own shotguns, so we needed to take care. The door opened directly into a kitchen. I called out hello again. Stale, lifeless air lacked any warmth, and not even the ticking of a clock disturbed the silence. The kitchen range was iron-cold to my touch.

'Not at home.'

'I saw someone, I'm sure I did,' she said, glancing behind her.

We advanced inside. It was a simple lodge, with an open door from the kitchen leading into a narrow hall, then another open door opening into a sitting room. A closed door on my left must be a front bedroom. I tapped on it, then opened it to find a barely used room with a few pieces of stacked furniture and accumulated belongings of the type often consigned to lofts.

In the lounge, a wooden-cased clock stood motionless on the tiles of the fireplace. I saw no party literature, no discarded uniform, no Union Flag or photograph of Mosley. If Neil Gotobed was a fascist supporter, he hid it well. A small pile of newspapers mingled with parish magazines sat on the floor by the sofa. The only book on show was a well-thumbed bible on the arm of what looked like his preferred reading chair beside the window. It was old, and inside its black cloth cover was a faded plate announcing it had been awarded in 1898 to a woman who most probably had been his mother or aunt.

Sissy sniffed the air, where the scent of tobacco lingered. 'Pipe smoke.'

'Recent,' I said.

'I did see someone.'

Six or eight burned matches lay in an old saucer, and a tin mug containing water stood on a small table by the window. Across the road, Windsor Great Park stood shrouded by trees, and just visible further from London was a road junction. Beyond it, a private part of the park climbed in wooded tiers. Somewhere in those grounds stood Fort Belvedere where Prince Edward had made his home and where he still lingered as king. I didn't like coincidences.

We checked the rear bedroom behind its closed door. A lack of fresh air added to the oppression of the small bedroom with its closed curtains and part-made bed.

'Pooh.' Sissy theatrically pinched her nose against the pervading smell of laundry left to mature. Nobody had been in that room for a while. She tugged open the wardrobe door, which wobbled on cheap hinges. Between us, we'd gained the arrogance of policemen, as if those Department Z badges gave us authority to poke around in someone's life.

'I'm getting a horrible feeling,' she said.

'Me too. I don't like the look of this.'

A tin-plated pocket watch sat on the dark wood chest of drawers that served as a dressing table. The watch had stopped, and next to it were a few shillings of assorted copper and silver. Gotobed had not been burgled.

'Look for boots,' I said. 'And a coat.'

We found only a pair of shoes and a summer-weight jacket. Out in the yard, I checked the privy.

'Oh, poor dears!' Sissy exclaimed.

Down one margin of the narrow garden was a chicken coop where three lifeless bundles of feathers lay amid a smear of broken eggs. A sole survivor blinked at us, scrawny but expecting the humans to save it. Sissy opened the coop, and the hen stalked into the garden and immediately started pecking at the ground.

'The man's dead too,' she said.

'Or he's the one who killed his brother and has gone on the run.'

But if Gotobed had ventured to Kent, he'd have taken his watch and his change. Otherwise, on a normal day, a groundsman should be able to sense the time from the elements, so would have little need of a watch he could easily lose in some thicket or pool.

'But someone was here, in the sitting room, smoking a pipe,' she said.

'Waiting,' I said.

'Someone who didn't care about the chickens.'

'They were still here,' I realised, quickly checking the gap between the cottage and the far fence. 'There's room to squeeze this way while we were prowling around the other side.'

Sissy tested my idea and easily brushed past an overhanging hedge. She cautiously peered around the front corner with me just behind her. 'Who's that?'

I saw it too, the face in the trees opposite. The watcher vanished.

'Let's find out.' I unbuttoned my leather coat, and Sissy did the same as we emerged from our corner, checked right and left for traffic, then jogged swiftly across the carriageway.

The face did not reappear. I peered over the iron fence into the gloom of the trees, then looked for a place to cross. 'Leg up?' I asked. Without so much as a whisper, she was helping me over.

'My turn.'

'No, move along the fence.' I gesticulated towards Fort Belvedere. 'Keep an eye out. We're miles from anywhere, so he could have a car at the back of the trees.'

'Down that road,' she said, pointing towards the road junction.

That made sense.

'Take care.'

I took out my Walther and moved from tree to tree until I could barely see the shine of the road behind me. With twigs and early fallen leaves scattered on the ground, it was not a place to move about silently. A crunch and a rustle betrayed my prey. He was somewhere not far ahead. I moved more to my right, intending to circle round so he'd be silhouetted against the road while my back would be to the dark. On instinct, I checked that no one else had the same idea and was sneaking behind me.

There he was.

'Come out with your hands up!' I commanded, faking authority once more. 'We are armed.'

So was he. Wood splintered and fell onto the brim of my hat. Only then did I hear the shot. I pulled myself behind the tree, thinking before I acted again. Who on earth could it be? Special Branch, MI5, Royal Protection Squad, Grenadier Guards…

'Department Z!' I shouted. 'We just want to talk.'

'You come out then,' a man shouted back. 'With your hands up.' His accent was neither foreign nor rough, but not exactly well-spoken.

I slid down the tree so the next time I looked round it, my head would be a good two feet lower. I removed my hat to change my silhouette. The barrel of my Walther would edge out first, and then I'd chance a look.

He fired again as I pulled back. The bullet zipped deep into the woods before striking anything.

'That's not very sporting!' I shouted.

'I'll give you sporting.'

Two shots snapped out from the direction of the road. My attacker yelled something, and before he could spot Sissy and return fire, I rolled back into position and unloaded three bullets at the birch that offered him cover. Enfiladed, he could retreat or die. He chose to retreat, scurrying quickly away from the pair of us.

'Sissy, stay where you are!' I shouted. 'And don't shoot me. I'm to your right.' I edged back towards the road from tree to tree until I saw her, using the cover of an elm that was leaning against the fence.

'Hugh, are you hurt?'

'I'm fine. You?'

She hesitated for a moment. 'Never better.' Her hesitation suggested otherwise. 'Did you get him?'

'No, and I don't think you did either, but you gave him a scare. Watch my back for a moment.' I holstered my Walther, tossed my hat over the fence, and then clumsily clambered over.

'We're not going to chase him?'

'And risk getting shot without knowing why, or who by? Let's get to the car before he comes back with friends.'

As we sped back to London, Sissy's hands were shaking as she put her Walther on safety.

'Well, that was...exhilarating.'

I spared her a glance, and she offered a quick smile to conceal her excitement or her fear, or both.

'Do you think that was Gotobed?' she asked.

'More likely the person who's killed him. Certainly, someone who knows he's gone, even if he's not dead. Whether they were waiting for him to come back or checking to see if anyone missed him, we can only guess.'

'Perhaps they were waiting for us. Someone knew we were going.'

'No, no, they'd have planned an ambush properly and not just posted one man with a pistol.'

'But they could still have been wanting to know what we were up to.'

It could not have been Special Branch, and a police officer wouldn't have shot us out of hand but challenged us formally. Detectives on royal protection duties would have no reason to lurk. There, my certainty ended, as I knew the Germans had an interest in King Edward, and Verity's team could also be in play. Not everyone in the British security services played by the rules, and other clandestine organisations could be getting in on the act. It could have been one of the chief rabbi's men shooting at us for all I knew. The field was becoming crowded.

Chapter Eighteen

I first met Hills when we shared guard duty for Mosley at a Stratford rally in the summer of '35. By degree I learned he'd spent five years in the army then twelve in the police, rising to sergeant before his cosy arrangement with a Brixton brothel-keeper was exposed.

'It wasn't just for the money,' he said with a smile. 'There was this one girl….'

He'd told me more than a gentleman should, but then Department Z had no need for gentlemen. Hills had been thrown out of the force for corrupt practices, or 'for being the one who got caught', as he put it.

When not occupied, he'd often seem to be in a trance as if searching for something he'd lost, or, indeed not yet owned. I'd seen that miles-away gaze in men who'd served in the trenches, but even though he was touching forty years old, Hills had never served in the trenches. He was at his best when kept busy and, at my bidding, was on the lookout for other ex-coppers down on their luck and for old lags hiding in the ranks of the fascists whose irregular skills could come in handy.

I parked my Alvis in George Street fifty yards back from an imposing seven-storey mansion block. Its portal was framed by Doric columns in white stone with the carved name Bryanston Court picked out in gold above it. Above the austere ground floor, its upper parts were red London brick.

Hills strolled across and slid into the seat beside me.

'The Simpson place. Nice, innit? *He* lives in one of the apartments, number five, but *she*'s not here anymore. She spent a fortune doing it up, too. Doorman's talkative. Might be able to get at the butler or one of the maids.'

89

'Thring tells me he's a shipping broker with a company called Simpson, Spence, and Young,' I said. 'Simpson's father was actually a British Jew named Solomon, who changed his name to found the firm.'

'I thought he was American?'

'Not anymore. Simpson was born over there but served in the Guards during the War and became a British citizen. Thring seems to think his business is struggling—his father knows Simpson.'

Hills nodded towards the building. 'I heard he wants to move out. Must cost a bit to maintain that place, staff and all.'

'Wallis is his second wife—they married in '28.'

Sissy was quick at digging up society news.

'He's her second husband, and it's just possible she's trying to make the king number three. We found a court circular from May. Both Simpsons dined with the king at York House.'

'Both of them? I've heard he's a bit of a bounder, but...'

'It set the tongues of the snobs and the socialites wagging. She went again to a court dinner in July, on her own this time.'

'No wonder they've separated,' Hills said. 'He spends a lot of time at his club—he's been living there much of the summer.'

'Which one?'

'Guards. Likes his drink and likes women. But don't we all? And he throws his money about, they say, more than he's got. That could be his weak point, if the nobs up top ever want to pay him off.'

Paying for the problem to go away was not a bad idea.

'The prince has been seen here, earlier in the year, coming and going,' Hills reported. 'Sorry, the king, I can't get used to him being king with him not crowned yet. Oh, and Simpson is a Freemason, and God knows what they get up to. Some of the top brass in the force are Masons. They could be running the whole show for all we know. I read a book about it. Well, one of them pamphlets.' Hills glanced at his notebook. 'This has cost me a few drinks, you know, buying favours. Bent coppers need a bit of bending.'

Employing disgraced corrupt policemen came with its risk, but also its advantages.

'See Thring. He'll reimburse you.'

'Is this money coming from the Party?' Hills asked.

'Coal mining,' I said bluntly.

It was a convenient fiction that my family wealth was supporting Section Z3. In truth, I had diverted a considerable sum of Nazi money the previous year and was still putting it to good use. My father quietly received credit for his unwitting support of the Party in that contracts were nudged his way, ensuring that the mines of R T Clifton Limited were, at last, working at full capacity. Shovelling money to their friends was an indication of the way the fascists would run the country if given the chance. Perhaps it was the way all parties would run the country.

'If I had as much brass as you, I wouldn't be here doing this,' Hills said. 'I'd be in my big house, drinking fine wines and...' He waved his hand as his imagination ran dry.

'It gets boring,' I said. 'Trust me.'

'I'd take the risk,' Hills grumbled. He directed me to drive a mile or so north, then around the eastern perimeter of Regent's Park. I still felt an acute pain in my arm each time I engaged first gear or made a sharp left turn.

'You all right, guv?'

'I owe a communist a punch on the nose.'

He directed me to turn off the Outer Circle by a strip of gardens that ran parallel to the park, then turn hard left into Cumberland Terrace where I parked against the kerb. I pulled on the handbrake, wincing.

'This is where your Mrs Simpson's moved to.'

The entire east side of the narrow road was taken up by a four-storey mansion block facing west across the gardens to the park. Cumberland Terrace had the appearance of a Greco-Roman palace, all in white stone. In the centre of its facade, a double row of ten fluted ionic columns supported a central pediment where sculpted gods and nymphs frolicked.

'How much of this is hers?' I asked.

'There're two or three dozen apartments in there, but she's hardly roughing it. She's at number sixteen—the rent's about thirty quid a week, if you believe. Must have a nice view—but for that price, it would have to.'

We were not the only ones taking an interest in the building. Two men loitered beside a parked black car some hundred yards or so ahead, and I didn't expect they were students of neoclassical Georgian architecture.

'Wait here, could you?'

I took an apple from the glove box and, as nonchalantly as I could, began to stroll down the road in front of the mansion. I was not a smoker, so the apple provided a useful prop I could pretend to be engaged with. Yes, two men, and the car was a Wolseley, so it was a pretty sound bet they were policemen. As neither was in uniform, I narrowed my bet down to Scotland Yard detectives. I crunched my apple, then glanced up at the building as if in appreciation of the opulent design.

I was not nonchalant enough, as one of the men broke away from the other, came round his car, and walked swiftly after me.

'Mr Clifton.' The disapproving eye of Detective Inspector Renton of Special Branch met me as I turned. 'Keep walking, Mr Clifton.'

'Fine building, isn't it? John Nash, the architect who built my father's house, copied his style.'

'My father's house is a two-up, two-down brick terrace in Edinburgh,' he growled. 'Now we're done with the family history, you can tell me why you're here.'

'My guess is I'm here for exactly the same reason you're here,' I said. 'Mrs Wallis Simpson.'

'Go on.'

'Alleged mistress of the king.'

'Why does Department Z care who the king might socialise with?'

'I'd ask the same of Special Branch.'

'And I'd ask you back to the Yard for tea and biscuits, but there won't be any tea or any biscuits. You're out of favours now, Clifton. We're even.'

I smiled. Renton liked playing that hard copper routine.

'Something fishy is going on, and you know that too, else you wouldn't be wasting the Exchequer's money standing around out here.'

Cocky and brazen was what the detective had come to expect from me, so I mustn't disappoint. Underneath, I knew he could easily trump up some charge and make my life very difficult. I was glad I'd left my Walther in the glove box of the car and stopped wearing the giveaway shoulder holster.

'Have you got friends at the German embassy?' Renton asked.

'A contact, possibly.'

'Do me a favour and have lunch with your "contact possibly." See what he knows.'

'Very well, but if we're trading favours, I also need a trade.'

'We don't trade, you know that.'

'So this is for free. A man's gone missing. Neil Gotobed. He lives on the London Road opposite Virginia Water and suspiciously close to Fort Belvedere.' I wouldn't mention the shoot-out. 'He's the brother of Alf Hardcastle, who was murdered in Kent.'

'The case you were poking your nose into? Have you any evidence this— what's his name?'

'Gotobed. Daft name, long story.'

'Was this Gotobed involved in his brother's death?'

'Not that we can prove, but he hasn't been home since. You've far more resources to investigate than I have.'

'Have we? Glad you've noticed.'

'Kent police are getting nowhere—this is a case for Scotland Yard.'

'Which novel did you rip that line from?'

I must have sounded exasperated. 'Call for the files, get hold of the post-mortem report—'

'Any more advice on how we should conduct a routine investigation?'

'Just a request that if you discover anything that could be mutually beneficial—'

Renton held up his palm. 'We don't work with fascists.'

Chapter Nineteen

I t had been a couple of days since we visited Gotobed's cottage, but Sissy hadn't talked about it since. As I escorted her from the door of her apartment building that Friday night, a car backfired, and she grabbed at my arm. Once in the back of the cab, I could feel her hands were still trembling. In India, I'd seen men react like that after returning from a patrol that had come under fire, especially young men fresh to the Frontier.

I gripped a trembling hand. Perhaps the new Errol Flynn adventure *Charge of the Light Brigade* was not the ideal movie for a woman anxious about violence. *Swing Time* might still be showing, and an evening watching Fred and Ginger could prove a better idea.

'You don't have to carry on with Z,' I said. 'There's no dishonour. Plenty would say it's not work for a woman.'

'Oh rubbish,' she said. 'You don't mean that at all. You're the one telling me you need women for this job, and you want them to be equal to the men. That you're more suffragist than the suffragists.'

'But *you* don't have to do it. I feel terrible for pulling you back into all this.'

She nodded. 'Shot at again. And we shot straight back, just like that, not knowing who it was we were going to kill.'

'We all missed,' I said.

'We won't always miss, though.'

'No, somewhere down the tracks, we're going to meet someone who's a better shot or who hangs around long enough for us to find a target.'

She gazed out at the bright lights of the West End.

'Did you ever think that changing the course of British history would be bloodless?' I asked. 'Three hundred years of parliamentary democracy ending without a whimper?'

'I hoped.' Sissy took a deep breath. 'Hugh, I don't want to watch a film. I'm hungry.'

'We could eat afterwards.'

She leaned forward. 'Cabbie, stop, will you,' she ordered. 'Outside the Ritz.'

It was quite early, so we were able to secure a table, though my rather casual suit saw us posted into an unfashionable corner. I ordered a good vintage champagne to deflate some of the waiter's snobbery, and Sissy took a rather unladylike first gulp. Her silk jersey suit, comprising a wide-shouldered grey jacket and blue pleated skirt, was high Parisian fashion, if again not quite in keeping with the pearl-bedecked women around us.

'When he comes back, I'll have salmon.' Sissy took a deep breath, then another sip.

'Better now?'

She nodded. 'So which brother was killed first?'

I smiled at her pluck. 'You still want to be a Blackshirt detective?'

'It's that, or it's cooking and babies,' she said. 'And neither of those light my fire, darling. So, Alf or Neil? I mean, they must both be dead. This Neil Gotobed, well, he wouldn't have just left his chickens to die, and why would he want to murder his brother and go all the way to the middle of Kent to do it?'

'Agreed. My best assumption is that someone has buried his body somewhere it's not been found yet.'

Her fingers switched from salt cellar to pepper pot. 'But was Alf killed because of Neil, or Neil because of Alf?'

'I don't think Neil was important; it's where he lives.'

I took her visual cue and rearranged the cutlery on the table. Two knives placed end to end became the London Road, and a fork quite literally marked where the road forked.

'Gotobed's house is here, just short of the junction.' I took the salt cellar

95

to act as the house. 'The woods where we were shot at are here.' A napkin in autumnal red served as the woods, then I placed a second on the other side of the fork. 'Parkland.' I planted my champagne glass. 'Fort Belvedere. Anyone heading there from London passes this way.' I ran my finger down the knives. 'Anyone wanting to nip over into the park unobserved could base themselves in this house.' I touched the salt cellar.

'So they killed Neil just to use his house? That's ridiculous.'

'We've seen people watching both Simpsons' flats, so why not watch the king too? Perhaps they asked Neil nicely at first, tried to win him onto their side, greased his palm.'

'But he didn't want to play,' she said.

A waiter came over and frowned at my rearrangement of the table setting, oblivious to its significance. 'Sorry, sir,' he said, 'madam.' He carefully re-set the table, then took our orders.

'What next?' she asked.

'Are you fine staying with the investigation?'

She looked off towards the next table of diners, no doubt engaged in far more trivial talk than murder.

'I am, so long as nobody shoots at me again.'

'I can't guarantee that.'

'Just give me something to do,' she took a sip of wine. 'Other than drink and eat and chat while men are killed.'

Chapter Twenty

Sissy knew she was a bad Christian. She drank, she smoked, she fornicated out of wedlock, she'd probably displayed much envy of whatever her friends possessed that she did not, and attaining the age of twenty-seven without doing a day's paid work probably counted as sloth. And she had killed. Over and again, she had reasoned it was not murder, but death at point-blank range was still death. No matter how justified she'd been, no matter how crucial it was that she'd pulled the trigger when she did, she would never escape the memory of that night.

She sat through the service at Christ Church, Virginia Water, quietly muttering words of hymns whose tunes she didn't know. It was just over half full and she took her time leaving after the service, loitering at the back, reading parish notices.

Christians Against Fascism were holding a meeting in the church hall on October the sixth. The leaflet had been printed by the 35 Group, and contained a suitable biblical quote she didn't even read.

'Oh, I'm sorry, that's terribly out of date.'

She turned to see the vicar, a youthful man full of smiles mixed with apologies. He reached to take the notice down.

'Could I have it?'

'Of course. I have the new one somewhere.'

As she removed the notice, the cleric went to fetch a new one.

'Here we go. They're meeting again, a week on Tuesday. Are you coming along?'

The new notice, with a new exhortation to fight the evils of fascism, replaced the first. This time with no 35 Group.

'What happened to the 35 people?' she asked, being as flippant as she could be.

'Oh, oh, I wouldn't know. It's just the printers,' he said.

'Was Neil Gotobed a regular member of your congregation?'

'I'm sure I didn't catch your name.'

'I'm a friend of his sister-in-law and, well, her husband, Neil's brother, has died in rather tragic circumstances.'

'Yes, yes, I heard. Our constable went to deliver the bad news. He's a parishioner, too.'

'Does he go to these meetings?'

'I can't say.'

'But you go.'

'Yes, yes, we have to fight the Nazis. Today, it's the Jews, tomorrow the Catholics, and after that, it's anyone who is not a heathen.'

'And did Neil go along?'

He frowned, sensing how her tone had changed. 'It's no concern of yours.'

'Where does your constable live? I'd like to talk to him.'

The vicar nodded, offering directions.

'You're a fascist, aren't you?' he asked. 'I can tell.'

'How?'

'Your arrogance.'

'So it's not like sniffing witches before you burn them?'

'I've been civil, madam, but this is God's house.'

'And God would like me to leave?'

His hackles rose, and she could see she was adding blasphemy to her list of sins.

Chapter Twenty-One

S issy gave me the details of her attendance at church, and her visit to the village constable. He confirmed he'd been to see Neil Gotobed on the Tuesday following Hardcastle's death, but he hadn't been at home. Scotland Yard had taken an interest, so he would say no more.

On Wednesday, she brought a copy of *The News Chronicle* from the day before up to Room Z.

'Wallis Simpson is divorcing her husband. It's in some of the others, but only a dull factual paragraph hidden away as if it weren't important.'

The young man from the outer office brought tea up for us, and I usually kept a packet of squashed fly biscuits in one drawer of my desk. Sissy declined a biscuit.

'Hidden perhaps because it *is* important,' I said, brushing away crumbs that had fallen onto my uniform. 'Beaverbrook loves this kind of thing usually: scandals, stories about royalty. It should be all over *The Daily Express*.'

'But Lord Beaverbrook is a friend of the king,' Sissy said.

'Lord Rothermere, then. They're rivals, wouldn't he love to steal a march on Beaverbrook? Why isn't it in the *Mail*?'

'Ah,' she said, holding up a finger to instruct me. 'Esmond Harmsworth, Lord Rothermere's son, is also a good friend of the king's. And they're both patriots. Neither Beaverbrook nor Rothermere would want to drag the king through the muck of a divorce scandal.'

I drained my tea, imagining the press barons round a table in the back room of some club, wreathed in cigar smoke, agreeing the king mustn't be embarrassed by even the whiff of scandal. *The Times* and *The Daily Telegraph* and whoever now owned the *Daily Mirror* must all be in on it, too. The *News Chronicle* was owned by the Cadbury family, by all accounts Quaker philanthropists. It had a radical edge and was critical of both the BU and the Spanish Nationalists. Perhaps it did not care for the king either.

'Of all places, she went to Ipswich for the hearing, presumably to avoid publicity.'

'Grounds?'

'Her hubby's admitted having relations with a lady called Buttercup Kennedy in some hotel.'

'Could we find this Buttercup?'

'It's a made-up name, obviously. They went to this hotel and made sure they were seen to be sharing a bedroom, the usual put-up job, a convenient piece of adultery by him to provide her with grounds. It's done all the time.'

'I suppose it wouldn't look good if he cited her infidelity with the king?'

'Oh no, and it would make the whole thing impossible. Only one party can misbehave, otherwise, the deal is off. That's why you can't get rid of Leonora. She'd have to be the one doing the divorcing.'

'She'll never do that. Not unless she snags someone more useful to her. You could divorce Vincent, though; you must have plenty of grounds.'

'Except even if we can drag him back from Venice, he'll never admit to sleeping with boys because he'd be thrown in jail. I'm useful camouflage. He can always scuttle back to me if things get really hot down there. The best thing would be to have one of Mussolini's men drown him in a canal.'

I was shocked, and she could see that I was shocked.

'I'm joking, darling.'

'I'm glad to hear it. I'll also take care the next time I'm walking close to a canal when you're miffed with me. How long does divorce take, given you're the expert?'

'Six months. She's got a decree nisi, which is a sort of promissory note.'

'That's awkward, it would mean she'd be free before the coronation next May. My, that would be complicated.'

'You mean what comes first? The royal wedding or the coronation? I can't imagine a Queen Wallis; it doesn't sound right. She'd have to choose a royal name—her first name is Bessie, so a new Queen Bess would be all right.'

'It's far from all right. He can't marry her; it's tradition; it might even be a rule. The king is Defender of the Faith, and she'll be twice divorced, so there's no question of their getting married.'

'Oh, nobody cares about that anymore.'

'I'm sure a great many people do, from the archbishop downwards. They're wedded to the status quo,' I observed. 'Joyce is always going on about how sentimental and conservative Britain is.'

'I can't believe the murder is just about the house—and it's nothing to do with tithes and fifty-pound debts. That's just a...' She whirled a finger in the air. 'You know, in your books, that clue that isn't really.'

'A red herring.'

'Yes.' She tapped the paper. 'There's more to it, and it's all to do with this.'

Sissy was at her finest when passionately engaged with an idea.

'Hardcastle had a jumble of old newspapers on his shelf, cuttings and things. I thought nothing of them when I was looking for his letters,' she said. 'But he must have been following this story, or his brother was following it and sending him cuttings.'

It made sense. Hardcastle saw himself as the crusading investigator, perhaps upholding his fascist values. He'd come too close and let the fact slip.

'You could be right,' I said. 'So we raise our eyes from arguments about cows and tithes, forget Kent farmers, and engage some Kent nobility. We need inside information. Could your mother ask Wallis to dinner?'

'Gosh, I doubt it. The king has a very tight circle, and my mother doesn't move in it.'

'Not both of them, just Wallis. If she's a social climber, she'd love dinner with Baroness Rockwell here—at a better table, obviously—or one of those new places ordinary mortals can barely get any table at. Can we see how she ticks?'

'You're getting very ambitious, Hugh.' She wrinkled her nose. 'I like it.'

Chapter Twenty-Two

Calhoun knew I had a contact in the German embassy but had not suggested I ask him about the Simpson affair, despite the assertion she could be a Nazi spy. It indicated that MI5 had a contact of their own, who clearly was not supplying information to Special Branch. Britain would surely be a safer place if all the arms of the Security Service worked together.

I invited Bruno Vogel to dine with me at Veeraswamy, the Indian restaurant in Regent Street. In part, this was to test him. I was reading too much about the German obsession with racial purity and the supremacy of the white peoples and it would be interesting to watch his reaction as he interacted with brown-skinned staff and tasted their food.

He was not thrown at all. To be fair to Bruno, he was about as far from a tall blond model of Aryan manhood as one could get: sallow-skinned, hollow-cheeked, with eyes that tended to fall to half-closed when listening.

'So, Hugh, how are you enjoying leading Department Z?'

'Just Section Z3,' I said.

'Give it time, give it time. You have Room Z, yes? At the very top of Black House. When people ask me what Department Z is, I explain you're building a British version of the Gestapo. It's a very logical move on this chessboard of a game. You know that in Germany, Himmler is consolidating all the police agencies under the SS—the Gestapo, the political police, the Prussian police. And the Sicherheitsdienst.' Bruno mimed moulding a ball of dough. 'It gives him a lot of power.' Bruno didn't say this with any relish or glint in his eye. 'So, a good model for your party to follow.'

He'd have been right if I had any desire for Britain to have its own Gestapo.

'I am enjoying this meal, you know,' he said after flinching at a spicy dish. 'It makes a change.'

I smiled.

'Is this purely social?'

'I always enjoy your company,' I said with complete honesty. 'But I'd be interested to know whether you've come across a Mrs Wallis Simpson?'

It was his turn to give a broad, impish smile.

'Of course, you in England are the last to know the story the world has been following all year.'

'We're catching up.'

'She toured the Mediterranean in a yacht with your king in August and caused quite a stir.'

I could imagine that British security services had tracked their every move. Then again, they did not come over as the model of efficiency.

'Would Germany be pleased if she became our next queen?'

Now, he sat back. 'You've been listening to the wrong tittle-tattle.'

'Tell me the tittle-tattle,' I said. 'If we're going to be Britain's Gestapo, we need to know everything. The Party worries about getting on the wrong side of the debate. Is Mrs Simpson a Good Thing or not, from a National Socialist perspective? Should we work to expose the scandal or hush it up?'

Bruno tapped the table. 'Mrs Simpson is a friend of von Ribbentrop, our new ambassador. I must invite you to meet him at the embassy. He's very close to Hitler.'

'A Good Thing, or a Bad Thing?' I asked more insistently. 'We don't want to step the wrong way.'

'King Edward is a friend of Germany,' Bruno said carefully. 'Von Ribbentrop's key mission is to build Anglo-German relations. We must be friends.'

'So Germany would not like the king to be in any way damaged by scandal?'

'No. This affair is...unfortunate. The Führer has no time for bourgeois prejudice, but we ask if your king will ruin himself with this woman. You are old-fashioned in England. It's part of your charm.'

'So Germany's hope is that the king gets bored of her and moves along to find a more suitable bride?'

'That would be good. Ribbentrop is looking for German princesses. Pretty ones, nice smiles. Ones ready to have lots of Anglo-German babies. It would create a new union between our countries. If Mrs Simpson leaves, everyone wins—including your king. Britain is our friend—we don't want a crisis in your government.'

He leaned forward and asked me a straight question.

'You must be watching Mrs Simpson's apartment. Have you seen any flowers delivered?'

'My men have.'

'Have they seen von Ribbentrop arrive?'

'They wouldn't recognise him—indeed, I wouldn't recognise him.'

'He's started to fly swastika flags on his car. You can't mistake it.'

'I'm sure if he wanted to make his arrival less obvious, he could do so.'

Bruno nodded as if this were an entirely reasonable idea.

'He sends her roses.'

'So Germany disapproves, but is also making friends with Mrs Simpson?'

He smiled at the sari-clad waitress who delivered a fresh jug of water and thanked her in German. His grin broadened.

'We can never have too many friends.'

* * *

'You have news about the Germans.' Detective Inspector Renton paced beside me as we strolled through Bloomsbury.

'Von Ribbentrop is sending flowers to Wallis Simpson,' I said.

He nodded as if ticking a question off his personal enquiry list.

'Have your men seen this Von Ribbentrop character turn up at her apartment?' I asked.

He cocked his head as a half-admission.

'The Germans like our king but disapprove of Mrs Simpson,' I told him. 'But I think they're hedging their bets with the flowers, and I imagine plenty of Prussian flattery. They're cosying up to her, but it doesn't look like anything more sinister at the moment.'

'Sinister, says the man who parades around in a black uniform, giving Hitler salutes. As you're in a talkative mood, tell me why the Hardcastle murder has you entertained when you should be busy taking over the country.'

'That farm raid was heavy-handed, but murder isn't a logical consequence of a dispute over fifty quid.'

'I've known men killed for less.'

Renton indulged me because in late 1935, I'd given him possibly the juiciest tip-off of his career. What I'd never shared with him, or even with Calhoun, was that the events of the previous autumn left me with a deep suspicion I'd uncovered only half a plot. I'd not been able to tie up more than a few loose ends, and on the face of it, neither Special Branch nor the Security Service was interested in the ones left dangling. Whoever was trying to reset the British political agenda could still be at work.

We approached the gate of University College Hospital.

'Tell me—is Guy Trundle on your Department Z books?' Renton asked.

'Never heard of him.'

'Ford Motors executive from Mayfair. If you hear the name, you'll let me know. Like a good citizen.'

He stopped outside the hospital gate.

'You've been here before and know where to go. I don't want us to be seen together, it wouldn't do either of us any good.'

Chapter Twenty-Three

When Renton made arrangements to have me released from the Kent cell, it was using the excuse that Scotland Yard had taken an interest in the murder. The ruse had become reality, and Hardcastle's body had since been brought to London with the agreement of his widow. Dr Pascoe at University College performed the post-mortem. To an extent, I owed the pathologist a favour and wanted to repair the damage I'd done to her self-esteem the last time we'd met.

Her little office looked unchanged from my last visit the previous autumn, apart from possibly even more journals and bundles of files that had been squeezed onto the shelves that hemmed Pascoe in from two sides. A patter of rain began against her small window as she greeted me with a look of suspicion and a twist of her head to show genuine interest in what the case had to offer.

'There's no doubt it was murder,' she said. 'This time.'

'Sorry about last year.' My investigation of a suspicious death had made nonsense of the coroner's verdict based on Pascoe's post-mortem.

'You kept it to yourself,' she said. 'For whatever reason. It didn't harm my career. And now you're this, what, Blackshirt detective?'

I had to smile. 'Yes.'

'Working with Special Branch.'

'Informally.'

She was too bright not to realise that things were happening behind the scenes and bright enough not to ask what they were.

'Well, Hardcastle had alcohol in his system but not enough to make him an easy target. He was attacked from behind, probably by surprise. I take it that no witnesses heard any screams?'

'No.'

'Then someone clamped one hand over his mouth and slit his carotid artery with a single stroke.' She paused. 'Do you know a lot about anatomy?'

'No.'

'I thought with your being a writer of murder stories as well as a fascist, you might make a hobby of researching how to kill people in nasty ways.'

'How do you know I write detective novels?'

'I asked,' she said. 'Research is never wasted. I hear your pen name is Vincent Hammer, but I couldn't find any of your books in the library. Or in the Charing Cross Road bookshops.'

'I'm not surprised,' I said quickly. 'My first novel isn't due out until next month.'

'Put me down for one,' she said, wrinkling her nose so her tortoiseshell spectacles twitched.

'I'll sign one and drop it by,' I said. 'You were saying. Carotid artery?'

She mimed the cut. 'High under the left ear, down across to the right. It's the best way to slit a throat—he'd have been dead in moments. The blade also sliced through his windpipe, so if he'd been free to make any sound, he'd have choked on it.'

'He was a hard case by all accounts—to match his name. He'd have gone down fighting.'

'But he didn't. There are no defence wounds, no cut knuckles or bruises to suggest a fight. He wasn't as tall as you, but he was well-built. I counted seven scars and two healed fractures, so Mr Hardcastle was, as you say, a hard case. One of your Blackshirt street brawlers.'

'I gather by that remark you don't support our Leader?'

'No, I don't.'

'Well, I respect holders of all political opinions. We do live in a democracy.'

'For how long?'

I had to play the loyal Mosleyite every day and hated it.

'Look, politics apart, I owe resolution of the case to Hardcastle's family.'

She gave a shrug. 'The attacker was right-handed, but that's not much help.'

'So let me posit a scene. Mr Hardcastle came out of the Green Man pub after a couple of pints, then walked across the village green as far as the maypole which was a recognisable rendezvous just far enough from the pub lights so nobody would see. He met somebody by arrangement, and that person was either sufficiently skilled to take him by surprise or engaged his attention while a right-handed accomplice sneaked up from behind.'

'That's it, case closed,' she said. 'It wasn't something that happened in a red rage, like most stabbings outside pubs. Whoever killed your man only made one stroke, there was no sign of hesitation. He knew exactly what he was doing.'

A disturbing thought came to me.

'A doctor would know how to make that cut.'

'Depending on what kind of doctor he was.' Pascoe inclined her head and gave me a smile, almost of pity. 'Or she was. There are female doctors these days.'

'A female doctor?'

She smiled at my reaction. She half opened her mouth as if to say more, closed it, and then straightened up before delivering her next line. Then she smiled again in a different way, a dangerous way.

'May I enquire if you are married, Mr Clifton?'

If Dr Pascoe was daring to make an advance, I was flattered, but life was already complicated enough, and I was in no mood to add more lies and betrayal.

'I am indeed married,' I said, hoping I did not bash a hole in her self-esteem.

'Ah.' She blushed. 'Another fascist, I suppose?'

'No, as it happens.' My estranged wife had as little time for Mosley as Dr Pascoe.

She closed her file briskly. 'Does the killer know you're looking for him—or her?'

'He must by now.'

'Well. Be careful on dark nights, Mr Clifton.'

Chapter Twenty-Four

The communists were holding an Aid for Spain rally in Hyde Park. It gave a focus for the Crusaders who had marched two-hundred-odd miles down from Jarrow to protest about poverty and unemployment. It was supposed to be a non-political campaign, and the Labour Party had shunned it. Even the bishops were against men marching to protest about hunger, thinking it smacked too much of revolution. Most practical support for the marchers ironically had come from Conservative-controlled councils, Rotary clubs, and the like.

I mixed among them, not declaring my allegiance. Ruth and Nigel Fritton also mingled with the crowd. They had excellent ears for snippets of information and were always keen for the next task. The rest of Sissy's women were far too upper-crust to get away with it, and Lucy insisted on not working weekends. My men were busy keeping an eye on the Simpsons and chasing leads.

The Jarrow Crusaders had hoped the king would receive them in London and their cause would be debated in the new session of parliament, but of course, neither was allowed. So, the suffering would continue through another winter. I'd always said I was not political, but as I marched beside the Crusaders for their last few hundred yards towards the park, I knew something must be done. The democratic parties of Britain needed to address the grievances of the poor, the badly housed, and the downtrodden, or the anti-democratic forces would take matters out of their hands.

And there was Verity, just for a moment, clad in a knitted cloche hat and long grey overcoat. I zig-zagged through the crowd but lost her. For a woman who couldn't walk quickly, she'd made an art of the vanishing act. She must have seen me, or someone else who wished her ill. I was sure Renton would enjoy a long talk with her, with no tea and no biscuits. I'd already spotted him, sitting in a car with another officer, probably noting down the names of the communist leaders as they arrived. Plainclothes men would be mingling just as I was mingling, looking for faces and noting who was talking to whom. At least at a Blackshirt rally, it was harder for spies to hide.

Some spies, at least.

* * *

I washed away the grime of pretending to be downtrodden and dressed for dinner, feeling rather guilty that I'd be dining at Kettner's while the Crusaders ate at some charity kitchen. Perhaps I'd lingered too long during those impassioned speeches and was turning into a socialist. Perhaps communist propaganda was more effective than I'd realised.

Time to dine, and to romance. I once spotted Agatha Christie in Kettner's but fought off the urge to engage her in conversation as she must tire of public attention. However, it would be infinitely preferable to be famous for murdering people in my books rather than infamous for shooting them down in the street.

Britain had put the clocks back to Greenwich Mean Time, so it was dark by five o'clock. I left Havelock Mansions at seven with a spring in my step, deliberately pushing guilt aside. Sissy was right to be afraid about that fight in the woods. Life could end swiftly and suddenly, so we should make merry while we could. It was a pleasant evening, with birds straining to be heard above the traffic.

I saw motion in the shadows and spun round, hand already inside my coat pocket, just as the woman reached into hers.

'Don't!' I warned.

'I have a comrade watching.' Verity stepped into the light, approaching cautiously with that step, half-step gait of hers.

I couldn't see a comrade, but it didn't mean he wasn't there. I was no longer a newcomer to this game. Ever since our first encounter a year before, Verity made up half the reason I continued to walk out armed.

'I wasn't surprised to bump into you in the East End,' I said, not relaxing my hand. 'But I'd expected you to turn up long before.' I'm pretty sure she'd burgled my apartment the previous year, so could have come for me at any time of her choosing.

'If I wanted you dead, you'd be dead.'

'Do your comrades feel the same?'

'They don't know it was you who killed Sean.'

'Who is Sean?'

'He told me his name was Sean. I didn't believe him.'

'No, I didn't believe the name he gave me either. Whoever he really was, I liked him. I'm sorry he died.' I wasn't going to tell her that it was Sissy who actually pulled the trigger. 'I saw you today, hoped we could talk.'

'Did you see how many police spies there were in that crowd?'

'I spotted a couple.'

'And I spotted you,' she said. 'Clearly you want to talk to me, so talk. You put another little lonely heart advert in the *Daily Worker*, but I assume you're still seeing Sissy, so not that lonely.'

'I need your help.'

'Give me one good reason.'

'Here's two. When I had a chance to shoot you, I didn't. Twice now. I'm also keeping your existence a secret. From what you've just said, you're returning the favour by not exposing me?'

'Something like that. What's so important that you want to meet?'

'The Establishment wants to crush the socialists, and the fascists are giving them as much encouragement as they can.'

'Do you care?'

'If Stalin wants to overthrow Britain, I'm on Britain's side, but I'm not going to peddle lies about a communist threat that doesn't exist, because the winner will be Mosley.'

'You still want me to believe you're an anti-fascist and that this whole

Department Z thing is just an act?'

'Yes. There are people in the British Union trying to build Mosley into Britain's Hitler, but there are others who want to nudge him towards being nothing more than a taller version of Winston Churchill.'

'They'll both hang together.'

'Verity, drop the dogma! You're not on a podium in Hyde Park preaching to the masses. We both know there's an evil side to the Blackshirt leaders, but we also both know there's little difference between their rank and file and yours. Poor people, jobless people, angry people who need someone to blame.'

'I'll accept that,' she said.

'I'm working at...making things better.'

'So why do you want to see me?'

'A Blackshirt trade unionist was murdered in Kent on the tenth of October.'

'That sounds like a good start.'

I could not see her expression in the half-light.

'It was carried out efficiently and deliberately, as if by a trained assassin.'

'Good men and women died in the Battle of Cable Street, you know. A child was thrown through a window, so don't be surprised if people want revenge on your Blackshirts.'

'They're not *my* Blackshirts.'

'So you say. What's so important about this one man?'

'He wasn't important, which is the puzzle.' I was saying nothing about the royal connection. 'Yes, he was rubbing up against the unions, but at best, they'd rough him about, give him a kicking and a black eye—not arrange for his throat to be slit.'

'But why should I care?'

'Because it could be another Byzantine plan by the BU Research Committee to create a red scare and give Special Branch further excuse to round up more of your trade union friends. Nobody is admitting anything, so I'm trying to eliminate other motives. Were your people behind it? If he finds out, William Joyce will make a meal out of this.'

'If it was a sanctioned execution, who says I'd know about it? And even then, I wouldn't tell you.'

'I understand, but a hint would be welcome.'

'And if you discover it was Blackshirt killing Blackshirt, you must tell me if you genuinely want to fight the fascists. We have a propaganda department too.'

'Agreed. One more question. Do you get involved with Christians Against Fascists?'

'Plenty of Christian groups oppose the fascists.'

'Not in Spain,' I commented.

'We're not Spain. Not yet.'

'How about the 35 Group?'

'Never heard of them. I'm going to leave now.'

'How do I contact you?'

'I know where you live.'

'But how do I contact *you*? I can't keep using the lonely-hearts ruse, or one day someone will smell a rat.'

She grunted agreement. 'There's a tobacconist's kiosk near Holborn Tube station. Put a card into his rack with the word Athens and the day's date. I'll telephone you.' She turned to walk away. Her first step was awkward.

I called after her. 'Did you ever identify the men who tried to kill you?'

She stopped, self-consciously letting one hand rest on her crippled right thigh.

'I know who led them.'

'And what did you do to him?'

'Before he left me to die, I took his eye out,' she said.

Suddenly, I knew. 'Parker?'

'Yes, Parker.'

Verity was a woman who could take care of herself, quick to pull a knife and a pistol, and who once had no compunction in shooting at me. Somehow Parker had managed to cripple her, meaning the dog was not all bark.

'And yet you haven't revisited him to finish the job?'

'His time will come. Right now, he's the best recruiting officer we have. He's putting the Jews firmly on our side. And the churches, by the sound of it.'

That was pretty cynical, even for a communist.

'Who do you work for, Verity?'

'The people. And you're still working for Calhoun, I suppose. And he tells you he works for M, who works for K…. But have you ever met K, or M, or anyone else who claims to work for MI5?'

I was not going to admit I was at the bottom of the heap.

'Of course you haven't. You know that M's wife is a leading fascist out in the West Country? Not one of Mosley's, but one of the other nasty right-wing groups. If you've never met any of these people, never been to their offices, how do you know whom Calhoun is really working for?'

In truth, I didn't, but Calhoun's motivation had seemed genuine, even if whomever he was working for had re-framed my spectacular success of the previous November into something that suited their purposes.

'You've nothing to say to that, have you?' she taunted.

I had at last spotted the watchman. Two of them, indeed.

'I spy with my little eye,' I said. 'Your men over in the Austin.'

She didn't try to look. 'My comrade is on foot, and there's just one of him.'

'So are those two over there watching you or me?'

Verity glanced ever so slightly to where her comrade should be.

'If you go down to the bottom of the Mews, there's a way through to the main road,' I said. 'Right then left.'

'I know which way to go.'

Of course, she would.

'I'm off to dinner, and it would be rude to be late,' I said, 'but I'm taking a scenic detour t'other way. Let's see which one of us they follow.'

Chapter Twenty-Five

Verity set off immediately, limping away down the poorly lit mews. The first time we met had been when she pounced on me in a narrow alley, and I'd learned a trick or two from the times I'd seen her since. And indeed, the times I hadn't. Since moving to Havelock Mansions, I'd made sure I knew all the streets and the snickets and the nooks and crannies of Bloomsbury. As Verity vanished north, I went south across the road and along past a narrow garden fenced off for residents. Behind me, I heard a car door close.

Along the right in a hundred yards or so, was an arched entrance to some mews or service yard. At the grey rendered arch, I turned in. It would look like the kind of route I would take if trying to avoid a tail, and my tail would hurry to catch me. The inner face of the arch offered a perfect cover in complete darkness. I drew my Walther and took off the safety.

The man hurried through. I allowed him to make two paces down the yard to put him beyond where he could grab my weapon then levelled the gun.

'Stop right there!'

He froze, his tan raincoat glowing in the pool of distant streetlight.

'Clifton?' Valentine said.

The other man must either still be in the Austin or had tried to follow Verity. She may not play so nicely if he caught her.

'May I turn around?'

'Slowly. And keep your hands away from your pockets.'

He half raised his hands in surrender and turned to face me, glasses glinting in the light. I remained in total shadow.

'Are you pointing a gun at me?'

'No, it's a milk bottle—of course, it's a bloody gun.'

'That's not wise.'

'You know my reputation. If I were a spy or a traitor, you'd now be dead. I'd drag your body behind those bins, and the rats would have a feast until you were found in a couple of days' time.'

He nodded.

'You're not very good at your job, Dr Valentine. I run training courses for my team on how to follow people and how to throw spies off your tail.'

'And where did you learn that?'

'I read. Someone once told me research is never wasted.'

He nodded his head slowly. 'Don't tell anyone about this.'

I gave one of my nervous coughs in lieu of a laugh.

'Why, because it dents the mystique of Z1?' I took my left hand off the pistol grip and lowered my stance, but still kept the muzzle pointed his way.

'Can I put my hands down?'

'Gently.'

'You're making a mistake.'

'By not shooting you?'

'In terms of your career in the Party. Can we talk about this?'

'Briefly. I've a dinner date.'

'With that woman back there?'

'God no, that's Peg Leg Sally.' I adapted a character I'd already composed for my next novel. 'Plies her trade around King's Cross, men find her a novelty act. She lets me know which of our lords and masters are slumming it. A shilling a name.'

'Names for your files. You keep your own, don't you?'

'As does Z1.'

'We must talk.'

'Yes, but somewhere that doesn't involve firearms and dark alleys. Let's have dinner somewhere with witnesses, but perhaps booths for a little privacy.'

'Very well.'
'And you're paying.'

Chapter Twenty-Six

The morning after I avoided the temptation to put Dr Valentine into an early grave, I attended the funeral of Alf Hardcastle at the London Road cemetery in Bromley. His coffin was carried out of the cemetery chapel by six Blackshirts in full uniform, their boots and belts polished. I could see the discomfort of the vicar, who looked to the skies for a little salvation.

Mrs Hardcastle looked around herself as if more than her husband were missing. She also wore uniform black under her coat. Reporters had turned up, including a photographer from *Blackshirt*, so there was a clutch of people she didn't recognise among the mourners. I'd sent both Frittons down too, briefed to mingle with the mourners and use their innocent, winning smiles to learn what they could.

I wore my uniform, as it was the blackest garb I owned, with the leather coat on top, but I omitted the armband. Hymns sung, lesson read, earth was thrown into the grave, and we walked away from a Blackshirt martyr.

The wake was held at Mrs Hardcastle's sister's terraced house, which was more or less identical in design and layout and choice of cheap furniture to the Hardcastle home. Amid the press of Blackshirts and civilians, there was not a great deal of room, and the kitchen table had been pushed to one side and was covered in potted meat sandwiches. A jaunty man pushed a bottle of brown ale into my hands and removed the top for me.

'Get that down, squire. A toast to Alf—a Blackshirt to the end!'

I raised the bottle in salute, then looked for a glass.

The widow Hardcastle bustled through.

'Could I have a word, please,' I asked her.

'I'm just going out for some air,' she said and led me through to the back door and out into the yard. A few men were smoking, talking quietly.

'We went to your brother-in-law's cottage, and he wasn't there,' I said, waiting for a reaction that did not come. 'We think he hasn't been home for some time. He went out one day and never came back.'

'Oh.' She took half a step back towards the brickwork of the coalhouse.

'It's too much of a coincidence, with your Alf having died around the last time Neil was seen.'

'Neil wouldn't have done it! He was a gentle man; two more different brothers you'd never find.'

'I never said he was a suspect.'

'But that means...'

'Yes, it could mean he's dead too,' I said bluntly, trying to read her. 'And I'm sorry it has to be today, but I need to know more about Neil—was he in the Party?'

'No, no, he was High Church. Sometimes him and Alf would argue politics, and Neil wanted a better country, yes, but he didn't hold with our uniforms and marches. God's way is peace, he used to say. Onward, Christian soldiers, Alf would tease back.'

'Did you see him often?'

'Once or twice a year. Family funerals and christenings. He'd come down for Christmas, and once we went up there. He had a young wife, but she was taken early. That only strengthened his link to the Almighty.' She shook her head. 'It did the opposite for me.'

'You said he hadn't written. Did Alf and Neil write to each other often?'

'Alf would send him his articles sometimes. Neil would write now and then but didn't have much to say.'

This was starting to fall together. We hadn't seen any correspondence or snippets of articles during our visit to Virginia Water.

'You told my lady colleague that Alf was working on stories about conspiracies with Jews and spies and...well, the usual things for *The Blackshirt*. Exactly what conspiracies worried him?'

119

'Communists in the unions. The Church throwing poor farmers off their lands. And spying on the king.'

'Precisely who is spying on the king? The Church?'

'That's what Alf said.'

'Was it Neil who told him? In one of his letters?'

Mrs Hardcastle nodded slowly. 'Yes, that one came from Neil. He was disgusted.'

At any other time, this would have been an eccentric idea, but having seen the fire in Isby's eyes and the invective of the 35 Group leaflets, I was less certain.

'Who else did Alf tell about this?'

'I don't know. He said he was going to write about it, but he didn't get a chance, did he?'

No, he was properly silenced. Neil's house offered a good base for spying on Fort Belvedere, and whoever wanted it was prepared to kill both brothers to keep the secret safe.

* * *

I couldn't share my wildest suspicions with Calhoun at our usual Tuesday meeting. It was back to Lyon's Corner House and to coffee and seed cake, which I merely nibbled to keep my mouth clear. As usual, we had a table in that awkward corner close to the lavatories where we may as well have been alone amid the clatter of teacups and hubbub of conversation. The House of Commons had begun a new session after the king's speech, and in the report on business in the House, a question was raised over Mrs Simpson's role in the coronation arrangements. I related to Calhoun what little new information I'd learned about the Simpsons, wondering how much he knew already.

'Who is directing our strategy?' I asked, still contaminated by Verity's cynicism.

'That's an odd question.'

'Do we even have a strategy?' I asked.

'We gather intelligence.'

'To what end, and for whom?'

'The stability of the country.'

'That it?'

'Pretty much.'

He didn't elaborate to include the words 'government' or 'monarchy' in his brief, suggesting both could be sacrificed.

'What's your ideal objective? Our objective, the brief from on high.'

Calhoun considered my question. 'The best outcome is the king decides to drop Mrs Simpson of his own volition, or Mrs Simpson drops the king.'

Britain's aims seemed perfectly aligned with those of Germany, as espoused by Bruno.

'Is that what we—you, my team—must aim for, then?'

'What would be really useful is for you to rake up more dirt to smear her with, so the king will realise how unsuitable a match she is.'

I was genuinely shocked. 'Is that right? Manipulating the king, destroying that poor woman's reputation—'

'If that's what it takes to maintain stability, yes.'

'My country, right or wrong, eh?'

Is a democracy that needed to play dirty tricks to survive worth defending, I had to wonder. Stability, indeed, seemed to trump even democracy and the rule of law, which was much the way Mosley would run a government. I doubted Calhoun would tell me whose interest this course of action served or who on high had decided this was the best outcome.

'If we don't find the dirt, the newspapers will,' he said, 'and we'll end up with a queen whose name is mud.'

'Special Branch are all over this case. I've seen their officers staking out both Simpson residences. Surely they'll have found scandal if it were there.'

'So we need to find it too.'

It wasn't only the British Union that was hobbled by rivalry.

'Britain would be better served if our agencies worked together,' I said. 'The Germans have brought all theirs under one roof.'

'Except the *Abwehr*,' Calhoun corrected. 'Military intelligence. They're still not under the Nazi party's direct control. That's worth remembering.'

Bruno. Suddenly the distance he seemed to maintain from the Nazi party made sense. Perhaps he could be trusted rather more than I'd given him credit for.

'I've another question for you. The case of the murdered trade unionist grows more complex.'

'Oh, stop wasting time,' Calhoun said. 'I thought you'd be bored by now.'

'On the contrary, his brother has also disappeared. Scotland Yard is on the case, but I'm keeping an eye on it. Now, if you recall the series of unexpected events that led up to last year's excitement, this feels like another one. The murder was too clean, too planned.'

'And the question?'

'Did your boys in the Security Service do it?'

'We don't behave like your Nazis and just kill people we don't like.'

'I suppose if you did, someone could just push Wallis Simpson under a bus. Problem solved.'

'Stop joking, Clifton: it's all one big jape to you, isn't it? Well, you'll need to take extra care from now on. The Home Secretary is sharing intelligence about your party's funding with the Commons. The Italian money and the Nazi money.'

'When?'

'Next week, probably. Inevitably, questions will be raised about how the Home Secretary has come across this information, and when he cannot disclose it, all eyes will be on the Security Service. Expect fear and recrimination in your camp.'

'As if we don't have enough already.'

It was to Britain's benefit the BU remained a squabbling, fractious bunch, but it did make my job more dangerous.

'Don't get caught, not now.' His warning was pretty superfluous.

'I've given you nothing on funding since last year, so where's all the new information come from?'

'Our resources might be stretched, but you're not Britain's only agent.'

'Can you tell me who it is?'

'Of course not.'

'Well, you need to warn this other person,' I said. 'Last year, I thought Department Z were just playing at spies, but not anymore. I know they killed one of your agents—Verity.'

He rolled his eyes at me. I gave him a chance to deny it, correct or reprimand me. Nothing.

'I've found out who did it. If you're interested.'

'You're assuming I don't already know,' he said.

Chapter Twenty-Seven

'A T-Type, very nice. New, is it?'

'Yes, rather,' Sissy said. It was the first car she'd ever bought for herself, and she was quite proud of it.

The man in the mid-market suit and smart hat walked round the front, then back along the pavement side.

'But you'd like a Ford? American styling is so modern.'

She glanced back at her MG, which felt modern enough. Of course, she had no interest in replacing it, and was here solely to gain a close look at Guy Trundle. Somehow, he was connected to the Wallis Simpson affair.

'I thought I'd show you a model 48,' said the salesman. 'See how clean the lines are.'

It was a smoother, rounder car in a rather fetching bright blue.

'This is the sedan, but you can buy a coupe. V8 engine. Right-hand drive, of course, for England—they drive on the wrong side of the road in America. Would you like a spin?'

'Very much.'

'We'll head out of town to the west to be clear of the traffic, then you can try her out on an open stretch of road.'

Trundle drove at first, chatting of this and that. He enjoyed dancing and asked Sissy which clubs she favoured. She named a few and recalled many dancing partners as handsome as Trundle with equally smooth and well-practised patter. He had charm, but was of that category of men who knew he had charm and deployed it as a tool. It would help in selling cars, and it would help in other spheres of life, too.

Once out of the London traffic, Sissy took the wheel, managing to stall twice when starting the car and then gradually mastering the controls. She'd slept badly for a few nights after that brief skirmish in the woods, worrying over how it might have turned out, but her enthusiasm for detection had returned.

'What do you think?' asked Trundle.

'It feels quite heavy.'

'Compared to your little car, it will.'

So her new car was little, lacking in style, and old-fashioned. Trundle was not scoring as many points as he believed. It was time to come to the point.

'Does Mrs Simpson drive one of these?'

He didn't respond.

'Have you sold her one?' Sissy gave him a smile. 'Or taken her dancing, perhaps?'

'I don't know who you're talking about.'

'Oh, come on!'

'Who are you, a reporter?'

'Have reporters sought you out?'

'Not until today.'

'Well, for the benefit of your nerves, I'm not a reporter. Call me a concerned friend. Tell me, is anyone watching your house?'

For a chatty, self-assured man, he suddenly became very quiet.

'Eighteen Bruton Street, Mayfair,' she reminded him.

'You've...not talked to my wife?'

'No, silly, I wouldn't do that. A man's got to live, what?'

He glanced down the road, then behind as if the car were being followed. 'We should turn round here and head back.'

'No, I'm enjoying this.'

'I have to pay for the petrol.'

'I'll pay for your petrol. And you tell me about Wallis. I'm not a reporter, honestly.'

He gave a harrumph.

Sissy sensed that in Trundle's world, women were for dancing and flirting with, for seducing over dinner, and for impressing with new motors. They were not confidential investigators.

'We danced,' he said. 'We met at social occasions. Last year—it's all over. Well, she's....'

'Yes?'

'You know. Dancing with the king now.'

She wondered how closely Trundle and Wallis Simpson had danced but suspected she'd never find out, short of dragging him into that all-black cell in the basement of Black House.

'Have you told anyone about your friendship with Wallis?'

Each of his responses came reluctantly. 'No. I was hoping everyone had forgotten. Of course, people saw us and might have jumped to the wrong conclusions.'

'Or the right conclusions.'

'I'm saying nothing. I'm taking it to my grave.'

People might yet arrange that, she thought.

'Unless someone spills the story to the newspapers.'

'Oh no, here we go. What do you want, money? I'm not that well off, I'll tell you now.'

'You have a nice house in Mayfair, but no, I've no need of your money. Ooh, I can turn here.'

'I can drive now.'

'No, no, I'm enjoying this. Ford 38?'

'48.'

Sissy used a road junction to swing the car round to face back in the direction of London. Another driver honked his horn. Trundle looked anxiously over his shoulder to verify that no, there hadn't been a collision.

'Did Wallis have German friends?'

'Germans?' He turned back to watch the road. 'One or two.'

'Who?'

'I don't know. Businessmen, people from the embassy.'

'But you don't remember any names?'

'No, no, I'm a Ford Motors executive, not a private detective.'

That was a little too close. Perhaps her quizzing was becoming clumsy.

'I need to ask you, very nicely, not to breathe a peep about Mrs Simpson to anyone.'

'That sounds like a threat. Who sent you? Was it her husband?'

'No, but I need to warn you there are some rather nasty people about who wish Mrs Simpson harm. And no doubt there are reporters who'd love to pose a photograph of you beside that of Mrs Simpson on the front page of their newspaper. So, as a gentleman, you'll give me your word. Utmost confidence.'

'Of course, my word. I don't want anything more to do with this wild goose chase of yours. Can I drive now?'

'Yes, I think I've had enough fun for one morning.'

Before Sissy got out of the car in front of the garage, she passed Trundle a slip of paper.

'That's my phone number. If you're contacted by anyone on the same wild goose chase, as you call it, ring me straight away. Your life could depend on it.'

'My life? Who in God's name are you?'

'Department Z,' she said sweetly.

'Never heard of them.'

She showed her badge at last.

'Like Special Branch…but more special.'

* * *

Julian was checking the menu at the Young Britain Club, just off St James's Street. He had an arrangement to dine with his father, who had changed his own club from Gresham's to White's, which was only a short walk from Young's. He was anticipating the enjoyment of treating his father to dinner at *his* club for once.

Odd, there was a slip of paper with his name on it inserted into the little leather folder. He unfolded it.

Thring. Dept. Z has no more need to chase the 35 Group.

They have been dealt with.
It was not signed.

Chapter Twenty-Eight

Guy Fawkes Night concentrated the mind. I hoped Sissy had taken the point about how people who plotted to overthrow the government often met a sticky end. We dined at Prunier's, St James, not so far from White's club, where I'd learned Valentine was a member, and a little further from Young's, where Julian was no doubt enjoying another evening with his new chums. Fish was Madame Prunier's speciality, and it came with a respectable price tag.

'I was only joking when I said you could pick up the bill for the meal,' I said.

'It's no problem.' Valentine glanced at Sissy as he opened the menu. 'I'm surprised we're not meeting at Black House. It would be far more convenient.'

'Room Z is not very cosy and you don't have your own office yet,' I said.

'There are meeting rooms.'

'Rule one of intelligence work is to meet in public places. Nobody can eavesdrop here, if we speak softly. Nobody is checking us in and out on their notebook.'

'Very well, play your spy games,' Valentine said, glancing at the menu once more. 'Turn me into a character in your next book. A villain with a monocle and a suspicious *Cherman* accent.'

'Too predictable.'

'What I did not predict is that it's not just the two of us.'

'Can you imagine there's anything I hear that Sissy doesn't hear?'

Sissy's presence complicated Valentine's mission while not adding to the danger we faced.

'And if I were the traitor working for Special Branch, there's a pretty good bet that Sissy would have found out about it and told you.' I inclined my head towards her in a manner that could be interpreted as patronising.

She touched my ankle with the toe of her shoe. It wasn't quite a kick, meaning she'd spotted my game.

'And if I were convinced you had evidence against me, you wouldn't have made it out of that alley,' I added.

'He once shot a man in an alley,' Sissy commented lightly. 'I was there.'

'Yes, the Blackshirt hero of Kensington,' Valentine said. 'And also the villain of the Swat Massacre.'

It had become futile to deny my responsibility for the so-called massacre out in India. I'd carried the can for more senior officers when everyone thought I would die of my wounds, and the ironic legacy of the story was that fascists rated me as being ruthless. It did me no harm anymore.

'I'm public property. There's nothing to learn about me that's not in the newspaper clippings and files at Black House. My book will be published in a couple of weeks, so hopefully, my publisher will slip my picture into the newspapers again.'

'You've come a long way in a short time.'

'So have we all. Men of action—and women of action.' I smiled at Sissy again, and again she tapped my ankle.

'From all the evidence I've put together, you're not the person your reputation suggests,' Valentine observed. 'Are you a northern man pretending to be sophisticated, or a sophisticated man using your northern roots as a stage prop? Are the guns and the stories you perpetuate about yourself just part of a veneer, or is this mild-mannered no saluting, no ranks, chummy behaviour the veneer?'

'Rule two of intelligence work. Keep people guessing.'

Valentine gave a harrumph. 'What's your choice from the menu, Woman Unit Leader?'

'We don't use ranks when out of uniform,' she chided, almost in a whisper. 'And I'm having the poached salmon.'

'Again?' I observed.

'I like salmon.'

'I'll have that as well.' Valentine snapped his menu closed. The waiter came, and Valentine named a white burgundy that was clearly a favourite.

'What kind of doctor are you?' Sissy asked as the wine arrived.

'My guess is military surgeon,' I added. 'You're just about the right age to have served in the war.'

'Only just. I was studying Italian literature and philosophy in Florence when war broke out.'

'So that's what you're a doctor of, Italian literature and philosophy?'

'Broadly.' Valentine smiled and sniffed at his wine.

'You've never even dissected a rat?'

'No. And I assure you I haven't stuck a scalpel into one of our own men.'

'Philosophy is hardly a reserved occupation—how did you skip the war?'

'I didn't skip it. I slipped into doing military liaison with the Italians. Second lieutenant, like you, spent the war at this headquarters or that and never fired a shot. But that's when I became interested in fascism. I stayed in Italy and even saw Mussolini's march on Rome.'

Sissy was impressed. 'Gosh, you were a witness to history.'

'And it wasn't exactly like it was later reported. More protracted, less dramatic—Mussolini didn't even lead the march, but it's the story people believe that matters. I've read most of the leading fascist thinkers. Have you read any of my papers?'

'I can't say I have,' I admitted.

'Sorry.' Sissy shook her head.

'If you're writing fascist philosophy, it sounds like you should be in the Research Department or Propaganda, not hunting spies,' I said.

'No, no, I have my own theories of how to establish a fascist state, but the Party has just one leader. His path is the one we will follow. It's the only way this will work; we're not anarchists with everyone having their pet idea on how to run the country. Fascism can only have one voice.'

'*National Socialism* can only have one voice.' Sissy emphasised the new party line.

Valentine looked bitten. 'Exactly. Do you disagree, Clifton?'

'Oh, I'm just infantry. I let the men at the top do the thinking.'

'And the women,' Sissy added.

'But you write books.'

'For my own entertainment.'

'I suppose the sons and daughters of the wealthy need something to occupy themselves beyond fine dining and drawing room chit-chat.'

'We may,' Sissy said.

'So, Valentine, can you please take your eyes off my people,' I said. 'They don't have time to be police spies. The poor ones are looking for work, and the rich ones have full social calendars.'

'I can never take my eyes off anyone. You understand how this works now.'

'Are you watching Parker too?'

'Of course.'

'Was he in Kent the same time as you?'

Valentine considered his answer. 'No.'

'Because last year he was doing what you're doing now. Purging the party of undesirables. At knifepoint.'

'Captain Parker has a different focus now.'

I gave a little cough. 'We're a secret police force in all but name. Some are calling us the British Gestapo, and that's what Parker wants us to be. If there's dirty work to be done, he'll do it.'

'Parker wasn't in Kent—he was embroiled in the East End battles. I have checked, I'm not an amateur. You know what military liaison is, don't you?'

'Spying, of a sort,' I realised. Valentine could have accumulated many useful contacts during his time in Italy, and since. 'So tell me the real reason *you* were in Kent. Turning up the day Hardcastle was killed, going home as soon as his body was found.'

'I was there because I read his file. Your man Hardcastle served time for blackmail.

Eighteen months; '31 to '32.'

This was a bouncer.

'He found out some draper was having it away with his young assistant, so tried to make money out of it,' Valentine said. 'Sadly for him, the draper didn't care who knew, reported the blackmail letter, dumped his wife, and moved the girl in as his mistress. They're married now. Hardcastle pleaded guilty, apologised, and said he hadn't done anything like it before. Not been caught anyway.' Valentine let it all sink in.

'A blackmailer,' Sissy said. 'Oh buggeration.'

Valentine nodded slowly, a look of triumph on his face.

I had begun to regard Alf Hardcastle as some kind of patriotic hero, a crusader for the truth. Tipped off by his brother about a threat against the Crown, he'd pitched into a one-man investigation, much as I might have done with that information in hand. It appeared I'd been misled. I had to admire a man who would try to blackmail the Archbishop of Canterbury—or was amazed by his stupidity, at least. No wonder Hardcastle didn't pass the information back to Department Z. The Party's careless recruitment of crooks and society's failures came with a price.

Chapter Twenty-Nine

The Kent investigation had run into a brick wall, and my assumptions were scattered like broken headlamps on the highway. With Valentine on the prowl, it was time to get my team out of harm's way and treat them to a holiday. I hired a motor coach and took Z3 on a long drive to West Yorkshire. My father was away, so we would have the run of Moat Hall and in Lucy's words, 'play cowboys in the woods'. Farmers were having a tough time in the north, too, and as was his way, my father bought up each parcel of land sold in desperation in the vicinity of Moat Hall. The estate was expanding. He'd even tried to wave money under the nose of the local rector in an effort to buy church lands.

My team were almost all unpaid, and many were down on their luck, so a weekend in a country house at the expense of the boss appeared great fun.

A pair of crates rested in a stable block that was out of use, as my father had no interest in horses. Hills knew a man who knew a man who was able to buy what I wanted for a pretty price and plenty of pay-offs along the way. I'd been waiting until I knew I could trust my team before opening the crates.

On Saturday morning, we carried our hunting rifles and pistols openly out of the hall and made for the woods around the mound where the original moated manor had stood, but we carried the crates padlocked closed. They created much interest and speculation.

Hills opened them with a flourish.

'Ta-dah! Won't you look at those beauties.'

Those not in on the act gave a gasp. The crates contained a pair of

Thompson submachine guns, the kind used in American gangster movies, but ours had straight box magazines rather than the drums seen in the films. I'd heard the fifty-round drums were heavy and awkward to use in real life.

'This is dead secret,' I said, 'like everything we do. It's illegal to own these, and we'd all go down for it if the police knew.'

I calculated that as long as the weapons stayed on private land, I was within my legal rights, but I was testing the discretion of Z3.

'London gangsters would kill to get their hands on such weapons, as would communist terrorists. Indeed, a few of our Blackshirt friends are impatient for a stand-up fight and would have them off us tomorrow. Anyone not happy, walk away now.'

I had no need to worry, as they were all keener than I pretended to be.

Sissy nodded slowly. I'd told her about the guns straight after I'd bought them and explained why I'd bought them. Sensing events ratcheting towards a crisis, I deemed it time to be ready. We walked over to an old barn that slumbered under a moss-covered roof where holes gaped between the slates. The team got their eye in with standard rifle and pistol practice, and then it was time to play with our new toys. Practice used prodigious amounts of bullets, but fortunately, the tommy gun used standard pistol ammunition, even if this came at the cost of hitting power.

Disappointment came swiftly. The women found the weapon too heavy to hold steadily, and most of the men struggled to hit the barn door from further than twenty paces. The gun jerked up after a few rounds, so the next shots went high and wild.

Unexpectedly, Julian was the best at taming the bucking beast.

'It's mathematics.' He tried to explain by using his hands to mime angles and employing terms I'd not heard since officer training school, but mathematics had never been my strong suit.

What did impress me was the noise, the staccato beat of lead into wood as splinters flew in all directions. We would have to be very close to the enemy to hit what we intended, but with that rate of fire, even an amateur could strike a target by accident. Only a fool would face up to a tommy gun.

The Frittons were awed by what they saw. Both made pretty good attempts with pistols, given I doubt they'd shot before. I didn't allow them to touch the Thompsons as they could work their way there in time, and neither seemed to carry much muscle.

It was a weekend to out-Valentine Valentine and see if I could spot anyone whose loyalty to the party was divided. If word seeped back to Black House about what we were up to, I'd have a pretty good indication there was someone I couldn't trust. Taylor seemed to have dismissed Nigel Fritton's attempts to join, so he owed no loyalty to Z1 and was certainly not the kind of racialist thug sought by Z2. Ruth was simply quiet. Relaxing away from the intensity of the capital, men and women alike would be unguarded and ultimately loud and drunk.

Adding the Thompsons to our growing stock of pistols and rifles meant Department Z3 could pack a fair punch in a crisis. The team imagined one day we'd be storming a communist headquarters, but in my mind, the guns pointed in the opposite direction. If Mosley ever made his bid to seize power by force and my friends were caught in the middle, we'd have a chance to fight our way out of trouble. Until then, they would remain deeply hidden.

'That was great fun,' Julian said as we walked back to the Hall. 'Didn't help my headaches, though. How's your arm?'

'Still pretty useless—I could barely lift the thing. Almost shot my foot off. I'm glad you were up for coming.'

'Wouldn't have missed it.'

'Julian.' I stopped walking. 'The reason we came up here to practise is because Sissy and I were shot at last month, and we've no idea who pulled the trigger. One or probably two men have been murdered, and again, we've no idea who's wielding the knife.'

'We have to do what we have to do,' he said, 'if we're going to win power.'

He wouldn't be prised away from the fascist dream anytime soon.

'There's also a reason I said no when you asked if Melissa could come. This war we're in isn't black against red, us against the communists. This is a game with lots of players, and there's at least one faction I don't understand. I don't know whose side they're on or what they want.'

'And you think my fiancée is part of this faction?'

'No.' Melissa was too obviously on the William Joyce would-be-Nazi wing of the party to be concealing anything. 'But we need to protect her from knowing things she doesn't need to know.'

'In case she tells Valentine?'

'Or anyone else. The Party is a leaky ship.'

Melissa was busy with a project to infiltrate female societies such as the Women's Institute, so had been eased aside without fuss.

'Can you trust all the others, then? Hills got you these guns, which makes me wonder about whom he associates with. He's been making some hefty calls on petty cash, too.' Julian frowned to emphasise his accountant's concern. 'Handing out money without receipts goes against the grain. And Hills, well, he has a history of not being the most honest copper on the street. Are you sure he's not pocketing it himself?'

'Would you dare to cross Department Z, knowing what you know?'

'No,' he said after just a moment's thought.

We both knew the black-walled interrogation room beneath Black House too well, but for most of the Party, its existence was a dark rumour that encouraged obedience.

'Your new chums at that club, Young Britain. Do any of them work for the king? He's young, so he'd favour young men to work with him. It's a long throw from the outfield, but it'd be worth keeping a quiet ear to the ground. We need someone on the inside if we're going to get the full Simpson story.'

'I think Viscount Lyle does something with the king. I can find out.'

'Fine—but be subtle. Don't try to pull him on board yet.'

'You know some of the chaps there are pretty important,' he said, with a tinge of reluctance. 'I'm never quite sure what I should pass on to you about what I hear.'

'Our first loyalty is to Section Z3,' I said, making a mockery of my own true allegiance. 'Not to any club or drinking chums.'

Julian gazed off at the distant Pennines.

'The chaps at the club know I'm with Z3,' he said. 'One of them slipped this to me.' He dug in the pocket of his jacket and took out a slip of paper. 'I wasn't given this in confidence, so I think I'm supposed to act on it.'

'35 Group have been dealt with,' I read.

'Someone knows we're interested in them. I mean, Sissy has been out asking questions.'

'And we sent Ruth along to a couple of Christians Against Fascists meetings,' I added. She'd not reported hearing a word about the Group. 'And then, of course, there's Isby who must know who they really are. Or were.'

'As it says, they've been dealt with,' Julian said with a shrug. 'Closed down, put out of business. Told to stop whatever they're up to. They're not a problem anymore.'

It explained why their name had vanished off any leaflets printed later than the Battle of Cable Street. Lucy had ferreted through our piles of anti-fascist literature and confirmed it. Perhaps 35 Group's involvement in the battle had been a step too far, and they'd offended the wrong people, or someone had exceeded their orders. It made me wonder.

'When we get back, we're going to continue our bible studies. Isby accused me of wanting to raid their office and smash up their printing presses. At the very least, we should find that office.'

* * *

To make Saturday's grand dinner a levelling occasion, nobody sat at the end of the great oak table under the portrait of my late mother, and the fit was tight. I asked the staff to serve plain fare, but plenty of it, and even the servants seemed to enjoy the riot of cheerful young people. Hills was, by several years, the daddy of the group. My own father was clueless about wine, but Hopkins, the butler, stocked the cellar with an expert's eye and served choice bottles with a smile. He had a Yorkshireman's good taste for beer, too.

Sissy and copper-haired Eleanor could be riotously funny after a few drinks, and it amused them to see how quickly young Ruth Fritton became drunk. Her brother urged her to slow down, take things gently, but the other men told him to lay off and pushed a bottle of John Smiths beer his way. Julia changed places to sit next to Ruth, sternly promising to chaperone her against all these brutish men. Nobody's mask slipped. The team remained the team.

At the end of the evening, I led the choir of drunks singing 'The Blackshirt Marching Song' I'd been talked into writing the previous year. Rewritten after the party changed its name and the design of its flag, it ran to the tune of 'Auld Lang Syne'.

> *Hold high the Party flag, my friends,*
> *Hold the standard high!*
> *Advance to victory today,*
> *The Blackshirts marching by.*

Crushing the country under the heel of a dictatorship had never been so jolly.

Despite the camaraderie and bonhomie, a cloud of depression came over me. These were not evil people at heart but were marching to the wrong tunes. The more they respected and admired me, the greater would be the betrayal when I finally revealed myself as that traitor Valentine was hunting for. And if Calhoun was right, the Home Secretary was about to release the evidence of how German and Italian money was funding the British Union. It was not a good week to be an agent embedded within the fascists, an agent who wanted to lurk unseen.

Chapter Thirty

Julian Thring called early at the Young Britain Club that Friday evening. The porter said a gentleman had been trying to contact him urgently and would be at the club by seven if Julian could spare the time.

The bar seemed the best place to wait, so he took a whisky with water and was about to unfold his paper when one of the club committee men walked in. Frederick Douglas, known as Dougie to his friends, was one of the chubbier members, often seen at the centre of one group or another, invariably with a brandy in hand. He carried a furtive look when alone, looking to left and right as if in search of the next meaty issue to become involved with.

'Thring, my good man.'

'Julian, please. I've not sure we've been fully introduced.'

'My friends call me Dougie. Can we, ah, talk quietly?' The bar wasn't crowded, but Dougie acted as if it weren't quiet enough. 'I have a room here.'

Julian narrowed his eyes.

'You have Mosley's ear, I understand.'

It would have been honest to say that it was his father who had the ear of the Leader, but a man got nowhere by feigning humility.

'I have contact with Mosley.'

'Could you spare me five minutes for a quiet word?'

Julian downed the last of his whisky in one gulp. He'd never stayed overnight at the club but had heard the rooms were small and cold, and the rumours proved correct. On the credit side, the one into which Dougie led looked like it had been freshly repainted and refurbished. It had a single bed; a wardrobe painted the same white shade as the door, one easy chair, a dresser, and one tall window behind lime-green, patterned curtains. Julian took the chair, expecting to be offered a drink followed by a little conspiratorial talk. He wondered whether Dougie was the one who'd slipped that note into his menu the other week.

'You run Department Z,' Dougie stated.

'Section Z3.'

It was Hugh's baby, but in truth, Julian did run it, as Hugh was keener to gallivant on hair-raising missions than bother with office work. He might be an inspiring leader of men, but Hugh Clifton was no administrator.

'I need the utmost discretion,' Dougie said.

'Agreed.'

'Do you know where I work?'

Julian understood he worked for the Cabinet Office but didn't want to presume.

'Whitehall?' he ventured.

'Close enough.' Dougie took a sheet of paper from a slim case on the dresser. 'This is a matter of national security, so if you're not comfortable with what I'm going to show you, please leave now. I won't think any the worse of you.'

Julian nodded, staying put.

'This is a very dangerous piece of paper.'

He held out his hand. Dougie paused for a moment, then handed over a handwritten note in a wildly swirling script that included a number of crossing-outs.

When Your Majesty was pleased to receive me on 20th October...

Julian skipped to the foot of the letter. It was not signed. 'Who wrote this?'

'Stanley Baldwin. But it was written by the Chancellor, Neville Chamberlain. Baldwin's having his arm twisted to sign this. He's facing a Cabinet revolt if he does nothing. Which, frankly, is his style.'

'Do you work closely with the Prime Minister?' Julian asked.

'Read, read.'

The letter was a pretty blunt ultimatum addressed to the king.

'Is this a draft?'

'Yes. Baldwin's original was softer, and there has been a further revision by Fisher, the Permanent Secretary.' He paused. 'My superior. As you see, it's a demand the king must give up this Mrs Simpson, or the government will resign.'

Julian drew in breath sharply. Hugh's wild goose chase had not been off target—he clearly had a nose for trouble.

'You do know who Mrs Simpson is?' Dougie asked.

'Of course—you do know what Department Z does?' Julian retorted. 'We've been following this story for weeks.'

Dougie raised an eyebrow in approval.

All sorts of unpleasant outcomes were flooding Julian's thoughts. 'What happens if the king refuses?'

'He'll have to abdicate.'

'It doesn't say that.'

'Of course, it doesn't, not in writing. That's not how the civil service writes letters to the king. It's firm but polite and will be delivered with sighs and shrugs about how unfortunate it all is, but the true meaning may as well be scrawled across it in red ink. Baldwin is threatening to resign, and the government with him, so forcing a general election with a single issue at its heart and every newspaper in the world knowing the intimate details of the king's private life. I'm sure they have detectives following him and Mrs Simpson.'

'They have,' Julian asserted. 'We've seen them.'

Dougie gave that approving twitch of an eyebrow again. 'I've clearly given this to the right man.'

'Where's the final copy?'

'It's being redrafted again by the king's private secretary to rub the sharp edges down.'

'The king's private secretary is in on this too?'

'Yes—terrifying, isn't it? There's a cabal of senior civil servants and a small number of Cabinet ministers led by Chamberlain driving this whole affair. Baldwin is just a passenger, as he has been since appointed.'

'If I were the king, I'd tell them to go to hell,' Julian said. 'Jump off London Bridge if they want to.'

'But they won't jump off the bridge. And this isn't just about getting rid of Mrs Simpson. The men in the dark suits want rid of the king himself. He's young, he's progressive...like we are. He's a king for the modern world who doesn't like bureaucrats telling him what to do. Neville Chamberlain is playing kingmaker and will put the Duke of York on the throne. A king who will do what he is told.'

'How on earth is all this being kept from the public?'

'In the same way, we keep everything else from the public. By the time the people of the Empire know the truth, it'll be too late, and the ink will be dry on the Instrument of Abdication.'

'Mosley would stop their game,' Julian asserted.

'Would he indeed?'

'Can I show this to him?'

'No, it needs to be back in its dossier before anyone notices it's gone. And nobody, but nobody, can know that I'm the one showing you this, especially not Hugh Clifton.'

Julian gave a sharp intake of breath. 'But Hugh—'

'We know you're friends, but he has a tendency towards brute force rather than subtlety. And this requires the utmost subtlety. Agreed?'

Reluctantly, Julian agreed. What Hugh didn't know wouldn't hurt him, and Julian had picked up that word 'we'. Dougie wasn't just scoring runs off his own bat.

'How about Viscount Lyle? He's on your committee—does he know about this? He works with the king, doesn't he?'

'He does, but don't talk to him about it. He has his part to play.'

That was a chance gone, but worth taking.

'So, read this carefully, commit it to memory, make a few notes, take as much time as you need, but tell Mosley tonight. Mosley has to speak up for the king.'

Chapter Thirty-One

I enjoyed a quiet week, staying at home to work on my book. Mosley had been laughed at in the House when he'd protested about the allegations about BU funding, and I wanted to steer clear of Black House as much as I could get away with, knowing it would be fizzing with yet more angry informant-hunts.

Sissy giggled, following a fit of hiccoughs in the taxi. After an intrusion last year, Havelock Mansions had changed its policy and now had a porter on duty all night. As we passed his desk, Bass called me across and passed an urgent message. I called Black House from the front desk while Bass retreated to his room to offer me privacy. Sissy leaned on the newel post, hand clasped over her mouth to suppress more hiccoughs.

The switchboard girl brought Parker to the phone. Mosley had called an emergency meeting at Black House, and it was essential I attend.

'Now?'

'Yes. Sooner if possible.'

The idea that Parker wanted me to go anywhere on a cold November night filled me with chills. I'd once been down in the black room in the basement of Black House, staring across at Parker and Taylor and wondering what my fate would be. Afterwards, I'd convinced myself they were paper dictators with nowhere near as much power or menace as they believed. Ever since Verity had told me of Parker's attempt to kill her, I'd re-appraised the man. Beneath his cruel, bullying, antisemitic exterior lay something worse.

As for Valentine, goodness knows what habits he'd picked up from associating with Mussolini. I could outsmart Parker and out-fight Valentine, but the pair made an uncomfortable combination.

I apologised and invited Sissy to stay in my flat while I went back out. She went into the kitchen for a glass of water. I swapped my coat for the black leather one with its newly modified inner pocket that would serve in lieu of a holster. I checked the Walther was fully loaded before slipping it into the pocket, though I was in no doubt I'd be soft-soaped first, and only when I was off my guard would Parker's henchmen dare pounce. Perhaps my apprehension was misplaced, but I saw little alternative than to follow the order if I were to maintain my charade. Once I broke cover and ran, I'd be running for the rest of my life.

If I failed to show up before breakfast, Sissy would pull together the team and start asking questions. Perhaps they were by now sufficiently loyal to take my side over the rest of Department Z.

Lights burned from several windows at Black House as I climbed out of the cab, wishing I'd not bothered with the brandy after dinner. Then again, it bolstered my courage. Two stormtroopers normally stood guard at the door in daylight hours, but this was the first time I'd seen sentries on duty this late, and tonight they were Black Guards. I entered the building at a swift pace so I'd at least have some momentum if suddenly pounced upon. A regular Blackshirt stood in the centre of the vestibule, acting as an usher.

'The Club Room, sir.'

Not the sinister basement, then. Nor Taylor's new office nor the small meeting room, but the Club Room. This really was urgent. It had to be the fuss over the leaks about Nazi money, but I hoped to God nobody had worked out it was me supplying the information to MI5.

Half filling the room was a disorderly gathering of men plucked from their dinners, their theatre dates, their wives, or their mistresses. Neil Francis-Hawkins had taken the most prominent seat at the front, with one pretty young henchman on either side. Only these three and Parker had found time to pull on their uniforms. Perhaps they slept in them for comfort, as a toddler clings to a favourite blanket. The rest of us had turned up at National Headquarters in whatever we were wearing when the call came. With no discernible arrangement of seats, I chose one in the back corner of the room where I could see everything. Parker nodded to acknowledge my presence.

Many of the big names in the movement were present, including Julian's father. Amelia Symes, one of the women MPs, was the sole representative of her sex. Of every person there, I was the most junior, the least important in their top-heavy hierarchy. I could not suppress uncomfortable conclusions as to why I'd been asked along. At least no one had searched me for a weapon.

Joyce burst through the door, quickly followed by Mosley. He was still dressed in a dinner jacket, but with his tie cast aside emphasising his wild mood.

'We will begin!' Joyce commanded, glaring at Francis-Hawkins for occupying the most dominant seats.

Mosley pushed a chair aside and stood before the table at the head of the room.

'There is a conspiracy!' he boomed.

The Leader looked hard at one man in the room, then another, then glared at me, then looked away. I glanced right and left, sweating. If this was the great unmasking, who would it be?

'Traitors, the Tories, communists....'

Traitors plural. I relaxed a little as the rant continued.

'The king is in danger. The country is in danger. We must act and must act now!' The Leader thumped the table again, and his tirade ran on for another minute or so to pump up the room to the maximum level of expectation. Far more important affairs than internal witch-hunts were in train. 'Stanley Baldwin. Has written a letter. To the king. It threatens him! It demands that he give up the woman of his choice.'

'Disgraceful!' someone said.

'Or if not—and listen to this—the government will resign.'

Amelia Symes spoke out. 'Hurrah, about time!'

The Leader stayed the cheers with the palm of his hand.

'The government has no intention of resigning. This is nothing less than blackmail. The king must kowtow to Baldwin, or the king must abdicate.'

The Club Room erupted in outrage.

'Abdicate,' he repeated.

I was stunned by the news, but shouldn't have been. Perhaps Calhoun knew, but things must have been happening feverishly out of public sight to come to this pass so quickly.

Mosley allowed the fury to bubble before calling for quiet.

'Action. This is the time for action! No committees or debates. We must act tonight. We have been waiting for this moment. We have been working towards this moment. We have a hundred thousand stormtroopers ready to stand by the king.' He thumped the table in time to the numbers.

Joyce indicated he wished to speak. 'This is the crisis we knew must come. If the king is forced to abdicate, there will be revolution. If he does not, the national government will fall. In either case, British Union will step into the void created. I need plans from all of you—'

'We need plans,' Mosley corrected. His eyes swept the room like the beam of a lighthouse.

I stood up.

'What, Clifton?' Joyce asked.

'Section Z3 has been following these rumours for a month.'

'Why the blazes didn't you let us know!' Major Taylor demanded.

'It began as gossip, tittle-tattle in foreign newspapers. We began to collect it, investigating whether there was any truth in what was being said.' I wondered quite how much I should reveal. Enough to keep me at the heart of their plans, but not so much that I provided fuel for their revolution. 'Mrs Simpson is divorcing her husband, which means she could be free to marry the king in the spring.'

'That can't happen!' one old hand snorted. 'This Wallis must go.'

Mosley pointed at him. 'That is the attitude of the old gang.' The beam turned to fix on me again. 'You, Clifton, have you seen this letter?'

'No, it's the first I've heard of it, sir.'

Mosley was not waving a letter around, which suggested he didn't have it on his person. Perhaps he'd not read it either. He could be operating on hearsay, but the intensity of effort from MI5, Special Branch, and others suggested something of this nature was taking place behind the scenes. I wondered who the source was, and whether he was a genuine monarchist or a troublemaker.

The Leader shifted his tone into the one he used for prepared speeches.

'British Union stands beside the king, and if the king stands his ground, this is our great opportunity. I want everybody, everybody to prepare. You, Clifton, put all your men onto finding out whatever you can.'

'Sir.' I would, and all my women, too.

He pointed at Francis-Hawkins. 'FH, I want the regional inspectors on the alert to bring their men to London at a day's notice. We want a codename. Joyce?'

'We'll break the story in the *Blackshirt* and pass it to all our friends in the newspapers.' Joyce, as Director of Propaganda, had clearly already set his own ideas in motion. 'Operation Mercury.'

'Good, good. I want more ideas.'

I needed to know who else was in on the plot and whose interest it served to draw Mosley into the fight. I stood up again.

'Sir, do we have allies? Is anyone else on the king's side?'

'No one. The victory will be ours alone.'

Chapter Thirty-Two

The British public may know little of the relationship between the king and Wallis Simpson, but the leaders of the land clearly knew much more and did not like what they saw. I was of course in the middle, knowing more than Mr Braithwaite on the Halifax omnibus, but so much less than the flies on the walls of the Cabinet rooms. I'd always worn my patriotism lightly, not feeling the urge to wrap myself in the Union Jack and sock it to Johnny Foreigner, but loyalty to my country and the late King George had been instinctive, drilled into me by my schools, by the church and then by the army. I was now unsure where I stood.

Could Mosley possibly be on the right side for once?

Accepted, he wanted to bring the lawfully elected government down and replace it with a dictatorship. But that same government, allegedly, was plotting to depose the lawful head of state and replace him with a puppet of their choosing. From the back-and-forth sharing of shreds of information, Mrs Simpson looked to be no more than a pawn in the game; an excuse to remove a monarch the men who wielded the real power found inconvenient.

I'd now been ordered to investigate the Simpson affair by both my masters, and all the threads I'd been following since Hardcastle's death seemed to be merging. Somehow the murder had become just another loose end.

Sissy roused me late on Saturday morning. There was none of the usual play, despite her sleeping only in one of my oversized pyjama tops and wrapping a naked leg around me as I came round. Without betraying too much confidence I let her know in which direction the affairs of the country had suddenly lurched.

'That's appalling,' she said. 'Baldwin has to go. He can't just order the king to abdicate.'

'No, I'm not sure he can, constitutionally.'

'So it's Baldwin who must go,' she asserted. 'And Mosley must take his place. This is the best chance we'll get to take power.' She paused, propped herself up on an elbow, and stuck a fingernail into my chest. 'And I'm sorry, Hugh, but if your mission is to stop us, then my mission is to stop you.'

This could be the end of something beautiful and the start of a nightmare.

'I can't stop you,' I said with complete honesty.

'But you don't want Mosley to lead the country?'

I thought carefully how to answer her. 'There's no right and wrong in this matter. You and I, we just have to do the best we can. You know that doctors have a Hippocratic Oath? There's a line that reads something like "do no harm, do no injustice". That should be our oath, whatever happens now.' For the time being it would serve as a plan.

'Fine, I'll agree with that,' she withdrew the finger. 'But what about your secret spymasters? What do they want?'

I had no idea what Calhoun and his masters really wanted. 'For all I know, they're the ones trying to get rid of the king, or they might secretly want to see Mosley in power.'

'I do mean it,' she said, frowning earnestly. 'Really and honestly.'

'Despite everything?'

'You're not winning me over with a few dinners and goodnight kisses.'

'I enjoy our dinners and goodnight kisses.' I made to kiss her and failed to make contact.

'Stop it.' That fingernail was back. 'You'll be on our side in the end. Those invisible spymasters of yours will be gone, and those invisible enemies of yours will be gone too. You'll back Mosley, or you'll be his enemy, out there for all to see.'

Frighteningly, she could be right. Britain could so quickly turn into Spain, where Nationalists murdered Republicans and Republicans murdered Nationalists and if you were not one, you were the other.

'Sissy, darling, we're just little people in the end. Nobody cares about us or our happiness. Whatever happens, you and I mustn't fight.'

Her fingernail folded into a full fist, and she gently thumped my chest twice.

'Punch, punch. Can we do something nice today? Something that doesn't involve civil wars. I'd like to leave my gun at home and be a normal person for the weekend.'

'I'd love to, but I need to pull the team together and tell them what's happening.'

She gave a sigh and rolled onto her back. 'Lucy won't come in on a Saturday, and nor will the Chelsea Wives.'

'They will today.'

I had to drive around London picking up the ones who didn't have telephones, and once I'd brought Walsh to the bakery, send him out in a bread van to find more. One of the bakers was persuaded to stay behind and make cheese sandwiches for everyone. It was time to share all the facts about Baldwin's letter and how it fitted with the surveillance we'd been carrying out on the Simpsons and the Hardcastle murder.

I didn't expect so much silence from my audience.

'Black House is drawing up plans, and we'll be a key part of those plans. We don't know what Baldwin, the government, or the king's advisors are doing behind the scenes, so things could happen very quickly. We're going to man this office seven days a week, twelve hours a day.'

Lucy started to object. 'But—'

'There'll be a rota.'

Other than Lucy and the Chelsea Wives, most of the team disliked office work. Some disliked work of any description.

'A king hasn't been deposed since the Glorious Revolution of 1688,' I said. 'There could be trouble on the streets at the very least. If the government falls, then we're into an election with no notice.'

'It's a big opportunity for the Party,' Julian added. 'The best we've had.'

He was right, and the others nodded in agreement. Mosley had been waiting for a crisis to justify the Blackshirts taking to the streets, and one of this magnitude might never come again.

A tinkling bell in the main office demanded attention.

'Phone again,' said Lucy.

I nodded to indicate she should go through and answer it.

'Major Taylor for you, sir. In your office?'

I went through and picked up the line.

'Taylor here, where the hell have you been? I've been ringing all bloody afternoon.'

'Just doing my job, sir.'

'Well, your job is to get down to Black House and meet The Leader. Seven o'clock sharp. No uniform, but look smart. Best suit—and shine your shoes.'

* * *

I'd never ridden in a bulletproof car before, if in truth it was bulletproof. I sat beside Mosley, and while his chauffeur drove westwards, he explained why he wanted me along. We were heading for Fort Belvedere, a drive of twenty miles or so, which offered half an hour for exposition.

'I invited you along because you're a thinker,' the Leader said. 'You've been on this case for weeks, and at last, we have time to talk candidly. Did you know I was married last month?'

'I heard a rumour. Germany?'

'We're keeping it quiet to avoid embarrassing Diana. Her divorce is quite fresh.'

Not only to protect Diana, I suspected. Conservative opinion frowned on divorce, more so on hasty remarriage. The middle class were particularly prurient about such matters, and Nazi Germany made most right-thinking people nervous.

'And yes, we married in Germany, your intelligence is correct. Diana is great friends with Magda Goebbels, and the ceremony was conducted at their house.' He waited for me to be impressed. 'Hitler came.'

Now, I was impressed. And disconcerted.

'I found time to discuss our progress, and Hitler was most supportive. This is, of course, highly secret.'

He was testing my confidence. If I were to start gossiping about the wedding and Hitler, it showed I couldn't be trusted. Calhoun and his cloak-and-dagger cousins must know the details even if the newspapers did not.

'So you see, the king and I share a conundrum. He wishes to marry a woman who is getting divorced, and of course, by convention, that isn't allowed. I say hang convention, this is the 1930s. Being a leader is a lonely job at the best of times, but imagine the misery of a man in his position being told he cannot marry the woman he loves. Told, as if he were a callow youth with one of those domineering Victorian fathers. Let the king marry whom he pleases.'

'What if the government falls?'

'The sooner, the better! We need rid of small men like Baldwin and his gang and all the baggage of democracy. Did you read what Lady Houston wrote about the needs for a benevolent dictatorship?'

'I did, but wasn't she arguing the king should in effect be that dictator?'

'No, no, that's just her choice of words,' Mosley asserted. 'The king will remain the head of state, of course, but he's above politics. King Edward makes a fine figurehead the nation can love and admire, but it's also up to the king to choose his Prime Minister.'

'You, sir,' I said without hesitation.

'Who else will support him?'

I'm sure Mosley believed he was benevolent and that his objectives and those of the British people were perfectly aligned. Blinded by their own sense of righteousness, even the worst of tyrants would not consider themselves to be evil.

'If the government falls, we don't need Parliament. We clear Whitehall of the plotters, the dead wood, and put vigorous young men in charge. You'll go far, Clifton. You've backed the right horse.'

In truth, I had a two-way bet. With horribly high stakes.

'And when we have power, what's our first priority?' I asked.

'We re-arm.'

'But you're on good terms with Hitler.'

'Yes, but I want to look him straight in the eye, as an equal. Britain will be too strong to challenge. There will be no second Great War because the fascist powers will be in alliance.'

Mosley's zeal to avoid war was perhaps his most redeeming feature.

'I want you to set your agents to making a list of names of men connected with this plot of Baldwin's,' he said, almost offhand. 'Men who need to be dealt with.'

And here, the benevolence ended.

We passed Neil Gotobed's house. No lights shone. Mosley might be fired up with his plan, but he was not the only one making plans.

Fort Belvedere topped Shrub's Hill, surrounded by a hundred acres of woodland. Its extensive grounds kept the king's affairs private, and I assumed they were patrolled by soldiers or armed police. Our identity was checked by a constable in uniform before we could enter the main gate. In the dark, the Fort resembled the golf club we'd visited earlier, another mock-gothic folly with a crenelated tower.

For all my father's nouveau-riche pretensions and for all Sissy's mother's high-born connections, I never imagined I'd ever meet the king at his home. It wouldn't have been impossible that one day I might have been at a royal garden party, at which I'd be politely introduced and exchange a line about the weather, but never did I think I'd play any part in an intimate meeting with a monarch.

'Are you carrying…?' Mosley asked, not looking me in the eye.

'I can leave it on the floor.'

'The best idea.'

I took the Walther from the deep inner pocket of my coat and laid it on the floor of the car. In the event, nobody checked what we were carrying into Fort Belvedere, which was worrying given the escalating state of affairs. I could have been a revolutionary planning to clear the decks with a couple of well-chosen shots or a modest bomb.

On the inside, the Fort had the feel of a Scottish hunting lodge. After a doorman admitted us and took our coats and hats, an impeccably dressed man not so much older than me came to greet us. He was very tall, hawkish, and I felt he was looking down his nose at both of us.

'Good evening, Mosley,' he said.

'Ah, Lyle. I heard you were up here now. The right men in the right place, what?'

Lyle nodded in polite sympathy with Mosley's assertion. This must be the Viscount Lyle of whom Julian had spoken. One of the Young Britons. The sort of younger man who, in Mosley's words, would replace the dead wood when he came to power.

'And this is Commander Clifton.'

'Clifton, yes. Your reputation precedes you.'

I often felt like the world's worst secret agent. Everyone knew who I was.

'And speaking of which, no arms, please.'

I opened my jacket and displayed empty pockets.

'His Majesty is expecting you, so if you'll kindly follow me.'

The drawing room into which we were shown appeared to be lined with pine panelling, but at a second glance, this was clever paintwork. Stags' heads added to the Highland feel.

A man in tweeds came through the far door.

'Mosley, my dear man.' The king approached, offering a hand to the Leader. He was shorter than both of us, lean and quite pale.

'Your Royal Highness.' Mosley shook the king's hand and gave a bow of his head.

'And your companion?'

'May I present Commander Clifton of my personal staff.'

That was a promotion I was unaware of.

'Clifton.'

'Pleased to meet you...Your Royal Highness.' I stumbled over protocol as I shook hands with the man who would not be king for very much longer if the men in Downing Street had their way.

'Clifton is concerned that you're being observed. You may be in danger.'

'What about Wallis?' The king asked anxiously, speaking with an odd lisp.

'Mrs Simpson is being watched too, sir,' I replied.

'This is terrible, terrible... Mosley, you had better take a chair. And...' The king glanced my way.

Mosley nodded to me. 'You can wait outside, Clifton.'

'Sir.'

I gave a curt nod of my head and followed Lyle, who was already opening the door.

'Lyle,' I said as soon as the door closed. 'Have you read Baldwin's letter?'

'I have.'

'Is it as outrageous as we've heard?'

'It is.' Lyle turned to the butler. 'Look after Mr Clifton, would you?'

The hawkish viscount gave a nod of his head in farewell, and the butler edged around to catch my attention.

'Would sir like to read the newspaper while waiting?' he asked. 'And would sir like a drink?'

Sir would certainly like a drink.

* * *

'Baldwin was here last night wheedling the king into abdicating,' Mosley said as his car wound back down the hill towards the main gate. 'I told the king that we'd fight at his side. Winston Churchill is his only other ally at the moment—Churchill, for God's sake. He's an adventurer, an opportunist. Would you believe we're in the same dining club?'

Churchill was a maverick Tory, strangely held in respect despite the number of times he'd switched parties or been implicated in major policy disasters. He was only a backbencher now, campaigning against the independence of India, warning about German rearmament, and making the government's life difficult with sharp and often witty speeches.

'He's always got his eye on the next rung up the ladder. There's a motto among Tory MP's: ABC; anyone but Churchill.'

We drove on towards London.

'Lord Beaverbrook is all for launching a public campaign,' Mosley said, 'but the king doesn't want Mrs Simpson's name all over the newspapers.'

'But isn't Joyce going to break the story in *Blackshirt*?'

'We can't stay silent. If Beaverbrook thinks he can keep this quiet and control affairs, he's mistaken. He's taken ship to America, so what can he do? Lady Houston is also going to publish relentlessly, and damn whatever the Tory press barons are trying to do to suffocate the story. We'll steal a march on them all. The king's off to Wales tomorrow, and he's agreed to meet again as soon as he returns. We'll dine together, and I'll pump some fire into him. Baldwin's already got him half defeated.'

'Does Mrs Simpson have any influence over the king?'

'I hear she's a very determined woman.'

'Could you speak to her?'

'No, because it will look to the king like I'm scheming too.'

It was time for me to show some initiative. 'How about a woman having a go?'

'Lady Houston is already doing her damnedest.'

'I thought perhaps lunch with Baroness Rockwell?'

Mosley thought about this briefly. 'Excellent idea, make it happen. And get yourself off to Wales in the morning. If we know the king is going, so do the men who would bring him down.'

Chapter Thirty-Three

I hurried to Wales early Sunday morning. The king's schedule for the next two days would be hectic, as he moved from depressed coal mine to closed steelworks then on to a renewal project that offered hope. There was no prospect I would be able to match his progress even if I'd been privy to the timetable, so I aimed to catch his arrival in Merthyr Tydfil.

A rail strike had been threatened but called off, and my train from Paddington departed only seven minutes late.

'At least Mosley will make the trains run on time!' the woman seated opposite me declared to her companion.

I said nothing and buried my head in a biography of Napoleon. When I found myself nodding off, I swapped it for Christie's *The ABC Murders*. I was slightly thrown by the change of viewpoint from first to third person in the novel, which is something I wouldn't have dared attempt in *Blackshirt Detective*. Perhaps I could try it in *Bretton's Second Case*. England passed by, then we entered Wales. I laid the novel down and scribbled some notes for my next book. Perhaps there might be a climax on a train. I had no illusions of earning fame or fortune from my writing. Being an author had begun as a front and was now more of a hobby and talking point. In reply to the question, 'And what do you do?', I could hardly reply, 'Hunt down communists on behalf of a would-be-secret police arm of a fascist party while in cahoots with the Security Service.'

The weather was cold but fine, the town a drab and unloved metaphor for the state of Britain. Bunting and waving Union flags offered colour and the policemen were kitted out in parade uniform with spiked helmets and silver chains. I didn't expect trouble, but if Verity were there anything could happen. In my last contact with 'Athens' she said she was heading to Wales and now I knew why.

A group of St John's Ambulance volunteers were assembling, suggesting they were to be inspected, so I found a good vantage point in the third rank of the crowd. A procession of black cars drew up, and men in long coats emerged, with policemen opening the doors. The king wore a tan raincoat and black bowler, standing out from his more somberly dressed companions. Was that a flower in his buttonhole? It was too late for daffodils, surely. The crowd bobbed about, cheering and singing what sounded like an anthem in Welsh. My mood was lifted by the crowd's sentiment that now the king was come, everything would be put right. Then, the king was off to a grand reception with aldermen and Rotarians.

'Three-quarters of the men have no jobs,' said a woman's voice from behind me. At last, I had picked out a touch of an accent in the way Verity pronounced *quarters* with a 'd' instead of a 't.' She was American.

'Howdy,' I said, almost on reflex. I did enjoy Westerns.

'Come to see how the ordinary people are suffering?'

'We've enough deprivation up north to keep any poverty tourist happy. Please tell me your squad aren't planning an outrage.'

'Nothing is planned. See the cameras? That's *Pathé News*, showing the world the poverty of this region. Yes, the headlines will be about your king and all the waving flags, but this is a political act. He's not visiting a flower show in Harrow.'

'My, my, don't tell me you're a royalist.'

'Far from it. But won't this annoy Baldwin and the Tories?' she said with glee. 'They can ignore the Jarrow March, but they can't ignore this.'

'Just out of interest,' I asked, almost as if passing the time of day. 'Are you aware of the Wallis Simpson story?'

'Yes, it's going to be an exciting few months for the monarchists and the moralists.'

'The king wants to marry her. What would you think of an American queen?'

'Very modern—and she's a commoner too. But I can't see that being allowed, I mean, it's only 1936,' she mocked. 'How would the Empire survive if common people even come near the throne?'

'The Empire will survive, because the marriage isn't going to be allowed. Baldwin wants the king to abdicate.'

Verity stared at me with her bright blue eyes wide open. For the first time, I was telling her something she didn't know.

'He's written the king an ultimatum. Some of the fascists are saying it's a communist plot.'

'They think the sun coming up in the east is a communist plot.'

'But wouldn't you like to see the king toppled and England in turmoil?'

She was still absorbing what I'd told her. 'Not this king,' Verity said. 'Until we overthrow the whole system, if you do away with one king, you just get another. Next in line is stuffy, malleable Albert with those two terribly cute princesses. And if he dies without having any sons, you get a Queen Elizabeth the Second. A new Elizabethan age—won't that excite the monarchists?' She raised both her eyebrows in mock alarm. 'We have to destroy the very idea of monarchy.'

'So your people are just going to sit back and let affairs play out?'

Her eyes shifted this way and that as she played with the idea.

'If anyone must be on the throne, we want Edward—a weak playboy married to a money-loving American divorcee. They'll do a better job of discrediting the monarchy than any amount of propaganda. In a few years, nobody will man the barricades to defend them.'

'So, if push comes to shove, the workers will support the king?'

'I can't promise that. They're traditional, used to believing the lies they read in the newspapers, and they're so downtrodden they do what the ruling class tell them to do.'

But there was nothing in the newspapers, lies or otherwise, and the people waving flags at the king had no idea of the turmoil in his private life or the intrigue swirling around him. Keeping the scandal secret robbed Edward of any mass support. The first thing most people would know about it would be when they read the abdication speech the day after it was delivered.

'Oh, your murder,' she said. 'It wasn't one of the comrades.'

Inwardly, I knew this would be the case. 'Tell me why I should believe you.'

'How many Russian agents would you say there are in Britain?'

'A couple of hundred,' I guessed.

She laughed and slapped me on my arm. 'Oh, Hugh Clifton, you do believe some nonsense. You could fit them all in a large car and have room for the Nazi spies too.'

'Honestly?'

She shrugged. 'It is very, very difficult to plant a spy in a foreign country and keep them unobserved. And very expensive. Your Hardcastle would need to be really important to put an agent at risk.'

Really important. The words rattled around in my head.

'Someone could have overstepped the mark, an excess of enthusiasm.'

'Nobody I've spoken to even knows who he was.'

There was no logical reason I could pin the death on a communist, much as Black House would love me to do so.

'And what about the Blackshirts?' She asked, inclining her head in a manner which I found unsettlingly appealing. 'Did they kill him?'

'No.'

'Honestly?' she echoed me, with a little sarcasm in her voice.

'I haven't met anyone who thought he was worth killing.'

As I spoke, I realised this wasn't true.

Chapter Thirty-Four

'I've spent a jolly two days in Wales following the king around.'

We were walking slowly through Green Park, enjoying a little winter sunshine. Calhoun and I had met in a cafe by the tube station, but I'd suggested we walk. Too much of what I had to say could be easily understood by a nosey patron at another table or an overly attentive waitress.

'The politicians don't like what the king said at that steelworks,' Calhoun said.

'Something must be done,' I quoted.

The crowd had cheered.

'British kings don't dabble in politics, but that speech smacked of politics all the way. He could almost have been campaigning for votes. I've heard the phrase "fascist king" bandied about by fretting politicians.'

'If Baldwin has his way, he won't be king much longer.'

Calhoun frowned. It was childish, perhaps, but the idea that he was in the dark over Baldwin's letter delighted me.

'You don't know?'

'What am I supposed to know? You're an informer, I know things because you tell me them.'

Supressing any temptation to grin, I sketched what I knew of the ultimatum. Calhoun looked away.

'Does K know?' I asked. 'Or M?'

Calhoun shook his head. 'If they do, I haven't been told.'

If the Security Service had been kept in the dark, the Cabinet scheme must be a closely guarded secret. If Calhoun didn't know, then Verity was no longer working for him else, she'd have been on the telephone straight away from Wales.

'Someone leaked Baldwin's letter to Mosley,' I said, 'and he sees it as his big chance. He's planning a coup.'

'As in an armed uprising?'

'I'm not sure about armed. The stormtroopers have little more than clubs but pour ten thousand into Whitehall at short notice, and nobody short of the Brigade of Guards is going to stop them. From what I've seen, the police certainly won't. The BU regional inspectors are assembling recruits, rallies are being planned, and printing presses are going flat out with leaflets and a special magazine.'

'When will this happen?'

'The propaganda war starts in the next few days. Other plans are being drawn up, but they'll wait for the right moment. If Mosley takes to the streets to support the king, will the king support Mosley?'

'If it's his only hope,' Calhoun said slowly. 'And as for your quip about the Guards, they worry us. They could take their oath of allegiance to the king literally, so if he digs in his heels, things could become sticky. A lot of the young officers admire Mosley, and the generals are rubbing their hands at his promise of rearmament.' He nodded rhythmically as the crisis stacked up in front of him. 'And the navy loves the king, even if the admirals don't.'

'He's popular out in the country.'

'Or will be until they find out about his bedroom shenanigans, and even then, I wouldn't put money on which way popular feelings will run. There could be some bigotry about her being American and prudery over the divorce, but we can't rely on petty sentiment stopping a civil war. Look how quickly Spain turned into chaos—this nonsense has to stop.' He was thinking aloud. 'I'll go and see K directly to see whether he's inside Baldwin's confidence.'

'Just arrest Mosley and his gang,' I said. 'I'll give you the names and addresses of a hundred top men. Chop the heads off the hydra, as you've said before.'

'I hope it won't come to that.'

'If Mosley takes power, be sure he has a list of names and addresses, too,' I warned. 'He won't hesitate to round up anyone not firmly on his side. He used the phrase *deal with*, which you can interpret any way you like.'

'Yes, yes,' said Calhoun, 'but we're not there yet. I'm going to verify that your news about the letter is genuine. If we have to act against Mosley, we may need you to throw a spanner into the machinery; tell us when the leadership is all in one place so we can collar the lot. Will you be able to do that?'

'If I can.'

'And can you trust your Z3 shipmates not to take Mosley's side?'

I had to tell the bitter truth. 'No.'

'We'll have to collar them too.'

Chapter Thirty-Five

Two men in the black uniform of the SS guarded the door of the German embassy, with a swastika flag fluttering from a pole above them. Von Ribbentrop was certainly marking out his pitch as the new German ambassador to the Court of St James. The occasion was another reception for the Anglo-German Fellowship, celebrating the creation of its sister organisation the Deutsch-Englische Gesellschaft. I spotted a number of prominent men in the room, including the Governor of the Bank of England and the editor of *The Times,* over by the portrait of Hitler. Sissy and I were, as far as I knew, the only BU members invited. Mosley was still officially keeping his distance from the Nazis.

'Philby, Kim,' a young man introduced himself. 'And this is Litzi, my wife.'

Sissy commenced a conversation with Litzi, dressed plainly in brown velour, who it transpired was Austrian. It was good to see Sissy in a colour other than black. Her satin dress was a shade of purple, with a high neck and sequin-encrusted half-sleeves that shimmered as she raised a glass to her lips.

That flash reminded me of a shoal of fishes making a turn, distracting me from what Philby was saying about journalism.

'I started working on an Anglo-Russian trade magazine, but do you know what? Britain does hardly any trade with Russia. So I'm writing about Anglo-German trade. Are you in this AGF?'

'No, no, we're personal friends of one of the embassy staff. I'm a writer, too.' I proceeded to talk crime writing while Philby threw in his ideas for new plot lines.

'Have you been to Spain?' he asked.

I had, but I wasn't going to share any details of my Spanish interlude with anyone.

'Not recently.'

'It's a very, very sad state of affairs. I'm hoping to get there before it's all over.'

'I doubt if it'll soon be over; they're just warming up. Are you volunteering? Which side, Nationalists or Republicans?'

'Neither; I'm hoping for a commission as a journalist.'

'I did see the editor of *The Times* earlier.'

He glanced around. 'Do you know him?'

'No, but he's over there. Below Hitler.' I indicated where the newspaper-man stood.

'Oh, thanks, old chap. I'll... Good to meet you, Clifton.'

Bruno Vogel, at this point, took the opportunity to introduce us to Von Ribbentrop, a blond six-footer carrying a frown for every occasion. He was the most senior Nazi I'd met, and we shook hands genially.

'Clifton is with the British Union,' Bruno said.

'*Ja, ja.* And you're on the side of the king?' Ribbentrop asked bluntly.

'All the way,' I said.

'Vogel,' the ambassador said, as if signalling a pre-arranged order.

Bruno led me aside.

'What do you know about the king?' I asked.

'And what do you know?' he challenged.

'Do you know about....' I deliberately paused.

'A certain letter?'

'The letter, exactly. But how did you, and presumably von Ribbentrop, find out about it?'

'If you can find out, we can find out. It's unexpected. It makes difficulty for Britain.'

'And Germany is not pleased that things are difficult for Britain?'

'No. The Anglo-German Fellowship is not an empty slogan.'

And I'd thought it was just something dreamed up by von Ribbentrop to lull Britain into a false sense of security.

'Can you and I, somehow, co-operate on this?' I asked.

'We are already.' He smiled. 'I invited you here, to see what we can do together, as friends.'

'If this goes wrong, there could be disorder. Young Philby over there wants to cover the civil war in Spain, but at this rate, he won't need to go to Spain to see blood on the streets. Whose side are you putting money on, Baldwin's or the king's?'

He wiggled his hand as if it were an uncertain bet.

'The king, but Baldwin must not fall. You'll get a socialist government or some old fool like Winston Churchill who hates Germany.'

'Has it occurred to you that someone could be making trouble? Leaking that letter, knowing what harm it could do?'

'Communists,' he said.

'Come on, it's more subtle than that. What I really need to know is who told you about the letter. Let me guess; the king told Wallis Simpson, and she told von Ribbentrop?"

He smiled again and then looked off into the crowd beyond me, as if noticing something for the first time but in a rather stagey manner.

'Ach, I see someone who you may wish to meet. Or not, perhaps.'

Bruno was not as subtle as he was half pretending to be. As I looked around, I spotted the blonde curls of my wife Leonora. Her soft red shoes perfectly matched her high-waisted evening dress, which featured applique roses across her bosom and frills below her naked shoulder.

'I'm sorry to embarrass you again,' said Bruno, 'but it appears she's arrived with a guest.' He paused. 'And now, if you'll excuse me.'

He did this last year, bringing me eye to eye with an enemy so we both knew there were boundaries we should not cross. I'd not seen Sissy for some minutes now, and she would certainly avoid being anywhere near Leonora, so I was on my own as I approached my wife.

'Leo.'

She was in the company of a man who matched her perfectly in age, blondness, and sparkle. I'd thought he was German when I first encountered him in the spring until I learned he worked for the British government in a capacity he kept obscure.

'Hugh,' Leonora said with a purr. 'Fancy you being here, with all the other Nazis—you fit in well.'

'Don't sneer. Why the hell are you here?'

'Oh, and may I introduce AA.'

Even though we had met before, neither of us was going to admit it.

He shook my hand and smirked. 'Arnold Alexander Thorne.'

'But everyone calls him AA,' Leonora explained.

'And you're the Blackshirt hero,' AA said with no attempt to hide the mockery in his voice. At least he didn't call me the Coward of the Swat Massacre or worse.

'And now a top-selling novelist,' my wife added.

'It's not published until tomorrow,' I said.

'You'll have to let me have a free copy.'

'I won't get rich giving away free copies.'

'Darling, I thought you were already rich? Or has Daddy cut you off?' Leonora touched the arm of her companion. 'AA is very big in the Foreign Office.'

I was not fond of the Foreign Office. Given the imprecise nature of AA's role, it was quite plausible he was privy to my mission to infiltrate the Blackshirts, which increased his advantage over me. To add to my discomfort, he was another one of those blackballing Young Britons.

'What's your angle here, AA?' I asked.

'Angle? You mean *Anglo*, as in German Fellowship.' He gave a laugh at his own wit.

I'd not seen Leonora since another embassy event almost exactly a year before. It had unsettled me to see her back then, and I suspected it was some trick by whoever was trying to manipulate me, but this year, her presence didn't need to be explained by intrigue. Perhaps.

'So, AA, you could be an ambassador yourself one day,' I said flippantly. 'Spain, maybe.'

'Who knows?' he said.

Leonora would not let the sparring continue any longer, and I wasn't about to fight a duel for her honour.

'Lovely to see you again, Hugh, but we must mingle. I'm sure I saw that girl of yours here. Very sparkly.'

Bruno's little pause a few minutes before had come with a glance towards AA, and I finally grasped what the German spy had intended.

'AA, tell me,' I said. 'I need some insight into the way Whitehall thinks. Although most people in my party would say that Whitehall doesn't think.'

'I say, Clifton, what do you mean?'

'If a politician on the inside or some official wanted to stir things up between the king and the PM, any idea who that might be?'

'None at all. Now, I know that politeness isn't one of your strengths, and it's not one of mine, either. So you need to go and find that fascist brunette, and I need to go and look after your wife.'

'You don't get rid of me that easily.'

'On the contrary. You would be very easy to get rid of.'

Chapter Thirty-Six

My fascist brunette was all teeth and smiles on the evening of my book launch. Without her connections, it would never have happened. Within a small bookshop in Cecil Court, off the Charing Cross Road, I signed thirty-seven copies of *Blackshirt Detective.* Hills stood beside me, decked out as my token Blackshirt, though his uniform was very tight around the waist. He aroused some curiosity from members of polite society who hadn't seen *a real Blackshirt* in the flesh.

I expected A K Chesterton's new biography of Mosley would sell better, if containing fewer twists.

Loudly, I declared I'd be 'going on to dinner' later. I did no such thing. In the back of a baker's van Hills stripped out of his uniform and into a much-worn suit and overcoat. I dressed down into a selection from my second-hand clothes collection. Both of us had at least the makings of an alibi. To bolster it, I'd booked a table in my name, which would be enjoyed by Julian, Melissa, Sissy, the Chelsea Wives, and their husbands. Waiters would remember the tip more than the exact details of who sat where.

Walsh drove the van down to Lambeth, and we collected Rinker on the way. Hills had recruited this boy-sized, half-starved-looking man. His lean physique had enabled him to slip through far more unlocked windows and poorly secured grilles than had ever featured on a charge sheet.

Heavenly trumpets almost blared out the involvement of the Church in the circumstances surrounding Hardcastle's death, wound up as it must be in discussions over the suitability of Mrs Simpson. My team had identified where the Christians Against Fascist posters originated, and since then, we'd been waiting for an opportunity to strike. I had no intention of putting them out of business, more of understanding how they fitted into the jigsaw.

Hills and his tame burglar had already scouted the New World Bookstore in a side street off Waterloo Road, situated close enough to the station for travellers to drop by. Rinker said there was a back way in, through a passageway three doors down, then along another that ran behind the shops.

'No other way out,' Rinker reported, 'and can't tell which 'ouse is which.'

We had to chance it. I silently counted fifty-two steps as we walked from the shop doorway to the passageway. It had an arched roof but would be wide enough to admit a small lorry. At its end was a small yard suitable for unloading. As Rinker had said, a narrow passage open to the rain ran down the back of the shops. Each had some form of rear extension, one amounting to a substantial outhouse. Rinker went first, moving silently, head stooped. I counted forty-eight paces until we reached a back gate in a plank fence about eight feet high.

'This it?'

'Could be. Give me a leg up, squire.'

I formed a saddle with my hands, and the featherweight man placed his foot in one and then placed the other on my shoulder and was over the fence. It shuddered as he released his grip and landed on the far side. In a moment, the gate was open. A padlock had offered little resistance, and the bolt was well-greased.

No lights shone from the building. A single-storey wing filled most of the space between the fence and the three-storey block of the shop. Rinker's gloved hands tested the windows that ran along one side, checking for any that were loosely secured. He briefly examined the door at the back of the main building then decided to try the door on the extension. I'd learned how to pick locks the year before, but this man was a master of his trade, and we were inside within the minute.

I had to chance using the torch. The long windows at the side had no curtains, so I cupped my hand to restrict the beam. Hills did the same while Rinker rattled the door at the far end and went into the body of the building.

The smell of ink and machinery gave away what the room was used for. A printing press reared at one end, with piles of newsprint, racks of letters, and drums of ink sufficient to produce Christian pamphlets and posters. Previous editions were pinned along one wall as a gallery testifying to the output of the press.

Rinker found a little lobby connecting the press with the back door of the shop, the street door, and a staircase. He slipped up the first flight of stairs, and I followed. It turned to continue upwards, but I was interested in the door marked 'Office.' It, too, was locked, and after our thief had worked his magic, it was indeed revealed to be an office overlooking the street. Nobody down below could see in through those first-floor windows, so we could afford to move about with more freedom. Immediately I saw ledgers and some boxed-up stock awaiting unboxing. Rinker pushed open the door of a room at the rear.

'Safe,' he whispered. 'An easy one.'

'Find out what's there.'

So far, *what was there* amounted to exactly what one would expect from a bookshop with a biblical bias in its stock. A door adjacent to the back office where Rinker was working was locked. That intrigued me. It was a Yale-type pin cylinder lock, so I took out my tools and started to rake the pins in the way I'd been taught. Hills held the torch steady, but Rinker was by his side just as I finished.

'Well done, squire, we'll make a villain of you yet.'

I made sure the door was not going to close on my success, then went to examine the contents of the safe that Rinker had already opened. It contained a cash box.

'Are we nicking this?'

'No, we don't want anyone to know we were here.' Plus, fundamentally, I had no axe to grind against Christians opposed to Britain sinking into a new Dark Age.

The main ledgers of the business were also in there, but after a moment's inspection, I told Rinker to lock it all away again. I wanted to see inside the other office. It was small but neat, and it was rewarding to confirm it belonged to Isby, who appeared in several photographs framed on the walls. One was of Isby himself with the archbishop. In another, he was in a captain's uniform, and I made out a short row of medal ribbons on his breast. Four or five, so he'd likely served in the Great War but saw no further campaigns. In a third picture, he was all togged up for dinner with a bunch of toffs. On the dark polished desk, neatly laid out for the ink to dry, were four stamped letters, each in a different style of envelopes and each addressed in a different hand. The name and address on all of them was the same, barring what must be deliberate spelling mistakes.

'He's writing to our Mrs Simpson,' said Hills. 'Go on, open one.'

I wished I could without betraying our intrusion, but the wastepaper basket carried what looked like drafts in pencil. 'They're poison-pen letters,' I said.

Quickly, I flipped the four envelopes over, took a pencil from a holder on the desk, and drew a short tick in the bottom right-hand corner of the back of each envelope before putting them neatly back in place.

A filing cabinet was locked, although not for more than the few seconds it took Rinker to open it.

'We could put a torch to this place, you know.' Hills said. 'That'll knock 'em out of business for a few weeks. We could write communist rubbish on the walls to show who did it. Red stars and 'ammers and sickles.'

'That's what Captain Parker's section is for,' I said, not wanting to develop the idea further.

I quickly sorted through correspondence addressed to Mr N Isby, sometimes to Captain Isby, sometimes to Nathaniel, or Mr N Isby MC. A transatlantic telegram from three days before read simply. AGREED SEND LETTERS B. I carried on searching but quickly found multiple candidates for B, Mrs B, Mr B, Lord B and so forth in copies of outgoing correspondence.

The 35 Group had its own folder. Minutes of meetings coordinating the publication and distribution of leaflets, and the organisation of public gatherings. Cable Street seemed to have been its swansong, but there were no minutes after July. It had clearly been Isby's baby, but its cries had been stifled. A folder marked C.A.F. continued the story from August, but the names and initials in the minutes and notes were all different. One had the pencil note 'for information', indicating Isby had not even attended the meetings as an observer.

'And this, sir,' Hills said.

In the first drawer of a wide chest was a sketch diagram of Cumberland Terrace, drawn possibly with reference to an architect's plan. Number 16 was clearly marked. A few Ordnance Survey maps were in there, too, both one-inch and six-inch, chiefly Surrey and Kent. There was a diagram of an airfield, offering no clue as to where it was. Other diagrams were of country houses, villas, apartments. I'd sketched one or two like that when plotting the first murder of *Bretton's Second Case*.

We heard a thump, then a voice. Our torches clicked off instantly. No way out, Rinker had said. One stairwell, one lobby, one passageway and none much wider than a man. We would have to fight to escape. I eased the filing cabinet door closed, then the door of the back office, so we were all inside. I heard a woman, shrill, giggling in that night-on-the-town way. Then, a man, directly outside the door. Thumps recorded their ascent up the second flight of stairs and into the room above our heads.

'Must be a flat up top,' Hills said.

'Let's lock up, creep out,' I said.

We reversed our path, checking nothing was out of place. Now we had the layout of the place we could always return. Parker's barbarians, indeed could return. Upstairs, the man's voice said something that provoked the woman into another cascade of shrill laughter. We needed to get out before we heard bedsprings.

Chapter Thirty-Seven

Sir Oswald Mosley was shouted down in the House when he tried to raise the issue of Baldwin's ultimatum. He was unable to catch the eye of the Speaker, even in a debate on the Public Order Act that Monday afternoon. The legislation was deliberately targeted to undermine the Blackshirts, but all the debate was over the fine print of the clauses. Eventually, the Leader interrupted, shouted out accusations about Baldwin's letter, accused the Prime Minister of dishonesty, and was promptly suspended from the House for his pains. The other British Union MPs marched out in solidarity. If Mosley had no time for democracy, democracy had no time for him.

* * *

Wallis Simpson arrived at the Ritz twenty minutes late and was ushered quickly to the table. Most striking were her eyes, surmounted by dark arching eyebrows. She struck Sissy as elegant, very well dressed in a dark woollen suit, edging towards forty years of age and trying valiantly not to show it. She did not fit the model of either a fairy-tale princess or wicked queen.

Mrs Simpson seemed nervous and unsure, this woman who mixed with royalty and was on the brink of plunging the world's most powerful empire into chaos. Baroness Rockwell introduced herself, then Sissy.

'I did not respond to your invitation straight away,' their guest said. Her voice was high and nasal, her accent was American, yet far more refined than that of the cowboy and gangster movies. 'I've become…a novelty. I wanted to be sure I'm not just here to satisfy curiosity.'

Oh, but she is, thought Sissy. One or two diners were glancing their way. Even if the secret was not yet front-page news in England, it was filtering out through the class who felt they had a right to know.

'I read your letter with interest,' Wallis said. 'Then your second letter. Thank you for your kind words.' She was clearly trying very hard to adopt the voice of an English aristocrat, framing her speech as a BBC announcer might train to do. 'I've not met your Sir Oswald, that I recall, but I am familiar with your party.'

'Our women's section is very strong,' the baroness said.

Wallis reached into her handbag and brought out her cigarette holder and smoking apparatus, but also a sheaf of letters.

'I accepted your kind invitation when you mentioned these. You said to keep the envelopes, so I kept the envelopes. I was going to burn them all."

'Could I see them?' Sissy counted nine.

Wallis slid them over with some reluctance. Sissy sorted through the envelopes, flicking to the back in each case, and sure enough, three had a little pencil tick down in the right-hand corner.

'Someone is organising a poison-pen campaign against you.'

'You don't say?'

Sissy took out a letter from an envelope that had once rested on Isby's desk and quickly ran over its hurried, angry, abusive content.

Wallis peered over to check what she was reading. 'That's not the worst one. I've burned that already. Some lunatic threatened to kill me, simply for my friendship with the king.'

'Are you not going to marry him, my dear?' the baroness asked.

Wallis stiffened. 'That's a reporter's question. They're outside my apartment day and night, the police have given away my address.'

Sissy made to withdraw a second letter, but Wallis reclaimed the whole pile.

'Can we keep those?'

'No.'

'They'll help our investigation.'

'It's all lies and innuendo. There's a letter here about my time in China. How did the writer know about that?' She packed away the lies and innuendo.

'Do any mention Guy Trundle?' Sissy asked.

Wallis stiffened again, as a cornered cat might.

Sissy apologised, 'We're trying to protect you.'

'Yes, everyone says they are on my side. While I'm in the room. Back in the States they have the Federal Bureau of Investigations questioning my friends. As if I'm a gangster or a revolutionary.'

'Have you thought of going home until all this cools down?'

'And abandon David?'

'Sorry, my dear, but who is David?' asked Baroness Rockwell.

'The king. All his friends call him David. And as for his enemies—they want me out of the way so they can work on him.' Her expression had already been hard, but if possible, it became harder. 'I'm not going to play the game the way the British Establishment wants me to play it. This is a great country, but some of you just can't imagine having an American as queen.'

'Well, we have no problem with it,' Sissy said. 'The Party.'

'Can your party stop this? Because your police can't. I'm here because… well, it was David's idea, or a friend of David's. One of his people. He suggested I take some of your women as guards. You are the Blackshirt girl?'

This was unexpected. 'Well, I have reliable women in my section,' Sissy said.

'I don't like having guards like I'm in jail. Your lady Blackshirts would need guns, but nobody carries guns in this country.'

Sissy lifted her handbag onto the table, opening it just so far that Wallis could see the black handle of her Walther.

'Some of us carry them. And the idea of having a guard is a good one. The people behind these letters have plans for your apartment. And you say one threatened to kill you.'

'My Aunt Bessie is staying with me,' Wallis said.

It was unlikely Aunt Bessie was trained in jujitsu and packed a Walther PPK.

'That friend of the king's was right. You need more protection,' Sissy said. 'We could do it—Department Z would see it done.'

The waiter came over.

'You order,' Wallis said. 'I don't have time to eat.' She stood up. 'And your lady guards, come around tonight. I may be out dining, but there will be someone there.'

'Is dining out wise, ma'am?'

'I have a position to maintain. Be there at six. And I want you, not some girl.' And then the woman who was rocking the kingdom was gone.

'Well, I say!' declared the baroness. 'She doesn't have manners.'

'Any manners she had are drowned by her problems,' Sissy said. 'She arrived late, with no apology. Was that rudeness, or is she having to dodge reporters? She said she doesn't have time for lunch, but perhaps she's just not eating. She needs friends, she needs us, no matter what we might think of her as queen-in-waiting.'

'You're right, dear.'

'We're building a new Britain, and the second Edwardian age must not be as stuffy as the first. An American queen would freshen things up, show the world that we're a modern nation not wedded to the past.'

'I'm a baroness,' her mother said sharply. 'Our family is wedded to the past.'

Sissy merely nodded, as if reprimanded. Class and privilege represented one barrier to modernising the country—even the Leader was Baronet Ancoats. If the king chose a bride from outside the European nobility, it would send a powerful reformist message. Several slices of English society wouldn't like that, and it was easy to imagine the lengths they would go to in order to stop it.

Chapter Thirty-Eight

Barred from the House of Commons, Mosley took to wearing his uniform routinely. Joyce and the other MPs followed suit; the pretence of playing by the rules of the game was over. The Westminster offices were shunned in favour of the Club Room at Black House, the National Headquarters, guarded around the clock. Sentries were all picked from the Black Guard.

I was called in for ten-fifteen on a cold and crispy morning and allowed precisely fifteen minutes to summarise what I'd discovered for the benefit of the Command Group. Mosley, Joyce, F-H, Taylor, and one of the regional military inspectors I didn't know sat and listened.

'Woman Unit Leader Poe and her team are now guarding Mrs Simpson. We have reason to believe an attempt will be made on her life.' I gave as much detail as I thought wise.

Joyce demanded to know more.

'Sir, with respect, there are some things you don't want to know.'

'I need to know everything.'

'No you don't, sir. Major Taylor?'

Taylor nodded his support.

'Sometimes in intelligence work things must be done that are not strictly legal,' I said. 'The fewer who know, the fewer are culpable. You can put your hand on the bible in court, say you know nothing, and be telling the truth and the whole truth.'

'So how can we trust what you're telling us?' Joyce demanded.

'You must use your judgment. Intelligence is not facts; it's hints, it's

180

rumours, it's hunches. I find it, but you're the ones who decide how to use it.'

'I like you, Clifton,' Mosley said.

I don't think Joyce concurred.

The Leader narrowed his eyes. 'What are you planning next?'

'Something else you don't want to know about. We have a lead on the plotters and are going to pay them a call.'

'Communists?' asked Joyce.

'No,' I said. 'If only it were that simple.'

The meeting ran on, so I was late for my usual Tuesday meeting with Calhoun, and he'd chosen a cafe that was a good twenty minutes' journey from Black House for our rendezvous. He was checking his watch when I arrived, on to his second cup of tea, and crumbs betrayed he'd also consumed a cake.

'Busy morning?' he asked once I'd hung my dripping coat on a hook.

I took my seat, then asked for another pot of tea and a ham sandwich. The owners were Jewish, and of course, they didn't serve ham sandwiches. I was happy with salt beef and the knowledge that a BU man wouldn't be seen dead in there.

'Mosley's Command Group is in permanent session,' I whispered. 'I've seen a whole procession of officers in and out of Black House. The Research Department, Propaganda, Women's Section, Fascist Police.'

'Fascist Police?'

'They're just jumped-up parade marshals, for the moment. And there's talk of re-forming the Women's Auxiliary Police, too. The most worrying thing from your point of view is that all the regional inspectors have been up to town, which means there's a plan to bring Blackshirts into the capital. My agents in the regions have confirmed plans are forming for *stand by the king* marches, again probably London. They won't rely on trains because the unions can stop them, so they're hiring motor coaches and using private vans.'

'When?'

'The word is early December.'

'Just protest marches? Will they be armed?'

'There are BU rifle clubs all across the country; the north London one is on alert, so the rest must be too. The cadets are taught to shoot on their adventure weekends, but I've no idea how many weapons we're talking about or if they're planning to bring them.'

Calhoun pondered this for a moment.

'Mosley will want this to look like a lawful demonstration until the very last minute,' I said. 'Any guns will stay well hidden, so if it all goes wrong, he can play the victim again without being arrested for treason.'

'He wouldn't make it that easy,' Calhoun said.

'No, I've not found anything you can drag the top men to court for. They'd claim habeas corpus and be out in a day to continue the plot.'

'We can't arrest him,' said Calhoun. 'Not without firm evidence. But we can apply to put a wiretap on the phone lines at Black House and listen in on their calls.'

'They think you're doing that already. Calls are brief and coded, and detailed messages are sent by motorcycle courier. There's a whole bevy of plans with mythical names doing the rounds; Mercury is the propaganda plan, and Artemis is Sissy guarding Mrs Simpson, but at last count, there were also Gorgon, Trident, and Pegasus, which I don't have a clue about. Have your boys listen out for classical-sounding codewords.'

'Gorgon...Trident, they do shout codewords,' Calhoun agreed. 'Dramatic lot, your fascists.'

'And to maximise the drama they're going to break the story in *Blackshirt*; this Saturday's edition, I'd guess. And we'll probably see a piece in Lady Houston's *The Saturday Review* at the same time.'

'Very well, I'll feed this up the chain, and we might finally be able to clear for action,' Calhoun said. 'Do you have a plan of your own, with a suitably natty codeword?'

'No, but I've a suspect: Nathaniel Isby. He's on the staff of the Archbishop of Canterbury. Does his name ring any bells?'

'No.'

'So not one of ours? Please tell me if he is, because somebody shot at me last month and I shot back. Next time, I won't miss.'

Calhoun pulled back into his chair.

'Oh, for God's sake, don't start shooting people again.' A patron at another table glanced round, so Calhoun lowered his voice. 'I can't defend you—you know that.'

'I know—but Isby? He runs an organisation called Christians Against Fascism, or he hides behind it. I've got a man watching their shop at Waterloo.'

'By the sound of it, he's not going to support a Mosley coup.'

'I'm not sure what he's supporting. I spoke to our friend Viscount Wickersley, and he hunted round. It turns out that Isby won the MC at Passchendaele. After one gruesome attack, his acting colonel was missing, so he crawled out under the wire at night, found him wounded, and pulled him back. After that, he became quite a star of trench raids and was awarded a bar. He must have become a skilled killer.'

'And this skilled killer now works for the Archbishop of Canterbury?'

'He must have had some road to Passchendaele conversion.'

'A lot of men found God their only friend during the War.'

'And now he's doing God's work in stopping the fascists.'

'Top marks to him, then,' Calhoun said.

'Trench raids were unpleasant close-quarter affairs. It's not hard to imagine Isby becoming quick with a knife in the dark. He was on the scene when Hardcastle was killed.'

'So that makes him your suspect? War hero and committed Christian?'

'Yes. Hardcastle picked up Isby's spying on the king and Mrs Simpson. I think he tried to blackmail the archbishop.'

'So the archbishop had him killed? That's rather fanciful.'

'People want to destroy the king, and other people want to destroy the government. It's not a trivial motive for murder. Out of interest, did you find all the explosives that went missing last year?'

'Not every ounce,' Calhoun admitted cautiously.

'And you never caught the men who took it.'

'Don't tell me the fascists have it?'

'No, Mosley's far too wedded to peace to start throwing bombs around. But Isby has a plan of Mrs Simpson's apartment. Suppose some of those explosives wound its way into his hands? You need to pass the word to Special Branch, have them round him up, and see what he knows.'

'Do I?' he asked. 'Where's Isby now?'

'We don't know. We're going to pay a visit to his place—'

'I don't want to know things like that.'

'If I turn up with my throat slit, you'll know who to haul in. Or if I don't turn up at all.'

Chapter Thirty-Nine

We could have marched straight up to the front door and bawled out, 'Department Z, open up!' but in reality, I had all the legal clout of a scout troop leader. Isby owned a small farm just to the west of Canterbury. Four of us took a sandwich lunch at Baroness Rockwell's estate and made our final plans. Just Hills and I would be armed. Walsh drove delivery vans when working and had become my driver of choice. Young Fritton came along to learn. We travelled down in late afternoon, allowing enough light to locate the address. The baker's van was pulled into a gateway while we checked the scene with field glasses. A thatched-roof cottage stood close to a lane, and further back was a farm proper, with the land falling away into a valley beyond. We looped around the lane until we found a track along the valley-bottom stream. Outbuildings beside the stream would be our first objective as soon as night fell.

It would have been a boggy path in the rain, but the mud was frozen into waves and crests. It would be a clear night with the moon close to full and already waiting in the sky when the sun set. We moved as silently as we could manage until opposite the shed, then found a place to cross the stream using a couple of planks placed haphazardly for the purpose. Over a gate was a pair of outbuildings, one quite new and of brick, the other older and ramshackle.

A padlock was no longer a barrier to entry. The new building was revealed to be a quarter full of straw bales, but otherwise almost empty.

'Something was here,' Hills said. 'A vehicle.'

Muddy straw on the floor had been crushed into wheel ruts. It could be something as innocent as a farm truck, but the spacing was wrong for a tractor. I could smell petrol, possibly exhaust fumes, so it hadn't long moved away. We poked and prodded and moved bales to no reward. Outside, a rough track led up the hill, its surface too solid to reveal new tyre marks.

The old barn looked less promising and was not even locked. As I flicked a torch over the door to check, I moved my light closer to one point, then another. I recognised the scene. The heavy timber was pock-marked with the impact of bullets.

'They can hit a barn door,' commented Hills. 'Not like our lot.'

I looked over my shoulder. The shooters must have been positioned further up the valley. We formed a tight line and began to walk that way, risking our torches after twenty paces or so, looking intently at the ground. Ankle-length grass was freezing into glittering spikes.

'Here!' Walsh said.

We stopped moving, and I edged over. A glint of copper drew me to a bullet case, probably from a .303 round. After another minute's search of the same area, we found two more. Isby or his friends had tried to clear up the scene but not succeeded completely. Night may have fallen to curtail their work.

A rusted iron barrel stood drunkenly on the slope a few yards further on. We were now perhaps fifty yards from the barn, and a shooter might appreciate a rest for his weapon. Isby was clearly not acting alone, and his confederates were practising in precisely the manner mine had. Judging by the grouping of impacts on that door, they were making better work of it.

Discreet enquiries had revealed a real farmer occupied the distant brick farmhouse from which lights shone, but Isby himself lived in the thatched cottage closer to the road. The four of us cautiously advanced up the slope, guided by the farm lights but keeping our own torches off. Dogs started to bark, so we edged away and made a wider circle to reach our objective, and the dogs calmed down. The thatched cottage was dark. A low hedge ran around its back garden, with a convenient wooden gate allowing us to creep up the garden path.

A beam of light lit up the side of the house as a car or small van drove past, continuing sedately down the lane.

'Walsh—go to the corner and keep an eye on the road,' I ordered. 'Fritton, stay here and watch our backs.'

A large and old-fashioned three-tumbler lock on the back door proved easy work. Inside, the cottage had a musty smell, as if the owner could never quite eliminate damp. Hills took the door on the right, and I moved left into what proved to be a sitting room, with another door inviting me to investigate beyond Isby's study.

He liked displaying photographs. Several were of relatives, presumably. One looked like a senior school or university group. I leaned in for a closer look as a face or two seemed familiar.

I could spend a week in here, checking the drawers, reading his letters, riffling through the books on his shelves for concealed notes, but I was not granted more than two minutes.

Bright lights swept the window, then another set, then another. The sound of motors died, and doors rattled open. I reached for my Walther and rushed to the window. Two vans and a car were disgorging policemen. I wasn't going to shoot my way out of this one.

'Police!' Hills said. 'Hide your shooter.'

After just a moment's hesitation, I pulled three thick hardback tomes from the end of a series on a shelf, then propped the Walther vertically behind them.

'Police, open up!' Hammering on the front door announced their arrival.

I remembered the lockpick in its little canvas pouch, dropped it onto the floor, and kicked it under the bookcase. Calming myself, I took a few steps into the hall as Hills emerged from the kitchen. We still had a few moments, so I turned for the back of the house.

A shot shattered the night, then another, then another.

Before we reached the rear porch, we halted. Instead of seeing Fritton, a clutch of dark shapes confronted us. I stepped back into the hall and snapped on a light to reveal a uniformed sergeant armed with a revolver.

'Don't you move!' A plainclothes officer came to reinforce him, and a twitch of the sergeant's pistol suggested we raise our hands in surrender.

A constable found a key to open the front door, and in stepped Detective Inspector Renton.

'Mister Clifton, what a surprise.'

'Good evening, Inspector.'

'Search them both.'

I helpfully stretched my arms wider so the policeman could reach into my inner pockets.

'No weapons, sir.'

'Check them properly.'

Another plainclothes officer came round behind me and patted and prodded.

'What was that shooting?' I asked.

'You tell me,' Renton said. 'Are you guests of Mr Isby, sitting here quietly with all the lights off?'

'We're doing what you're doing.'

'Except I have a legally enforceable warrant, and you are breaking and entering.'

'The back door is unlocked,' I said. 'We didn't break in. We've stolen nothing.'

'Clever arse, as usual,' said Renton.

Walsh was pushed through the front door, shamefaced.

'Sorry, they came up across the fields at me. Had me trapped.'

A commotion announced another bunch of coppers coming in through the back. A man in a civilian coat struggled to drag a casualty through the doorway. Nigel Fritton.

'Kitchen table through there,' Hills suggested.

I couldn't see a wound, but his journey from the back door to the kitchen was marked by a smear of blood. His head lolled towards the floor and his eyes stared into infinity. I knew he was dead.

Chapter Forty

'One of yours?' Renton asked.

I nodded, barely able to speak the words.

'Nigel Fritton. He was nineteen.'

'He's not going to be twenty.'

This was my fault; no, it was Renton's fault.

'Did you shoot him in the back?'

'Firing at my officers isn't clever.'

'He wasn't armed.'

A sergeant opened a bundle of cloth to reveal a snub-nosed revolver. I could smell it had been fired.

'But he wasn't armed—'

'You're all going down for this. We're going to kick in the doors on your Department Z and end your circus.' He pointed at Walsh and Hills. 'Put them in a van.'

My men were bundled outside to the waiting Black Marias.

'Does that telephone work, or have you cut the wires?' Renton asked. 'We need a doctor before we move that one.'

'You need to search the barns at the bottom of the field,' I said.

'Thank you,' Renton said. 'We will.'

'And phone Mrs Wallis Simpson and warn her that her life is in danger.'

'Is it?'

I was handcuffed and pushed into the rear seat of the black Wolseley, with a uniformed driver and a plainclothes officer in front and Renton sitting beside me. Despite the icy road, we sped towards London. I thought I saw

189

another car parked in a field gateway, but only for a moment.

'I'm not armed, so don't think you can grab my weapon,' Renton said. 'You can try diving out of a moving car if you wish, but my men will happily shoot you down when you try to escape.'

'You'd shoot me in the back, too?'

'It's dark, there're no witnesses, and you're a bloody fascist whose gang just fired at my officers. How much sympathy do you expect to get?'

None, I knew.

'Why were you inside Mr Isby's house tonight?' Renton asked.

'He's waging a campaign against Mrs Simpson, and tonight we discovered he's been carrying out weapons training. Isby's an army officer and a religious fanatic and he's capable of anything.'

'Go on.'

'I think he's the one who killed Alf Hardcastle and his brother Neil Gotobed.'

'Do you know for a fact that Gotobed is dead?'

'No, but you were tipped off about him disappearing, and you were also tipped off about Isby's involvement,' I stated.

'Claiming you're my pet informant isn't going to save you. We didn't ask questions about those dead communists last year or how you came to know all about what they were up to, but you've chanced your arm just once too often. You're going inside, Mr Clifton. For a long time.'

Chapter Forty-One

Sissy sat beside the window of Mrs Simpson's apartment, looking out at bare trees and a wintry sky over Regent's Park. Becoming a confidential investigator had seemed an exciting prospect, but in reality, Sissy found it too much like having a job. At first, it had been a break from the endless round of parties and lunches and afternoons of mindless chit-chat with female friends and relations, then evenings in the company of would-be seducers. Hugh had pulled her into an exciting joint enterprise, a marriage of souls as they fought against communism and helped build that better Britain. Hugh had thrown himself into forming Z3 with such gusto one could believe he was the most dedicated fascist of the bunch.

One could believe.

Just possibly, he was seeing the light. The corruption, incompetence, and double-dealing of the Tory government and the feeble compliance of Labour and the National Liberals must surely make Hugh realise that Britain had to take a new direction. The violence and the Russian-funded meddling of the socialists must shepherd him towards Mosley. Her resolve grew that the boredom would be worth the time expended and that the danger would be justified. The Party was mobilising to take power, at which point Department Z would become invaluable.

Simpson's Aunt Bessie was fussing at Slipper, a cairn terrier given to his lover by the king. The telephone rang at the far end of the room. Mrs Simpson 'call me Wallis, please, dear' had only just risen. She rushed to pick up the receiver. If it were the king, she'd signal with the back of her hands in a shooing motion, and Sissy would vacate the room and shoo through to the kitchen or the maid's room she used in rotation with the other five. Ruth Fritton was due to perform the afternoon shift today.

'Sissy, it's for you.'

Wallis made space, but not too much space. She sat down on the nearest armchair and searched out her cigarettes. The call was brief and came as a shock. Hugh was ringing from Scotland Yard. He'd been arrested again and had policemen standing beside him. Isby had not been at his farm, tipped off possibly. Worse was to come. The police had shot and killed Ruth Fritton's brother.

Wallis inclined her head. 'Bad news, honey?'

Sissy laid down the telephone, her hands trembling. It could easily have been Hugh lying dead, and she could imagine young Fritton throwing himself into the path of a bullet meant for him. A glance at the clock told her Ruth would be due in less than two hours, and she was usually early. The sister was as keen to impress as the brother.

'I need to make a call,' she said.

'That's fine, but don't be too long. David should call any minute.'

'I understand.' Sissy telephoned Julia and asked her to come back before two and take the afternoon shift. The Chelsea Wives were on the duty roster but always needed notice and were much less flexible. Eleanor was due to do the overnight stint, so despite Julia having already spent the night at the apartment, Sissy needed her back.

Next, she telephoned the bakery and asked Lucy to find Julian and have him ring back. Lucy also needed to telephone Black House to make sure a solicitor was on his way to Scotland Yard.

Wallis keenly watched each move and overheard each call. It can't have settled her nerves.

The job was no longer boring, but as she accepted a sherry from Wallis, Sissy wished to go back to the comfortable tedium of the morning. As soon as Julia arrived, stern and serious-faced, Sissy gave her the news.

Normally reserved, tears came to Julia's eyes, and she bit her lip. 'He was so young.'

'Chin up, carry on,' Sissy said.

Julia nodded, touched a finger to stem the stray tears, then breezed in to announce her arrival to Wallis. Sissy donned her sleek leather coat and went out behind the apartment towards the link road. A detective on duty nodded to her. Just one detective, she noted. How effective would he be at stopping a determined attack? Once they were past him, it was just one Z3 guard, Aunt Bessie, and a little dog to stop the terrorists. Two men who looked like reporters moved in as if to ask Sissy questions, and she told them to go away using the least ladylike vocabulary possible. Slapping one would have made her feel a little better.

Ruth Fritton was a petite girl of twenty and moved with the lightness of a ballerina. She approached with a carefree gait down the link road from the park, with hands in the pockets of her raincoat and keeping warm in a matching knitted cap and scarf in purple.

'Sissy,' she said, clearly surprised.

'Julia's taking over this afternoon,' Sissy said. It was as good a prelude to easing out the truth as any other.

'Why? What's wrong? I can take my turn.'

'No, it's not that, it's Nigel.' There was no way to say it but to say it. 'He went out to Kent with the team last night, and the police shot him.'

'Shot—'

'He's dead. I'm terribly sorry.'

Sissy was prepared for Ruth to crumple up, to break down in tears, but she barely reacted. Her eyes switched left and right and down to the fallen leaves. 'Dead?'

'Hugh telephoned me this morning. He's been arrested with the others. Nigel was probably doing something brave.'

Ruth nodded.

'I say, you must talk to the police at Scotland Yard. They have to tell you what happened. What about your parents?'

'They're dead too,' she said. 'There's just me.'

'I'm sorry. Can I walk with you? I can drive you home. I'll stay with you rather than see you alone, or we could have tea. Tea calms the nerves.'

'Tea would be nice.'

* * *

Julian glanced out of the window at the commotion in the street. A police car and a police van had pulled up outside the bakery. Another black car disgorged a pair of men in plain clothes. Only Lucy was also in the office.

'Police,' he warned. 'They're coming here.'

'I'll lock the filing room,' Lucy said immediately.

A hubbub echoed up from the bakery proper, and by the time Lucy had returned to her seat, the bakery manager was knocking on the office door.

'Mr Thring, Mr Thring!'

Pushing open the door without ceremony, a weary-looking man in a drab raincoat strode into the room.

'This is Department Z?' The man had a slight Scots accent.' Directly behind him came another man, brandishing some document.

No fascist posters adorned the walls, no pamphlets urging action against the Jews or unions were carelessly lying about. Neither Julian nor Lucy were in uniform.

'Sorry, who are you?' Julian asked, not rising from his desk.

'Detective Inspector Renton, Special Branch, and we have a warrant to search this so-called bakery.'

'It is a bakery,' said Lucy.

Renton ignored her and challenged Julian. 'Are you in charge?'

'I'm the accountant,' he said, indicating a calculating machine by his right hand.

'And who are you?' he asked Lucy.

'I just work here,' she replied with a shrug and a smile.

Renton pushed his way into Clifton's side office and started to go through the untidy heap of paper that filled most of his desk. Much of it consisted of foreign newspapers carrying stories about Mrs Simpson.

'Is this Clifton's office?' he shouted back.

'Yes,' said Lucy. 'But he's not here.'

'No, he's in a cosy little cell,' Renton added. He opened a cupboard and found what looked like Clifton's fascist garb and what might pass for civilian disguises.

A uniformed sergeant came into the room.

'It is a bakery downstairs, guv. Ovens, bakers, flour and whatnot.'

Lucy smiled. It was, in truth, a bakery.

'What's through there?' Renton asked Lucy.

'Oh,' she said, springing to her feet. 'This is where, well....' Desks and chairs betrayed what it was. 'This is the meeting room,' she sang, as if trying to sell the property to a prospective buyer.

More newspapers lay about, largely relating to Mrs Simpson, and several shelves were filled by fascist papers arranged in date order. Communist pamphlets and papers occupied another set of shelves, along with handouts from Jewish organisations and peace groups. A few had been printed by Christians Against Fascism. Renton paused for a moment by each shelf, noting the contents. It was not the most exciting library. He pointed to drawers and cupboards, and Lucy either unlocked them or stood by as uniformed constables forced them open.

'What's through there?' Renton pointed to a plain door painted the same dull white as the brick walls.

'That's the shop next door,' she said. 'It all used to be one.'

One advantage of being young and blonde and female and owning an irregular set of teeth and a strong Essex accent was that men might easily take Lucy to be stupid.

'Open it.'

She made a show of hunting out the key and unlocked the door, pulling it inwards to reveal an unpainted patch of brickwork. A constable rapped his truncheon against it.

'You strike me as being a bright girl,' Renton said. 'If this is an intelligence unit, where is all the intelligence?'

She went over to the communist newspaper shelf. 'This,' she said. 'And this.' She picked up a copy of the *Chicago Tribune*. 'The American press are getting very anti-British over the Simpson affair.'

Renton was close to losing his temper as he urged the girl back into the main office and pointed to her typewriter.

'Where's all your work? What do you type?'

'It goes to Black House,' Julian said. 'It's filed there.'

'So why are you a bunch of clowns not at Black House?'

'They ran out of space.'

The other detective and the uniformed men were reporting 'nothing' or equally disappointing news. Either Hugh Clifton was as clever as he thought he was, or the whole Department Z thing was an act. They were playing at it.

'Would you like some tea, Inspector?' the blonde typist asked.

'No, thank you,' Renton said, 'but you, Mister Accountant, are coming with me.'

Chapter Forty-Two

Julian Thring called into Black House as soon as the police were through with 'routine questions.' He had no need to even call in Naburn, the solicitor who was somewhere else in the building fighting Hugh's corner. Knowing no details of the fatal nocturnal project helped his case enormously. As did Clifton's addiction to Agatha Christie, which inspired him to add that false door to the meeting room wall. The filing room itself was concealed by a sliding bookcase with a lock at toe level. How Lucy could have held the police off with a straight face was beyond him, but she deserved a medal.

Half of Section Z3 were in police custody or on the roster to guard Mrs Simpson, and Julian sent messages to the others to lie low until Special Branch became bored. He was still trying to get to the bottom of what had happened to young Nigel Fritton, and unsure whether he had any next of kin beyond his sister, who by all accounts was being a brick.

In need of a shave and a fresh shirt, Julian arrived at Black House just as a trio of police vehicles were leaving. A pair of Black Guards prevented him from entering until his identity was confirmed, then no sooner had he taken station in Room Z when Major Taylor put his head around the door.

'Thring. Where the hell have you been?'

'With Special Branch—was that them outside?'

'Yes, yes, but not feeling so special today. Two typing mistakes in their warrant and two solicitors in the building. They got no further than the front door.'

'They'll be back.'

'No, they won't. We have friends who'll make sure of that.' Taylor took a seat in the office that used to be his. 'How long did they hold you for?'

'Three hours.'

'And what about your bakery? Did they search it? I worry you've got guns down there and all kinds of documents that could be used against us.'

'No, no,' Julian said. 'They were very disappointed to discover it really is a bakery.'

'Good. With Clifton still banged up, you're needed in the Club Room immediately.'

Julian followed Taylor to the stairs. Trotting down to the ground floor, Taylor nodded to the guard who opened the Club Room door.

'You're now running Z3, and it could become a permanent arrangement,' Taylor said.

Parker was already seated in the room. 'Clifton was never reliable,' he commented.

The centre of the room was now dominated by trestle tables pushed together and covered with maps of London and its environs. The Leader was there, with half a dozen senior officers. Mosley checked his watch and called Joyce over from where he'd been staring out of the window.

'Intelligence briefing.'

Joyce strode back.

'Operation Mercury has begun.' Joyce waved his hand mystically over a series of publications. '*Blackshirt* will carry the story on the front page tomorrow, and I've created this special newssheet I've called *Crisis*. And a hundred thousand of these.'

He picked up a leaflet headlined 'Stand by the King.'

'Every local branch is launching a maximum effort. Distributors are to be *in uniform*. We want no one in any doubt who it is that's standing by the king.' He pointed to Julian. 'Did the police take those baker's vans?'

'No.'

'We need them.'

'After they've taken the bread...'

'Yes, of course, after the bread. Bring them here to help move this mountain of paper.'

'How many of your men are left?' Taylor asked.

'Fewer than a dozen still free,' Julian replied.

'No thanks to bloody Clifton winding up Special Branch,' Parker said.

'He was onto something,' Julian said. 'Someone is planning an attack on Mrs Simpson.'

'Well, that's what Operation Artemis is for,' Joyce said. 'You got enough women?'

'Just.'

'Armed?'

'Some.'

'And your men? The rumour is you've built up a private arsenal down at the bakery.'

'If we had an arsenal the size of the rumour, the police would have found it this morning.' Telling lies was not in Julian's nature, but telling the truth at that moment could prove far more dangerous. 'What do you need armed men for?' he asked.

'We have to be very careful about showing we have weapons,' Mosley said.

'We'll need them for Trident, surely?' Taylor asked the Leader.

Francis-Hawkins intervened. 'No. We don't want to get into a shooting match we can't win.' The military wing of the party was constrained to do little more than march.

'I'm sure the police didn't look as carefully as they might have.' Taylor said, narrowing his eyes.

Julian admitted nothing.

'Can we get Clifton out?' Mosley asked the room. 'He's useful.'

'He certainly knows how to get into trouble,' Taylor said. 'Naburn has been with him, Baroness Rockwell is working her contacts as usual, but his nine lives are running out fast. We don't want to waste Assistant Commissioner Mulholland on just one man.'

'Is it true one of your men was killed?' Parker asked.

'Yes, shot in the back by the police,' Julian said.

'He'll be avenged.' Joyce clicked his fingers. 'Name?'

'Nigel Fritton. He was nineteen.'

'I need his photograph for *Blackshirt*. Nigel Fritton, a martyr to the cause. Young, handsome, yes? His death is just one more example of the rotten state of British policing. There will be a reckoning.'

'Thring,' Mosley said. 'Don't expect to sleep much in the next week.'

'No, sir,' Julian straightened his back.

Mosley opened his palm to indicate the door. 'You too, Parker.'

Julian left the room with Parker just behind him.

'I could use some of those guns for Trident,' Parker said. 'Whatever FH claims. He's going to have ten thousand men, and I've got forty.'

'What is Trident?'

Parker shrugged. 'They'll tell us in time. But I've been told to move my men from the East End to Whitehall and Westminster. People are going to be very angry with Baldwin when *Blackshirt* breaks the news tomorrow.'

'And you're going to make them angrier?'

'That's the idea.'

Naburn, the solicitor, was back from Scotland Yard and caught their attention.

'Thring, could I have a word? Sorry, Parker, we need to talk alone.'

Parker clicked his heels and gave a salute, then Julian led the solicitor up to Room Z. As soon as the door bearing the faded letter Z was closed, Naburn reached into his jacket pocket and passed a slip of paper as though it were some underhand bookie's tip.

'Clifton wanted me to give you this. I never read it.'

Julian unfolded the piece of paper.

The solicitor didn't even take the time to sit down and was already opening the door to take his leave. 'Don't tell me what it says.'

As Julian read the short instruction, his pulse rose. He didn't exactly understand the cryptic message, but that burglar Rinker would.

'How is Hugh doing?'

'Bearing up,' said Naburn. 'He's up against it, though, and there's not a lot more I can do. I hope whatever's in that note helps.'

Julian needed Hugh free, for all the top brass wanting to push the load onto his shoulders. The next thing he must do was speak to Sissy. He had an idea.

Chapter Forty-Three

I was feeling like an old lag after two days in the cells. Naburn, the solicitor, had talked me out of custody before, but this time I'd been caught red-handed. It would all be down to the fine print of the law as to what I was doing in Isby's house and what I intended to do. And if the police found the pistols we carried, these needed to be accounted for too. I was helped by Isby remaining suspiciously invisible and not popping up to insist we were charged for invading his house.

The key clunked around in its lock. It was about time they brought tea; I was parched.

Renton came in and ordered the cell door closed behind him. He had of course tried to interview me in the usual way, on the record, with Naburn urging me to say as little as possible and preferably nothing. After contemplating me for the best part of a minute, the Inspector spoke.

'Friends in high places.'

'Oh, Baroness Rockwell does her best.'

'I'm not talking about a mere baroness.' He let that hang. 'Your girlfriend is staying with Mrs Wallis Simpson, correct? And we know with whom Mrs Simpson associates.'

I smiled inwardly. 'Don't say the king rang you?'

'I'm sure we'd have had a pleasant conversation, but...' Renton pointed a finger above his head. 'The string-pullers don't ring me—they ring people up there who have an eye on the Honours List. And I listen to what they say, because I have an eye on my pension.' He was still contemplating me, measuring me up.

'You know that I'm onto something with Isby,' I said, sensing a route to escape from my predicament.

'What's he planning?' Renton asked bluntly.

'I'll tell you now, but you need this to stay off the record.'

'Why off the record?'

'Because men are being killed for coming too close to the truth. And those people, high up, with their eyes on the Honours List, might not be happy that you know what I know.'

'Thrill me, thriller writer.'

'Isby has been running a poison-pen campaign against Mrs Simpson, but it could just be the start. I fear he's planning to kill her and possibly the king as well in some sort of moral cleansing.'

'That's stretching the evidence.'

'He has plans for Mrs Simpson's flat, and I know you've not accounted for all the missing explosives from last year, else you'd have trumpeted it in the newspapers. And you found the bullet casings and the shooting ground at his farm?'

He nodded reluctantly.

'Do you know there's an Establishment plot underway to depose the king?'

Renton reached into his jacket pocket and took out a crumpled newssheet entitled *Crisis*. 'This?'

'Just because it's written by William Joyce doesn't mean it's not true. Baldwin, Chamberlain, and the top rank civil servants are all in on the conspiracy.'

'Let's say I believe you. Do you know where Neil Gotobed's body is?'

'No.'

'I do,' he replied. 'Isn't it marvellous what simple policemen can achieve?'

'Where?'

'A shallow grave in woodland, about five miles from his house. Discovered by a groundsman, ironically.'

'Shot?'

'Stabbed twice, throat slit. He's now in the company of our mutual friend Dr Pascoe. Can you give me a motive?'

'Someone, Isby and his 35 Group possibly, wanted Gotobed's cottage as either a reconnaissance base or an ambush point. Someone from his church may have approached him, singing a song about the king being a godless adulterer. Gotobed resisted, told his brother what the church was up to. Neil Hardcastle did a little research of his own, but instead of blowing the whole plot, he decided to use whatever he'd found out about the Church's activities to extort something out of the archbishop. Perhaps.'

'More than perhaps. He demanded a hundred pounds,' Renton said. 'We found the letter. Anonymous, but the dates fit.'

What a fool Hardcastle had been for a hundred pounds when the fate of the nation was at stake.

'I imagine the archbishop denies any knowledge of receiving it,' I said.

'I imagine he does.'

'But Isby works for him!'

'And is part of this great plot against the Crown?' He waved the crumpled copy of *Crisis*.

'If you don't believe in the great plot, you won't believe there's more than one in progress. The 35 Group decided to become invisible at some point this summer or were told to keep their heads down as they shifted from words to action. Isby may be some lone religious fanatic, but he could be part of someone's reserve plan. If the king refuses to abdicate and the problem can't be resolved any other way, Wallis must die.'

'And Department Z is going to save her? You, your accountant, and a typist?'

'If you let us. Did you have to shoot young Fritton?'

'He tried to run off into the dark, firing at my officers. I'd rather stand over a dead fascist than have to console a police widow.' Renton paused. 'Searching Isby's property, we found a Walther automatic on a bookshelf and a Webley revolver in a kitchen drawer. It's a pity you and your man were wearing gloves. Stupid criminals are the easiest to convict.'

He was teasing me. His words didn't veil a threat, more a promise or a prize.

'No more burglaries, no matter how well your brief can argue,' he ordered.

'No more touting guns around the capital and no more playing at policemen.'

I wasn't inclined to agree, but this was not the time for fascist insolence either.

'But if you—or your typist, or your crooked ex-copper Hills find Isby or discover anything else about this plot of yours, it's your lawful duty to tell me.'

'I understand.'

Renton rapped on the cell door. 'Open up.'

The inspector was trusting me, confirming I was on the correct scent. With luck, the weight of Scotland Yard would break the plot.

'Finally, we're on the same side,' I said.

'We are not on the same side.'

'We will be if Mosley takes power.'

'Over my dead body. Get out of here, you patronising bastard.'

Chapter Forty-Four

Once back at my apartment, and even before taking a shave, I telephoned round to discover what was happening. Sissy was over at Cumberland Terrace, the Simpson place.

'That was a brilliant move, Sissy.'

'It was Julian's idea, and Wallis was wonderful about it. As soon as I explained, she was on the telephone to David straight away.'

'David—the king?'

'All his friends call him David.' Sissy talked as if she'd now become one of those friends.

'Was he the one who actually made the call to Scotland Yard?'

'No, I think it was Viscount Lyle. The king, after all, has an empire to run as well as worry about Hugh Clifton.'

'I suppose.'

'Oh, Hugh, you could have been killed!'

'It's starting to be a hazard of the job. Poor Fritton, if only he'd kept his head and stayed put. Instead, he ran off, blasting rounds over his shoulder like some bloody bank robber. I should blame the police, but I can't. I should never have taken him. He needed more training. He needed to settle in more.'

'You shouldn't have let him take a gun.'

'I didn't even know he had one. It was a puny little thing, looked like a detective special. God knows who he thought he was.'

'You, Hugh. He thought he was you.'

I blinked this thought away.

'How's Ruth taking it?'

'Impossibly well, considering. I thought she'd want to run and hide, but she says its strengthened her resolve, and she's still keen to carry on. More keen, if possible.'

I sighed. Martyrs demanded respect, but a martyr to the wrong cause was just a waste.

'If we didn't need everyone we had, I'd say send her on leave—even let her go. Whatever happens, she must not be armed. Give her light duties until we're completely sure she'll hold up.'

'I've not brought her back here yet, so I'm having to rely on the Wives more than I'd like,' she said. 'They're happy pistol shooting in a field, but I wouldn't trust them in a crisis, not yet. Melissa would be here in a shot—'

'Not Melissa. We need to keep this inside the tent as much as possible. The police must have been tipped off about our raid on Isby's farm. On the other hand, it might be down to me putting them onto the trail of Hardcastle's killers, and it was just hard luck they turned up at the same time as us. What worries me is that Isby was well gone, together with whatever he was keeping in that barn and all the weapons he was practising shooting. He knew the police were coming—or knew we were coming.'

'Or he's about to strike,' Sissy said.

* * *

Julian waited for me in Room Z, swinging to and fro in the second chair.

'The police raided the bakery, but they clearly don't read as much sensational fiction as you.'

We were alone, apart from Julian's man on duty at the outer desk. I stood and gazed from the window down at King's Road.

'I thought if we burgled the Christian place again, they'd be waiting for us,' Julian said. 'But your man Rinker said with you banged up, they might think their problem was solved. I sent him in alone. I just sat in the car. I wasn't doing anything heroic at all, and if he'd been caught, I'd have been off like a hare from a trap.'

'Did you get them?'

Julian slid open the middle drawer of his desk and took out three framed photographs. He paused before handing them over, as if guilty.

'I paid Rinker. He told me the frames weren't worth much.'

I sat at my desk and glanced at the first photograph. A younger Isby was in a captain's uniform. In the second he was with Archbishop Lang. It was the third that piqued my interest and was the one that provoked me into asking Julian to burgle Christians Against Fascism a second time. I'd half noticed something on our last visit but disregarded it. Four men in dinner jackets featured in the photograph. One was Isby, and one was Viscount Lyle.

'This man is familiar with my wife.' I tapped a finger on Arnold Alexander Thorne's face, imagining I was punching it instead. 'He's known as AA.'

Julian came across. 'Ah, yes, I've seen him at the club.' He took a deep breath before tapping another face. 'That's Viscount Lyle. He's also a member of my club.'

The pieces were starting to fall together, and I hoped Julian could see the picture emerging.

'He's attached to the king's personal staff,' Julian said.

'I met him when I went with Mosley to Belvedere,' I said. 'And he was the one who talked me out of jail. He could even be the one who came up with the idea of Sissy guarding Mrs Simpson. Strange bedfellows. Is Isby a member of your club?'

'I've never seen him there.'

'And the fourth chap?'

'I've seen him at dinners, but don't know his name. AA works for the Foreign Office, but I'm not sure what he does there.'

'I'd put a pound on him working for the Secret Intelligence Service,' I said. 'That's the overseas branch of British military intelligence.'

'I've never heard of them,' Julian said.

'Because they don't officially exist. All these different agencies and departments get rather muddled together, and that's probably deliberate.'

Julian's lips moved, but he said nothing, trying to assemble a scenario where a man who worked for the king, one who worked in the murky parts of the government, and one who was clearly following a reactionary agenda fitted into the same frame.

I shared my theories aloud. 'Isby has it in for the king—or at least for Mrs Simpson. He works for the archbishop, who can't approve of her. Your man Lyle works for the king, so should be on his side. But God knows who's pulling AA's strings.'

Something unspoken hung between us.

'Julian, be really careful with anything you do or say at that club,' I said hurriedly. 'Remember what I said about how we were played for fools last year?'

'And this year,' he said, then fell silent.

'Julian?'

'Hugh, I'm sorry, but, well, I was sworn to secrecy.' He pulled himself up to full height as if about to confess to the headmaster. 'It was me who gave Mosley the letter to the king, the one that got him all fired up.'

This struck me hard. They were even using my friends as part of their schemes.

'Ah, a chap at the club gave it to me,' Julian continued.

'Who?'

'Dougie, Frederick Douglas. You have to understand, I was sworn to secrecy.'

'Of course, you were. And you still are.'

He slapped my desk hard. 'Golly, this is why they blackballed you! They didn't want to risk you picking up these clues, but they thought I was the sort of chump who wouldn't rumble them.'

And I'd put it down to snobbery.

'But they wanted you because of your father's influence and Mosley's ear,' I said. 'They saw you as one of them, whereas I—'

He gave a nervous laugh. 'You're just a northern oik who asks too many questions.'

I had to laugh too.

'And I'm in Department Z,' he said. 'So when I told Mosley, it looked like we gained the information through one of our informers. If my father had presented the letter, it would've looked like another one of his schemes. And he's got enemies at Black House. They wouldn't trust him.'

'And if your father knew the source, he'd interrogate it because he's suspicious like that,' I reasoned. 'He'd dig into the motivations of the man who exposed this letter. Whereas, as you say, Department Z has ears everywhere, and we don't betray our informers. You were no doubt mysterious as to how you came by the letter, so improving the credibility of the information.'

He nodded vigorously. 'I do feel an awful chump. I've let you down.'

'But you're not a chump anymore, and now we know your new friends are the ones playing power games. But did they give that message to Mosley to help him into power or set him up to be destroyed? Help the king or bring him down?'

Chapter Forty-Five

Sissy studied the growing crowd outside Cumberland Terrace, restless and constantly shifting. Inquisitive members of the public mixed with the reporters and policemen. Slowly the story was leaking out, or someone was spreading rumours maliciously. Thank God Hugh was free—or thank Wallis, more like.

'Don't mention it, honey.' Wallis looked anxiously out of the window, then turned to Aunt Bessie, who was pouring coffee. 'Did David ring while I was napping?'

'No, dear.'

'Perhaps you should telephone him today,' Sissy suggested, trying to be helpful.

'I do not ring men,' Wallis said tartly. 'They must ring me. That's a lesson you need to learn, young woman.'

So she was no longer honey but a young woman. Firmly put in her place, put her attention back to the crowd. Gosh, this was boring. Eleanor would be in later, but Hugh had to go to Black House and then the bakery, so might not get out to Regent's Park at all that day. The maid announced that two plainclothes police officers were at the door, and Sissy went to see. Perhaps the boredom was about to be broken.

His raincoat was wet, but he removed his hat respectfully.

'Detective Inspector Renton, Special Branch.'

So this was the infamous Inspector Renton who had thrown Hugh in jail and shot Nigel Fritton. As soon as Mosley took power, Renton would have to be removed from his post, she decided; retired or shipped off to join the colonial police. Special Branch could even be closed down and replaced by Department Z. While plotting the termination of Renton's career, Sissy led him into the apartment and announced him.

'Inspector?' From her chair beside the silent telephone Wallis sounded rather shrill as she turned up her entitled English accent to the full. 'You must drive those people away. They have no business to be lurking out there.'

'I'm afraid I can't, madam.'

'Don't call me madam, I don't run a brothel. Whatever you might have read in your grubby little files.'

'No, ah…' Renton ran dry on how to refer to Mrs Simpson. 'I see the Blackshirts are guarding you well.'

Sissy forced a smile.

'Yes, yes.'

'So this warning is for you ladies as well.' He held Sissy in a hard stare. 'There is a suggestion of a bomb plot.'

'A bomb?' Wallis could not turn any paler or smoke any harder.

At last, the police were taking the threats seriously, thought Sissy.

'Just a rumour, nothing to be alarmed about, but we're putting more men outside. Which means you won't be needing your Blackshirts. Or Blackblouses.'

'Oh, Sissy is a friend. She's the daughter of Baroness Rockwell, don't you know?'

'I know,' said Renton in a manner that suggested this was of great regret. He cocked his head in Sissy's direction. 'I hope you're not running around with guns as well, *madam*.'

'Me?' Sissy said innocently, spreading her arms as if offering to be searched. Her blouse hugged her figure so well she'd struggle to conceal a fountain pen. 'You wouldn't be such a cad as to search me?' Her weapon was concealed in her handbag beside the second armchair.

The telephone rang, and Wallis snatched it up. 'David?'

'King Edward,' Sissy explained to Renton in a hushed voice. 'David to his friends.'

Renton fidgeted with his hat.

'I expect the phone call will last an hour,' Sissy added. 'It often does.'

The policeman placed his hat on his head, and his colleague followed suit.

'Take care, *madam.*'

* * *

Wallis was not the only anxious one in the apartment, and even the dog Slipper became edgy. When Eleanor arrived, Sissy did not leave. As it grew dark, policemen in uniform were making themselves more obvious outside, which only increased the interest of the crowd. Eleanor had been advised to come unarmed, and the first thing she did on entering the apartment was complain she had been searched.

Sissy knew nothing about bombs and how they worked, whether one concealed in a car or a suitcase outside could blow up the apartment. It would certainly send a shower of broken glass to shred any flesh in its path. Something like a hand grenade might be hurled through the window like a cricket ball. She tapped the glass, remembering having seen a cricket ball bounce off a window she'd been convinced was doomed, so perhaps a grenade would do the same. She was taking no risks and closed the heavy curtains.

'Why are you closing the drapes?' Wallis asked.

'In case they... To stop photographs.' With luck, they might just stop flying glass. 'It will be dark soon, anyway. We should keep well back from the windows.'

'Until David fetches us.'

'Is the king coming here?'

'He is. He's coming to rescue me.'

It was not Renton, but another detective who escorted the king to the door of the apartment that evening. Wallis, Aunt Bessie, and the dog were packed and ready. Sissy, Eleanor, and the maid hung back in awe. The king completely ignored them, having eyes only for Wallis and fussing over her. She didn't seem relieved to see him. It was just one more crisis for the day.

'You two,' Wallis said, turning to the women in the black blouses and grey skirts. 'Come close.'

'It's not necessary—' the detective began.

'It is,' the king asserted his authority as king. Only now did he notice the two women. 'Come on, ladies!'

The king and the detective led the way, meeting two uniformed men before the main door. Sissy grabbed her coat and snatched up her handbag. Eleanor put her own coat on as they waited for Wallis to follow.

Sissy glanced right and left as they emerged into the evening air. Already, she could hear the crowd. If the other side employed agitators such as Parker, this was their moment to cause trouble. She and Eleanor walked one each side of Wallis, both taller than the American and masking her with their unfastened coats flapping. Aunt Bessie and Slipper came last, plus the maid struggling with a suitcase.

'We could take you in my car, Wallis,' Sissy said. 'They won't expect that.'

'David? David?' Wallis called to the king. 'How about I travel with Sissy?'

The king either did not hear or ignored the suggestion.

'Mask her, mask her,' Sissy urged Eleanor, remembering the last time a sniper had tried to kill a woman under her protection. Surely, he wouldn't waste a shot against a target he couldn't see.

Someone yelled an obscenity. More shouts came, and a stone was thrown. The king reached his car and pulled open the passenger door.

'Quick, quick,' he said with that funny royal intonation.

Wallis ducked inside, then Sissy moved to block the passenger window. Eleanor held the dog while Aunt Bessie climbed into the back. The king started the engine, then the police car in front began to move off. Sissy darted across to her own car, and with Slipper duly passed over, Eleanor joined her. The crowd made the exit slow, but the little yellow T-type was able to catch the royal car before it reached Regent's Circle. A photographer leaned in close and photographed Eleanor, her glasses flashing as his bulb went off. One thump against the wing of the car, then all three were driving free.

No bomb exploded, no shot rang out, and nothing more than a single stone was thrown. Perhaps Hugh had been wrong, perhaps the enemy had been thwarted, or perhaps they had another time and place in mind.

Chapter Forty-Six

The king and Mrs Simpson were ensconced at Fort Belvedere, assumed safe behind police and guardsmen. Isby hadn't yet popped back into sight, but at least Walsh and Hills were released from police custody. The Club Room at Black House was closed to anyone who didn't need to be there, so I put my mornings into cracking on with the second Bretton novel.

I described a chase across those Welsh hills I'd seen from my train and a manhunt involving an aeroplane. Bretton was up against communist spies, and I was hurtling towards a finale in which his trusty Parabellum (that his father brought back from the Boer War) saw him triumph after a shoot-out in a railway goods yard. I paused as I was about to start typing that scene. Memories came back to me of shots in the dark, and the blood of a man I'd thought was a friend. There was no glamour in the corpse I concealed by throwing my coat over it, the lies that surrounded that death and continued to shackle me. Some author I'd once met advised 'write what you know,' but I didn't want to write what I knew. Bretton should solve his second case by brains, not violence.

Julian had a busy time organising the fleets of vans distributing copies of *Crisis* and handbills bearing the appeal 'Stand by the King'. The *Blackshirt* newspaper laid bare the machinations of the Cabinet that Saturday, but Joyce had pushed the issue of Mrs Simpson into the background. Nobody in the Propaganda department was quite sure whether the public would be awed by the romance or disgusted by the scandal. Lady Houston's *Saturday Review* revelled in the idea that it was all a communist plot. Now the story was out, it would be a busy week for Fleet Street, with editors and newspaper barons finally getting the chance to have their say and to take sides.

I hosted a dinner on Monday evening with Sissy and Julian, and Melissa. To reach the Savoy, we avoided Trafalgar Square and Whitehall, as an almost-permanent crowd had taken up residence, demonstrating their support for the king, booing every official car that passed. I knew Parker and his men were busy out there.

When shown to our table, I made sure I sat opposite the arch-fascist blonde, keen to hear her every word and opinion. It would be interesting to discover how the moral, hard-faced right wing of the party viewed the prospect of the king marrying a divorcee. Melissa's opinions were confused for a change. The Church made an inconvenient bogeyman for her conservative outlook. She clung on to ragged threads of ideas that the crisis had been cooked up by communists and Jews.

As the soup dishes were being cleared, we became aware of diners drifting towards the windows amid a growing hubbub. One opened a door, and we followed the curious out to the terrace. From every direction came the sound of jangling bells, a fire engine dashed across Waterloo bridge, then another, then another. A great glow came from the horizon in the south. Something large and prominent was on fire several miles away.

'Julian, have you heard anything about a planned attack tonight?' I asked. 'The start of Operation Gorgon, or Trident perhaps?'

'No, I've no idea what those plans are. The Leader's keeping his cards close to his chest.'

'This could be one of them kicking off.'

'Surely Black House would tell us if operations were starting.'

'Not necessarily.'

'That's a big fire,' Melissa added.

More bells could be heard, and more fire engines, police cars, and ambulances crossed the bridge. One of the head waiters came out, sharing news with one group of spectators, then the next. Julian called him over.

'Have you heard the news, sir? That's the Crystal Palace going up.'

The site of the Great Exhibition. I had a soft spot for its life-sized dinosaur statues.

'If that's a diversion, it's a spectacular one,' I said.

But diverting attention from what?

'Julian, find a phone, round up as many men as you can to the bakery. We might be called yet.'

I strode through to the phone booths in the lobby and telephoned Black House. I spoke to a young man, rather cockney but presumably handsome. He said he'd no idea that Crystal Palace was on fire.

'Is Gorgon tonight?'

'I don't know what you're talking about.'

'Trident?'

'I'm sorry, Commander Clifton, but you're using meaningless words.'

He must be assuming Special Branch or MI5 were listening in on the calls.

'Sorry, I've had rather a lot to drink,' I said for the benefit of any snoopers on the line. 'I read rather too many adventure novels.'

I dialled another number but couldn't locate Calhoun. Our foursome went out into the night and called a pair of cabs—one for Melissa, the other for the rest for us. She sulked a little as we packed her off to safety. She was a standard-bearer, not a stormtrooper, and I didn't trust her an inch. Our taxi negotiated through streets teeming with people. Buses and taxis headed south towards the great firework show as we headed west.

My team assembled one by one, Hills and a few men moving the sacks of flour that concealed the trapdoor below which the weapons were stored. Walsh warmed up the engine of each van in turn. Midnight arrived.

Chapter Forty-Seven

No call had come by dawn, so I sent my men home. An act of God had destroyed the Crystal Palace, not a fascist plot. As the twisted ruin smouldered, I returned to Havelock Mansions tired and deflated by anti-climax. A few hours' sleep wouldn't go amiss, but I enjoyed barely two before my telephone rang. It was Mosley, not entrusting his message to any of his underlings. He instructed me to go to the Albert Hall that evening with men I could trust.

I drove Sissy's yellow T-Type with Julian at my side. Sissy and I had agreed to switch cars as she needed to be able to move her women at short notice and refused to stuff them into a bread van. Walsh, Hills, and the others were not so squeamish and completed my team. I'd asked Mosley why he wanted my section to perform the duty, and he replied, 'because you don't look like Blackshirts.' I took it as a compliment.

Julian and I were given tickets to the great rearmament rally, and as the platform included Winston Churchill, we expected to hear speeches on the growing threat of Germany and the evils of Nazism. I spotted Bruno in the audience, no doubt marking the maverick politician's card.

Churchill was a rather short and chubby man, wide-faced with a flabby neck. He had a growling, rousing voice and spoke not so much about Hitler's Germany, but attacked the plot against the king. A cabal within the Conservative-dominated Cabinet was planning a coup in all but name. Baldwin, Chamberlain… He spat out the names as if they were venereal diseases. It was not a speech to win him any love in the Tory party, and not one to be delivered by any politician licking up to his masters. He was either launching an unstoppable moral crusade or committing political suicide. I was inspired by his fire but wouldn't put money on his survival.

Applause followed Churchill out of the hall. The moment I identified myself by the stage door he nodded acknowledgement and made for where a chauffeur held open his car door. Our little yellow MG tagged along behind, and I was reassured to see a bread van in my wing mirror.

Churchill's car stopped outside an apartment block in Mayfair. We pulled up behind and Julian stepped out smartly and held open the politician's door. As I joined them, Churchill signalled to his driver to leave.

He nodded his head towards the T-Type. 'Is that yours?'

'Yes,' was the easiest answer.

'A daffodil yellow car. And you're working incognito?'

'Well, sir, would you guess that was a Blackshirt's car?'

Churchill shook his head, then strode up the steps to the portal. I left the car parked where it was while Julian and I guarded the door, discreetly standing half in shadow beside Doric columns.

Other men arrived, their chauffeurs hurrying away immediately. I'd been asked not to salute or shake hands, but to simply nod. Lord Beaverbrook was the first I recognised; he must have rushed back from America. Possibly he'd been the Lord B in Isby's correspondence, possibly not. This would be a good place for Isby's group to strike, and an opportune time as something clearly was afoot, so Walsh's bread van was parked around the corner. I couldn't identify every man in the dozen who came up those steps, and none were keen to be recognised. Mosley's name was poison in political circles, and Churchill's not much better. Strange bedfellows were assembling, and none of them featured in Isby's photographs. The Young Britons were notable by their absence.

We fidgeted a little at the top of those steps, part-concealed by the columns. A policeman on his beat gave us a glance, and I nodded to him.

'Evening, sir,' he replied, suspicion not allayed. He checked the yellow car, then moved on.

Sentry duty had always been boring, but I so wanted to be inside with my ear to the door of that first-floor room from which the lights shone.

After half an hour, Julian went to fetch Hills to replace him and, a little later, roused Walsh to take over my duty. We were unarmed of course, as Renton had given notice that his tolerance was at an end, even if notionally acknowledging we were on the same scent. I sat in Sissy's car and waited. For over three hours, we took turns, eyes open for potential threats, then the first of the men of power left, a footman signalling one chauffeur, then another.

Mosley emerged long past midnight. I was on duty again.

'Right, chaps, you can go. Many thanks. Top secret, as always.'

'Is this Gorgon, sir?'

'Don't worry about Gorgon. But I need your men ready for Operation Pegasus.'

'Pegasus?'

For goodness sake, had someone at Black House swallowed a book of Greek myths?

'Sir, we need to know what all these plans are about. Can you share more details?'

'No,' said the Leader. 'You'll be told when necessary.'

Chapter Forty-Eight

It was hardly peace on earth that December.

'Two-Four-Six-Eight, the king must not abdicate!'

A crowd booed Baldwin outside Downing Street, while another crowd threw stones at Cumberland Terrace. Carol singers adjusted their words to mock Wallis Simpson, and the Bishop of Bradford came out strongly against her. In the press, battle lines were drawn. No longer muzzled, newspaper editors took sides in the most partisan way. Mrs Simpson was either the most hated woman in the country or the victim of a most heinous conspiracy, depending on which editorial the reader wanted to believe.

It was too much for the American, and her fair-weather friends found the seas around her a little too stormy. Sissy took a call she'd been half expecting, but had never imagined she'd be heading to France. Thank goodness she'd swapped cars with Hugh. Her T-Type was perfect for a summer spin around the continent but not for a dark night in December. She was soon driving around collecting her ladies in the much more practical Alvis. 'Look after it,' she'd been told, unnecessarily. Knowing Hugh's propensity for impulsive action, she was less confident she'd get her little yellow car back in one piece.

Where was Eleanor when Sissy needed her most? That excuse about the sick aunt was wearing thin. It was far more likely a new young man was on the scene. The Chelsea Wives didn't hold passports, but fortunately, Julia did.

'Looks like it'll be just me and you.' Julia dropped her bag into the luggage pannier, then opened the passenger door.

'And me,' Ruth Fritton spoke up from the back seat. 'Hello, Julia.'

'Hello, Ruth,' Julia said, shooting Sissy a questioning look.

'I speak French.' Ruth rattled off a few lines asking the best way to drive to Calais.

'But are you all right?' Julia asked. 'After everything?'

'Yes, I want to do this. For my brother.'

'Good for you.' Julia didn't sound convinced. 'But have you got a passport?'

'She has,' Sissy snapped, turning on the ignition.

'Sorry to sound like a prig,' Julia said, 'but Eleanor can shoot, and Ruth can't.'

'Eleanor is otherwise engaged,' Sissy said. 'Apparently, there are more important things than saving the whole future of the country.'

'And I'm not planning to shoot anyone,' Ruth said. 'I speak French, and I can drive. That's why I'm coming with you.'

Sissy engaged gear and drove away from the kerb.

'I've only had time to pack a few things, and most of that's my uniform,' Julia said. 'Will we be away long?'

'They have shops in France.'

Sissy knew the route out to Fort Belvedere well by now, which helped as the night was dark and the weather unpleasant. She pulled the Alvis up outside the back gate of the estate with only a few minutes to spare. A police officer came across to challenge her. He wasn't even aware Mrs Simpson was leaving. Wallis had already told Sissy she disliked travelling— and travelling by air was the worst.

A car emerged, followed by a police car. They halted, engines running. A man came across.

'Inspector Evans,' he introduced himself after Sissy wound down the window. 'Three of you?'

She offered their names.

'I don't like this at all,' he said. 'Are you armed? Yes? Hand the weapons over.'

'I can't be a bodyguard unarmed,' Sissy objected.

'We're providing protection; you're just window dressing to keep the lady happy. Hand them over.'

Julia fished in the glove box and brought out a pair of Walthers. She'd bought her own just recently.

'Only two?'

'I'm just window dressing,' Ruth said.

'Follow our car and keep up,' the detective ordered.

'I need to tell Mrs Simpson we're here,' Sissy said.

'Be quick.'

Sissy nipped across and waved to Wallis, who was just visible through the rain-splashed glass. In response, she raised a hand in recognition. A man sat beside her in the back and there was a chauffeur at the wheel. It was an American car, a Buick, a difficult vehicle to keep inconspicuous.

The convoy set off into the night, setting a good pace, but after twenty minutes there was an abrupt halt. Sissy stepped out to investigate, walking up beside Inspector Evans who was speaking to Wallis's companion, discussing directions to Lincolnshire. Wallis was insisting they went to France.

'France it is,' came the tired voice. 'France, Evans. As planned.'

'Who's the man?' she asked Inspector Evans.

'Lord Brownlow. He wants to divert to his Lincolnshire estate.'

'Why?' Changes of plan roused her suspicions.

He ignored the question. 'Just follow us. Newhaven. I hope you brought maps—we're not waiting for you.'

Chapter Forty-Nine

Sissy was gone from London, and I'd heard no news from her beyond a short late-night call from the port of Newhaven. Calhoun took my call, and we met on the rainy riverbank short of the tower of London. I didn't tell him of the disaster at Isby's Farm, and he didn't ask.

'I've heard whispers of something called the King's Party being formed,' I said.

He listened to every detail I could recount about the late-night meeting in Mayfair.

'It explains a lot,' Calhoun grunted satisfaction. 'A few dozen Tory MPs are inclining Churchill's way, and from what you say, it looks like Beaverbrook is backing them. Lady Houston must be, too—her car was seen entering the grounds of Fort Belvedere. Only her chauffeur was driving, so goodness knows what he was carrying in the boot.'

'Money? A war chest for the King's Party? And by the sounds of it, you've got a man up there.'

'We may have.'

'Not this mysterious M I've never met?'

'No, his wife has died suddenly; she'd come up to London and was staying in one of the clubs. It's been in some of the newspapers if you look hard enough. M is having to deal with her affairs.'

'You know she's a fascist.'

'*Was* a fascist—British *Fascisti*, not one of Mosley's crew.'

'You said *suddenly*. Is someone investigating how—'

'The usual inquest,' said Calhoun sharply. 'Whatever transpires, I don't think we'll see M back at the crease this year.'

The Security Service must be a little tidier with that embarrassment out of the way.

'So, is anything else happening at Belvedere I should know about?'

'Churchill and Baldwin are playing shuttlecock, alternating turns up there, one urging the king to stand his ground and the other trying to make him buckle.'

'If the king does stand his ground, and Baldwin resigns, that means Churchill has a fair stab at being the next Prime Minister,' I said.

'That will be his objective,' Calhoun said. 'Else he wouldn't be seen dead associating with Mosley.'

'But if he offers Mosley a juicy post to bring him inside the tent, and if the new Public Order Act disbands the Blackshirts, that's the end of the BU.'

'We can hope.'

And it would end my masquerade. For purely selfish reasons, it would suit me very well if Churchill were the winner.

'Then I suppose the king can marry Wallis if that's what he wants,' I said brightly. 'Happy ever after.'

'Not so fast—he'd have to climb over several dead bishops first, and I can't see the unions taking a Churchill–Mosley coalition lying down. It's going to be anything but happy ever after.'

Yes, that scenario would be too neat to be true. Verity would be rushing to the barricades, red flag in hand.

'And I suppose the Germans wouldn't like a government headed by Churchill, either.'

'No.'

'So do we make it happen?'

'*You* don't make any of it happen,' Calhoun said. 'Not Pegasus, or Peter Pan or Tinkerbell for that matter. Don't forget we work for the government, which happens to comprise Mr Baldwin, Mr Chamberlain and all. The Security Service doesn't decide who rules the country.'

But it could, I realised. Or at least nudge an outcome in one direction or another.

Chapter Fifty

I n the middle of France, at an inn in the middle of nowhere, it still felt like the middle of the night. While the woman who checked in as 'Mrs Harris' tried to sleep, detectives watched the doors and even had a grudging word of thanks for the three young women who took turns keeping eyes out for reporters. Somehow, a pack of pressmen had latched onto the convoy soon after it arrived in Dieppe. Loose tongues had been at work long before 'Mrs Harris' had left England, and her Buick stood out from the ordinary. An over-eager pursuer had already nipped his vehicle around the Alvis, tried to squeeze into the gap, and smacked into the rear bumper of Wallis's car. Sissy had taken its door off as the reporters tried to get out, just as she was overtaking once more. The Alvis carried a few scrapes along its wing as honourable battle scars.

Before it was fully light, a car carrying at least four men pulled up in the road beyond the inn. Ruth gave Sissy a signal she should wait and ran over to challenge them. For three, perhaps four minutes, she employed her French, with many assertive hand movements before the car drove off.

'Who were they?' Sissy asked as Ruth returned.

The young woman didn't seem happy with her success.

'French policemen,' Ruth said with some hesitation. 'Except not normal gendarmes; no uniforms.'

'Their version of Special Branch?'

'I guess so. They're keeping their distance.'

'Did they say anything else?'

Ruth gave an almost Gallic shrug. 'You know what the police think of us.'

'Go and have a little breakfast, and I'll keep watch.'

Sissy was still on duty when another car swept up by the gate of the inn. One of the male detectives waved it away.

'Reporters,' he called back. 'They've found us!'

She went to locate a weary-eyed Inspector Evans, who was sitting in the dining area, and repeated the news.

'If reporters can find us, anyone can find us,' she said. 'I wish you'd let me have my gun back.'

'Are you familiar with French firearms laws?'

'I—'

'I won't bore you with them.' He stood up. 'We need to move, sharpish, before the whole pack arrives.'

'I have a plan,' she said.

While the reporters, photographers, and onlookers gathered in front of the hotel, Julia took over the duty of keeping them back, wearing full Blackshirt garb. It grabbed their attention, as did Sissy bringing the Alvis round, also in uniform, then Ruth carrying out the bags one at a time. The other cars remained parked at the rear and could drive away unseen. It meant climbing out of a window, but Wallis, Lord Brownlow, and the detectives made a clean getaway.

With all three Blackshirts aboard, the Alvis set off at pace, soon pursued.

'It's like the Keystone Cops,' Ruth said, her body twisting to watch the cars on their tail.

Sissy drove as fast as she dared while Julia fumbled with Michelin maps bought at a petrol station. One car hurtled past, a photographer leaning out with a long lens camera, hoping perhaps Wallis had sneaked out hidden under a blanket. She was under a blanket, no doubt, but in a different car on a different route. The photographer's car tore ahead, and the reporters would soon learn they'd been fooled.

'We can turn left soon,' Julia said, frowning at the map. 'That will put us back en route. It's about ten kilometres—what's a kilometre?'

'Two-thirds of a mile,' Ruth said.

'You can drive once we've made that turn, Ruth,' Sissy told her.

Sissy had taught Julia to drive the previous summer and had never been happy with the result. Being on the wrong side of the road would be doubly nerve-wracking if she was entrusted with the wheel. The press were not duped for long, and with Ruth driving, they caught up the reporters' convoy some way short of Nice. It was a grey winter afternoon even on the Riviera and dark by the time Ruth found the way to a villa perched on the forested hills behind Cannes.

Villa Lou Viei had once been a monastery, apparently. Sissy had hoped to find it walled like a fort, easily defended from prying eyes and unwanted attention. As Ruth drove up the steep drive, her optimism grew. It was a tall, ancient-looking structure with a tower towards one end. In daylight, it might be quite pretty.

Servants showed Ruth where to park and took their bags. Once inside, an American man with film star good looks greeted them.

'Herman Rodgers,' he said. 'Pleased to meet you all.'

The trio shook his hand and introduced themselves.

'Wallis's Amazons,' he declared. 'My wife is arranging rooms for you, down there. Two of you will have to share. We don't normally use that wing, so it may be a little dusty.'

'Thank you, but I'd like to check the grounds immediately,' Sissy said.

'Of course, be my guest.'

Once she began the circuit of the villa, Sissy was disappointed, then worried. A small lane ran close to the north side, and a wall topped with railings barely served to keep back the onlookers being herded by French gendarmes. A smaller lane ran down the eastern side, and two other houses stood close by. Beyond the swimming pool and gardens to the west, a dark mass must be woodland. She could smell poorly maintained drains, and through the rain, the lights of Cannes were strung out in an arc far below.

She was pleased to be playing such a leading role in keeping Wallis safe, but felt the weight of the responsibility. The woman inside that villa could be the next queen of England. This is what Sissy had been looking for since her mother badgered her into joining the fascists; a chance to make a difference.

Chapter Fifty-One

'The king has requested time on the BBC to make his case to the nation,' Mosley said. 'Baldwin has refused.'

The heads of Department Z had been called into the Club Room for an intelligence meeting. Mosley and his inner circle were all there; all male, everyone in uniform. Parker, Taylor, Valentine, and I ranged ourselves down the opposite side of the planning table to Francis-Hawkins, the commander of the Black Guard, and the military inspectors who sat with their arms crossed.

'The king is a virtual prisoner, unable to speak to his people.' Mosley paused for effect. 'We have powerful allies now. This is our chance to take power.'

'I thought,' I dared ask, 'that the plan was to achieve power democratically, by winning elections.'

One of the crossed-arm militarists opposite gave a derisive snort.

'Do you know what democracy is?' Valentine asked rhetorically. 'Every five years, the sheep are allowed to bleat. Then they're sent off for shearing just like before.'

Several of the others laughed, putting my liberalism firmly in its place.

'Britain is sinking,' Valentine added. 'The question is, will it capsize to the left or the right?'

I'd have to read one of his books.

'Very philosophical, but I've seen Special Branch outside—we're being watched,' I warned. 'There are police everywhere.'

'Losing your nerve?' Parker sneered. 'Because you got one of your men killed?'

'Nobody loses their nerve!' Mosley asserted. 'Especially not you, Clifton. We need whatever armed men you have and your vans to stand by for Operation Pegasus.'

'What is Pegasus, sir?'

'You'll be told when you need to know.'

'With respect, I need to know. My people are scattered all over the city. Some of them work, they have homes and families, and most don't own telephones. It takes half a day to round them up. And the guns, such as we have, are not just hidden under my bed.'

'Pegasus.' Major Taylor spoke with gravity, and Mosley nodded assent he could continue. 'The king is thinking of flying off to the Continent while all the fuss dies down.'

'And that can't happen,' Joyce added. 'It will look like cowardice, and the men ranged against him will use it to bury him. You, Clifton, will stop him.'

Gosh, that was a bouncer I never saw coming.

'You want me to stop the king? How? Shoot his plane down?'

'You're resourceful. Work it out,' Joyce said.

'Can't you get whoever's feeding you this information to tell the king it's a bad idea?'

'I'm sure they are doing exactly that,' Mosley said.

I was not so sure. For all I knew, Viscount Lyle could be the one putting the idea of flight into the king's head. Or be the one betraying his plans to Mosley.

'Don't we also need Clifton for Trident?' Taylor asked with some concern.

'If Pegasus fails, there won't be a Trident,' Joyce said. 'Or a Gorgon.'

Francis-Hawkins stood up, erect.

'I need two days' notice to assemble my men for Gorgon. At least.'

So, Gorgon was a monster. A particularly hideous monster, no doubt. F-H could have a thousand times more Blackshirts awaiting his call than Department Z could muster.

'The men are ready, but you need to give the order, sir,' F-H continued. 'I need two days.'

The commander of the Black Guard nodded his square jaw in agreement. 'Initiate Gorgon,' Mosley commanded.

'We'll hold the rally on Saturday,' Joyce announced. 'Stand by the King, Trafalgar Square.'

One of the regional inspectors spoke up. 'So we start men moving on Thursday?'

'No, today,' Joyce said. 'Get them moving today.'

'But sir.' Parker stood to his feet and spoke with hesitation. 'I was in the Royal Corps of Transport. If the men arrive too early, they'll need to be housed, fed...'

'Details,' said Joyce.

'Details matter,' Parker insisted. His fists clenched as he spoke.

'Not your concern, Parker.'

'Well, at least let me know about Trident,' he said, sitting back down. 'What's expected of my section. I'll need to give orders. Like Clifton's men, mine live all over the city.'

He looked to me for support, and I nodded agreement. If Parker was at the sharp end, Trident meant trouble. A swift jab, followed up by the mass of Blackshirts summoned in the name of Gorgon.

'Make your men ready, Parker,' Mosley said. 'And you, Clifton, Valentine. I'm taking a suite at the Langham Hotel from tonight. To be close to the action when it comes. Gentlemen, the hour is at hand.'

Department Z was asked to leave the meeting. I imagine the logistics of the great protest rally would be next on the agenda, but I wondered if that was all the operation codenamed Gorgon entailed. The level of secrecy was out of proportion to a straightforward rally—the BU held them routinely.

Major Taylor went upstairs to his office, followed by Parker who was based along the corridor from Room Z, but Valentine caught my eye and loitered. Once we were alone, he led me down into the basement and a tiny windowless room, which he unlocked with two keys. A single seat and a couple of small crates almost filled it. On a narrow shelf, a telephone had been jury-rigged to a box of electronic tricks.

'Sit, sit,' Valentine said. 'For all your picking locks and listening at keyholes, this is the future of intelligence work.'

I sat on a crate and waited for a revelation as Valentine closed the door, pulled up the small stool, and inserted plugs into the apparatus. Presently, a small orange lamp flicked on. Valentine put his finger to his lips and raised a telephone earpiece ever so gently, sharing it so I could also hear.

Major Taylor was speaking. '...Gorgon needs two days and has been set in motion.' He went on to describe Pegasus in hasty detail. 'Nothing new on Trident. Nothing from Artemis.'

The man he spoke to said little beyond the occasional single-word response. The way *aye* was pronounced suggested he was Scottish. Taylor mentioned my name in connection with Pegasus, which elicited a knowing sigh from the man at the other end.

After Taylor's call clicked off, Valentine leaned close to me.

'And who do you think Taylor was speaking to?'

'Sounds like Detective Inspector Renton of Special Branch,' I said. 'And Major Taylor is the traitor?'

'An informer, at least. And we have to act now. We can't afford to wait. This isn't the first call Taylor's made that's given away our secrets. He betrayed details of our latest courier from Germany and other things.'

I'd started to guess this might be the case, and there was no benefit to defending Taylor's corner now.

'Please tell me this isn't just a way of your getting the top job?'

'I wish it were. Imagine our head of intelligence feeding information to Special Branch. But then you also have a relationship with this Renton.'

'It keeps him off my back if I throw him a communist every now and again.'

'But this is more than tipping him off about communists. Taylor is privy to all the Leader's plans, which means that Special Branch know everything. The Leader will be arrested the moment he gives the order for Trident. And Renton now knows all about who will have to carry out Pegasus.'

That wouldn't make my life any easier. I pondered the options that were the best for Britain, weighed up against those that were best for my own interests. Patriotism has its limits, especially when everyone from the king downward was playing the game for their own ends.

'I'm not the only one who knows this,' Valentine added. 'Just in case you're firmly in Taylor's camp.'

So knocking Valentine on the head was ruled out as a way to protect Special Branch's sources.

'I've briefed Parker already—he thought you were the spy. But he knows the truth now, and his compliance means we have the manpower to cut out the Taylor loyalists even if you don't play the game.'

'We'll play,' I said, undecided whether I was telling the truth. 'What's our plan, kill him?'

'In the end. But first, we need to learn what he's let slip.'

'Across in the black room?'

'That's the idea. Though we may have to find a more remote venue.'

I was being asked to collaborate in a programme of torture and murder worthy of Hitler's gang, and even if I could somehow thwart Valentine, Parker would relish taking over the task.

'So we kidnap him, torture him, kill him, then bury his body in a remote location,' I stated.

Valentine inclined his head as if it were all in a day's work.

I had only moments to avoid being dragged into crimes I could never escape from.

'What kind of Britain do you want to build? Start this way, and it's all downhill. Next month, it's you tied up in a cell with Parker breaking your fingers. Then, after that, he's in the chair, and I'm breaking his fingers. There's a better way. A British way.'

Chapter Fifty-Two

Not trusting any telephone line connected to Black House or the bakery now, I waited my turn at a public telephone box on Fulham Road. The man before me had smoked his way through his call, and I held the door open with my toe to let fresh yet icy air inside. I dialled the international exchange and asked for the number in France Sissy had told me to call. It took an agonisingly long time to get through. I failed and stepped out so others could take a turn. At the third attempt, I began to run short of small change.

Distant and crackling, a male American answered and called Sissy over to the telephone. I longed to hear her voice, and she began to tell me of her adventures, but my coins wouldn't last long, and I had to interrupt her.

'Quickly,' I said. 'The king has a plan to fly out of the country, get away from being bullied by one camp and wooed by another. If he does, it's game, set, and match to Baldwin.'

'I see.'

I had no time to debate the morality of what I was doing or saying, but I was playing with history, manipulating events as so many others were trying to do at that very moment.

'I've been ordered to stop him. God knows how, but it won't end well. So you're the one who needs to stop him.'

'Wallis will tell him to stay put,' she said immediately. 'She's always telling him what to do, she wears the trousers in that relationship. Or wears the crown.'

'Can you ask her?'

'I will, straight away.'

The French operator started speaking, and I laid down the phone as my last coin fell away.

* * *

Churchill began what should have been an epic speech to Parliament in defence of the king and in defiance of Baldwin. He was shouted down from both sides of the House, but dozens of Tory MPs rallied to his side, and what *The Times* described as a 'raucous' row developed, with the Speaker eventually suspending the sitting. Mosley and his cohort were of course still absent, making their own plans to take power.

While the great men battled in public, Department Z continued to fight in the shadows. It was little surprise that the man Taylor was leaking information to would be Renton. Special Branch could not have that many officers of his rank detailed to keep an eye on the Blackshirts. I knew the pub Renton used to meet his best-placed sources. It was not frequented by what he called his usual customers, nor by off-duty policemen, and was well away from both Scotland Yard and the Security Service's office at Millbank. The Coachman had table service, too, so drinkers didn't even need to present themselves at the bar.

When Taylor prepared to leave for one of his long lunches, Valentine knew within a minute and was able to tip me off such that I left Black House before either of them. It needed to be a long lunch as Taylor required time to journey to Marble Arch by underground train, then walk down Oxford Street and around to the Coachman by an indirect route, stepping into shops seemingly at random to avoid anyone who might be on his tail.

I was on his tail, but I'd worked out where he was going and that he'd time his arrival for a rendezvous neatly, in this case, 12.30 p.m.

Knowing the BU's penchant for exaggerating its own importance, there was a fair chance all Mosley's dramatically titled operations would flop. Plucking one of his top men out of the game would pull away another prop to his confidence and trigger yet more in-fighting. The more insecure the

Party felt, the less effective it would be. If Renton knew we had his man, he might spring whatever action he was planning, which in turn might deter Gorgon, Trident, and the shopping list of Greek farces or set them off half-cocked. Using this mishmash of logic, I allied myself to Valentine's scheme, guiltily grateful he had hooked a bigger fish than me.

That guilt was less than it might once have been. All the rumour and innuendo that had come to my ears in the past year nagged at me. Mosley's key men were closer to officers of Special Branch, MI5, and the Secret Intelligence Service than felt comfortable. Were the British security services working for the fascists, or were the fascists working for the British security services? I did not like either option.

I glimpsed the conspirators in close conversation in a dim corner of the pub. One glance was enough to confirm Renton was the second man, and I retreated outside rather than risk being spotted. I'd chosen not to arm myself, given Renton would gleefully throw me back in a cell if the encounter ended in a fracas.

After almost an hour, Taylor emerged flush-faced from his lunch and the odd drink. I made no attempt to hide and strode straight towards him, staring him down. He halted, and Valentine caught up with him from behind. The cornered man glanced over his shoulder and knew the game was up. I had the reputation as a killer, Valentine was still a man of mystery, and Taylor could assume one or both of us would be armed.

'Shall we call a cab?' I said, flagging one down.

Taylor worked out the scene immediately and got into the taxi without a murmur. If our intention had been to kill him, we'd have bundled our captive into the back of a baker's van and driven out to the Essex marshes. Then he mightn't have come so calmly.

I sat across from the traitor, with Valentine seated next to him. I gave the cabbie Taylor's home address in Sloane Square. He looked sharply at me, but Valentine was the one to stick in the proverbial knife.

'James McGuirk Hughes,' he began. 'British *Fascisti* in the 1920s, Makgill Organisation, Unit K on anti-communist operations. Shall I go on?'

It was all just a list of names to me, but the man who called himself Taylor squirmed a little. He'd clearly lived an adventurous, if clandestine, life.

'You've had plenty of help from the police over the years,' Valentine said. 'And you, of course, have helped them.' All the way back, he whispered his suspicions and accusations, and Taylor simply listened, calculating his chances of survival. If Department Z lived up to its fantasies and had indeed become Britain's Gestapo, those chances would be slight.

It was time to throw him a lifebelt.

'Back on the North West Frontier, we had a way of dealing with failure, betrayal,' I said. 'A chap would be left alone in a room with a bottle of whisky and a revolver.'

Or that's what I'd been told as a gullible young officer—I didn't know if it ever happened.

'What do you two want?' Taylor spoke at last.

'A written confession and your resignation from the Party,' I said. 'We're offering you a gentleman's way out. More pleasant than the whisky and revolver thing.'

'You're no gentleman,' he said.

* * *

Late in the afternoon, I went into a pub and changed a ten-shilling note, receiving scowls from the barman, which a shilling tip barely drove away. A young woman occupied the nearest telephone box and seemed to be spending her weekly allowance on one call. At last, my turn came. I rang the Security Service switchboard and asked to speak to Calhoun.

'I hope this line is secure,' he growled.

I told him about Taylor's fall, then repeated all the facts he'd betrayed that led to his downfall.

'There was no way of saving him?' Calhoun asked.

'Parker and Valentine would have had him killed. Tortured first, no doubt. He's probably managed to keep things back that you wouldn't want revealed under torture.'

Calhoun sighed.

'Did you know about him?'

'I knew Renton had a well-placed source. And,' he paused. 'I know Taylor's history. He used to work with M in the twenties, and M used to work with Joyce at the same time. It's a complicated world.'

'Any more complications I need to know about? Because we're on short notice for this Operation Pegasus,' I said.

'Not Achilles?' he asked.

'No, why?'

'A plan called Achilles would have a weak point.'

Calhoun didn't often try to be witty, but the BU was an easy target for mockery.

'The king has an idea that if he flies out of the country, the press will get bored, and the politicians find more important things to worry about than who he's sleeping with,' I said. 'Then, I'm not sure if it's the king's idea or if someone has put it into his head. He's being pulled this way and that as though he were a puppet. I've been phoning France half the day to find out what's going on from that end.'

'Mrs Simpson and the king do spend an awful lot of time on the telephone,' Calhoun said. 'The number is often engaged.'

'How do you know they spend a lot of time on the telephone?'

'Oh, use your imagination.'

I didn't believe what I was hearing. 'Don't tell me. You've tapped the king's phone, the line from Fort Belvedere. Is that even legal?'

'It is, with the right signatures on the right piece of paper.'

'So, you're listening to the king's private chatter? For God's sake, what's the country coming to?'

'Don't be a pompous ass, Clifton. You've just allowed a valuable informer to be exposed because it was necessary to keep you at the wicket. By now, you should know there are no rules in the intelligence game. None at all.'

Chapter Fifty-Three

Villa Lou Viei had been under siege for four days. Photographers hung over the fence and climbed trees. The old monastery clung to the hillside, so had vaulted walls on the uphill side and was left short of windows. Although good for security, it gave a dungeon-like feel to the winter nights once the magnificent view was taken away. Keeping curtains closed in the daytime just added to the gloom. This was not picture-postcard French Riviera, nor romance-novel Cannes.

The Rodgers's butler reported an attempt to bribe him, and Evans sent one of his detectives home following a nifty piece of detection by the women of Z3. At least now they knew who had been informing reporters of their every move. Sissy had worried it was Ruth at one point, as she developed a habit of engaging with male members of the crowd over the rear railings, all smiles and bi-lingual chat. The black uniform seemed to add to her confidence with men and to their interest in her. Ruth was proving her worth.

A crowd formed every day, curious, intrusive, and sometimes abusive—demanding the head of the whore who was wrecking the life of the king. In desperation, Wallis had written a letter which her friend Herman Rodgers read to the assembled press at the Grand Hotel. That man was a real hero and clearly adored Wallis. He'd even had a bed made up in the tower so he could sleep outside her room. Quite what his wife thought about the arrangement was a different matter.

Sissy was in that anteroom now, talking to Herman quietly.

'I wish the inspector had let us keep our pistols,' she said.

240

With a wink, he lifted the pillow on his little bed. A revolver nestled there. 'Just in case,' he said.

Wallis's voice could be heard through the door, yelling down the phone.

'Do not abdicate! You goddam fool. Do nothing reckless, listen to your friends.'

Herman glanced anxiously at Sissy, and she grimaced, wondering if he'd be unhappy if his friend married another man, or more unhappy if her dream of becoming queen was shattered. The bedroom door flew open, and Wallis shot out of the room, glancing from Herman to Sissy as if jealous he was giving attention to any other woman.

'Would you like a coffee?' asked Herman.

Wallis snorted as if it were the last thing in the world she wanted, then agreed without thanks. Wan and exhausted, she'd only been outside once to visit a relative since the siege began.

Another evening of waiting passed slowly. Sitting around the ground-floor lounge, smoking, drinking coffee, running out of small talk, the besieged became increasingly edgy.

'Is that lawyer Goddard still coming?' Herman Rodgers asked.

'Tomorrow, I expect,' Wallis said without emotion. She turned to Sissy. 'This Goddard is being sent to talk me out of marrying David.'

'But you won't agree?'

'You know what, honey, if that's what it takes to stop him abdicating.'

It would be a good outcome for the Party, Sissy knew. Mosley would be pleased. Although she felt for Wallis, coming so close to becoming queen, then seeing it pulled away from her, it had to be the right outcome for the country. Perhaps if the couple waited for the fuss to die down in a year or so, attitudes would mellow.

'When Mosley becomes Prime Minister, all those stuffy rules will change,' Sissy said. 'And then you'd have a chance.'

'What chance does Mosley have of becoming Prime Minister?' Wallis said tartly. 'If they can stop me from becoming queen, they can stop him.'

And if the king abdicated, it would push Mosley even further away from power.

Wallis turned to Herman, touched his hand. Sissy glanced at Mrs Rodgers, but she made no reaction. Perhaps she was used to this.

'If he abdicates, that stuttering idiot becomes king, and that fat Scottish cook...' Wallis turned to Sissy again. 'You're not a friend of the *Duchess* of York?'

'Grief, no.'

'She hates me, sneers at me, looks down her nose at me. The snob. She'll be enjoying all this. She'll be cheering the plotters on. And A-a-a-a-albert is just a feather in the wind, Baldwin can blow him around whenever he likes.'

Wallis fretted and smoked heavily as the evening drew on. She paced across the lounge, momentarily pulling aside the curtain, confirming only that the rain was still spattering down.

'So, folks, how about a game of poker?' Herman said, rubbing his hands together. 'Or bridge? Sissy, do you play?'

'Not very well.'

'We could hunt Brownlow out,' he said. 'Unless you're a poker player, Julia?'

'I'll partner Sissy at bridge.' Julia broke out of the bored spell that inflicted the whole group.

The game was set up, but Wallis showed more interest in the silent telephone.

'David usually calls,' she said. 'I do hope he's holding up. That horrible man Baldwin went to see him again yesterday.'

Sissy took her seat, Julia followed, then Herman brought the cards over. Wallis, still by the telephone.

'I'll score if you like,' Julia said, taking up a pad of paper and a pencil.

'Why doesn't David ring!' Wallis declared. 'Yesterday I told him what you said, about that silly idea of flying to Switzerland. I don't know who put that goddam idea into his head.'

Sissy dreaded what this Operation Pegasus could draw Hugh into.

'If he tries to leave the country, people will stop him.'

'How, how will they stop him?'

'By whatever means necessary,' Sissy said.

'But he's the king!'

'Wallis, people have been killed over this!'

Ruth was there, over by the archway, and Sissy caught her eye.

'I talked him out of it,' Wallis said. 'But I wonder how you know more about what David is planning than I do.'

'We're Department Z, we're investigators.'

'Spies,' Wallis said tartly. 'You need to go home, all of you.' She picked up the telephone receiver. 'It should be him ringing me, this just ain't right.'

Julia nodded her head forward, as if bored of all the melodrama, and Herman tapped the card pack on the table more than necessary to sort before a shuffle. Sissy passed a smile of encouragement to Ruth, but she didn't return it. The young woman faded into the shadow of the porch.

'Herman, the phone won't work,' Wallis complained.

'It was fine earlier.' He rose and took up the receiver, tapped the switch hook, and shook his head. 'It must be the storm.'

'This goddam country.'

'You say that about England too. Come and play. And be kind to Sissy and her ladies. They only want to help.'

Sissy no longer wanted to play bridge, if she ever had. She was in a beleaguered villa full of strangers in the growing night, in a rainstorm in a foreign land. And the phone was not working.

Chapter Fifty-Four

The bakery felt a safer place than being trapped in Room Z, at the very top of the building with no way out if Valentine's witch-hunt spread further or suffered a backlash from Taylor's confederates. I'd happily step aside while they fought among themselves.

I arrived earlier than usual on Wednesday, and Lucy ran through the information trickling in from our regional offices. Black House might be keeping its intelligence department in the dark, but we had intelligence of our own. Three contacts reported that Blackshirts had set off to travel to London for a march at the weekend. Just about every branch in London reported the same, with their men asked to come to the branch offices and sleep there overnight.

Hills echoed Parker's concerns about the cost of feeding all those mouths and putting them up in hostels, never mind busing them down or paying rail fares. It was a big stretch for a party that allegedly had no money.

Lady Houston and Beaverbrook came to mind—deep pockets, and a pleasure in meddling.

A couple of the team commented it was curious Joyce wanted the Blackshirts on hand well in advance of the weekend. Perhaps he anticipated obstruction by the police or unions, they suggested.

After Julian came in, the bakery sent up ham sandwiches for the four of us. Eleanor made an appearance early in the afternoon, asking if there were any news about Sissy and Julia. Her young man had cancelled their dinner for that evening as something had come up. He was a Party member and one of the Black Guard, which set my thoughts whirring. Gorgon needed two days to organise, but Eleanor's beau lived in Mayfair, so had no need to sleep overnight at a branch until the weekend.

A cold sensation rippled down my spine. Those two days had elapsed. I asked Lucy to find the Chelsea Wives, and they came in happily, as their husbands had some corporate event in the City. I set them to calling in as many people as they could reach. Hills went out in a van to collect the men without telephones, telling others to hurry to the bakery the moment they could. I hoped this wouldn't turn out to be another Crystal Palace.

A young man rang the doorbell of the bakery, as the shop was now closed. One of the Wives brought him upstairs. He was wearing motorbike overalls and carrying a helmet, but his haircut would have given him away even if he hadn't delivered a perfect Roman salute. From a pouch, he produced a brown envelope.

'Your hands only, sir.'

The note was simple and direct.

Standby Trident immediate. All men and vehicles.

'Any reply, sir?'

'Verbal reply. Received and understood.'

The courier saluted again, spun round on his heels, and marched out. No sooner had the sound of his motorbike faded than Lucy transferred a call through to my little office.

'Fulham Bakery?' Detective Inspector Renton asked with more than a shot of sarcasm in his voice.

'Yes. We're happy to deliver fresh rolls to Scotland Yard in time for breakfast.'

'Come outside, turn right, phone box on the corner.'

I'd come to know that phone box well. Renton was waiting close by, hands in the pockets of his raincoat and collar pulled up.

'Motorcycle couriers?' he observed.

'We can never be too careful who's listening.'

'Or which motorcyclists are stopped for speeding or having a faulty lamp.' He was carrying a cloth-wrapped bundle and made to hand it over. 'We haven't found Isby yet. If he's what you say he is, you might be needing these before the week's out.'

My Walther and a Webley revolver clinked against each other as I peeked inside. I was surprised.

'For self-defence, Mr Clifton.'

'Of course.'

'You're the closest I have to a source within the Blackshirts now.'

'Please don't take our exposing Taylor personally; he became careless.'

'At least you didn't saw his arms off. Informers always know the risk they're taking.' He nodded sagely as if trying to read my true allegiance. 'The coroner's inquest on your man is tomorrow.'

'Fritton? The verdict should be easy: murdered by the police.'

'Except that your man Fritton is not called Fritton. It's an assumed name—who was he really?'

'Nigel Fritton, of Maida Vale.'

'There's no such person.'

I felt a heavy thump in my chest and gave a little cough in response.

'Clifton, did you hear that?'

'I've picked him up from his house,' I said. 'He must have carried something in his wallet with his name on when you dragged his body in.'

'Forgeries.'

'But there must have been some official record of him: fingerprints, dentist, driving license—'

'Nothing that isn't forged. At the address you supplied, we even found a forged passport in his name. It was a good forgery, too.'

All that innocence and enthusiasm had simply blinded me, and his feigned devotion only pumped up my ego and reinforced my trust.

'Bastard,' I spat. 'No wonder he ran.'

'Looks like you've got a traitor of your own,' Renton pushed the point home with relish. 'Or at least, you had a traitor. Do you know why we turned up at that farm just in time to nab you?'

'My tip-off about Isby?'

'No, we were tipped off about your little burgling expedition. Exact time and all. Someone wanted you out of the way—arrested or killed in a shooting match. My guess it was your so-called Fritton. Which makes his death ironic, poetic justice, call it what you will.'

'He wasn't one of your informants as well?'

'No.'

'Ruth!' I exclaimed. 'Did you find out anything about his sister, Ruth Fritton?'

'She doesn't exist either. Her name was on a few papers at the same address, but also forged.' I felt even more of an idiot. 'No passport,' he said. 'Though being a woman—'

'She's carrying it,' I said. 'Right now, she's with Wallis Simpson in France.'

'Bugger.' Renton looked off into the growing gloom. 'One of your black-blouse guards? Is she armed as well?'

'Shouldn't be.'

'Oh Jesus, you've dropped us in the jobby now.' He began to speak quickly. 'Tell you what, Clifton, just this once, we might be on the same side. I'll check from my end, and you check from yours. Let me know what you find out straight away. Ring the Yard, ask for me, and don't let them fob you off with a duty sergeant.'

He hurried off round the corner while I stood transfixed by my own blindness. Christians Against Fascism; I should have seen it. That innocence, the dream of a better world, and dogged performance of their duty had been easily faked by the Frittons because it was only barely faked. Mosley's party were not the only fanatics on the loose.

Chapter Fifty-Five

I ran up the stairs and burst back into the office.

'Hills, I need everyone ready for action. Lucy, I need to make an international call.'

'Sissy's villa?'

'Yes.' I no longer cared who was eavesdropping and this was far too important to trust to a handful of change.

Lucy started to ferret in her telephone directory, then began the cumbersome process of calling the international exchange. I fidgeted while the men clattered around downstairs. Seven minutes felt like forever.

'I've got somebody French,' Lucy said and held out the phone. 'I can't speak French.'

A very distant voice could be heard between the crackles. Her accent was thick, and she spoke far too quickly for me to separate one word from another. In my slowest, loudest, clearest schoolboy French I asked for the telephone number in Cannes. I waited. She said something. I waited another minute or so. She apologised for something. The call died.

'Damn, damn, and blast it!'

Lucy cocked her head. 'It's not my fault, Commander Clifton.'

It was back to the phone box. I called Calhoun, and he was easy to reach, also standing to.

'Don't leave your phone this evening,' I said. 'I think tonight is the night.'

'What is tonight?'

'Gorgon and Trident.'

'Which are?'

'I don't have the details yet.'

'As soon as you do, let me know instantly,' Calhoun said. 'The police are already out in force—including every man Special Branch has. Every key government building is guarded. We expect disorder, even rioting when the news breaks. The king will abdicate tomorrow.'

I paused only for a moment. 'Are you sure? Because the whole point of Gorgon and all the rest is to stop that. Blackshirts are flooding in from all over the country for a big march at the weekend in support of the king.'

'And it will be too late.' Calhoun sounded very certain.

So Baldwin and Chamberlain and the mandarins plotting the king's downfall had won.

'There's still danger,' I said. 'Ruth Fritton, one of the women who's guarding Wallis Simpson, isn't whom she claims to be. She's infiltrated us very neatly with a man claiming to be her brother and they put on a very good act. They're all wound up with this plot to force the king to abdicate. Are they anything to do with the Security Service?'

Calhoun became quiet.

'They're not your other secret source? I know they don't work for Renton because we've just bagged his man.'

He stayed quiet.

'Calhoun, are you listening? I've tried putting a call through to the villa, but it would be easier to contact the moon. Have you any idea what's happening down there?'

Now, he deigned to speak.

'Get yourself up to Green Park, and you'll see a Post Office van by the little exchange on the Piccadilly side. Ask for Taff and tell him I sent you.' Calhoun put down the phone.

'Walsh, you're with me,' I shouted. 'Eleanor, did they teach you French at that awfully expensive finishing school of yours?'

'*Un petit peu*,' she said.

'Phone the villa and keep phoning it. Sissy must know that Ruth Fritton is a traitor. And she's not even called Ruth Fritton.'

Eleanor gawped. 'Ruth? She's so sweet.'

'Yes, yes, she fooled us all. She's to be searched for weapons, then locked in a room or got away from that villa entirely. Straight away.'

'Sir.'

'And Sissy's not to shoot her unless she has to.'

* * *

Walsh sat beside me in Sissy's T-Type as we edged along the King's Road in habitually heavy late afternoon traffic. We swung around the back of Buckingham Palace, then turned into Piccadilly at Hyde Park Corner. Sure enough, a Post Office van was parked beside a small building at the edge of Green Park. I judged my moment to turn across the traffic and bumped up the kerb to park behind it. Cables ran from the van and into the building.

A man stepped around the van with his hand dug inside his coat on the left side. I told Walsh to stay in the car and got out cautiously.

'I'm here to see Taff. Calhoun sent me.'

'We don't report to Calhoun.'

'Still, Calhoun sent me. It's very urgent.'

Taff was crouching in the back of the van. Within an open suitcase, valves flickered on equipment I couldn't even begin to name. He held a telephone receiver to his left ear and was making notes on a pad with his right hand, nodding rhythmically. He made to shush me. After three or four minutes of nodding and jotting, he put down both pencil and earpiece.

'Good evening, sah. And you are?'

'A messenger from Calhoun. Was that the king speaking to Mrs Simpson?'

Taff admitted nothing, clearly considering whether he should speak to me.

'I know which line you're tapping,' I said, 'and I know why. Was that the king and Mrs Simpson on the line?'

'No, but they were earlier.'

'For a long time?'

'Oh yes. I wouldn't like to be picking up his telephone bill. It was over an hour this afternoon. That was one of his staff calling a Marylebone number.'

'Can I call Mrs Simpson's villa in France from here?'

'No, we just listen.'

'Everything is calm down there?'

'No. She shouts at him a lot, the poor man.'

'Have you heard anything that sounds like a codeword? Something Greek like Pegasus, Trident—'

'Yes,' said Taff.

'And?'

'Calhoun will be briefed by K.'

'Tomorrow, next week? I need to know now. This is very urgent. Mrs Simpson is in danger, and the king could be in danger too.' I opened my coat to display the Walther in my pocket, then closed it again. 'I'm not mucking about.'

Taff gave a sigh. 'Well, it's Calhoun's neck, not mine. Pegasus was cancelled, if you must know. Then it was back on. Trident is happening tonight, says a man calling from a public telephone box speaking to someone at Fort Belvedere. I have his name, but unless you also have his name, I can't share it.'

'Viscount Lyle, by any chance?'

'By, you are well informed.'

'And has the king talked about flying to Switzerland, or France, or anywhere?'

'Yes, Mrs Simpson shouted at him about it, so I don't think he dare,' Taff said. 'The Air Ministry would have to approve the flight, so we'll know well in advance if he changes his mind again.'

And so could stop it, if they wanted to, I reasoned.

'But you said Pegasus is still happening?'

'I just listen. I don't make up the silly names.'

'Gorgon? Is that tonight, too?'

'Yes. They also talked about Artemis.'

'I know what Artemis is. When was the last call to the villa?'

'Early afternoon. They've tried a few times tonight, but the line is down. The last call from the Fort mentioned a car arriving for the king at six thirty.'

'Who made the call?'

'Your friend Viscount Lyle, speaking to that number in Marylebone.' Taff said. 'Oh, here we go again.' He picked up his earpiece.

There was no value in my loitering there anymore. Royalty had no more luck getting through to the villa than I had. I was worried where Isby had vanished to, what Lyle was up to, and indeed, where the king was going when presumably he should be polishing his abdication speech.

A green coach passed by as I was reversing the car back out onto Piccadilly. I only caught a glimpse but afterwards realised I'd seen the word Leeds beside the operator's name. As I drove towards Hyde Park Corner another coach cruised past, red and from Sheffield. It was an unusual time for tourists to enjoy London, even without the unrest and the vile weather. Even more unusual were the windows covered up by newspaper.

Unusual things were also dangerous things. I sped back to the bakery as quickly as I could. Some copper blew his whistle at me, but I was past him long before he could record my number plate. In the bakery yard, a bread van stood ready, rain hammering down on its roof.

'Warm the engine up,' I told Walsh.

Upstairs, the air was by now an almost liquid mix of smoke, coffee, male sweat, and female perfume. The whole of Section Z3, still in London, was assembled waiting for orders.

'Any success?' I asked, rushing into the office.

'No,' said Eleanor, standing up from Lucy's usual seat. 'But we've put more coffee on and scrounged some scones from downstairs. They're a bit stale. Like one?'

'Please.'

A telephone rang, and Lucy plucked it off the desk. 'Fulham Bakery.' After a short conversation, she mouthed the words *the leader*.

I'd been told to stand by but did not expect the Leader himself to call. I darted into my office in time for Lucy to put the call through to my extension.

'Clifton?'

'Sir.'

'Commence Trident.'

Chapter Fifty-Six

'Sorry, sir, I'm not privy to what Trident is. And what about Pegasus?'

'Pegasus is not needed, so your part in Trident starts now. Baldwin went to see the king again last night and is forcing him to abdicate tomorrow.'

The king must have told Mrs Simpson about this, so the eavesdroppers must have passed it on to Calhoun.

'That's terrible!' I reacted as if I were hearing the news for the first time.

'A solicitor named Goddard is flying out to Nice tonight to persuade Mrs Simpson to give up the king so he can draw back from abdicating, but he may not get there in time. And she may not agree, even then.'

'What's Trident, sir? I imagine there are three prongs.'

'Prongs, yes. Well, your prong is to take a car out to Fort Belvedere and escort the king back to Central London. Take your best men and arm them if you can. Can you do that?'

'Yes, sir.'

'You need to be there by six-thirty, so you need to get cracking. Make sure that you and your men are in uniform. Be at the gates just before, not too early, or you'll raise suspicion. The king should emerge promptly and be on the road before Baldwin and his gang realise what is happening. He'll be driven directly to the Langham Hotel with one police escort in front and your car behind.'

I'd never been to the Langham and couldn't even place where it was.

'You may experience difficulties when you reach the end of Oxford Street. Pull rank if the police try to stop you.' He meant pull a gun. 'This is crucial,

Clifton; it must not fail. This is why I've entrusted this job to you.'

If I were the black knight of fascism I claimed to be, my ego would be thoroughly inflated by now.

'Thank you, sir, I'll see it done. And the rest of Trident? I assume it has two more prongs.'

'You'll learn more when you need to know. Get your men together. You don't have much time.'

No, and not much time to stop it. The Leader put down his phone.

'Julian, a word?'

Julian came into the office and pushed the door shut.

'How much do you know about Trident?' I asked.

'Three prongs, as you'd expect. Parker's mob have one, F-H has another—'

'We're the third. Have you ever been to the Langham?'

'Why yes, it's—' he shrugged—'of a good standard. The end of Portland Place, up from Oxford Circus.'

'Marylebone,' I said, knowing now who Lyle had been talking to.

'Handy for the BBC,' Julian said offhand.

Of course, Broadcasting House. I'd walked around the impressive building, making notes on the Eric Gill carvings in preparation for writing a scene in *Blackshirt Detective*. I'd cut it out after Sissy said it was too flowery. Mosley and the king were not going to be discussing architecture or planning novels. The government had blocked the king's wish to broadcast an appeal to the nation, but it looked like he was making the broadcast anyway, suggesting Mosley was employing considerable sleight of hand. Most likely, he was employing brute force. I knew where a second prong of the trident would strike.

If I were mounting a *coup d'état*, I'd secure the king, arrest the Prime Minister, and take over the BBC to announce my triumph. The other prongs of the trident must already be in position somewhere in central London. It made sense for the Black Guard to seize Broadcasting House while Parker's plainclothes thugs attacked something else, possibly to divert police attention. A riot-in-waiting was already thronging Whitehall, only needing a spark, which Parker would delight in igniting.

Those motor coaches came back to mind. If Blackshirts were being bused in from as far away as Sheffield and Leeds, the capital must be full of them by now. The men had been told the parade was at the weekend, so no doubt that's what the police were expecting. The BU was full of spies and informers, so why should the authorities think otherwise?

'Go get your uniform on,' I said to Julian. 'We're off to meet the king.'

I had possibly a minute alone to make one more call with the certainty none of the others could overhear me. So many people were involved from so many different angles I had to make that call right. The police? Renton? Calhoun? Downing Street itself? Would they act, could they act, or were they in on the plot?

I popped my head out of the door and called to Lucy to give me a line. I closed my door once more. My hand paused over the dial. Should I join Mosley and Churchill and stand by the king? Should I allow the Prime Minister to force the king to abdicate? Should the coup be stopped, then let fate dictate what happened next? These were not my decisions to make, so if Calhoun was in on the act, I had nothing to lose by tipping him off, as he already knew who I was and what I was. If he were not one of the plotters, he could be the man to stop the coup.

Calhoun came on the line quickly this time.

'You probably know more about this than me, and you've probably got my line tapped as well, but I know what Gorgon and Trident are, and they're happening tonight.' I glanced at my watch. It was already twenty minutes to six. 'That big show of force isn't at the weekend, it's tonight. Get yourself up to Broadcasting House. It may be a diversion, but I believe Mosley is going to take over the BBC. At the very least, he's arranged to make a broadcast.'

I hung up, allowing no time for debate or cross-questioning. The mystery would add urgency, and Calhoun should be on the spot to see whatever transpired and hopefully had the wherewithal to call in loyal reinforcements.

The office was a hubbub of expectation, so I clapped my hands for attention.

'Right! Every man ready. Uniforms. Hills, break out the weapons, including the rifles and Thompsons.

'Already done,' he said, lifting a Thompson from a desk.

'Good. I want you with half a dozen men in a van. Pack all the spare magazines. Walsh, you'll drive. Julian, you're with me. Everyone else, stay here. Arm yourselves, too. Lucy, Eleanor, keep trying to get through to France.'

They all stared at me.

'This is what we've been practising for. Move!'

I could of course lead my band straight to the BBC and try to stop the Black Guard in their tracks, but I couldn't rely on the others following my lead. They were as likely to join in the coup as try to stop it. At best, they would be confused and ineffective.

Or this could be a test of my loyalty. There might be no assault on the BBC, and it was a double-bluff for me to feed back to Calhoun and expose me as a traitor. Or I might have overestimated the BU's capacity for cunning, and the march would indeed be at the weekend. I'd never felt so powerless.

Chapter Fifty-Seven

The last office workers and shop staff were making their way home, and others lingered for an after-work drink or meal. Marcus Calhoun put up his umbrella when he stepped out of the cab. London was quieter than usual, with shoppers avoiding the central areas due to the daily demonstrations and near-riots. He had been dropped off on the section of Regent Street north of Oxford Circus, allowing a couple of hundred yards' walk to gain perspective on what might be happening. Clifton's tip-off had been oblique, and there was a fair chance it was wrong, or he'd been deliberately misled.

Two police cars and a Black Maria whizzed past, their lights and bells signalling emergency. They were heading south, just possibly to Whitehall, where the monarchist demonstrators should by now have decided enough was enough for one day. Perhaps this might not be the spot at which Mosley would strike. Trident did suggest three attacks, or one attack and two diversions—unless someone with a classical bent was having a laugh, and it was nothing of the sort.

Calhoun checked each way for the unusual. Three motor coaches were parked along Margaret Street with drivers at the wheel but with newspaper taped over the windows to bar the view inside. Clifton was clearly onto something. Down Little Portland Street, he could see a parked furniture van, again with a man at the wheel. A pair of taxis loitered outside the Langham Hotel, but far more sinister was the plain black van just beyond the circular vestibule of All Souls church. The spire was almost lost in the darkness and rain, but beyond it, lights shone from the bull-nosed prow of

Broadcasting House, newly built bastion of the BBC.

A pair of policemen swathed in greatcoats were pacing towards him, heads down, water dripping from the peak of their helmets. How could he explain what he didn't fully understand? It was like navigating by committee, sailing a hazardous archipelago with just one square of a chart in his hand, the other squares all jealously held by others.

Calhoun stepped in front of the constables and asked where the nearest police call box was.

'You can call us, sir,' one quipped.

'See that van, the black one? It belongs to the fascists, to the British Union.'

'Are you sure, sir?'

At that moment, its doors swung open, and a dozen men in black uniforms poured from the back and began to run around the front of the church.

'I'm sure.'

Another van tore down the road from the north, screeching to a halt. More men in black appeared.

'Blimey,' said one of the constables.

'You need to get to that telephone,' Calhoun urged. 'The fascists are attacking the BBC.'

Two other officers had been stationed to guard the main door of Broadcasting House but stood little chance against the black wave. Four Blackshirts came rushing round the corner in front of Calhoun, armed with staves of wood and taking up the whole pavement, driving civilians before them.

'Get back, clear the street!' one bawled.

'We can't have this!' one of the constables said. 'Oi, you lot!'

'Don't try to stop them,' Calhoun warned.

A motor coach drew up, and more of Mosley's men clattered down its steps. People began to run. Before he could be crushed, Calhoun retreated towards the marble columns fronting the Langham, aiming to find a telephone, but Blackshirts barred his progress, a gang of them pushing past the concierge and invading the lobby. It would be a perfect position for the police to position snipers, but the police would not get the chance.

'Move along, mate,' a young Blackshirt said jauntily.

Six of his less jaunty friends set about the two constables with their sticks.

Calhoun swiftly moved along, pulling up the collar of his coat and taking down his umbrella in case he needed to use it as a weapon. Traffic had petered out, meaning the approach roads had been blocked. This was Mosley's coup. It was no longer a case of contacting the police. It was time to call in the army.

Chapter Fifty-Eight

It was a filthy night. Mosley had said a lawyer was flying out to Nice, and I didn't envy him. My first flight had been both frightening and exhilarating, and frankly, I didn't believe I was aloft. Flying on a night such as this meant placing trust in both an excellent pilot and a merciful God.

Only Julian could squeeze into the T-type beside me. We carried just pistols, as I was still wary of being set up, and the car offered little scope to conceal a Thompson so as not to scare the policemen protecting the king. Racing out of London as fast as I could without being pulled over, I parked outside Neil Gotobed's silent cottage and loitered until the time grew close. It would have been a perfect position from which to ambush the king, should someone wish him harm. I allowed myself a little self-congratulation that we'd eliminated at least one threat.

With a couple of minutes in hand, I drove sedately to the gates of the Fort. A police Wolseley was drawn up beside them, pointing towards London. I brought Sissy's yellow car round in a wide sweep and stopped behind it. A detective was by my door before I'd switched off the engine.

'You can't stop here, sir.'

'I'm sorry, but I'm here by express order of the king.'

'And I'm a Dutchman.'

The gates opened, and a Rolls Royce eased out. It stopped, and a man scuttled over, ducking his head against the rain. I recognised the figure of Viscount Lyle and was immediately on my guard.

'Sergeant, is there a problem?' Lyle asked in that upper-class manner which made this more of a rebuke than a question.

'Loiterer, sir, I think they're reporters.'

'Commander Clifton, Department Z,' I said.

'Clifton, so glad you are here. Mosley speaks well of you.' Lyle checked my face and then recognised Julian. 'Ah, Thring too. Just the two of you, I see. Are you...?'

'Yes,' I said, guessing he was asking if we were armed.

'Very good. Could you follow the royal car? Sergeant, you will need to drive in front.'

'I don't have orders for this, sir,' the policeman protested.

'Now you do, and they come from the king. Would you like to speak to the king?'

'No, sir.'

'Clifton, as I said, follow the royal car.'

'Central London?'

'Ah, there's been a slight change of plan. We're driving to Harmondsworth.'

I'd never heard of the place. My suspicions had been right, and Mosley had no intention of storming the BBC. Or perhaps Mosley would be the bride left waiting at the altar and it was he who had been fooled. If so, the move would destroy the British Union. Someone, somewhere, was playing the game with a touch of genius.

Some technical wizard needed to invent a radio small enough to fit in a car, and then I could tell my men in the bread van of the change of plan. For all the talk of modern Britain, I may as well be back in the age of semaphore and carrier pigeons.

The police car moved off, followed by the Rolls Royce. We came third. I asked Julian to take the map and torch from the glove box and work out where we were going.

'Got it, it's not far, a few miles dead ahead,' he said after a little ferreting. 'London direction.'

'What's there?' I asked. 'A castle, country house?'

We were fast coming upon the pub where I'd asked the rest of the team to wait by the telephone.

'Not much…an aerodrome?'

'Bloody hell.' I stomped on the brakes just as we reached the pub. 'This isn't Trident, it's Pegasus. Warn the others we're headed to an airfield, and there will be trouble. Tell Walsh to step on the pedal and catch up. Hurry!'

'I won't let you down this time.'

Julian had barely closed the door when I shot off again after the Rolls. In my head, I ticked off the plots one by one. There was a plan to force the king to abdicate, one to persuade Wallis to ditch him, another for him to speak on the BBC and keep his throne, and now one for him to go to the little aerodrome and flee the country. What niggled at me was the fair chance somebody had concocted a fifth plan, one that relied on everyone else thinking their own little scheme was working. With luck, no one had bargained for a bread van loaded with Blackshirt detectives.

King Edward was the first British monarch to learn to fly and had his own plane, but surely he wouldn't contemplate flying himself on a night like this. I had no idea how an aircraft could be navigated in the dark or how on earth it would land at its destination. He could just possibly be heading for Scotland and the safety of one of the castles up there, but more likely, he was headed to see Mrs Simpson before that lawyer Goddard arrived, or indeed to hide in Switzerland. I had no idea if either course would prevent the abdication. A king fleeing the country in the dead of night only underlined what all his detractors said about him.

If it were the king's idea at all, and he was not being manipulated by Lyle as well as by Wallis, Baldwin, Mosley, and all the others. And if this were Pegasus, I was somehow expected to stop the king's flight.

I glanced in my mirror and could see no lights pursuing us. We were driving at a fair lick, and a bread van is no match for a Rolls travelling at full tilt. At least Julian knew where we were headed.

All too soon, we took a sharp left turn onto a side road. I hoped to goodness Walsh didn't drive straight past it. A sign advertised Fairey Aviation, and somewhere ahead, a bright light stabbed into the sky, so there was hope these provided enough clues.

No gatekeeper manned the entrance hut by the aerodrome, and its gates stood open as if expecting us. Our three cars turned in through the gates one after the other. Rain slanted across a strong landing light mounted on what looked like a tractor. Otherwise, lights only shone from a hangar out on the field. The sound of aero engines grew louder, and a Dragon Rapide biplane bounced out of the night, rolling across the grass into a pool of light shed from the hangar.

It was all timed perfectly, and the king obviously employed a top-notch pilot. His personal aeroplane was painted red over blue, with silver wings shining wet. It swung round and put its tail to the hangar, then the propellors died. A small, obscure aerodrome would witness history being made.

The police car lurched over the wet grass and came to a halt short of the aircraft, and the king's car stopped behind it. I brought the T-Type to a halt. A glance in my mirror showed the headlights of the bread van turning into the gate.

Thank goodness.

The policemen stepped out of their car. One held the door open for the king and another for Lyle. I kept my engine running. Without engaging in a shooting match with those detectives, my best way of preventing the king's flight would be to disable his plane. In doing so, I'd be supporting Mosley's plan and frustrating what looked like a double-cross by Lyle, but by the time daylight came, more sensible counsels may arise. I had just moments to compose a plan of my own; I would nip the T-Type around the back of the Dragon Rapide, knock its rudder off, and then hope to escape into the night.

I was reaching for the gearstick when the windscreen shattered. I sprawled down onto the passenger seat as more shots rang out and bullets smashed glass and punctured metal. Firing was coming from the hangar, and common sense said I could not be the main target. Squirming forward, I pushed open the passenger door and rolled out onto the soaking ground on the opposite side from the hangar and out of the light.

Legs stuck out from beyond the king's car; one of the detectives had been hit. Everyone else was taking refuge behind the Rolls.

Viscount Lyle stood over the crouching king, as if victorious at last.

'Don't let them get away with this, sir. Stand firm. Do not abdicate. Be strong. Be the king we need.' He raised himself to full height and waved towards the hangar. 'Cease fire. Lyle here. I'm with the king.'

Lyle fell dead without another word.

I drew my Walther and edged to the front of Sissy's car, the bonnet shuddering with the impact of bullets. I started coughing with the excitement.

The surviving detective levelled his gun at me. 'You, don't move!'

'I'm on your side!'

After a moment, he said, 'They're in the hangar. Three or four of them. If you're on our side, shoot at them.'

I bobbed up and fired towards the hangar with little hope of hitting anything, then bobbed back down again. The detective rose up next and fired into the night. The night fired back.

'Damn!' The detective ducked back behind the car, holding his shoulder and dropping his pistol.

The king had his head down, and his driver was half hiding, half shielding him. Lyle lay between us, and the injured detective was crawling to find a safer position. Bullets pinged off metal and through metal, and the legs of the corpse twitched with another impact. I blinked rain out of my eyes.

'Move behind the engine, sir,' I shouted. 'That's bulletproof.'

The king edged along. 'I was in the Guards, you know,' he called back. 'In the trenches.'

He was scared. Dammit, I was scared, but the bouncing lights of the bakery van drew closer.

A man darted from the shelter of the plane and rushed our way.

'No, no, I'm the pilot!' He held his hands up as I pointed the Walther at his chest.

'Dammit, Bernie, are you armed?' the king snapped.

'No, sir,' said the pilot.

'If I had a gun, I'd give them what for.'

'Pilot, pilot!' I shouted. 'There's a pistol on the ground.'

With a groan and a 'here you go,' the wounded detective rolled over and passed his weapon along.

The ambushers were only using pistols, I was certain, and that conclusion gave me confidence. I guessed the range was a good thirty or forty yards, so we would now make challenging targets with our backs to the dark. The first detective may have stood little chance, but Lyle had been foolish, and the second copper just unlucky. Unless they rushed us, the attackers had missed their opportunity to kill the king. The bread van slid to a halt as a bullet took out one of its lights.

'Good Lord, bread?' the king declared.

My men were little more than shadows as they tumbled from the front and rear doors amid a volley of shots. I fired two quick rounds towards the hangar to distract the attackers. One of my team cried out, he must have been hit. I grasped the wing mirror of the T-Type and gave it a good heave until it came away. Someone shot at me, but only found the windscreen again.

'Hills!' I shouted. 'Julian!'

'Boss!' Hills shouted back.

'The king is safe. He's behind me.' I edged the wing mirror over the bonnet to obtain a backwards view of the hangar. A figure was behind an oil drum, another beside a parked car. 'The bastards are in the hangar. Plaster it with bullets.'

'Good God!' the king exclaimed as Hills let rip with his tommy gun, then Julian joined in. Sixty bullets slammed into the hangar, the parked car, the grass, and anything else that got in the way.

'Excuse me, sir,' I shouted to the king. I darted across the wide gap to the van.

Hills offered me his tommy gun.

'Keep it.' I wasn't going to entrust my life to a new toy.

Julian clipped in a new magazine, then let rip at the hanger again. Four others were lying prone, taking more considered shots with rifles. The young paperhanger called Jenkins was nursing a leg wound with his back to the rear axle of the van.

'I'm fine, sir,' he said. 'I've had worse.'

I gave him a pat on the shoulder.

'Hills, you and me are going to break to the right, out of the light. Julian, keep shooting, and for God's sake, don't hit us in the back.'

The mayhem was renewed, and the heavily outgunned assassins kept their heads down. If indeed they still had heads. I darted right, slipped on the grass, recovered. We reached the side of the hangar by the time the latest fusillade of shots died down. I imagined magazines being changed once more. We could keep this rate of fire up for a few minutes, but no longer. Light spilled from a side door, and I peeked around it carefully. A yellow-painted biplane stood leaking fuel. A man was sprawled on his back beside a pair of barrels that gushed petrol all over him. The car outside had caught fire. Nobody else could be seen.

'Hold fire!' I shouted, then advanced cautiously into the hangar. Hills followed, gripping the tommy gun at his waist like a gangster.

Propped up against the barrels beside the dead man was the ungainly form of a Lewis gun, a pile of drum magazines by its side. That should have changed the narrative. It had the firepower of a Thompson and the range and hitting power of a rifle. If the Lewis had come into play, then me, the king, and everyone with us would have been minced.

I shouted outside. 'We're in the hangar. Don't fire unless you have a target!'

Now, the chief sound was rain hammering on the hangar's tin roof.

I edged down one wall. 'Keep an eye on that door,' I commanded. There was another door on the far side, partly open, and anyone who ventured through would be tommy-gunned. The young man by the barrel had been hit in the shoulder and in the centre of his forehead, and his blood mixed with fuel on the dirt of the hangar floor.

A shot rang out. A rifle.

'Got him!' Walsh exclaimed.

'I'm coming out!' I shouted. I waved my hand so they could see it, and nobody shot it off.

Walsh led two others heading my way in a clump. 'Over there,' he said.

A few yards beyond the burning car, a man lay prone with part of his head missing.

'Bloody good shot, Walsh,' Hills said.

'It wasn't that one I got.' Walsh pointed off into the dark. 'The one I hit was running off.'

'Yes, there were at least three,' I said. 'Walsh, take one man and check round the back. Take care. You, watch that door. Hills, watch my back. Where's Julian?'

'Caught one.'

Damn. I just kept pulling my friends into danger.

Coughing, I waited for the spasm to subside, then cautiously moved off into the night, making sure I wasn't silhouetted against that burning car. I could just make out a shape on the grass ahead. As I grew closer, the shape became a man curled on his side. In the flickering light, I could see that both his hands gripped his stomach. He issued quiet panting sounds.

'Don't move!'

'I couldn't if I wanted to.'

'Isby?'

'Oh, Clifton. It's you. It would be you shooting me in the back.'

But he was gripping his stomach. A rifle bullet striking him in the back had ripped its way through his body and made a messy exit.

'Can you stand?' I asked.

'Do you care?'

'I want someone to tell me what the hell is going on.'

'Hell, yes. A man such as you will never have read the Book of Deuteronomy, Chapter 32, the Song of Moses. "They are corrupt and not his children...they are a warped and crooked generation...I will heap calamities on them and spend my arrows against them...they are a nation without sense."' Each pause was filled with a short grunt of pain.

'Random lines from a five-thousand-year-old book don't justify treason and murder.'

'Ah, but read Verse 35. "It is mine to avenge; I will repay. In due time, their foot will slip; their day of disaster is near, and their doom rushes upon them".'

'They? The fascists? Are the Frittons your people? I know they're spies.'

'Useful.' He was panting, clearly in agony, but holding back as best he could. Perhaps his faith kept him strong. I checked he wasn't armed, then shouted back for help.

'Don't shout, I'm a goner. You got me, you got me, Clifton.'

I could have kicked him. 'We're on the same side, you idiot! I want to stop the fascists, too, but not this way. Not by killing the king. You and your bloody sanctimonious religious act.'

And it could all have been an act.

'Was the whole Christians Against Fascism a charade?'

He started to laugh, a weak gurgling laugh.

'Oh Clifton, Clifton. You fell for it. You fell for it all the way. They get the last laugh.'

'They—who are they? Who will be laughing over your grave? Which side are you on?'

'"…He will avenge the blood of his servants; he will take vengeance on his enemies…"'

Isby died. If anyone was going to avenge him, it would have to be me.

Chapter Fifty-Nine

She had taken the name Ruth Fritton and accepted the idea she had a younger brother, especially as they shared a passing resemblance. Over the past year, they'd eased into their new identities and worked their way into the British Union. The fascists were easily gulled by youth and feigned enthusiasm.

'Ruth' found Eleanor annoying and was glad she'd not come along. Julia was rather too serious, and Sissy simply overwhelming, so she could find reasons to remain detached and not grow to like them. The fact they were rich, and fascists made the job simpler. The whore Wallis Simpson was easy to hate, and her very hospitable American friends were damned by the fact of being her friends.

The easiest approach to the villa was from the lane at the top, but a French gendarme and one of the British detectives stood there. Another pair were currently posted down by the front gate, leaving only Inspector Evans inside on that foul evening. She tapped on the door of his room.

'Inspector, Inspector.' She was young and female, so in his eyes totally unsuited to the task of a bodyguard. 'Don't scare the others, but come and see. One of the reporters is sneaking round the woods.'

Pulling on his coat, muttering oaths against the weather, he followed her past the pool and along the terrace.

'You!' he challenged the shadow emerging from behind a tree.

A grunt, a scuffle, and a thudding, sickening, squelching sound ended his inquisitiveness. One problem had been solved.

* * *

'What will you have to drink, ladies?' Herman Rodgers asked. 'It's still a while until supper.'

One of the westies started to bark, then the other. Lord Brownlow came up at the noise.

'Ah, bridge, splendid.'

'You could take young Julia's seat,' Herman suggested.

'I don't mind,' Julia said, clearly minding.

'No, you play,' Sissy said. 'I'll sit out. I'll fetch the drinks.'

What she wanted was a little space, a little moment away from the tension. If it were not for the rain, she'd go outside. She walked up and through the cellar-like doorway into the little sitting area, wondering where Ruth had got to. Those bloody dogs were making a racket, and three people were now raising the noise even higher by trying to calm them.

Glass shattered behind her, and the world exploded. Her ears popped, and for a moment, she could hear nothing. When her hearing returned, all she heard was shooting. So much shooting. She threw herself behind one of those doorway arches, crouching low in the gap beside a sofa. Chunks of plaster blasted from walls above her. Machine guns! And her Walther had been confiscated, as much use as it would be against machine guns. Every item of glass or china was breaking. A man was yelling, a woman screaming, and a dog barking. Julia rushed through the doorway from the living room, twisting as she stumbled and slipped. Bullets followed her, smashing everything in their path. Julia hit the hard floor with a sigh, and Sissy curled closer to the sofa and the pathetic cover it offered. *Whup, whup*: bullet holes burst in the fabric and knocked plaster fragments onto her head. Something nicked her arm. She supressed a yelp of pain.

Suddenly, the shooting stopped.

'*Bon*,' a man's voice said.

A woman was groaning back in the lounge.

No, don't groan. They'll find you.

Three shots rang out rapidly.

Most of the lights had been snuffed out, and a sharp smell of smoke stung Sissy's nostrils. Her ears sang and buzzed. A lamp still shone down the tower end. Someone rushed from the lounge, skipped over Julia's body as if it were just a rug, and gave no thought to the sofa.

Ruth!

Ignoring the mayhem, without pausing to look back, Ruth ran towards the stairs and thumped her way up the tower. Through the confusion, Sissy remembered Herman as noble sentry, sleeping with a pistol under his pillow. She edged out, took one glance at Julia's terrified staring eyes, then sprang after Ruth, pausing at the foot of the stair, then climbing more cautiously. From outside came more shooting. A woman screamed out in French, one of the maids perhaps.

Sissy reached the little anteroom where Herman slept. Ruth was already inside Wallis's bedroom, rummaging through drawers. A few steps to the little bed and Sissy slid her hand under the pillow and pulled out the revolver. She checked it, pulled herself back into the corridor, checked the weapon again, and took the safety off.

Another shot came from outside.

Ruth rushed from the room, a bag over her shoulder. She froze.

'Sissy?'

Sissy's hands were trembling as she took aim on Ruth.

'Don't point that gun at me. Point it at them,' Ruth said. 'Quick, we have to get out of here.'

'What are you doing?'

'Saving the jewels. They're old, they're important.'

And worth a fortune, no doubt.

Ruth edged to the right. 'We have to get out of here.'

'Don't be silly; don't get shot like your brother trying to be brave.'

Such a tactless line should have wounded Ruth, but it had no effect.

'We have to get out, come on!' Ruth made a dash for the stairs.

'Stop!'

Was Ruth an enemy, in on the plot? Sissy couldn't shoot her in the back on a hunch, and the moment had gone. *Oh God, the jewels!* Sissy ran down the stairs in pursuit.

'Ruth, stop!'

But Ruth ran straight towards the danger, towards the smoke curling from the lounge. She slipped in Julia's blood, regained her footing, and ran on into the arms of her confederates.

Now Sissy fired, but only hit the far wall. Ruth yelled some warning in French. Reaching the arch to the living room, Sissy saw chaos; furniture and curtains on fire, smoke clawing at the ceiling, bodies scattered. Rain streamed in through the smashed doors, and Ruth rushed out between two dark figures.

She fired at one of the figures, and he jerked sideways with a loud '*Merde!*'. Quickly, she ducked back into the archway before more machine-gun bullets scarred the walls. She crouched down. Perhaps running away would be the wisest thing to do. Wiser still, hide and make them think she'd run. Something metallic bounced off a wall, then rolled to rest by Julia's armpit. On reflex, Sissy threw herself behind the feeble cover offered by the sofa. The explosion popped her ears again, brought down a light fitting, threw back the sofa. Pain lanced into her leg, her back, her face.

I mustn't scream, I mustn't scream.

Her ears roared, drowning out any footfalls or groans or shots. Pain grew and grew until she could think of little else. Surely, they must leave her alone now. Be satisfied with the death and carnage and the bag of jewels. She waited, trembling, touching her numb face where the blood gushed, putting the other hand to her side where it burned. That was the most serious wound. The leg still worked well enough for her to squirm around.

Shivering against shock, Sissy pushed the sofa away and crawled past the horrific scattered mess that had once been her friend. A friend whose body may have been enough to shield her from worse injury. Leaving a gory trail along the carpets and floors, she crawled in the direction of the kitchen. She spat out a tooth and spat blood—and something was sticking out of her cheek. A long splinter. She tugged it out, feeling wood or, please God, not bone.

A glance down at her left leg showed blood running from under her torn skirt and down her calf. Black blouses don't betray blood so easily, but hers was sticky and wet. Propped against an American-style refrigerator, she tore buttons away to reveal the oozing mess just above her waistline on the left. A towel hung from a hook, and she shuffled over to it, making a compress and pushing it down onto her wound.

The attackers were shouting in French. Jewel thieves, maybe. Communist terrorists. French allies of Isby and all those conspirators Hugh was unmasking. Surely the police must come, those special French detectives Ruth had spoken to.

If they'd been policemen at all.

From a distant part of the house, another woman was screaming and shouting for help in English. Mrs Rodgers, it had to be. At least someone had survived, someone who might help her. She couldn't die here, in a kitchen, murdered by enemies she didn't even recognise. Smoke crept into the room, and the whole villa could be on fire. It was time to leave. Her legs supported her, though her left was reluctant to move, and every step was bought with agony. Light-headed, she made for a side doorway step by step.

Two men rushed towards her. Both in odd, boxy caps, both with pistols in hand.

Chapter Sixty

Wiping rain from my eyes for the umpteenth time, I left Isby dead on the grass and walked back across to the cars. So much for solving the case through brains instead of violence.

'Julian!' I yelled.

'Yes,' a voice cried from the dark.

'You're alive.'

'Yes.'

'Stay that way.'

The king was sitting in the back of his car once more.

'Are you safe, sir?'

'Yes, thank God. Where's Lyle? Has he buggered off?'

'Dead.' Surely the king must have noticed.

'Oh my. He said something like "stay strong, stand firm."' The king spoke in a trembling voice that was neither strong nor firm.

The wounded detective hauled himself into the front seat with help from Bernie, the pilot.

'Are those your men in that van?' he asked.

'Yes.'

'Do they have a medical kit?'

They did, and it was already being used on Julian's bicep and Jenkins's leg. The Blackshirts had saved the day, but now my mind was clearing, I began to wonder. Even without my bread van full of tommy-gunners there should have been at least four of us armed and ready to take on the three assassins. Bernie, the pilot, would be ex-service and probably handy with a

275

pistol, and Lyle came from the hunting and shooting aristocracy. With a fair chance, we could have saved the king without help. That is unless the villains had used their Lewis gun to tip the odds.

'I need to call Wallis,' the king said.

'Are you not due to speak on the BBC?' I ventured.

'Hang the broadcast, I need to phone Wallis.'

The woman he loved came before his duty and his country. From a certain point of view, it was far from admirable, but from another it contained a kind of poetry. At least he'd confirmed what Mosley's plan had been. A plan now in tatters.

Only slowly did I realise the rain I'd been blinking out of my right eye was blood from a neat slice just above my eyebrow. By luck, I'd avoided gaining an eyepatch like Parker.

Both the king's Rolls Royce and Sissy's T-Type were undriveable. As soon as we could get our act together, we rushed the king to Windsor Castle in the police Wolseley. A detachment of foot guards were enough to ensure his security for the time being. Walsh drove the bread van to find a hospital, carrying the wounded detective, Julian, and Jenkins. For now, the bodies of the second detective, Viscount Lyle, and all three assassins had to be left lying in the rain.

My forehead was dressed by a local matron called to the castle for the purpose, and I sat in an anteroom within the great palace, drinking tea and wondering what the hell was going on. London was in chaos, and reliable news filtered out slowly. Oswald Mosley's Blackshirts had stormed the BBC building, and rumours flew that the king had been killed. The king repeatedly tried to telephone the villa in France but couldn't get through.

If there was, in truth, a coup underway, the plotters would be headed for Windsor Castle sooner or later. And if they had the army on their side, the game was up. With luck, someone might put in a good word for me when the dust settled. Or dawn might find me standing against the castle walls, staring down a firing squad.

I was shaken awake from an unintended sleep. Some bodyguard I was.

'Where's the king?' demanded a young Guards subaltern.

I unfolded myself stiffly from the chair and indicated a staircase.

'Can you tell me what it's about?' I asked.

'I need to speak to the king.'

I called up the staircase to the nearest flunky. The officer paced, agitated.

'Could you tell me what's happening?' I asked.

'Mrs Simpson's villa in France has been attacked. Everyone is dead.'

For a moment, I was robbed of the power of speech. 'Everyone?'

'Mrs Simpson too.'

'But what about the others… I had people down there.'

'The message said everyone.'

All strength left me, and I sagged back into the chair. I'd sent Sissy to her death almost carelessly, allowing her to be sucked into this evil scheme I'd blithely gone along with. My failure was complete.

Dawn arrived without a firing squad, though I deserved one. The king sat in an ancient chair, pale, exhausted, smoking constantly, knocking back one brandy then the next while we sat or stood and watched him consumed by grief. Nobody would care about Sissy—the story would all be about Mrs Simpson when the newspapers went to print. Instantly, she'd be transformed from the scheming mistress to Sainte Wallis the martyr.

'Baldwin,' muttered the king. 'This is that bastard Baldwin's doing.'

A female aide came across. 'Mr Mosley's on the telephone, sir.'

After a moment, the words seeped through. 'I'll take it.' The king stumbled over to the telephone, and we followed in a hushed group; soldiers, the pilot, a couple of policemen, a nurse, assorted members of the castle staff, and my men.

'Yes,' said the king into the mouthpiece. 'Thank you. Yes. Yes. Windsor. They tried to kill me too. Yes. Yes, I will. Oh, I need to dress. An hour.'

He put the telephone down and pointed to me.

'Your Sir Oswald is besieged at the BBC. He wants me to ride to his rescue. Like a king of old, on my charger.'

Chapter Sixty-One

The king drifted through the courtiers.

'Get my car. And you.' He stopped in front of the young Guards officer. 'I need all your men, so the blighters don't get another chance to have a pop at me.' He pointed back to me again. 'Tell Mosley we're coming.'

Something needed to be salvaged from the night. I owed this much to Sissy, but what did I owe her? Make her dream of a fascist government come true? All I could do was play my small part and see what transpired. The yellow car was still at the aerodrome, peppered by bullets, and one tyre shot out, so I rode back to London in a car driven by a police sergeant, with Hills and two others squashed into the back. We were all drained of energy and had shot away most of our ammunition, so there would be no question of joining another battle.

Our car was stopped at Marble Arch. Wearily, I allowed a police constable to tell us we were allowed no further, then the policeman by my side passed over the note hastily scribbled by the king on royal notepaper. 'That's signed by the king,' I said.

'Lumme, who'd have thought?'

The constable conferred with a sergeant, who came across to peer at us after re-reading the note twice.

'You can come through, but we're going to have to escort you.'

We drove round the pair of police vans forming a blockade and were met by a police motorcyclist. More time was lost as he received his instructions. He led us past Marble Arch along an Oxford Street lined with army lorries and London buses pressed hastily into use. Troops stood in squads, sheltering in the lee of shops awaiting orders. What must be a troop of the household cavalry, dressed now in khaki with bandoliers over their shoulders, were standing by their horses. Our car was halted again short of Oxford Circus and allowed no further. I asked the police driver to take Hills and the rest back to the bakery to regroup.

On foot now, I buttoned up my coat to conceal much of my black uniform. Perhaps a hundred yards north, where Regent Street met Margaret Street, the road was sealed off by a mixed line of soldiers and police, plus two Rolls Royce armoured cars shining wet from the overnight rain.

I explained to a sergeant I needed to speak to Mosley and was directed to a Lieutenant Colonel of the Coldstream Guards, then to a police superintendent.

'Clifton!' Calhoun made his way across to me. 'Why didn't you warn me?'

'I did.'

'Not about the attempt on the king's life!'

'I didn't know about that until the bullets started bouncing off my car.'

He raised a finger to indicate the plaster on my brow. 'Another close one?'

'I'll live. The attack came out of nowhere. It was Isby and his gang—he's dead and so's Viscount Lyle. What happened in France?'

'Mrs Simpson is dead.'

'And Sissy?'

'I'm sorry—'

'Sissy?'

Calhoun looked grim. 'We don't know the details yet, but it sounds like a simultaneous attack was mounted on the villa at the same time as Harmsworth aerodrome. Your girl Ruth was probably part of the plot.'

'Damn Ruth, I need to know what happened to Sissy—and her friend Julia for that matter.'

'I'll let you know when I know. But now we've more urgent things to take care of. Blackshirts have blocked Westminster bridge, there's a small army of them occupying Trafalgar Square, and it's turning very ugly around Whitehall—there's a few thousand people baying for Baldwin's blood, and the police have completely lost control.'

'Parker,' I said, half to myself.

'And you can see the state of affairs here,' Calhoun continued. 'Your warning was pretty cryptic, and I arrived just in time to see a thousand Blackshirts storm the BBC building. They're still there, and William Joyce is telling the world the king's on his way to make a speech.'

'He is.'

'Couldn't you stop him?'

'People tried to stop him and failed. Any idea who gave Isby his orders?'

Calhoun offered no answer.

'The king is pretty shaken up,' I said, 'and he's had a few brandies, but he'll be here in an hour. I need to get through to see Mosley.'

'There's someone you need to speak to first. Are you still carrying your popgun?'

'No, I thought best not.'

The sun was trying to break through the sheet of lead grey clouds as I was led towards a portly man in a homburg and raincoat sheltering under someone else's umbrella.

'Clifton, this is Mr Churchill. I'll leave you two to become acquainted.' Calhoun vanished into the crowd.

'Ah, you again.' Churchill frowned at me. 'No yellow car this time?'

I showed the king's piece of paper, which was by now rather soggy.

'The king asked me to get through to Mosley. He'll be here within the hour.'

'Then I have to talk to Mosley first,' Churchill said. 'You, man, let us through!'

'We can't, sir,' responded a soldier.

'Don't you know who I am, private?'

The soldier nodded towards me. 'But he looks like a—'

'He's with me.'

An officer intervened and allowed Churchill to push his way through the ranks, and I followed, slipping off my coat to display my black uniform. Goodness knows what happened to my cap. The officer tagged on behind us and called a sergeant to join him. I glanced back to see both kept hands resting on their unclipped pistol holsters like a pair of gunslingers.

A hundred yards in front of the line of soldiers, a pair of London buses had been pulled across the road before the end of Cavendish Place. Dustbins and crates filled the gaps between them. A rather pretty church spire reared beyond it.

'This is not my first siege, you know,' Churchill said. 'I was at the relief of Ladysmith, in the Boer War.' He puffed at the pace I was setting. 'I was younger then.'

I marched confidently up to the barrier, making sure I reached it first and announced myself. One of the Blackshirt commanders came over. I recognised him as the inspector for the London area and saluted him neatly with all the dedication of a true fascist. He returned the salute as Churchill scowled disapproval. I explained who Mr Churchill was and the urgency of our mission.

'Sir, we need to come with you,' the Guards officer said as Blackshirts blocked his way.

'Mosley won't harm me,' Churchill said. 'And if he does, fix bayonets and storm the place. No prisoners.'

'Warn your men the king is coming,' I said to the lead fascist. 'You'll need to make room for his car.' I glanced at his squad of young stormtroopers, wet and tired and uncertain as to whether they'd live to see another nightfall. 'And they might want to smarten up.'

The officer straightened his back in acknowledgement.

I did not see a single firearm. That was a clever move. BU solicitors could still claim this was a protest and not a rebellion. Unions occupied factories and threw stones at the police all the time, they would argue. If the troops did, in fact, storm the barricades with bayonets fixed, it would be a massacre and quickly grow into a folk legend that would only strengthen Mosley's cause.

It was almost silent as we walked between the Langham Hotel and the church and up to the curved façade of Broadcasting House. Above its door was a statue of an old man with a naked boy, which would be disturbing if I didn't know it was intended to be Prospero sending Ariel out into the world. I could also see Eric Gill's bas-relief of angels around a naked figure with a caption of *obsculta*, which disturbed me more. In Latin, it means 'listen' but also 'obey.' If the BBC projected Britain's cherished values to the world, Mosley's BBC would imprint his authority on the minds of listeners. His truth would become the only truth.

Black Guards stopped us at the door, and Parker trotted down the steps.

'Clifton. Where's your cap?'

'It was shot off,' I said.

Before I could introduce Mr Churchill, Parker recognised him and saluted. 'Mr Churchill, sir.'

'Good God,' Churchill muttered. 'Where's Mosley?'

'I'll inform the Leader you've arrived,' Parker said.

Instead of going upstairs or into some anteroom, Parker set off towards the Langham. Of course, Mosley had been there all the time. Not soiling his hands during the assault, not making broadcasts that might be held against him as treasonable, and keeping all options open to distance himself from the violence. It would be very hard to charge a man legally booked into a hotel suite with sedition.

We were allowed in through the portal under the statue of Prometheus. I imagined that in ordinary times, Broadcasting House was an orderly building with church-like reverence for its mission, with Lord Reith, the all-powerful Bishop of Enlightenment. It was now in a state of chaos, with papers strewn around and furniture broken. A rather untidy young man hurried up to us.

'Ah, Mr Churchill!' he said, as if they were already familiar. 'Burgess. I'll be your producer.'

Churchill gave not a flicker of recognition.

'I'll... When you're ready.' Burgess trotted off up the main stairs.

We looked around at the chaos and drifted back to the front doors. A few minutes passed before Sir Oswald Mosley came down the Langham's steps in full uniform and cap and a bodyguard at each elbow. He marched towards us.

'Churchill!' he bellowed.

'Mosley.' Churchill delivered the name with a deep rumble to his voice, as though ticking off a dog for misbehaving. He waited for the Leader to come to him. 'The king will be here within the hour, and we have a speech to write.'

We entered the vestibule once more, but partway across the floor, Churchill turned and stopped me.

'Thank you, young man. You can go now.'

Redundant, exhausted, hungry, and parched, I drank tea with a couple of Blackshirt women and one of the BBC telephonists who had been trapped by the attack. All the engineers had been told to remain at their stations waiting for the king. It was over two hours before King Edward VIII arrived in an old model of Rolls Royce, preceded by two police motorbikes and one of the armoured cars, and followed by a car containing plainclothes detectives and a truck full of armed guardsmen.

The king was still pale but stepped out smartly dressed in a dark suit, black coat, and black bowler, head down as if destined for a funeral. He wore a black silk armband and walked without great purpose in his stead. Assorted Blackshirts turned and saluted as he came in, and I offered a military salute, tiredly, instead of the fascist one. The telephone operator looked unsure what to do, then performed a half-bow, half-curtsey.

'We need a radio,' I said.

* * *

It was a masterful speech, just four minutes long, delivered in a wavering voice that cracked at times. I could hear Mosley's rhetoric and Churchill's clever choice of Anglo-Saxon words in a script that must have been written with both the greatest haste and maximum tension. With utmost regret, the king announced the murder of his great friend Mrs Wallis Simpson and the attempt on his own life. He refused absolutely to bow to threats from those who wanted him to abdicate. He had summoned the Prime Minister to Buckingham Palace at noon to accept his resignation and that of the

283

government. A new Prime Minister would be appointed forthwith, and order would be restored. He thanked the people of Britain for standing by him in this moment of national crisis and resisting those who would plunge the nation into chaos. This would be our finest hour.

We applauded the king as he left with Churchill at his side, but there was no question of Mosley or any of the Blackshirts being allowed to leave without submitting to arrest. I was trapped with the rest of them.

Chapter Sixty-Two

I could have been witness to the siege of Rourke's Drift out of a *Boy's Own* adventure book, except the baddies were on the inside. On reflection, from the Zulu point of view, the British redcoats had been the baddies even then.

Mosley had been snubbed by the BBC in recent years, but now had the run of the place. Sufficient staff were coerced into helping to keep the station on the air and chose sombre music in memory of those who had died, with a patriotic tune immediately before and after the news bulletin delivered fifteen minutes before each hour. The new television studio was up at Alexandra Palace, but as precious few people would be able to receive the broadcast, Mosley hadn't given it any attention. I bumped into Valentine, and we set up an impromptu Department Z in one of the side offices so at least I could get a sense of who was in control. The army could crush us in fifteen minutes if they had the will, but who had the authority to order an attack?

'Telephones are back!' shouted a voice along the hall.

I beckoned to a switchboard girl. 'I need to make calls.'

She indicated an empty office and gave me a line. A weary-sounding Eleanor answered the telephone at the bakery. Lucy was asleep, she said. No, there had been no news from France, but was it true about Julia and Sissy?

'I'll bloody kill them,' she said, voice breaking. 'When we find who did it, we'll bloody well hunt them down and kill them all. If it was that fucking bitch Ruth, I'll shoot her myself.'

I'd never heard her inject so much passion into anything.

'Yes, we'll hunt them down.' How could I disagree?

Nobody else had come into the room, so next, I called the Security Service switchboard. Calhoun wasn't available, but I told the woman who answered I needed to be let out. An hour or so later, a grey-shirted cadet runner came calling for me by name. I was asleep on a bench and not easily roused.

'Commander Clifton, you're wanted at the barricade.'

Now I felt like a character in that interminable book *Les Miserables*. The cadet led me back towards the commandeered buses, and I slipped my coat on as I passed through. An army subaltern escorted me back to their lines. Sappers were completing a staggered wall of sandbags, including a gap just wide enough to admit the passage of an armoured car. On either side, Vickers machine-gun teams were setting up firing positions.

The young officer directed me to walk east along Oxford Street, and the familiar chants of anti-fascist demonstrators grew louder with each step. Another cordon was manned by the Territorial Army who were keeping the demonstrators back by a combination of fixed bayonets and coarse threats. If this were civil war breaking out, goodness knows how many sides there'd be.

A man in plain clothes stood away from the Territorials.

'Belt up your coat, or that mob will tear you apart.' Calhoun said, and then guided me to a black car. 'We'll go to your flat. It's, what, a couple of minutes round the corner?'

Once at Havelock Mansions, I changed out of the soiled and bloodstained black uniform and ran a bath. I could hear Calhoun's muffled voice using my telephone and giving out its number at the end of each call.

The water was a little hot as I eased myself into the tub, but I deserved all the pain coming my way. Sissy was gone, and the country was in turmoil. Plots within plots within plots had brought us to this state: one group of men thinking they were smarter than the next and leaving a trail of bodies to testify to their incompetence. I could see there would be a logic to eliminating the king to ensure Britain had a more traditional monarch in the shape of his brother. Killing Mrs Simpson would end the scandalous relationship and remove the risk of the king abdicating. Killing both of them served nobody's ends. Something was distinctly off.

The king lives, but Wallis dies. Even the hostility of the stuffy middle class towards her would melt. A king alone, a king in mourning, a king betrayed by his government would have the sympathy of the whole Empire. I couldn't accept Sissy had been killed for no purpose. There had to be a reason for the massacre at the villa. If the plan had run exactly as intended, who did it benefit?

Dressed as a civilian once more, I served Calhoun coffee with no milk and crunched some rather stale crackers while I went through what had happened in as matter-of-fact manner as I could muster.

'There's more to all this chaos than meets the eye. Baldwin bullied the king into abdicating, but someone else persuaded him to stand his ground.'

'Churchill or Beaverbrook perhaps,' Calhoun said, frowning at his over-strong coffee.

'So Churchill trumps Baldwin's plot. But Mosley went one better, thinking this was his moment to seize power. He persuaded the king to come to the BBC and give a broadcast which the government had already refused. He gambled, poured unarmed men into the BBC, and sent me to escort the king. But meanwhile, someone else talked the king into fleeing the country instead. Who?'

Calhoun shook his head.

'So far, that makes four plots by my count,' I continued my analysis. 'And the fourth wasn't Mosley's because if the king hadn't turned up at the BBC, it would have made him look a chump.'

'A traitor, in fact.'

'No, because he booked a suite in the Langham and stayed there until he knew the king was on his way. Keeping his hands as clean as he could.'

'So not arranging the murder of the king.'

'Killing the king wouldn't help his cause. Someone else planned that, someone with a different agenda. The move to get the king to the airfield and the ambush were well synchronised because the plane flew in right on time—I can't imagine it's normally stabled out at Harmondsworth.'

'Hendon RAF base,' Calhoun said.

'Where an ambush wouldn't have been possible. And this plan wasn't just thrown together overnight—Isby had been practising for it. Dammit, I even found plans of an aerodrome at his office a month ago. They waited until the king was out in the open, with only a couple of detectives protecting him.'

'And you.'

'Once we were out of the cars, we had literally nowhere to run. It wasn't as risky as storming Fort Belvedere or trying to shoot up his car when it was haring along at fifty.'

'They didn't bargain for a bread van delivering Blackshirts,' Calhoun said.

'They didn't have to; they had a Lewis gun. It would have cut down the king and everyone else before we knew what hit us. It would have shot up the plane, the cars, and even the bakery van. They had half a dozen drums of ammunition and could have stopped a battalion.'

'But from what you're saying, the Lewis wasn't used.'

'Thank goodness,' I said. 'But it gives me the nagging feeling the attack was supposed to fail. Only three men with pistols and a Lewis gun that wouldn't work.'

'They do jam easily,' Calhoun commented.

'Yes, and I'm sure a tap with a hammer in the right place or a few bulged cartridges would guarantee failure. So either that was the fourth plot all along, or double-crossing Isby so that his attack failed was yet another one: Plan Five. Lyle is dead, so we can't ask him. He led the king into that ambush, but God knows if he knew it was going to happen. He was shouting at the ambushers when he was killed, as if they'd cocked up his scheme.'

Calhoun put his head in his hands.

'The king survives, but the government falls. Wallis is killed, so there's no reason at all for him to abdicate.'

'And we don't get an American queen, who the middle class and half the newspapers thought a tart.'

Calhoun cocked his head, looked off into an imagined distance, then gave a little laugh.

'Marvellously crafted. I hate to say it, but for the country, this is the best outcome.'

'My friends died,' I said.

'Not just your friends. Goddard's plane crashed last night, and he was killed along with the crew and his doctor.'

'I hadn't heard that.'

'His doctor was also a famous obstetrician. The newspapers would have made a meal of it if they knew Wallis was pregnant.'

The plot had thickened so extensively it was virtually baked solid.

'Was she pregnant?'

'We'll never know. There will be no smear on the king's reputation.'

An even better outcome for the country. We needed a second coffee, replete with a splash of scotch. Calhoun made another phone call while I boiled the kettle and numbly acted as host for want of anything better to do. I handed over the cup.

'That was a powerful speech this morning, almost Henry V,' Calhoun said. 'King Edward's going to be famous for it.'

'He didn't write a word of it. A script was pushed under his nose the moment he arrived at the BBC.'

'Yes, I could hear Churchill's turn of phrase. He'll be off to the palace soon, and once he has the keys to Number 10, we can start to prise the king away from his German friends.'

'But if we do that and Churchill becomes PM, it could be downhill to war with Germany.'

'In time—if we keep playing our cards wrong.'

'Can Churchill survive without Mosley's support?'

'No.'

'But will he even want to be associated with him?' I asked. 'Mosley's broken the law, even if what he did wasn't strictly an armed rebellion.'

'I've just been discussing that with K. Nobody wants a bloodbath at Broadcasting House with Mosley giving the world a running commentary over the radio. He's making a deal right now. He's masking what he did as patriotism, citing all these plots of yours. Churchill is an opportunist but also a realist. He'll have to give Mosley a plum job, which means we'll need you on the inside more than ever.'

And there was me thinking the cost had already been too high and I could discard my black shirt and look for peace somewhere.

'But it might cure Mosley of this fascist nonsense,' Calhoun added. 'In which case, we can pension you off.'

That was better.

The phone rang and Calhoun picked it up. 'Calhoun.' He passed it to me. 'I think this is the call you've been waiting for.'

I grabbed the receiver in a surge of hope.

'Hugh?'

'Sissy! Are you all right?'

'Yef, but nobody elth ith.' She sounded very far away, and as if she were talking with her mouth full of pudding. 'I'm forry, I ffouled up.'

'But are you all right?'

'I'm in hofpital. In Franth. Fot in the mouth, forry can't talk propery.'

I tried to remember her beautiful smile, but all that came to me were the images of the war-wounded with hideous damage to their jaws and faces. Men without noses, eyes, or ears.

'Julia gone. Mitthith Rodgers liffed. Not Wallif. Rufe traitor, fe ftole diamonds.'

Calhoun was waving at me frantically. 'Speed it up.'

'Go to blazes—no, not you, Sissy. So you were what, shot in the mouth?'

'Bomb. My fide ath well, leg too. Efcaped. Frenth police thaved me from fire. Can't talk proper, haf to hang up. Ah wing again.'

'Love you,' I said, not knowing if Sissy heard before the line went dead. I put down the receiver and the weight of the world went with it.

'Your lady is alive?'

'Yes, somehow.'

He clapped me on the arm and grinned.

'Not such a black day. And at least now we'll get some idea of what happened.'

'Oh, definitely. You'll get your action report now, you heartless bastard!'

'If I weren't a heartless bastard, I wouldn't have this job.' The phone rang again, and Calhoun took it up with a snappy, 'Yes?' He listened, frowning. 'Are you sure? Be very sure!' His frown grew deeper, if possible. He laid the receiver down slowly.

'What now?'

'The king has called Mosley to the palace. He's asking him to form a government.'

Chapter Sixty-Three

I'd always persuaded myself that I was unimportant, not even making the board as a pawn in this game, but perhaps this modesty was misplaced. My reputation as a communist killer had grown in the telling, and if few people knew I was routinely armed, many would suspect it. On several occasions, I'd made sure my operations were backed up by a van full of Blackshirts, and perhaps loose tongues had let slip about the tommy guns. Who better to send on a mission to escort the king to a broadcast than gun-toting Commander Clifton, who could summon a squad of armed men at the click of his finger? If whoever organised the ambush at the airport wanted it to fail, Z3 was an essential part of the planning. The king would survive, and Clifton's crack killers would eliminate the attackers. Moreover, the authorities would look even more foolish if it were left to Blackshirts to save the day.

And if we had failed, who would care if a bunch of fascist thugs were killed? Hugh Clifton, the Coward of the Swat Massacre, would carry the blame once again.

Calhoun must have worked out the pieces didn't fit, but his assertion the outcome was best for Britain could echo right up his chain of command. In my wildest scenarios, the Security Service could have decided the outcome in advance.

Yet the whole crisis had come up so quickly that much of what happened must have been improvised at very short notice. I was giving the Plan Five plotters too much credit if they'd mapped this path out perfectly from the outset. Mistakes must have been made, and pieces would still be out of position on the board. Once Calhoun had left me alone, I considered not what I knew but what I did not: where the gaps were and what didn't fit. My mind went back to an embassy reception in the autumn of 1935 where, for the first time, I suspected someone beyond the obvious villains was pulling the strings.

* * *

I'd not visited the house in Surrey since I shipped for India over four years earlier. As an invalid with no say in the matter, I'd been spirited straight to Yorkshire on my return, and Leonora hadn't even visited me. She'd probably intended to wait for my funeral before coming north. Even the widow of a coward exacts some sympathy.

My wipers slashed ineffectively at the sleet pounding on the windscreen of the Morris 10 I'd borrowed from Julian. He wouldn't be driving for a month with that bandaged arm. Despite the Dickensian scenes beloved of greeting cards, I'd not seen proper snow in the south this side of Christmas since the twenties.

Woolacres was a lovely house, modest but well positioned, barely visible through the grey mist stretching down from the greyer sky. I pulled up right outside the main doors, where one of the staff appeared to be removing a red ribbon.

'Mr Clifton?' she asked with obvious surprise.

'Is Mrs Clifton at home?'

'I'm not sure she's receiving.'

'She's receiving. What are you doing?'

'Removing the Christmas bow and replacing it with a black one. In memory of Mrs Simpson. Have you seen the papers, Mr Clifton?'

'I am aware—please find Mrs Clifton and announce me.'

I stood in the hallway, a smaller but much brighter space than my father's gloomy hall with its obligatory suits of armour. Leonora had de-militarised her family's country home and favoured pot plants and pastoral paintings over martial glory.

'Ma'am will receive you in the morning room, sir. Will you take tea?'

'Please.'

I'd shared many relaxed mornings over the newspapers in this very same bright room. Leonora would chat over the items that caught her eye, and we'd often swap one paper for the other. Her blue eyes looked up at me without any of the joy and sparkle I once saw. Of course, the person you remember loving is not the person who abandoned you.

'You're in the newspapers again,' she said. 'Saving the king, being a big hero.'

'Making up lost ground,' I quipped, choosing a seat without being invited.

'But with Mosley,' she said, turning down her lips. 'And now he's the Prime Minister. You should have shot him instead of those communists.'

'They weren't communists.'

'It's in *The Times*,' she said, slapping the paper with the back of her hand.

Reporters knew more than I did, clearly.

'Was I nearly a widow?' Her attention had shifted to the large sticking plaster on my right temple.

'Flying glass,' I said. 'Those communists couldn't shoot for toffee.'

'I'm sure you'll give them more chances. How's that pretty young lady of yours?'

'Not as pretty anymore. Somebody threw a hand grenade at her.'

Leonora blanched, some gory image surely passing before her eyes. As a girl in 1918, she'd helped nurse her horribly maimed brother in the weeks before death finally claimed him.

'Oh dear, you'll have to find a new one now.'

'Enough of the pleasantries, Leo, I'm here for a serious purpose.'

'The answer is no.'

'I wasn't surprised to see you at the German embassy the other week, but last year I was. Remember that night last autumn? It was an odd mix of invitees, I thought. I never expected to see you there.'

'I was a guest,' she shrugged.

'Of someone in the Foreign Office, you said.'

'A very well-placed someone in the Foreign Office.'

'Arnold Alexander Thorne, the same who escorted you to the embassy this year?'

'Yes, AA, he's in *The Times* too.' She ruffled through to an inside page where there was a column announcing new promotions in the civil service. 'Less heroic, but far, far more sound.'

She passed the newspaper across the me, and I read the list of names.

'AA strikes me as rather young to be given what...the top job?'

'Number two,' she said proudly, taking the newspaper back. 'If we must have a fascist government at least they're picking the right men to run the country for them.'

I'd lost count of the number of times I'd heard that already.

'Did you know AA well before the reception?' I asked. 'The one in '35, not this year.'

She took her tea from the maid and looked at first as if she'd ignore my question.

'No.'

This thought clearly troubled her. Leonora had a sharp mind as well as a smart tongue and knew I wouldn't have driven out here in the sleet to trade small talk.

'Do you see him regularly?'

'Now and again.'

'Divorce me, and you could marry him,' I said.

'Don't tempt me. Where's this leading?'

'Do you think he invited you on that first occasion simply to embarrass me?'

'I hope not, because it jolly well embarrassed me!'

I didn't recall seeing AA's face at that first reception, and only after bumping into him on an operation earlier this year had I become aware he could be more than just a time-serving civil servant. He clearly had connections to all the camps involved in the last two years' events.

'Whatever you do, don't mention I've asked about him,' I warned.

'I'll be straight on the telephone the moment you're gone.'

'That would be very inadvisable,' I said. 'A dozen people are dead, and I nearly joined them.' I indicated the plaster above my eye. 'The saga isn't over yet.'

'What's this to do with AA and me?'

'I bet he engineered your first meeting and casually asked you about me. Correct?'

'It was…' she paused. 'His interest was unexpected. I'm hardly a spring chicken anymore.'

'And amid the chit-chat, you told him everything he wanted to know.'

'Oh, so he wants to escort me not for myself but because of you? That makes a lot of sense in that little fantasy world you live in where nothing matters but Hugh Clifton.'

'You know what I do for a living now.'

'Some sort of—' she waved her hands—'fascist assassin.'

'And the people I'm mixing with and the people who oppose us don't mess around.'

She laid down her teacup with a clatter.

'Are you threatening me? You're threatening me. I don't believe you'd stoop to this. What are you, jealous of him?'

'No. Nobody will threaten you, and if you annoy the wrong people, you won't even see them coming. Be clever and don't get involved.'

'Terrorists…communists,' she said, shaking her head. 'What have you got us into?'

'If you'd taken me back when I returned from India, cared for me as most wives would, we'd be sitting here now reading about all this in the papers and both be none the wiser about what's really going on.'

'Are you saying this is all my fault?'

'We all play our part,' I said. 'And your part now is to say nothing. Except, I want to know everything you know about Arnold Alexander Thorne. Fair's fair, after all.'

Chapter Sixty-Four

I'd overlooked the significance of that article in *The Times*; it was too dull compared to the dramas of the front page. Leonora's phrase about the right men to lead the country stuck with me. Arnold Alexander Thorne was just slightly older than me, and the cohort promoted alongside him were all young men replacing either the senior civil servants implicated in the abdication plot or the dead wood Mosley always promised to sweep away. The new batting order in Whitehall would suit Mosley and King Edward's vision of an energetic Britain driven by youth.

Or Mosley and King Edward suited the vision of energetic young Britons.

Just perhaps I understood why AA had chosen Leo as his guest on both occasions he was bound to meet me. The first time, it was an attempt to deflect my investigation with a hint that bigger forces were at work. My nemesis at the time had shared the same experience. A plan was underway, and neither of us must ruin it in our determination to defeat the other.

Julian laughed at his latest injury when we met once more up in Room Z, and he wiggled his arm within its sling. The whole of Z3 had been shocked by Julia's death and Ruth's betrayal, mollified a little by Sissy's survival. Our success in defending the king outshone the failure to save Wallis, and every man and woman glowed with pride now Mosley had his feet under the desk of Number 10.

Except me, of course. I walked over to Julian's desk and laid down a copy of *The Times*, opened at the relevant page.

'Have you seen this?'

'Not paid the inside pages much attention, old man.'

'Check through these names and tell me whether any of them are in your Young Britons club.'

All of them, it transpired. These were the winners, the ones who benefited from the fall of the dice. It took only a stretch of the imagination to assume they loaded the dice in the first place.

'Dougie's done well from giving me that tip-off,' Julian observed. 'And AA. Shame about Lyle.'

'Or he'd no doubt have had a very shiny new title, too. Don't you think it stinks?'

'But Mosley's in power. We've won!'

'Who's won? British Union, or AA and his friends?' I flicked the list with a finger.

He nodded slowly.

'Lyle might have been deliberately sacrificed as part of their plot or just miscalculated, an ironic victim of his own subterfuge,' I said. 'We may never know.'

'Hang on, are you saying the Young Britons were behind the attack on the king?'

'No, I'm saying they were behind all of it: Hardcastle, Wallis's murder and Mosley's coup. AA has become the kingmaker. We've been played for fools again, but this time it's not just me and you; it's the whole country.'

* * *

Chastened, aware perhaps at last of the enormity of the affairs we were mixed up in, Julian sketched the layout of the Young Britain Club from memory. Rinker, the housebreaker, returned to perform another valuable service, and Verity provided everything else.

She smoked constantly as we sat and waited in an old Crossley van across the road from the austere frontage of the Young Britain Club. I tried not to cough.

'This will just give them another reason to round up more socialists,' she said bitterly.

'They don't need reasons anymore,' I said. 'The king was attacked, and his mistress murdered. Mosley can arrest whomever he wants for whatever reason he wants.'

'And you're helping him.'

'Tonight isn't about Mosley. It's about the people who pushed him into power.'

'Not just revenge for what happened to Sissy?'

'And others. The trail of bodies leads to this door.'

It was the Sunday before Christmas, and we were going to play Santa Claus in reverse. I would have dearly loved to break into that building personally and wreak havoc, but it was a job best left to the professionals. The hallowed arena of monied male privilege would be daubed with communist slogans as the safe-cracker plied his trade, and then Verity's crew would load anything worth stealing into their sack as their reward for the evening. All I wanted was the membership lists and the minutes of meetings. This was my ammunition for the war to come.

Chapter Sixty-Five

Prime Minister Mosley had been on the radio again, justifying moves against anyone and everyone who opposed him.

'He who insults the British Crown insults the history and achievements of the British race...'

The year 1937 promised busy times for Department Z.

As if no crisis could shake British traditions, a cluster of cheerful Londoners sang Christmas carols around a tree in Leicester Square. The army was still guarding key locations, more police were on the streets than usual, and patrols of Blackshirts and auxiliary police swelled the forces imposing order. I wore a warm but nondescript coat against the chilly night air and kept my hat brim pulled well down.

A year before, a man whom I didn't trust in the slightest had told me 1936 would be all about survival. I'd survived, Sissy had survived, so in this one respect I'd succeeded. Now, another man I trusted only slightly more was trying to shine a little light amid the darkness that had descended.

'He's made Churchill First Sea Lord,' Calhoun said. 'And throwing bones to other Tories to keep the list of his enemies down. Churchill's popular with the navy, so that buys their co-operation.'

He stopped speaking when a trio of men in dark greatcoats swaggered by too close for comfort. Their red armbands were embroidered with the letters FP—Fascist Police.

'You know we've failed,' I said once the men had passed.

Calhoun continued trying to sculpt a victory from the wreckage of disaster.

'We don't have a civil war, and the king didn't abdicate, so that's hardly failure.'

'There's fucking Blackshirts patrolling the streets, pardon my French. Working on an equal footing with the police and soon they'll be running the police. Is that mission accomplished for you, and K, and M, and all the faceless men?'

'No, don't paint MI5 into the pantheon of plotters,' he said. 'With all the security and intelligence failings since the summer, K's position is beyond saving. He's already past retirement age; he's overdue a rest.'

A young man would step into the shoes of the old man, no doubt.

'Who's replacing him?' I asked. 'M?'

'No, no, M is too much of a maverick. And there's still the circumstances of his wife's untimely death to iron out. They need someone sound.'

'A man with a naval background, perhaps.'

I'd read the membership list of the Young Britain Club and leafed through the shortlist of proposed new members. The name C M Calhoun had struck ice into my heart.

'We can't swim against the tide,' he said.

'You know we can still stop Mosley; I've got enough intelligence to bring him down.'

'Are you sure? We'd have one chance, then your cover would be destroyed, and all that evidence would be worthless. At best, I'd be dismissed, but more likely, some thug would put bullets in our heads.'

'We know who to arrest, I've got hundreds of names, addresses—'

'A mass round-up, arbitrary arrests, and detention without trial—is that what you're suggesting, Comrade Clifton? And where are all the secret policemen who are going to carry this out? The concentration camps where we hold our political prisoners? The firing squads to dispose of undesirables? We won't save democracy by destroying it. And, frankly, do we want to stop Mosley right now? The country has had enough upheaval, things need to settle down. Let the politicians play their games for the time being.'

'So we just stand and watch with our hands in our pockets?'

'No, no, MI5 will concentrate on defeating Moscow's spies and avoiding a European war. At least until Britain is re-armed and ready. I'd start to embrace the new reality if I were you. Now Mosley is in charge, Department Z will become even more powerful.'

'You mean the head of the Security Service becomes even more powerful?'

'That too.'

A Note from the Author

The conspiracy against King Edward VIII

The abdication of King Edward VIII in December 1936 and his love affair with Wallis Simpson has been covered from every angle in fiction, non-fiction, television and film. Wallis has been portrayed sympathetically as the victim of a male-dominated hierarchy, as a political pawn and as an open target for moral bigots. She's also been portrayed as a loose-living gold-digger, a social climber, a scheming money-lover, and even as a Nazi spy. All authorities agree she was the dominant figure in the relationship.

Edward can be viewed kindly as a reluctant monarch, harried by politicians, bullied by his father and boxed in by his ultra-formal family. At his best he was a dashing modern prince, frustrated by not having been given a real role during the Great War, and was the first British Royal to learn to fly. If he had remained on the throne he may have slimmed down and modernised the monarchy in the way Queen Elizabeth II and Prince Philip achieved in the post-war years. Edward clearly had a social conscience but wielded insufficient real power to make a difference.

The king's detractors point to his playboy lifestyle, his series of mistresses, his laziness, lack of intelligence and disinterest in the detail of ruling. As Verity observes, he could have become a very poor advert for monarchy. Worse, evidence continues to emerge of his Nazi sympathies, with some of his actions following the abdication tantamount to treason. Edward did not die until 1972 and if he'd continued to rule, married Wallis and remained childless we would eventually have seen Queen Elizabeth II ascending the throne, although two decades later than her early accession at age of 25.

Alternative history has a habit of self-correcting. However, British history in the run-up to 1939 could have taken a very different course if a malleable and selfish pro-Nazi monarch had remained on the throne.

This is a work of fiction and for purposes of the plot I've played fast and loose with historical facts. Where possible I have adhered to the overall timetable of historical events between 4 October and 9 December 1936. Very few British people were in on the secret that Edward planned to marry Mrs Simpson. He didn't discuss it with his mother Queen Mary and his brother Albert the Duke of York until 16 October (the day that in this book Clifton gets back from Wales). Only a small number of top civil servants and senior politicians became aware of the proposed marriage and an inner circle within the Cabinet quickly hatched the plot to prevent it. Some saw it as an opportunity to get rid of a king they considered unsuitable. The secrecy was helped by muzzling the press, which enabled the plot to gain such momentum the king was all but defeated by the time the news broke. Lord Beaverbrook rushed back from America to try to influence events, but the king didn't want him to launch a press campaign that would embarrass Wallis. Churchill overplayed his hand and almost wrecked his career by being a lonely voice supporting Edward in the House of Commons.

Wallis fled to Villa Lou Viei in the face of demonstrations, alleged bomb plots and the mounting conspiracy against her, but Blackshirt women did not join her detail of detectives. The king was talked out of his whim to flee the country to sit out the crisis. Pressure was applied to Wallis to turn down any plans of marriage, and technical measures were also discussed for a morganatic marriage whereby she would become a royal consort, not queen. More cynical moves were considered in order to undermine her divorce proceedings so she wouldn't be free to marry. Edward's few true allies urged him to bide his time, then bring Wallis to the fore after the coronation, but he was impatient. Refused permission to make his case to the people by broadcasting on the BBC, Edward bowed to pressure and announced his abdication on 10 December despite Wallis yelling down the phone at him not to do it. Strangely, despite this feeble submission, once in exile he engaged with his Nazi friends in schemes to restore him to the throne.

History was changed at the end of *Blackshirt Masquerade* to see Oswald Mosley back in Parliament and British Union reversing its decline in support. In fact, Mosley never again sat as a member of Parliament after 1931 and British Union never held any seats. Mosley found out about the conspiracy to remove the king too late in the day. He didn't manage to speak to the king during the abdication crisis and by the time British Union mobilised its 'Stand by the King!' campaign, public sentiment had swung against Edward. Julian's tip-off gives Mosley time he lacked in reality—it is the flap of the butterfly's wing that changes history.

The Public Order Act (1936) came in soon afterwards, meaning that militarised political movements such as the Blackshirts were banished from the streets. Plainclothes fascist support revived in opposition to a European war, but BU leaders increasingly resorted to antisemitic rhetoric and extremist behaviour as they grew desperate for success. In this book I have portrayed the BU more as the organisation they wished to be in 1936 than the weakened and splintering party they became in reality.

Department Z existed, but Z3 is all Hugh's invention. Major Taylor was the pseudonym of James McGuirk Hughes who was active in the anti-communist Makgill Organisation in the 1920s with Maxwell Knight ('M'). He probably acted as an informer to the Security Service even while Head of Intelligence for the BU and went on to perform shadowy roles in exposing Nazi agents in the early years of WW2. Taylor/Hughes was careful to avoid being photographed, or destroyed any copies he came across, and no image of him was found before 2005. There was no Christian 35 Group, but after WW2 Jewish ex-servicemen founded 43 Group to fight fascism, specifically Mosley's post-war Union movement.

Socialist narratives say that the Battle of Cable Street was the day British fascism was decisively defeated by the workers, but this is stretching the truth. It was overwhelmingly a battle between the police and anti-fascist demonstrators, as Mosley bowed to police advice to take a less provocative route. He was due to marry Diana Mitford in secret at Göring's house two days later and critics say this influenced his decision. Elements within the

Metropolitan Police were sympathetic to the BU, and here I've used sleight of hand by the Young Britons so the 'Battle' cannot even be framed as a fascist defeat.

Alternative history treads a line between the actual and the plausible. The events of this book are not fantasy; they play with the genuine fears politicians and civil servants in 1936 held of a fascist coup, a fascist king, and civil war. These fears were exaggerated, possibly to justify the actions of the men involved, but there was a logic behind them. Both Edward and Wallis expressed admiration for Germany and were wooed by the Nazis even after the abdication. During the Second World War the Germans concocted 'Operation Willi' to kidnap Edward and set him up as a puppet king.

If Edward had possessed more backbone than he showed during the crisis, more determination to be crowned and had more credible supporters, he could have refused to abdicate and gone on to name the guilty men. Opposition politicians had promised Baldwin they wouldn't form an alternative government if he carried out his threat to resign, but politics is a slippery game, and if public sympathy had turned in favour of the king, we could imagine many different scenarios. The historical outcome was by no means inevitable. Mosley was a man permanently in search of a crisis to justify his Blackshirts taking to the streets and the Abdication proved to be his best chance before 1939; a chance that evaporated. The BU began preparations to seize power but was overtaken by events.

By the end of *Blackshirt Conspiracy*, British history is heading down an unfamiliar path, but the progress of Hitler, Mussolini and Franco on the continent in 1936 continues as the textbooks tells us it did. The adventures of Hugh, Sissy and the agents of Room Z continue in *Blackshirt Rebellion*.

In writing this book my thanks go first to Dea Parkin at Fiction Feedback for her continued support and for her comments on the early drafts. I am grateful to many friends in the Crime Writers' Association, especially those running blogs and e-newsletters who supported the launch of this series and continue to show interest. I must also thank the Dames of Detection, in particular, Verena Main Rose and Shawn Reilly Simmons for bringing this book to completion.

If you enjoyed this book, please post a review or rating where you buy your books or follow Jason Monaghan on Bookbub.

About the Author

Jason Monaghan's life has provided plenty of inspiration for writing historical thrillers. He trained as an archaeologist studying Roman pottery, but his career took unexpected twists, including investigating shipwrecks, a spell in offshore banking, working as an anti-money laundering specialist, and ultimately becoming a museum director. Now a full-time writer living in his native Yorkshire, he travels as often and as far as he can.

SOCIAL MEDIA HANDLES:
 @jasonthriller (Twitter)
 docmonaghan (Instagram)
 Jason Monaghan Author (Facebook)

AUTHOR WEBSITE:
 www.jasonmonaghan.com

Also by Jason Monaghan

Agents of Room Z
  Blackshirt Masquerade

Jeffrey Flint Archaeology Mystery Series
  Darkness Rises
  Byron's Shadow
  Shadesmoor
  Lady in the Lake
  Blood and Sandals

Historical Novel
  Glint of light on Broken Glass

Historical Short Stories
  Islands that Never Were

www.ingramcontent.com/pod-product-compliance
Lightning Source LLC
Chambersburg PA
CBHW050017120726
47903CB00006B/1802